"Here Comes The Sheriff!" Crunch Radioed Elvis.

The two Super Phantoms peeled off and let The Wingman do his thing.

Hunter pulled out of his steep dive and pointed the nose of the Harrier directly at the lead F-104. One blast from his twin Aden cannons and the StarFighter disintegrated in a ball of fire and smoke. Hunter's attack was so sudden that the trailing jet plowed right into his leader's debris, ingesting burning parts into his jet intakes. Within seconds, he too was spinning out of control to a fiery grave below.

"I suppose that's another bottle of Scotch we owe you," Crunch radioed Hunter as the F-4's and the Harrier formed up.

"Just trying to make a hard job a little easier for you, boy," Hunter radioed back. "That one was on the house!"

ACTION ADVENTURE: WINGMAN #1–#6
by Mack Maloney

WINGMAN   (2015, $3.95)
From the radioactive ruins of a nuclear-devastated U.S. emerges a
hero for the ages. A brilliant ace fighter pilot, he takes to the
skies to help free his once-great homeland from the brutal heel of
the evil Soviet warlords. He is the last hope of a ravaged land. He
is Hawk Hunter . . . Wingman!

WINGMAN #2: THE CIRCLE WAR   (2120, $3.95)
A second explosive showdown ·with the Russian overlords and
their armies of destruction is in the wind. Only the deadly aerial
ace Hawk Hunter can rally the forces of freedom and strike one
last blow for a forgotten dream called "America"!

WINGMAN #3: THE LUCIFER CRUSADE   (2232, $3.95)
Viktor, the depraved international terrorist who orchestrated the
bloody war for America's West, has escaped. Ace pilot Hawk
Hunter takes off for a deadly confrontation in the skies above the
Middle East.

WINGMAN #4: THUNDER IN THE EAST   (2453, $3.95)
The evil New Order is raising a huge mercenary force to reclaim
America, and Hawk Hunter, the battered nation's most fearless
top gun fighter pilot, takes to the air to prevent this catastrophe
from occurring.

WINGMAN #5: THE TWISTED CROSS   (2553, $3.95)
"The Twisted Cross," a power-hungry neo-Nazi organization,
plans to destroy the Panama Canal with nuclear time bombs unless their war chests are filled with stolen Inca gold. The only
route to saving the strategic waterway is from above—as
Wingman takes to the air to rain death down upon the Cross'
South American jungle stronghold.

WINGMAN #6: THE FINAL STORM   (2655, $3.95)
Deep in the frozen Siberian wastes, last-ditch elements of the Evil
Empire plan to annihilate the Free World in one final rain of nu-
clear death. Trading his sleek F-16 fighter jet for a larger, heavier
B-1B supersonic swing-wing bomber, Hawk Hunter undertakes
his most perilous mission.

*Available wherever paperbacks are sold, or order direct from the
Publisher. Send cover price plus 50¢ per copy for mailing and
handling to Zebra Books, Dept. 2892, 475 Park Avenue South,
New York, N.Y. 10016. Residents of New York, New Jersey and
Pennsylvania must include sales tax. DO NOT SEND CASH.*

WINGMAN

—FREEDOM EXPRESS—
MACK MALONEY

ZEBRA BOOKS
KENSINGTON PUBLISHING CORP.

ZEBRA BOOKS

are published by

Kensington Publishing Corp.
475 Park Avenue South
New York, NY 10016

First printing: February, 1990

Printed in the United States of America

Prologue

The C-141 Starlifter cargo plane had been airborne for nearly ten hours.

Carving its way through the icy arctic air streams high over Free Canada, the huge jet was following no set flight plan. Nor did it have any particular destination.

The airplane, known by the call name Candlestick One, was in effect a flying prison, one of four C-141's configured for the job. The single prisoner it carried was considered so likely to escape that the only way to prevent such an attempt was to keep the person in question airborne for extended periods of time. This way, the only time the prisoner would even set foot on the ground was in switching from one of the four of prison planes to another.

The prisoner was awaiting trial for attempted murder. Not a month before, six shots had been fired into the disgraced former vice-president of the United States, he having been convicted of high treason just minutes before the assassination attempt. The traitor clung to life for days, finally recovering to the point where he was transferred to a special secret prison in Nova Scotia. The would-be assassin was apprehended seconds after the shooting and arrested. A trial was scheduled to begin in two months.

The fact that the prisoner was a celebrity—and a very beautiful woman to boot—had long ago lost its novelty on the flight crews of the Candlestick aircraft. They all knew her past history. The daughter of a famous scientist, she had been kidnapped by a gang of Nazis who exploited her extraordinary "deep zone" archaeology skills to find lost Mayan and Inca gold in Central America—bullion which would fuel their Panama-based fascist war machine. While being held captive, this beautiful, intelligent woman went mad. And in her twisted insanity, she had plotted and carried out the shooting of the traitorous ex-vice-president.

Ever since then, everyone in the country knew the name of Elizabeth Sandlake.

Sticking to the customs used before World War III had devastated America, most of the people assigned to guard the prisoner were women.

Every day they strip searched the prisoner, fed her, watched her as she bathed and sat outside her small prison cabin as she slept. Like just about everyone else who came in contact with her, these women guards couldn't believe that Elizabeth was the insane criminal that the media claimed she was.

So, inevitably perhaps, the female guards on Candlestick One became friendly with her—in the end, too friendly. The truth was they had unsuspectingly come under the influence of Elizabeth's considerable hypnotic powers. Soon enough, the time devoted to strip searching actually evolved into sensuous mutual massage sessions, as did the daily bathing ritual. The eating periods were filled with long, whispered conspiratorial conversations.

And frequently, the prisoner did not sleep alone.

Gradually, over the course of several weeks, the men in the flight crew aboard Candlestick One also came under Elizabeth's spell. Soon, they too were participating in intimate meetings with her. At one point, five of the six men had proclaimed nothing less than undying love for her.

Little did they know that their declaration would prove prophetically true.

On this night, Candlestick One had just completed a routine mid-air refueling when the pilots heard someone climb up to the flight deck.

Turning around and expecting to see one of the guards, they were stunned to find Elizabeth standing before them, stark naked.

"I've escaped," she said with a hint of her frighteningly unique laugh. "Who wants to be the first to help me celebrate?"

Right away the pilots realized their fraternization with the prisoner had gone too far. Before this, despite all the dalliances, she had never been allowed to roam the airplane alone, never mind naked.

Now the copilot stood up to escort her back to her cabin. But no sooner had he unstrapped from his seat when she suddenly produced a gun which she'd been hiding behind her back.

"Come over here," she told the man, pointing the revolver with one hand and seductively squeezing her lovely right breast with the other. "I want to give you something. . . ."

Seeing he had no other choice, the copilot obeyed. As soon as he was close enough, Elizabeth stuck her free hand down the man's pants and began fondling him. He quickly approached a climax, one that she could sense by his quickened breathing and groaning.

"Do you like it?" she asked, expertly moving her fingers.

"Yes . . ." the man answered breathlessly.

"Is it the best you've ever had?"

Again the man answered: "Yes . . ."

"Do you *really* love me?"

"God, yes . . ." was the reply.

With that she quietly put the gun to the man's head. Then, at the precise instant the climactic moment arrived, she pulled the trigger.

It was the frightened pilot who next felt the cold steel on his forehead and the soft groping hand inside his pants.

"I'm in charge now," Elizabeth whispered into his ear, her voice dripping with heart-stopping sensuality. "And you're going to fly me anywhere I want to go, aren't you?"

"Yes," came the terrified reply.

Part One
Other Voices

Chapter 1

"This truly is an *awesome* sight, ladies and gentlemen."
Nick "Red" Banner, newsman for KOAS-TV in Los
Angeles, was shouting into his microphone and trying not
to throw up at the same time. "There are thousands of spec-
tators on hand here today. They are stretching in lines along
the tracks that go back as far as I can see. And, of course,
all of them want to be here to witness this historic occasion."

Banner was delivering his report from a helicopter circling over downtown LA. And that was a story in itself.

When his station manager had first assigned the newsman to cover the "historic occasion" from the air, Banner
had told him that he was apprehensive.

Actually, scared to death was more like it.

Banner hated flying, and so he preferred to leave the aerial heroics to someone else. His station manager had other
ideas however. He reminded Banner that the people of Los
Angeles and the rest of California depended on his news
reports every day. The compliment was technically correct:
KOAS-TV was the only television station operating on the
West Coast these days, and because he was the senior anchorman, the audience had little choice but to watch Big
Red.

Still Banner had refused. He didn't trust aircraft or pilots, and nothing in his contract said he *had* to go up. It

11

was only when the station manager threatened to send a rookie reporter—a woman no less!—to cover this, the biggest story since the end of the war, that Banner changed his mind.

So now he was strapped tightly into the helicopter, trying to convince himself that he was being very courageous about the fact that he was hovering a couple of thousand feet off the ground with a hearty breakfast of scrambled eggs and bacon in his stomach that was barely an hour old.

Truth was, he had never felt so sick in his life. To combat his nausea and nervousness, Red was talking even louder and faster than usual.

"A *stream* of humanity has been *pouring* into downtown LA since early this morning," he boomed, over-emphasizing the so-called punch words in his commentary. "Everyone wants to be part of this *momentous* event. Everyone wants to be able to tell their grandchildren they were here on this *magical* day when the great train came roaring out of the east . . ."

It was not unusual for Banner to overwhelm his viewers with hyperbole, even when covering the most mundane events. But today, his inflated speaking style was almost appropriate.

After all, he really *was* covering an event of historical significance.

Three days before, a similar great event had taken place in Football City—the metropolis known as St. Louis before World War III and its bloody aftermath had torn apart the American continent. Football City sat right on the eastern edge of the heartland of America, the vast area that had been devastated by a Soviet nuclear sneak attack at the end of that war. Even today, five years later, the region from the Dakotas down to Texas and on through New Mexico and Arizona remained a ghostland of inconceivable destruction and desolation.

The region was appropriately called the Badlands.

Since the war, traveling across the Badlands by land was considered suicidal. In addition to some lingering effects of the radiation and the hallucinogenic gases the Soviets had sent over, the habitable portions of the region were now populated mostly by roving bands of cutthroat terrorists, common bandits, air pirates and other assorted varieties of human slime.

The Bads had also been the site of several huge battles fought after the war between the American democratic forces and those allied with the Red Star, the fanatical Soviet clique that had launched World War III in the first place. It was their aim to see the American continent stay divided in the war's aftermath, but after a handful of bloody years, the Americans had managed to throw them out. One side effect was that the Bads was now a kind of junkyard for military equipment, much of which still worked.

No surprise then that for anyone who wanted to travel from one coast of the American continent to the other, the preferred means of transport was in something high and fast — something that would fly over the nightmare landscape at about twenty-five thousand feet, going five hundred mph plus. Thus, for a long time, airplanes had become the sole means of long-distance travel between the civilized coasts.

But times were changing in America. Most of the Soviet-backed forces were gone, defeated by the democratic armies. The massive air convoys that traversed the continent had increased threefold. The water route through the Panama Canal had been secured, and the enormous task of rebuilding the eastern side of the continent — the scene of most of the battles against the Soviet-backed armies — had begun.

All that remained was to open a secure land route between the coasts.

Most of the highways had been long ago destroyed. But oddly enough, a vast majority of the railroad system was still intact, including the old Amtrak southern route. However, these tracks ran through New Mexico and Arizona — the most treacherous territories in the southwest Badlands — and no one had yet attempted to travel on them.

13

Until now.

The train had left Football City to a rousing send-off three days before.

An intrepid band of adventurers — they had dubbed themselves, The Modern Pioneers — had strung together a bunch of railroad cars and a locomotive on little more than a dare and had set out across the untamed country. Twenty-four of them in all, their well-publicized mission "was to relight the spirit of adventure and exploration on the continent."

Very few in the thousands of people crowded along the tracks leading to LA's recently rebuilt Amtrak station thought that one train making this journey meant it was again safe to travel across the country. No, this first trip would be more of a symbolic victory — another important step in the process of restoring the stability of the reemerging American nation.

Unlike most of the country, the West Coast had escaped much of the brutal fighting and destruction of the past few years, but the people of LA had still felt the effects of the horrors back East nevertheless. Many young men had left LA and joined America's freedom forces, now known as the United American Army, as they battled to restore liberty to the American continent. Many did not return. Even today, hundreds of well-armed soldiers circulated in the crowd, a constant reminder that America could never again lower its vigilance against the ever-present dangers from within and without.

Still, as the Pioneer Train's scheduled arrival time drew closer, the festive mood of the huge throng swelled into a patriotic fervor. A band standing on the station platform broke into a stirring rendition of "America, the Beautiful." Nearly every hand in the midst waved an American flag.

It was close to ten A.M. when somewhere at the far end of the crowd, several miles from the train station, a single voice suddenly called out, "There it is! I see it!"

Like a wave, the message rolled along the human pipeline

14

to the station: "It's here . . . the train is here. *They made it!*"

Suddenly all eyes were turned to the east. From his precarious perch in the sky, Red Banner should have been the first person to spot the train, it being a silver streak cutting through the foothills, rolling toward downtown LA. But Banner was so wrapped up in his efforts to verbalize the festive scene directly below him, that he neglected to watch for the historic train.

Finally his cameraman grabbed him by the shoulder. "Red! There it is!"

Banner swung around to look, just as the pilot swerved the chopper sharply to the left to give him a better view.

Banner felt his stomach roll up into his mouth.

"What the hell are you trying to do, kill me?" he bleated into his microphone, to the delight of several thousand viewers.

The newsman quickly regained his poise and resumed describing the scene below him.

"The crowd is *really* becoming excited now . . . we can see the Pioneer's train. It's *racing* toward the station. It should be pulling in within a minute or two . . . we're going to land very shortly so we can be on hand to greet the brave members of this history-making train crew. Until then, this is Red Banner for KOAS-TV."

This time Banner remembered to turn off his mike before growling at his pilot.

"Get this damn thing down," he yelled. *"Fast!"*

In his haste to return to solid ground, Banner failed to spot something that many of the people lining the tracks had already noticed as the train shot past them on its way to the station.

They had expected to be able to catch at least a glimpse of the crew members waving triumphantly from the train windows. Yet no faces appeared at those windows.

As the train approached the Amtrak terminal, an even greater concern began to grow in the crowd. Although it

15

now was only a few hundred yards from the platform, the train was still rocketing along the tracks at an incredible speed.

With growing horror, the crowd realized that this train, careening along at nearly one hundred thirty miles an hour, wasn't going to stop.

All along the tracks, people tried to flee. Only moments before, the air had been filled with the sounds of celebration; now it was filled with screams of terror and panic. Hundreds were trampled as the crowd quickly turned into a desperate, howling mob, scrambling for survival.

Under the feet of the unlucky ones, the ground began shaking. But this was no earthquake tremor. Like a giant metal monster relentlessly tracking its victim, the train charged into the mouth of the station.

The loading platforms inside the terminal were filled with dignitaries ready to welcome the heroic crew members. Although they had heard the shouts of panic from outside, there was no time for them to escape. The speeding train roared into the building, past the loading platform and, with a horrible, deafening crash, continued on into the back wall of the station.

As the wall collapsed, the roof of the building caved inward, raining tons of steel and concrete onto the crowd. The impact did little to slow the train, however. It rampaged on for several hundred yards, smashing out of the far end of the station and onto the crowded street before finally coming to rest in the middle of an abandoned department store. The resulting impact and explosion sent this three-story building toppling to the ground.

Behind the engine, the train's twenty cars were tossed in all directions. The crash sent some of the cars catapulting high into the air. Others shot off the tracks and into the path of the fleeing mob, crushing bodies underneath. In seconds, death and debris were everywhere.

The veteran pilot of Red Banner's helicopter had realized just in time that the train was going to crash. He managed to dodge the whirlwind of flying debris, rocketing the chopper back up to a safe altitude at the last possible sec-

16

ond. Now the aircraft was slowly circling the devastation, the video cameraman hanging halfway out the window, capturing the horror below.

Yet Banner's viewers were deprived of hearing his golden tones describe this scene of carnage and panic. He was too busy vomiting.

It would take almost a week for workers and volunteers to sort through the tons of wreckage surrounding what was left of the train and the station.

For days, the smell of seared wreckage and burned diesel fuel permeated downtown LA. The death toll finally was established at 502, many of the bodies burned or crushed beyond recognition.

The extent of the destruction made it virtually impossible for investigators to determine the cause of the crash. The locomotive was totally destroyed, so tracing any mechanical or electronic failure was out of the question.

But after dozens of hours of probing through the demolition, however, the city's Civil Guard investigators were able to come up with one indisputable, haunting fact: When the death train roared into the LA station, no one had been on board.

Chapter 2

"So what in hell happened to those guys?"

The speaker was General David Jones, the Commander in Chief of the United American Army. He and his top advisors were meeting in the conference room of his Washington headquarters in the mostly deserted Pentagon Building.

"And what does it mean?"

These were the two questions on just about everyone's mind this morning.

Although the United Americans were now in control of the major cities on both coasts, they had long considered the Badlands a double threat: first, as a too-perfect spawning ground for new terrorist groups that might eventually arise and challenge the security of the newly united American nation, and second, as a refuge where once-defeated enemies of America could gather to regroup and plot their revenge.

It was obvious that the American continent would never be completely secure and free again until the Badlands were tamed. So the high command of the United Americans—Jones and his most-trusted colleagues—had watched with more than a passing interest as the adventurous Modern Pioneers attempted to make the first train journey through that section of the country since the war.

Then came the disaster in LA.

18

Jones repeated his question. "The guys on the train. What could have happened to them? Any ideas?"

He turned to the man seated to his right. Major Hawk Hunter was tall, handsome and widely regarded as the best fighter pilot who ever lived. Better known to his admirers and his enemies as the Wingman, Hunter was probably more responsible than any other person for keeping alive the struggle against oppression and tyranny in the dark days following World War III. From the cockpit of his highly advanced F-16XL fighter jet, it was Hunter who had led the forces of freedom to victory after victory over a series of brutal, power-mad enemies.

Now he turned to his Commander in Chief and friend, General Jones.

"I hope I'm wrong, but I think there's only one reasonable explanation," Hunter said. "That train was attacked, and everyone on board was either killed or taken hostage. I'll also bet a bottle of booze that the accident in LA *was* no accident. I say it was planned. Someone wanted to send a message to us."

"If that's all true," Jones replied, "then it had to be a fairly well-planned operation."

"I agree," Hunter said. "I mean, we all know that there are probably hundreds of half-assed bandit gangs roaming around the southwest Bads, right? And we also know that they spend a lot of the time fighting each other. But to pull off something like this would take some coordinated thinking, and that's something the bandits are definitely *not* known for."

"That's for sure," agreed Mike Fitzgerald, the burly Irishman sitting next to Hunter. A fighter pilot who had become a millionaire entrepreneur and arms merchant after the Big War, Fitzgerald was one of Jones' most important advisors as well as one of Hunter's closest friends.

"And despite what the LA press might have led everyone to believe," Fitzgerald continued, "we all know those Modern Pioneers weren't a bunch of beach bums. They kept it quiet, but all of them were soldiers—trained by the Football City Special Forces Rangers themselves—and they

19

were well armed, too. Hell, they were carrying a howitzer, plus a few rocket launchers and even some SAMs. I know because my boys sold the stuff to them."

Next to speak was the Oriental fighter ace, Ben Wa, a colleague of Hunter's since before the war and a man who had provided strong aerial support on many of Hunter's most dangerous missions.

"So, we're saying that somewhere in the southwest Badlands there's an organized, well-armed group," he said. "One that was able to stop a well-defended train, overpower the small army on board, and then send it down through the mountains to crash into the middle of Los Angeles."

Just about everyone present nodded at the grim assessment.

Jones looked around the room at the dozen men who had gathered there. All of them had been fighting the foes of freedom for what seemed like forever. And still it wasn't over.

"I agree that it appears this was more than a random act of violence by a gang of roving hoodlums," the general said with a low voice. "But just how big or how organized they are is still pretty unclear."

"Maybe a few of the bandit gangs got together," Wa offered. "Formed a small alliance. . . ."

"That's a dangerous possibility," Jones replied. "If those other gangs see one alliance working, they might start to jump on the bandwagon, and it could get out of hand. Then we'd have a *real* problem."

"The question is," Fitzgerald said, "how can we find out what really happened?"

"We don't have much of a choice," Jones replied. "We have to track down whoever attacked that train and stop them before they turn into a bigger threat. But finding them in the Badlands is going to be like finding the proverbial needle in the haystack."

"A haystack filled with rattlesnakes," Wa added.

No one spoke for several moments. The men gathered in the room wrestled inwardly with their emotions, for the most part a mixture of anger and frustration. These were

20

professional warriors, patriotic men afraid of virtually nothing. They had proved that over and over again during the last few years. And if another threat had to be overcome, then they would do it.

Still, it was disheartening. After regaining control of much of America, wiping out the Nazi threat in the Panama Canal, and recapturing the traitorous vice-president who had plotted World War III in league with the fanatical Red Star, they had allowed themselves to hope that maybe the fighting was over for a while.

Obviously, it wasn't.

Even JT "Socket" Toomey, a highly skilled if rather impulsive fighter pilot, didn't have a quick answer. Usually his solution was to suggest an immediate air strike on the bad guys and ask questions later.

"I'd give anything to know who they are," Toomey said. "And where they are."

"Wouldn't we all," said Captain "Crunch" O'Malley of the Ace Wrecking Company, the free-lance F-4 fighter unit that had become a valuable part of the United Americans' team.

Hunter spoke again. "One thing we *do* know. It doesn't make sense to just send out a giant search party to look for these guys. There are several thousand square miles of territory out in the southwest Bads. They could be anywhere."

"Are you saying we're not going after them?" Toomey asked.

"Maybe not in the usual way," Hunter replied. "I've been thinking about this since we got the news from LA, and I've got a suggestion."

Jones leaned forward in his seat. Most of the world knew Hunter as the highly publicized, incredibly talented fighter pilot that he was. But Jones knew there were other facets to the Wingman. He had been a certified genius as a child and had earned a doctorate in aeronautics from MIT at seventeen. But even more, the man had an incredible intuition, one that went way beyond what some would simply call ESP. At times, Hunter's foresight was downright spooky.

"Well, let's hear it, Hawk," the general said.

Hunter ran his hand through his longish dark-blond hair and took a deep breath. "The next time a train tries to cross the Badlands, my guess is that our unseen enemy will be waiting to strike again," he said. "When it happens, we should be ready."

"You mean we follow the next train across the country?" Toomey asked.

"Not exactly," said Hunter. "We *are* the next train."

A silence enveloped the room for a moment as the others let Hunter's proposal sink in.

"Could you explain that, please?" Wa finally asked.

Hunter shrugged good-naturedly. "We assemble a train," he said. "Then we fill it with weapons and troops and follow the same route as the last train—"

"And when the attack comes," Toomey said, excitedly interrupting him, "Ba-*Boom!*"

"Well, more or less," Hunter replied. "But I think that should be only part of the plan. Just think for a minute about what the Badlands are like today. That whole territory has almost reverted back to the early days of this country. It's totally untamed, just like the Wild West. To make it secure again, we've got to do more than just go after some bandit gangs or get one train safely across the continent. We've got to literally resettle that entire part of the country. So why not use the same approach the frontiersmen did when the West was settled the first time?"

"You mean wagon trains?" asked Captain Elvis Q, another member of the Ace Wrecking Company. "Like scouting parties, forts, the whole cowboy-and-Indian bit?"

"Basically, yes," Hunter replied. "But more high-tech. We put together a *modern* version of the wagon train. I mean, a real goddamn train with powerful locomotives and dozens of railroad cars. Hell, *hundreds* of railroad cars. But some of these won't be ordinary cars—they'll be filled with weapons, medical supplies, food. Many of the cars can be, in effect, miniature, self-contained fortresses.

"As the train goes across the country, we drop off one or two of these special cars at strategic locations. Each one would have a contingent of soldiers on board. We can cre-

22

ate instant settlements — mini-forts. By the time the train reaches the West Coast, we've left behind a trail of forts that can serve as the foundation for the eventual resettlement of the Badlands."

"*And* fight these guys who attacked the first train?" Jones asked.

"Sure," Hunter replied. "Why not? In fact, there's a good chance that when they see what we're doing, they might just think twice about getting buddy-buddy with their slimeball pals and disappear."

"This is quite the flamboyant plan, even for you, Hawker," said Fitzgerald in his thick Irish brogue. "But I like it. The only thing is that unlike many of our operations, don't you think it will be difficult to keep this one under wraps?"

"Why should we have to?" Toomey replied. "At some point, the publicity could actually help us. I'm sure the lawful people out there will appreciate our coming. God, it might give them a chance to feel like they're Americans again."

There was a chorus of agreement from those gathered.

"However, I think we should try like hell to keep it quiet at first," Hunter cautioned. "The fewer people who know we are putting this thing together, the better. We'd be dumb to let our enemies out there get ready for us. But it will be a hard story to keep quiet once we actually roll into the Bads. And at that point, I agree, the publicity will probably work in our favor." He turned to Jones. "Well, General? What do you think?"

Jones pondered it all for a few moments, then spoke. "It will take a lot of planning," he said. "A lot of coordination and a *hell* of a lot of money. But I like it, too. I think it's the right time. Let's just hope we can pull it off."

Santa Fe, New Mexico Free Territory

At the same time the inner circle of the United Americans was gathering in Washington, another more sinister

23

meeting was taking place halfway across the continent.

In a dingy bar on the outskirts of the city of Santa Fe, two men leaned over their mugs of beer. Sitting a discreet distance away were no less than thirty bodyguards — fifteen for each man — on hand to ward off the myriad of dangers floating around the lawless southwestern city these days.

Once a thriving tourist and cultural center, Santa Fe was now a hotbed of drug smugglers, gunrunners and illicit sex — a suitable capital for the wild and wooly New Mexico Free Territory. Technically, the Free Territory was a protectorate of the Republic of Texas. Realistically, it was the underbelly of the southwest Badlands. And just like their staunch United American allies, the government of Texas had its hands full just securing and patrolling its own borders; they had neither the manpower nor the logistics at present to stamp out moral crimes like drugs and prostitution in places like Santa Fe. That would all come later.

But the two men sucking down the warm Texas beer weren't talking about cocaine or teenage hookers.

"Your guys really pulled it off," said a stocky, red-haired, cross-eyed Texan named Duke. "I'll have to admit, I didn't think you could do it."

The second man was lean, blond and spoke with a German accent. "It was hardly a challenge," he replied arrogantly. "Those fools on the train had no idea what was happening until it was too late."

"What did you do with them?" the red-haired man asked. "Are there any bodies to be found?"

"What difference does that make?" the second man replied, a twisted smirk crossing his face. "The job has been done."

The Texan rolled his oddly-spaced eyes in glee. "I would have loved to have been in LA with my camera to see that empty train roll in," he said. "From what I hear, it barrel-assed right through the fucking town." He laughed a little too wildly, and then suggested a toast. "Congratulations, my friend," Duke said to the blond man with the crooked smile. "You and your men will be a most welcome addition to our cause."

24

Their conversation was interrupted by the appearance of four teenage girls, all chained at the waist, who were brought through the cordon of bodyguards by a squad of black-uniformed soldiers.

"And what is this?" the German man asked.

"A thank-you present," Duke replied. "For a job well done."

The German carefully inspected each of the quartet of manacled girls.

"Interested?" Duke asked him.

"Why not?" the man replied, breaking into another rare, if nervously twisted smile. "We can talk business another time. . . ."

Chapter 3

Two weeks later

The AV-8BE Harrier jet streaked across the mouth of the Chesapeake Bay, heading out over the gray Atlantic.

Hawk Hunter was bathed in the rush of exhilaration that always came over him whenever he was at the controls of an aircraft hurdling across the sky. During the last couple of weeks, as he and the United Americans' brain trust shaped their plans for the cross-country train mission, he had done just about everything else *but* fly, and he had missed it terribly, both physically and mentally. For Hunter, climbing back into a cockpit after even a brief absence was a lot like being reunited with a passionate lover. It was a stirring experience.

He rolled the AV-8BE northward and started up the coastline. He had always enjoyed flying Harriers. Of course, they didn't have the power and range of his usual craft, the F-16. Few airplanes did. But the Harrier had one distinct advantage over his beloved F-16, and that made it the perfect companion for his next mission.

The Harrier was a VTOL jumpjet—a vertical takeoff and landing aircraft. It could take off and land vertically, like a helicopter, without the need for a runway. Not only that, but it could come to abrupt halts in flight at any altitude and at any speed and simply hover in midair. It could even move backward.

Its ability to come to sudden stops was certainly a major

advantage during dogfights with faster, but less mobile, aircraft. The attacker almost always became the attackee once the Harrier pilot "slammed on the brakes." But it was the vertical takeoff and landing feature that caused Hunter to select the Harrier jet for his next mission.

Now dubbed "Project *Freedom Express*" by the United Americans' inner circle, Hunter's assignment in the impending adventure was to act as the advance scout for the modern-day wagon train. Flying on ahead of the train's progress every day, he would check out the upcoming terrain, the condition of the track and whatever else might be lurking around the next bend.

His F-16 would still have fit the bill nicely except for two problems: There would be few landing strips along the Amtrak southern tier route that the train would follow, and even he would be hard-pressed to land an F-16 on top of a boxcar.

But a Harrier jet could practically set down on a dime.

Hunter had spent many hours during the past week designing and building a special flatbed "landing deck" railroad car. On the drawing board, its fold-down metal planks would provide more than twice the room required to land the Harrier. But the extra space would be needed. Dropping a jet out of the sky to land on a moving train wouldn't be easy. Most times the train would have to be stopped or at least moving very slowly when he set down, and even that would take all of Hunter's skill.

Once the special landing car was completed, Hunter turned his attention to finding and customizing a Harrier to meet his requirements. He had faced one dilemma: He didn't want to give up the myriad of computerized controls and special features built into the cockpit of his F-16. Yet the *Freedom Express* mission cried for the VTOL craft.

His eventual solution was rather simple: He decided to transfer the entire cockpit from his F-16 to the Harrier jumpjet.

He knew right off that this would require a Harrier with an unusually large cockpit. Fortunately, Hunter recalled seeing such a plane at Andrews Air Force Base several months before. He contacted a drinking buddy at Andrews and learned that the airplane was still there.

It was an old U.S. Marine AV-8BE, a two-seat, trainer version of the Harrier. The extra room in the enlarged cockpit would give Hunter the needed space to transfer the F-16's avionics, flight controls, and highly advanced weapons system controls into the jumpjet.

With JT's help, Hunter dismantled the F-16 cockpit and reassembled it, component by component, inside the extra-wide, extra-long Harrier compartment. Working nights and early mornings, the highly complex operation took just six days.

Now he was flight testing the hybrid airplane for the first time, and everything was working beautifully.

He put the airplane through a demanding series of rolls, flips, mid-air stops and starts, dips and dives, performing them all via his transplanted F-16 controls. It didn't take long for him to be convinced that the aircraft would respond to whatever situation he could possibly encounter in the skies over the southwest Badlands.

In addition to the special flying features, the Harrier was loaded for bear with weapons, including a pair of powerful Aden cannon pods and a slew of Sidewinder air-to-air missiles. He had to admit that the finished product was quite a piece of work — a flying arsenal capable of unlimited aerial acrobatics.

After three hours of flying, Hunter was more than satisfied with the Harrier's performance. Turning back toward Andrews, he knew he was ready to tackle the Bads.

Chapter 4

One week later

It was close to midnight when Hunter and Fitzgerald arrived at the Amtrak station in Washington, DC.

Having completed the final test out of the AV-8BE Harrier, the Wingman had flown into National Airport an hour before, anxious to see the progress Fitz and the others were making on their end of Project *Freedom Express*.

Now walking through the old train yard, he was so astonished at what he saw, he almost found it hard to speak.

Before him were two hundred armor-plated, gleaming silver railroad cars that had become the *Freedom Express*.

"I think you've created a monster!" Hunter was finally able to exclaim.

"I can only agree." Fitz smiled.

Quite simply, the train was a two-mile collection of rolling military might.

Its components had come together so quickly, even Fitzgerald felt he'd outdone himself. Calling in favors and working his multitude of contacts across the eastern half of the country, as well as up in Free Canada, Fitz and his procurement agents had bought or bartered for just about everything contained on the wish list compiled by the United Americans' planning team. The result was an astonishing assembly of weapons carriages, gun platforms, track-mobile missile launchers, radar cars, anti-aircraft cars, supply cars, sleeping cars, oil tankers and rolling storage beds.

Fitz explained that the train was divided into two sections. For the most part, the front section contained the majority of weapons cars, and the rear carried the sleeping compartments and mini-forts. In all, it stretched on for more than the length of thirty-five football fields.

Hunter tapped the side of one of the train's armored cars. Its metal skin looked thin, yet strong.

"Nice work," he said. "Who did this for you?"

"A guy I know who used to work for the Navy in the old days," Fitz replied. "He did research on protection systems for battleships. This stuff looks pretty lightweight, but it's bulletproof and pretty damn near missile-proof. Each car will be outfitted with it before we leave."

"But can we really expect to move all this?" Hunter asked over and over as they walked in and out of the cars.

Fitz chuckled mischievously and then led his friend into a tunnel which hid the very front part of the train. It was dark and musty inside the shaft, but when the Irishman dramatically threw the tunnel's light switch, Hunter saw for the first time the muscle behind the *Freedom Express*.

"Here's all we need," Fitz said proudly.

Before them were twelve powerful Dash-8 diesel locomotives, their red and black paint job still gleaming wet.

Transferred down from the old city of Erie earlier that day, each of the huge locomotives was a 16-cylinder, 4,000-horsepower colossus, a top-of-the-line model built by General Electric Company just before World War III. Miraculously, these engines had survived the war and were discovered by Fitz's advance men sitting in a railroad yard near GE's locomotive plant in Erie, far removed from the fighting that had defaced so much of the nation.

Fitz explained that the Dash-8's were the epitome of high-tech railroading. The first locomotives to be built with on-board computers, all aspects of each engine's operation was controlled by a collection of self-contained microprocessors located in the engineer's cabin. Once all twelve of the locomotives' computer systems were linked together, they would function as a kind of huge, electronic brain for the *Freedom Express*. The computers would drive the train, set the correct speed and control the amount of fuel used. Plus, their on-board diagnostic systems would be able to locate any problems anywhere on the train itself, report them promptly to the supervising engineers' video read-out screen, or in some cases, even remedy the situation without any human involvement at all.

Hunter and Fitzgerald knew that all of the people on board the train would have plenty to do during the trip, without worrying about running the train itself. With the Dash-8's, that operation would be as automated as possible.

"You've assembled an amazing piece of work," Hunter said as they left the tunnel. "I didn't think there were enough engines and cars left in the country to put together something like . . . well like *this*."

Fitz gave a modest shrug. "It pays to have friends," he said in his thick brogue.

The two men walked farther up the line and eventually approached the mid-point of the train.

The middle "keystone car" really stopped Hunter in his tracks. Mounted on a huge flatbed was one of the biggest guns he had ever seen.

He carefully studied the giant cannon. "Present from another friend?" he asked.

Fitzgerald, who at one time had run a profitable airfield operation in Syracuse before that city was destroyed in the Second Circle War, smiled again.

"Aye," he answered. "An old pal from my upstate New York days used to work in the Army's famous Watervliet Arsenal, making these big babies. He says this thing will toss a shell the weight of a Volkswagen about twenty miles."

"I believe it," Hunter said, admiring the gun's fifty-foot-long barrel, on which someone had painted the name *Big Dick*. "Good name for it," he said. "But how did you ever get this thing down here?"

"Well, that was a little tough," Fitzgerald admitted. "Had to take it apart up there and haul it down here. Took a half

31

dozen trucks the better part of a week."

The two friends moved on, inspecting the drop-off mini-forts. Arranged in blocks of three, one car contained sleeping and eating quarters, the second was filled with medical supplies and equipment, and the third contained weapons and ammunition. These sets of cars were to be left at strategic points along the train's route, equipped with all the necessities for a small, well-fortified settlement, including a contingent of one hundred highly trained United American Army troopers.

As the two men approached the end of the train, they were joined by Captain Lamont "Catfish" Johnson, a towering black man who formerly played defensive end for the San Diego Chargers of the old NFL. Johnson was a relatively new member of the United Americans' high command, taking the place of his long-time commanding officer and friend, Captain John "Bull" Dozer, leader of the U.S. Marine's 7th Cavalry. Dozer had died valiantly in a crucial battle between the United Americans and the Soviet Red-Star-backed Circle forces at the Washington Monument. Dozer still was greatly missed by Hunter and the rest of the group, both as a friend and a matchless warrior.

But Johnson was cut from the same mold. He had been tapped by Jones to recruit the best troops available for the train trip, and would be their overall commanding officer during the journey. With Hunter in charge of the aerial cover, the two would be working closely together.

Johnson greeted Hunter and Fitzgerald warmly.

"Quite impressive, no?" Johnson asked Hunter, as all three stood back and took one long look at the *Freedom Express*.

"A hell of a job," Hunter replied. "Now all we have to do is get this thing to LA."

Chapter 5

Three days later

"Are you that Wingman guy? You don't look so fuckin' tough."

The hulking, nasty-looking man was swaying drunkenly over the table being shared by Hunter and the Catfish.

This is trouble, Hunter thought.

It was their last night in Washington before the *Freedom Express* was to pull out, and Hunter and Johnson were trying to fortify themselves in a bar located in what formerly was the Georgetown section of the city.

"Yeah. I'm Major Hunter," he said, standing up to find himself eye level with the man's chest. "So what?"

"So what?" the man slurred. "So if you're such a big friggin' hero, how come you drink with niggers?"

Hunter instantly hit the man squarely on the jaw with a lightning left hook. The drunk staggered backward, stumbled a little, then fell forward, right across the table. Grabbing the man by the scruff of his neck, Hunter slammed his face twice on the table's beer-sticky surface, before shoving him to the floor.

At that moment, three other steroid-popping freaks— drinking companions of Mr. Flat Face—stood up and rushed the table.

Catfish was up on his feet in a flash. "This'll just take a second," he said to Hunter.

He picked the first drunk up off the floor and hurled

him right into his three charging buddies. All four went tumbling over the bar and crashed into a row of beer mugs, sending broken glass flying in all directions.

With a symbolic wipe of his hands, Johnson calmly sat back down. "How much do you suppose I'll have to pay for those glasses?" he asked Hunter casually.

The crowd settled down as the bar's delinquent bouncers removed the four semi-conscious men. At that point another man approached their table. Hunter recognized him as the bar's manager.

His own face a mass of scars, his nose a mountain range of broken bones, the manager nevertheless grinned toothlessly. "Drinks on the house for the rest of the night," he said with a wink.

After the man left, Hunter took a healthy slug of his drink.

"After all this country has been through in the last few years," he said, "all the fighting, the deception, the destruction . . . you'd think we would have gotten rid of clowns like those guys."

Johnson drained his own glass and motioned to the waitress for another round. "Sometimes I think it's never going to go away, Hawk," he said sadly. "Hell, the Nazis are the worst of all, and although we kicked their asses down in Panama, I bet some of them are still around."

Hunter knew Johnson was probably right. Even though the United Americans had recently destroyed the Twisted Cross, the Nazi-based operation that had taken control of the Panama Canal, he too had the uneasy feeling that the Nazis were not completely kaput. Already the United Americans had received reports that one of the most fanatical jet fighter groups allied with the Canal Nazis, the notorious Skinhead Squadron, was still roaming about Central America and had been spotted as far north as Texas.

The waitress arrived with two more drinks and a message.

"You see those two girls over at the bar?" she asked. "They'd like to meet you guys."

Hunter's radarlike vision scanned the rail. One of the

34

girls in question was an ebony-skinned beauty with long, inviting legs; the other was a very attractive and very shapely redhead.

He looked at Johnson. "Tempting, eh, Cat?"

Johnson smiled and then shook his head. "Already got a lady waiting for me at home," he said, quickly draining his shot glass of bourbon and getting up to leave. "And a family. They'll kick my butt if I don't get to it."

Several hours later, Hunter lay awake in his Washington apartment, staring at the ceiling.

Melinda, the redhead, was asleep next to him, one naked thigh still resting across his stomach, her full breasts warm and soft against his chest. She was snoring sweetly and contently. They had made love wildly for more than an hour until she collapsed, fulfilled but exhausted, and drifted off to sleep.

But sleep would not come for Hunter. The last thing Catfish had said to him just kept bouncing around his head.

" 'I already got a lady waiting for me at home.' "

Why can't I be like that? Hunter thought for the millionth time. Why can't I have a lady waiting at home . . . for me?

He pulled Melinda closer to him, and she sleepily rubbed his chest. She was bright, beautiful and one of the most creative lovers he had ever met. Still, he wasn't completely satisfied. It was always that way — a little corner of himself still ached for something more.

He knew, of course, the reason for this feeling was the beautiful Dominique.

Physically, they had spent very little time together. But ever since their first meeting in war-ravaged France several years ago, Dominique had never been far from Hunter, at least in his mind. And in his heart.

Sappy as it sounded, Hunter actually yearned for a world at peace, where he and Dominique could be together again, this time for good. But he loved her far too much to ask her to share the kind of life he was presently leading.

35

There were still too many battles to fight, too many enemies who wanted him dead.

He had nearly lost her once, when she was kidnapped by the ruthless terrorist Viktor during the black days of the First Circle War. Hunter had rescued her then, but he knew that she would be in jeopardy as long as she stayed close to him.

So he sent her off to one of the few "safe" countries left in the world—Free Canada—where she eventually joined a human encounter group somewhere in the Canadian Rockies. She seemed to be in friendly hands—maybe *too* friendly. Through his friend, Major Frost of the Free Canadian Air Force, Hunter had learned that people belonging to these encounter groups often shared everything, including their beds.

Not surprisingly, Hunter desperately wanted to forget everything else, fly to Free Canada and find Dominique. But he knew that was impossible. As much as he pined for her, he couldn't leave as long as his other great love—his country, America—was threatened by so many enemies. Someday, when the violence finally ended and the last foe of freedom was conquered, he would go to her.

But would that day ever come?

Chapter 6

The following day

Under a gun-metal gray sky, the *Freedom Express* slowly pulled out of downtown Washington and began its long and uncertain journey westward.

Hunter and Catfish were in the first car following the string of twelve locomotives. This car was specially outfitted as the control and communications center for the trip, and therefore was dubbed simply "Control." From a central console, they could monitor the dozens of video cameras mounted on the train, giving them a clear view of everything that was happening on or near them. A radar screen provided constant surveillance of the air space above; a unique land sonar device would warn them of the unexpected up to a mile ahead. A sophisticated radio/message center—complete with a retractable satellite dish on the Control car's roof—would keep them in secure scrambled radio and telex contact with Jones back in his Washington headquarters.

As the great train finally gathered speed, Hunter sat with his nose pressed up against the bulletproof window's remarkably clear glass, peering out at the Virginia countryside rolling past. It looked peaceful in the dim, early morning light.

Better relax now while I can, he thought, because it won't last long.

The United Americans didn't expect any trouble during

the first leg of the journey. The eastern part of the country had been secure for some time, except for a few stray bandit gangs occasionally spotted in the former Kentucky region. But they wouldn't be a problem; they didn't have the firepower or the guts to tackle anything as imposing as the powerful *Freedom Express*.

Since the eastern part of the route was considered safe, it had been decided to load the majority of their troops on in Football City. This way the weight of the train would be reduced for the first third of the trip, not only saving fuel, but also allowing the *Express* to make better time. To that end, elements of the United American 1st Airborne Division had been flying out of Washington and into Football City for the past three days, using a fleet of giant Free Canadian C-5 Galaxys as their mode of transport.

Hunter's Harrier jumpjet was securely moored on its specially designed flatbed car which was located several cars back from the Control car. Once they reached Football City and started into the Badlands, he would be flying surveillance missions several times a day. And, in case of an emergency, he could take off at any time if the need should arise, his living quarters/pilot ready room being in the car just behind the Harrier deck.

Nose still pressed against the glass, Hunter looked back toward the rear of the train. It seemed to stretch on forever, cutting its way through the countryside. He wondered if the original pioneers back in the 1880's felt as he did now: excited, yet apprehensive; anxious, yet curiously calm.

For him, he knew another great adventure lay ahead. Another mission to secure his country's freedom. And at its successful conclusion, he told himself, he would be one step closer to reuniting with Dominique.

"Coffee, Hawk?" Catfish asked him, shoving a mug of steaming java under his nose.

Hunter took the hot liquid thankfully. Then he and Catfish settled down for a couple of quiet, uneventful days.

They would be the last ones for some time.

Chapter 7

Over Oklahoma Territory

"We've got company," Ben Wa called over to JT as the radar screen in his A-7E Strikefighter started to crackle. "See the blips?"

"I see them," JT confirmed, checking his own A-7's screen. "Something tells me they ain't friendly."

They had flown the Strikefighters from Washington to Texas the day before to enlist the crack team of helicopter pilots known as the Cobra Brothers for the *Freedom Express* adventure. This done, they headed for Football City to await the arrival of the train.

Now, one hour out of Dallas and somewhere just above the old Oklahoma-Missouri border, the six bogies had appeared. The blips quickly turned into a flight of F-4J Phantoms that suddenly emerged from a cloud bank to the A-7's right. In seconds the Phantoms had turned and were taking dead aim on them.

Suddenly a warning buzzer went off in both A-7 cockpits. It meant that the Phantoms were preparing to fire air-to-air missiles at them.

"Damn! I thought this air space would be safe by now," JT shouted into his A-7's radio.

"I guess we were wrong again," Wa replied, arming his own air-to-air missiles.

"How about we give them the old scissors trick?" JT suggested as he too armed his Sidewinders.

"I'm with you, partner," Ben replied.

Toomey expertly put his Strikefighter into a stomach-wrenching dive while, at the same instant, Ben put the nose of his plane straight up and climbed a thousand feet in just a few seconds.

The perfectly timed maneuver momentarily confused the pilots of the attacking Phantom jets. After a delay of several crucial seconds, three of the jets dropped in pursuit of Toomey while the others went after Wa. But the Oriental pilot had disappeared into another high bank of clouds. The Phantoms followed — only to find Wa coming straight back down at them as they emerged from the cumulus, his nose cannon spitting fire and smoke. As he shot past them, one of the Phantoms exploded in flames, and the other was hit by a Sidewinder. Together, they began a deadly, downward spiral.

Meanwhile, Toomey had pulled out of his dive and brought his Strikefighter right under the belly of one of the pursuing Phantoms. Lining up the F-4's auxiliary fuel tank in his Head-Up Display, he pulled his cannon trigger, and the Phantom was blown to pieces.

"One down," he reported to Wa.

"I'm way ahead of you," Wa responded calmly.

Suddenly another Phantom loomed in front of JT's HUD. Without a moment's hesitation, he squeezed off another blast from his nose cannon. The F-4 snapped in half and plunged in flames.

The remaining two Phantoms had seen enough for one day; the Strikefighter pilots were obviously masters of their craft. The F-4's quickly gave up the attack and fled to the south.

Normally Toomey and Wa would have pursued them, but in this case, there was another priority to be considered. The 1st Airborne's C-5's were shuttling between DC and Football City just a few hundred miles away. The Phantoms' ambush might have been a diversionary measure to occupy the Strikefighters while another attack was heading for the C-5's.

It was an unlikely scenario — but JT and Wa couldn't take

any chances.

Quickly deciding they might be needed more as additional protection for the airlift, they kicked in their afterburners and headed for Football City.

Although they had no way of knowing, Toomey and Wa's quick and effective battle with the Phantom jets had attracted an audience.

A small group of men on horseback watched from far below as the planes exploded and dropped from the sky, crashing into the desolate wilderness of what once had been the northeastern corner of Oklahoma.

The leader of the group pointed to a funnel of smoke coming over a nearby hill.

"One came down over there," he said. "Let's take a look."

He spurred his horse in that direction, and the other riders quickly followed.

The men were American Indians—their bronze skin and high cheekbones bearing witness. They were remnants of the proud Oklahoma Shawnee Nation. Before the Soviet Red Star missiles of World War III had turned their homeland into a nuclear nightmare, they had lived peacefully on reservations in Oklahoma, somewhat forgotten by mainstream America, but basically more content than other tribes.

The leader of this small band of horsemen was Michael Crossbow. He was the son of the pre-war chief of the Shawnees and, before the war broke out, was expected to take his father's place at the head of the tribal council as soon as the chief retired.

But Crossbow had always had other ideas.

Going by the name of Michael Crosse, he left the reservation at the age of nineteen and joined the world of the white man—very successfully as it turned out. He won a full athletic scholarship to Princeton and surprised everyone by graduating with honors. He was working on his graduate degree in aeronautics at MIT when the war broke out. Enlisting almost immediately, he completed the Air Force's accelerated jet training program in record time and saw action in the last days of the war.

Most of Crossbow's family, including his father, were killed immediately in the Soviet's brief but awesome missile barrage. Others died from radiation poisoning during the next few months. Only a handful of the tribe survived, and bewildered and frightened at first, they wandered aimlessly through the desecrated land, trying to regain some of the long-dormant instincts of their ancestors for surviving in a hostile wilderness.

When he heard that American freedom fighters were striking back at the villains who had destroyed his country and people, Crossbow wanted to join them. But he could not turn his back on his people. To survive, they needed a leader; he was their only hope.

Calling on every ounce of determination, courage and intelligence that he possessed, he returned to the tribe and kept it together. Slowly, they rebuilt their lives, constructing primitive shelters, hunting for whatever game had survived the nuclear fallout, even beginning to grow some basic crops again.

Crossbow occasionally returned to his other world, venturing as far as Houston, New Orleans or Football City to trade and find out what was happening in post-war America. But he always came back to the tiny Shawnee settlement in the isolated, forgotten hills of Oklahoma.

He eagerly followed the successes of the United Americans. He had heard that the major cities in the East were free again, and he yearned to go there, to rejoin civilization. But not yet. He knew the survival of his people still could be threatened at any time by the continuing violence of the outside world. Just a week before, a small gang of bandits had raided his village; it was only his skill as a leader and a military strategist that enabled the Shawnees to repel the invaders.

And now, there was violence in their skies.

It took the small party of Shawnees only a few minutes to reach the nearest Phantom crash site. The fuselage was still in one piece, but it was charred and still smoldering. Pieces of the tail and the wings were scattered in several directions, the closest being several hundred yards away.

Crossbow dismounted and approached the wreckage. The pilot's partially burned body was still strapped into the cockpit. He reached into the scorched metal of the plane and pulled off the man's helmet. Staring up at him were the grotesque, twisted-in-death features of a man that had been totally bald.

The Shawnee leader had seen Skinheads before. He knew their reputation as the cruelest and craziest of all the aerial terrorists of the post-war world.

And he suddenly felt very afraid for his people.

Chapter 8

The *Freedom Express* pulled into Football City two days later, right on schedule.

Hunter and the Catfish were met on the platform by none other than Louie St. Louie, the beloved, uncrowned king of Football City. Always a high-rolling entrepreneur, it was St. Louie who just after World War III had turned the old city of St. Louis into the new gambling mecca of the continent. Rebuilding its decaying and bombed-out sections, St. Louie oversaw the construction of blocks of casinos, entertainment palaces, restaurants, saloons and high-priced cathouses.

And at the center of this universe was a football game.

But not just any football game—this was a 24-hour-a-day, 365-day-a-year football match between a pair of 500-member, free-substituting teams and played in a vast, 500,000-seat ultra-modern stadium located just outside the downtown section of the city. Bets could be placed on any part of this super game, from individual periods right up to an entire year's match. This constant action, along with the never-ending flow from the overcrowded, wildly popular casinos and nightspots, generated staggering amounts of revenue that dwarfed the glory days of the old Las Vegas.

Of course, the money brought problems to Football City, as all sorts of unsavory elements descended on it from all over the country. In a brief four-year period, a number of battles had been fought for the control of the city, and it had been occupied for a time by the Red-Star-backed Circle

Army. Now, with the United Americans back in charge of much of the continent, things had calmed down a little in Football City. But not completely. It still was a magnet for a lot of unscrupulous types who were out for a quick buck and anything else available for the grabbing.

Still, Hunter enjoyed his visits here, and he always liked seeing Louie St. Louie again.

After everyone on the train had disembarked and settled, St. Louie invited Hunter and his friends to join him in his private box at the football stadium for an evening's relaxation before the train left for the Badlands the next morning. Gladly accepting St. Louie's offer, they headed for the stadium in the man's thirty-two foot custom built limo.

The Catfish was especially enthusiastic about watching some football again; he had seen very few games since his NFL days.

"And now I can even bet on them," he said.

At the stadium, a reunion of sorts took place. Toomey and Ben Wa were there, along with Crunch O'Malley and his sidekick from the Ace Wrecking Company, Captain Elvis Q, both of whom had also signed on for the Badlands mission. Their role would be extremely important. As good as he was, Hunter and his Harrier would not be enough to provide air cover for the *Freedom Express*. It would be up to the Ace Wrecking Crew and their highly sophisticated F-4X Super Phantoms to seek out and, in some cases, secure the handful of airstrips that would be needed along the train's route. This way, their aircraft, as well as those of JT, Ben and other UA pilots, would be close enough to respond quickly if trouble arose.

The action on the football field was fast and furious when Hunter, Catfish and St. Louie arrived. Now, as the others settled in to watch, Toomey and Wa took the Wingman aside and told him about their skirmish over Oklahoma.

"No idea who they were?" Hunter asked.

"They didn't stick around long enough for us to find out," Toomey said. "And we didn't pursue because we figured we'd better get up here right away, just in case they

45

were part of a gang that was going for the C-5's."

"Which they weren't as it turned out," Wa added.

"Still, that was smart thinking, guys," Hunter said. "Plus, for all we know, those bandits may have been going for the Galaxys, and they ran into you first."

"I'd hate to think that was the case," Wa said.

"Well, in any event, it sounds like you were in the right place at the right time," Hunter concluded.

For the next hour, the others put all thoughts of the Badlands out of their minds as they enjoyed both the gridiron and the betting action. All except Hunter—the sneak attack by the F-4's was still puzzling him.

Gradually he filed it away to worry about later, and soon, he, too, was into the swing of the game.

But this enjoyment didn't last long. Just after the 314th quarter had ended, Hunter glanced over at Louie St. Louie and thought he detected a worried air about his friend.

During a rare time-out on the field, Hunter leaned over to him.

"Something bothering you?" he asked.

"I'm not sure, Hawk," the older, silver-maned man replied. He pointed toward a group of people seated a few rows away from his private box. "See that guy over there, with the red hair?"

Hunter nodded.

"His name is Duke Devillian. He's been hanging around this part of the country off and on since before the war. Used to be a small-time hood—just a pain-in-the-ass kind of guy."

"You must get plenty of that sort around here," Hunter said, devouring a foot-long hotdog.

"True," St. Louie answered. "But this guy has some pretty nasty political leanings. In fact there were a lot of rumors about him trying to resurrect the Klan in these parts."

The Ku Klux Klan?" Hunter asked, stopping in mid-bite.

"That's the one," St. Louie replied somberly. "Anyway, he dropped out of sight for a little while. Now he's back,

46

and all of a sudden he's a big shot. Tossing around money, traveling with an entourage. Look at those guys with him."

Devillian was surrounded by about a dozen rugged-looking men. Despite the generally festive atmosphere of the stadium, these apes wore solemn expressions. They also appeared to be more interested in looking around at the crowd than in watching the game.

"Almost looks like a gang of bodyguards," Hunter observed, finishing his dog and washing it down with a beer.

"That's what I thought," St. Louie said. "Somehow, he seems to have made some pretty powerful connections. And with scum like him, that sort of thing makes me real nervous."

One of the biggest reasons Hunter had survived his many brushes with death over the past few years was the fact that he possessed a type of extrasensory perception—sort of a built-in human early-warning system. In the cockpit of a plane, for example, he could always tell when a hostile aircraft was approaching, usually sensing it even before his radar kicked in. This special sense didn't desert him when he was on the ground. He just had a way of knowing when danger was present.

So whenever a vaguely uneasy feeling started creeping over him, he took it seriously.

"Would you do me a favor, Louie?" he asked.

"Name it," St. Louie said.

"After we pull out tomorrow, can you have a couple of your best guys keep an eye on Mr. Devillian and keep me posted?"

St. Louie looked down at Devillian and his gang and caught a stronger whiff of the trouble in the air.

"You got it, Hawk," he replied.

Chapter 9

The thunderstorm descended on Football City just after midnight and continued unabated until dawn.

Lightning lit up the sky for hundreds of miles around; thunder crashed with the volume of thousands of bombs going off at once. Yet there was no rain. Not a drop fell on the city or the two-mile-long armored train that waited in its station.

Hawk Hunter saw none of this display of Nature's ferocity. He was deep asleep in a penthouse suite provided by Louie St. Louie. But just as the city was being thrashed by the night storm, its air becoming saturated with ozone and negative ions, so too parts of Hunter's psyche were being filled with a different kind of ether.

Several months before, he had provided the bulk of testimony that led to the conviction of the ex-vice-president of the United States on charges of high treason. During this public trial, it was proved beyond all doubt that the ex-vp had conspired with the Soviets to start World War III. The traitor, having barely survived wounds suffered in an assassination attempt just minutes after his conviction, was now in protective custody in a hospital-prison secretly built in Nova Scotia, Free Canada.

Hunter's testimony for the trial had been drawn out in a most unusual way—by hypnosis. In a marathon twelve-hour session, Hunter spoke from a deep hypnotic trance about his participation in World War III and how it eventually altered the outcome of the conflict itself. The trance was induced by one Dr. Jocelyn Leylah, an attractive psychologist who specialized in hypnotic regression.

After the trial—and just before the startling events at the Los Angeles train station—Dr. Leylah had contacted Hunter with a request that he partake in another one of her experiments. Fascinated by Hunter's extraordinary sixth sense, the doctor wanted to test his capacity for subliminal learning through self-hypnosis.

Although Hunter already knew a few hypnotic tricks of his own, he was understandably skittish about anything that might tinker with his own, unique psyche. So he was very reluctant to partake in the doctor's experiment—at first. However, a weekend spent in the country with the pretty psychologist changed his mind. He agreed to take her specially programmed tape recorder and an extra-long-playing tape cassette and promised to listen to it while he was asleep one night.

And this was the night.

Hunter had no idea what was on the tape—after all, that was the key to the whole experiment. Theoretically, several hours of information would be pumped into his memory while he slept. If he remembered all or any of it over the next few weeks, then the experiment would be declared a success. If not, then it would be back to the drawing board.

As an extra added feature, the tape contained a hypnotic suggestion that would supposedly totally erase his knowledge of the experiment. The doctor claimed that when he woke up the next morning, he would simply remember playing the tape as a way to relax. Everything concerning the subliminal-learning experience would be forgotten, hidden away deep in his subconscious.

Hunter didn't believe any of this would even happen, but a promise was a promise—especially to such a pretty lady. So on this night, after he retired to the suite, Hunter hastily set up the recorder, put on the cotton-lined headphones and let the special tape play. The first hour was nothing more than the recorded sounds of waves crashing against a beach. This was to lull him to sleep—though at this point he needed no inducement. The many days of labor getting

49

the *Freedom Express* ready, combined with the half dozen beers he'd consumed at the game, were enough to send him to dreamland in five minutes.

So as the Wingman slept and the thunder and lightning crashed outside, his subconscious was subjected to a steady stream of subliminal data.

It would be some time before he would realize that the unusual experiment would save his life. . . .

Chapter 10

The next day

Hunter's customized Harrier jumpjet sliced through the early morning fog and quickly rose above the *Freedom Express* as the two-mile-long train pulled out of Football City and headed westward.

During the night, the troops under Catfish Johnson's command had loaded onto the train. Numbering nearly twelve thousand men, the army was composed primarily of the UA 1st Airborne Division, complemented by two battalions of Football City Special Forces Rangers, the force that had gained a place in post-World War III military history for their bravery during the first battle for Football City.

Thanks to Toomey and Ben Wa's mission to Texas, the Cobra Brothers and their famous Cobra attack helicopters also were aboard. Hunter was very appreciative to have the Brothers along for the ride—not only were their high-tech Cobra attack helicopters among the most deadly rotary aircraft ever built, but no one alive could fly them any better than the Cobra Brothers, who were not really brothers, but simply bonded together by their skill and experience. To handle the insectlike Cobras, two other platform cars, similar to the specially designed landing car for Hunter's Harrier, had been outfitted with landing pads for the choppers and had been placed toward the middle of the train.

The commanding officer of this small but renowned flying unit was Captain Jesse Tyler. He and his old friend, Captain Bobby Crockett, had been free-lance chopper pilots in the days before the Football City war. Since then, the two pilots and their gunners, Lieutenant John "John-Boy" Hobbs and Lieutenant Kenny Baxter, had worked almost exclusively for the United Americans.

They had returned to their native Texas for a short rest when Toomey and Ben Wa located them and recruited them for the train adventure. Actually, the recruiting part had been pretty easy. The minute Tyler and Crockett heard about Hunter's plan, they eagerly endorsed it.

The Cobra Brothers' role would be to stay close to the train, flying short reconnaissance missions and driving off any would-be ground attackers. Toomey and Ben Wa, with their A-7E Strikefighters, would join the F-4X's of the Ace Wrecking Company in hopping from one landing field to another as the train made its way across the country, trying their best to stay within striking distance in case they were needed. In addition to being the overall aerial commander for the journey, Hunter would stay in touch with the other jet pilots as well as fly his daily scouting missions. In this role, he felt like an old-time trail scout who rode on ahead of the wagon train.

Before heading westward along the first day's route, Hunter took the Harrier back over the train for one last look. He dropped down to five hundred feet and put the jumpjet into a slow, forward-moving, near hover.

Buzzing the entire length of the train in this manner, Hunter took a grim satisfaction in what he saw: dozens of cars carrying anti-aircraft guns, assorted assault weapons, banks of heavy machine guns, recoilless rifles, long-range cannons and SAM missile batteries, all of them inside special "turtle" armored cars that could cover up in case of trouble and then open automatically when it was time to go on the offensive. Mixed in close to the middle were the two cars carrying the ferocious-looking Cobra attack copters. Then, came the fifty-foot-barreled monstrosity called Big Dick and then the dozens of three-piece mini-fort cars that would be dropped off at scheduled intervals.

Hunter swung the Harrier back toward the west and contemplated the dark clouds that were ominously forming out there. For once, he chose not to be impressed by the omen.

It will take more than a few left-over air bandits or Badlands freaks to stop this train, he thought confidently.

The first stop for the *Freedom Express* was near the old city of Topeka, in the territory that once had been eastern Kansas. The first set of fortified cars would be dropped off in the vicinity of the city, thus becoming the first settlement on the road to recivilizing the country west of Football City.

Although most of the violence that had been reported in the Badlands in recent weeks had occurred farther west, in the New Mexico-Arizona areas, Hunter knew it was wise not to take anything for granted. Despite the fact that the first day's progress through Missouri was going smoothly, he knew the emerging open plains of Kansas held increasing dangers. While it might not be well-suited for an ambush from the ground, the train certainly would be a tempting target for an attack from the air once it reached the wide-open spaces.

Hunter's trained eye scanned the skies ahead of his Harrier. All seemed peaceful. Nothing appeared on his radar screen. He even allowed himself to relax a little.

Maybe the first day *would* be uneventful, he thought. That would be just fine with him—he had been feeling slightly edgy since taking off. He had caught several strange, conflicting thoughts creeping into his head. On one hand, something out there was making him feel more anxious about this mission. But on the other hand, he was feeling almost *too* confident about its success—and that bothered him.

Suddenly his specially designed cockpit scrambler radio crackled to life.

"Hawk . . . this is Catfish. We just got a radio message from JT and Ben. There's trouble up ahead."

Hunter turned back to the train and landed. Within ten minutes, he was in the Control car, getting briefed by the Catfish.

"They called in from the old Topeka airport," he told Hunter, pulling out a map. "You know, that was the first landing strip they were scouting as a possible forward base. Well, they were able to set down, but they say it looks like a battle zone."

Hunter was surprised at the news. "I thought that place had been abandoned."

"According to our information, it had been," Catfish replied. "But the guys say it's littered with bodies, about fifty of them."

So much for the easy first day on the job, Hunter thought. "Do they have any idea who they are? Or were?"

"They're not sure," Catfish said. "JT thought he recognized a couple of the guys he used to work with in his freelance days. And he says unless they had changed drastically, they were pretty strongly in favor of our cause. His best guess is that some ex-soldiers and free-lance pilots got together on their own to try and combat some of the crap that's been going on out here."

"And wound up being the victims of it," Hunter said grimly. "Could the guys tell how it happened?"

"From what JT and Ben said, it doesn't sound like just a band of roaming bandits raided the place," Catfish continued. "A couple of buildings had been completely leveled, and some of the bodies were pretty well blown apart. Looks like they were hit with some pretty sophisticated weaponry."

"Missile strike?" Hunter asked.

"Maybe," Catfish replied somberly. "Followed up by an air strike." Catfish paused, then added, "And they found something else that's a little strange."

"What's that?" Hunter quickly asked.

Johnson paused for a long moment. "They discovered one of our flags which had been pulled down from the flagpole at the airport and partially burned," he said slowly.

Instantly, Hunter felt anger rise from his belly. Though he recognized their Constitutionally-approved right to do it—after all, "Freedom" meant nothing less than total freedom of expression—he despised anyone who would burn the American flag.

"Another flag was waving over the place," Catfish continued. "It was obviously left behind by whoever staged the raid."

"Whose flag was it?" Hunter asked sharply.

"That's the weird thing," the army commander responded. "It's not one that we've ever seen before. The only insignia on it is a huge cross . . . in flames."

Chapter 11

Duke Devillian was feeling extremely pleased with himself.

Sitting in the front-seat gunner's cockpit of the Soviet-built Hind helicopter gunship, he was just about trembling with delight. The past few weeks had been very, *very* productive, and now, with several of his grand schemes going forward at once, the future looked very bright indeed—for him.

He couldn't decide which of his latest triumphs pleased him the most, though on examination, the meeting in Houston with Major Henrik Heck, former corps commander of the Twisted Cross, would probably rank Number One.

Devillian was surprised to learn that he actually enjoyed dealing with Heck and the leftovers from the Twisted Cross, especially since he was now their boss. A neo-Nazi organization, the Cross had seized control of the Panama Canal Zone the year before as the first step of a plan to extend its tentacles into North America and eventually rule the continent. But the United Americans had crushed this plot by winning back the canal in a savage land and air battle.

Although most of the Twisted Cross's war machine was destroyed, a handful of their officers, including Heck, had escaped.

In the months that followed their devastating defeat in Panama, Herr Heck and his cronies spent most of their time plotting their revenge against the United Americans—and especially Hawk Hunter. But without the military might of their former organization behind them, these men were basically impotent. Their plotting consisted mainly of rambling, drunken conversations in sleazy bars in the lawless towns of the Badlands, the only area where they felt relatively safe.

Then one day, Duke Devillian came back into their lives.

Devillian had actually been dealing with the Cross for several years. Long an ardent admirer of the Nazis and their doctrines, the cross-eyed Texan was also a slave to the notion that "White is Right," and therefore, like the Nazis, he had little patience for do-gooders who still thought that people of different races could live together in peace.

Colored? Asians? Indians? Mixing peacefully with pure White? How could anyone be that stupid? he would ask himself over and over.

Like his daddy before him, Devillian had jumped into the Ku Klux Klan with both feet as a young man, doing his best to stir up racial hatred wherever he went. In the violent days that followed World War III, he turned to gunrunning—both selling and buying—as a way of living. His customers needed only to pass one test: They had to be white. After that he would supply them with any and all weapons he could muster, no matter how perverse their cause might be.

Coincidently the Twisted Cross became one of his best customers, and for Devillian, it was like a dream come true. Nothing like a good mix of business and pleasure to bring out the best in a man, he thought. Being arms dealers themselves, the Nazi's procurement section hired Devillian as a sort of advance man for them, scouring the fringes of the American continent, his pockets full of Nazi money, buying up weapons caches that were for sale and stealing ones that weren't.

Then came the devastating defeat of the Cross in Panama. When that happened, Devillian was so despondent he nearly committed suicide. His dream of riding to power on bloody Nazi coattails seemed to vanish.

However, it didn't take long for him to see that the Cross's defeat could be a golden opportunity for him.

Over the years, Devillian had built up a fortune in gold and diamonds through his black market dealings. Even more importantly, he had made a lot of contacts with powerful people, including many enemies of America. One by one, those enemies had been defeated by the United Americans—vanquished, but not totally wiped out. Like Heck and his Nazi cohorts, they had retreated to lick their wounds and dream of revenge.

Somewhere along the way, Devillian decided he could be the one to make those dreams come true.

With his nefarious network reaching into many of the terrorist groups around the Bads, who was better positioned to unite all of the scattered enemies of America? Who was better equipped to build a new organization that could rise from the ashes of past defeats and launch a new, even more deadly challenge to the United Americans?

Once this grand idea came to him, Devillian wasted little time putting a plan into action. He recruited some of his old cohorts from the Klan, and together they began to quietly expand their power base by forming a secret alliance of Badlands terrorist organizations that had been operating in their own hit-or-miss fashions.

Supplying arms for his growing army was no problem for the cross-eyed terrorist. He knew most of the major gunrunners and weapons smugglers still operating in the world. Plus his contacts also included people who owned some fairly sophisticated military aircraft. Soon enough, Devillian had himself a patchwork air force containing a number of Soviet fighters as well as French Mirage aircraft.

Then another deal was added to this deadly air corps. It was no secret that the most vicious and feared of the Canal Nazi units was the Skinhead squadron. Eighteen pilots in all, the 'Heads flew their F-4J Phantoms with a bloody and reckless abandon that struck fear into enemies and allies alike. Temporarily "unemployed," they were only too happy to accept Devillian's invitation to join his evil crusade.

But Devillian still lacked a cohesive, well-trained officer

corps to keep his unruly bandit gangs in line. So when he finally approached Major Heck, he already had put in place the foundation for a military organization that would rival the Twisted Cross at the height of its power; yet it was one that lacked the needed discipline from the top. Heck jumped at the opportunity to round up what was left of the Canal Nazis' officer organization and join forces with Devillian.

To prove his value to Devillian's cause, Heck had been given a test assignment: stop the cross-country train journey of the Modern Pioneers. Heck accomplished this with typical, ruthless efficiency. Any lingering doubts Devillian might have entertained about Heck's ability to command troops again vanished when he heard about the fate of the train. The meeting in Houston completed the incorporation of the old Twisted Cross officers' corps into Devillian's new war machine.

News of this sinister union spread quickly though quietly through the Badlands, and hundreds of additional air pirates, bandits and other low-lifes decided to jump on the bandwagon. If there was going to be another war, they didn't want to miss out on the action.

With his still-secret army growing in numbers and power, Devillian's recent visit to Football City had been a kind of celebration-*cum*-scouting mission. He loved the very smell of money, and it permeated the very air of the place. Moreover, he dreamed of the day when his forces would march into Football City and he would take over the gambling empire.

But there was something that Devillian liked even more than money, and that was why he was sitting in the cockpit of the fiercesome Hind gunship.

Quite simply, he enjoyed killing people. And not just one or two murders at a time — he'd had enough of that during his Klan days. No, what really turned him on was slaughtering dozens, even hundreds, of people, all at once, and then filming the freshly killed bodies soon afterward. Just the thought of roaring out of the sky in a powerful airplane, with its nose cameras turned on and all guns blazing, blasting away at anything that moved on the ground, was enough to make his scrotum pulsate. Now he knew what the Nazi pilots of World War II must have felt like—strafing helpless civilians, bombing hospitals and schoolyards. Getting rid of the riff-raff.

Purify the country. That was the name of the game.

Of course, he couldn't actually fly an airplane, but he could function as a gunner, and that was even better: He got to pull the trigger that unleashed all that glorious havoc, all the while recording the carnage on his video gun cameras. As a favor from Heck, he had flown with the squadron of Skinheads that demolished the old Topeka airport just for the fun of it—and he had loved every bloody minute of it. When they landed and he filmed the death and destruction they had caused, he was overcome with a surge of sexual excitement so strong he nearly passed out.

It had been the best day of his life.

Now the whining of the helicopter's engines starting up knocked him out of his seminal daydream and back to reality.

"Buckled in?" the Skinhead pilot's raspy voice asked him over the intercom from the back seat. Normally an F-4 fighter pilot, this particular 'Head had drawn the shit duty of carting Devillian all around the Badlands.

"Shit, yes, I'm buckled in!" Devillian anxiously replied. "Now just get this fucking thing into the air."

The Red Star that formerly had adorned the tail of the Hind was gone. In its place was a large cross shown against a backdrop of fire—the symbol of Devillian's new organization, the Knights of the Burning Cross.

Devillian glanced back at his Skinhead pilot just as the Hind was lifting off.

He's an ugly bastard, but he sure knows how to put this baby through its paces, Devillian thought.

They turned west, over Oklahoma, heading for the secret headquarters Devillian had established in the wilds of the desert southwest. It was here that he was going to meet with his chief lieutenants to inform them of the news he had picked up during his visit to Football City.

Several days before Devillian flew to the gambling mecca, his spies had told him about a huge train that had rolled into town from the east, apparently headed for the West Coast. Devillian wasn't too surprised. He figured that someone would eventually be foolish enough to try and succeed where the Modern Pioneers had failed. However, from all reports, this latest train was much bigger and was hauling a tremendous amount of firepower.

By the time Devillian arrived in Football City, the whole place was buzzing about the super train. He had even traveled down to the railway station to get a look at it himself, though it wasn't much of a sight as all its cars had been covered over with canvas tarps.

But the trip had confirmed one thing: Just as Devillian had suspected, the United Americans were responsible for assembling and operating the train.

And for many reasons, learning this had made him perversely happy.

They flew along uneventfully, the Skinhead pilot keeping the Hind about a thousand feet above the wide open Oklahoma rangeland.

Suddenly, Devillian became erect with excitement. He grabbed his microphone and screamed back to the pilot: "Over there!" He pointed toward the ground. "I thought I saw something. Let's go down and take a look."

The Skinhead scanned where Devillian was pointing and saw a small band of horsemen. He immediately swung the Hind in that direction and put the chopper into a steep dive.

"Are they Indians?" Devillian asked, his voice murderously giddy. "They are! Fucking moccasin-sniffing Indians. Plug me in, I'm going to let 'em have it!"

The pilot nonchalantly flicked a control switch which supplied power both to the Hind's twin-barreled chin cannon and its nose-mounted video camera. No sooner was this done than Devillian was squeezing the cannon's trigger and screaming like a madman.

"You goddamn buffalo fuckers!" he roared with delight as the helicopter bore down on the horsemen who had all

61

now turned as one to escape.

The cannon was blazing away, spewing streaks of fire into the midst of the terrified Indians. One pass wiped out most of the men and horses, but Devillian wanted more.

"Go back for the rest of the bastards!" he ordered the pilot. "And keep the cameras rolling!"

They swung the Hind around and dove again, perforating the few remaining riders with two long blasts. Devillian then demanded that they make a third pass, just to make sure no one had survived.

Out of the corner of his crossed eye, he caught sight of a lone horseman dashing across a stretch of open prairie toward the relative safety of a nearby forest.

"Damn! we did miss one," Devillian yelled. "Quick — let's get him!"

The Skinhead pilot stifled a yawn and sent the aircraft hurtling toward the fleeing figure. He leveled off the Hind just a few feet above the ground, allowing Devillian to zero in for a final, killing shot. Just as he fired, the rider jerked his mount sharply to the right. A miss. Devillian fired again at the zigzagging horseman. Another miss.

Suddenly Devillian shrieked: *"Christ!* The goddamn trees!"

A look of mild panic distorted the Skinhead's face as he glanced up and saw the forest looming less than a hundred feet in front of the speeding aircraft. He yanked on the controls, and the Hind shot upward, its belly brushing the tops of the trees as it barely cleared the edge of the small forest.

"You stupid bastard!" Devillian was practically foaming at the mouth. "You almost got us killed."

"You're the one who told me to get him," the pilot protested angrily, not accustomed to taking such guff. If it had been anyone else that had talked to him like that, the Skinhead would have landed and bit the man's neck until he died of blood loss.

"I didn't tell you to ram us into the goddamn woods doing it," Devillian barked at him.

They circled the small clump of trees twice, but saw no

sign of their prey.

Devillian settled back and took some deep breaths.

"Aw, what the fuck, it'll give the SOB something to tell the squaws about," he roared crazily. "That is, if the chicken bastard stops running before he hits South America. Now, let's get out of here."

As the aircraft headed westward, the lone horseman re-emerged from the forest. Michael Crossbow's eyes blazed with tears of pure hatred as he watched the Hind disappear over the horizon.

Someday, he vowed, he would find whoever was in that aircraft. . . .

Chapter 12

The *Freedom Express* pulled into the old Topeka railroad station just before dusk.

Hawk Hunter gently set the Harrier down on the landing car and climbed out of the cockpit. Waiting for him at the side of the train were JT and Ben Wa, who had left their Strikefighters with a guard at the nearby airport and hitched a ride back to the train with the Cobra Brothers.

The men immediately went to the Control car where they met Catfish and Fitzgerald, who had spent most of the first day ironing out bugs in the Dash-8's combined computer system.

Hunter immediately asked JT and Ben Wa to describe the scene at the Topeka airport. They took the next few minutes doing so, in detail: the bodies, the widespread, indiscriminate destruction, the evidence of advanced weaponry.

"Nothing was looted though," Ben said. "We found weapons and booze and even money still laying around. Usually a raiding party would suck up all that kind of stuff. It was almost like whoever did it, did it as a lark."

"And of course they left that flag behind," JT said, finishing up his report by describing the banner.

"And I'm not real thrilled with their choice of symbols," Catfish moaned. "God, that's all we need, a bunch of yahoos running around under the banner of a burning cross."

Hunter rubbed his hands on his tired face. It seemed that in addition to all his other concerns, he'd been running into a disturbing number of racist acts over the past few weeks. Few things upset him so much. America was America, he had always preached. And *everyone* born here or citizenized was an American—equal, as spelled out in the Declaration of Independence, and guaranteed, as stated in the Constitution.

And while he was not so naive as to think that every American was a walking-talking angel, he couldn't believe anyone was stupid enough to think one group was worse or better than the other. It just wasn't natural. As such, he had no use whatsoever for people who were racists.

"What did you do with that flag?" he asked the two pilots.

JT glanced up at him with a look of mild surprise. "We burned it, of course," he replied.

The night in Topeka passed uneventfully, although once again, Hunter found his slumber interrupted by a series of weird dreams.

Despite this, he was up before dawn and joined the others in making preparations for the long day ahead. The first order of business was to disconnect the first three cars from the rear of the train: one filled with food and medical supplies, one set up as living quarters, and one filled with weapons, ammunition and communications equipment. They would form the nucleus of the first mini-fort settlement on the *Freedom Express* trail.

As an extra precaution, Hunter had radioed Jones and requested that a back-up squadron of six Chinook helicopters be sent to the Topeka Fort. He wanted to make sure that should the people who destroyed the airport happen to return, the men left behind in Topeka would have reenforcements to fight them off—or if it got desperate, enough airlift to evacuate them.

At first light, the Cobra Brothers took JT and Ben back to their Strikefighters at the airport. They too would hang around Topeka for a day or so, just to make sure the mini-fort would have some air support should they need it.

Meanwhile the two, single-seat F-4X Super Phantoms of the Ace Wrecking Company would fly ahead to the next stopping point, near the site of the famous old frontier town, Dodge City. In keeping with the pioneering spirit of the *Freedom Express,* the United American Command felt it appropriate to put a settlement near the town that embodied so much of the history of the Old West. Plus, there was a large civilian population reportedly living near the town — people who might appreciate some semblance of law and order returning to their land.

Hunter climbed back into the cockpit of the Harrier jumpjet at seven AM on the button. Moments later, the VTOL aircraft was rising straight up above the train. Hovering for a moment to check his in-flight systems, he then shifted the Harrier's thrust nozzles forward and, with a mighty roar, surged toward the west.

It was a beautiful, crisp day. As Hunter climbed to twenty thousand feet, he could see the flat plains of Kansas stretching on for miles beneath him. The land seemed as vacant as the endless sky around him.

He circled back toward Topeka and saw the train start to pull away, the Cobra helicopters hovering protectively nearby. A handful of soldiers stood next to the three railroad cars that were being left behind.

"Good luck, guys," Hunter whispered, taking the Harrier down to less than a hundred feet and flying directly over them, tipping his wings in a final salute. The men responded, waving and saluting as the Harrier turned westward again.

Two hours went by. Everything was as quiet as it had been the day before. Hunter was alone in the vast, calm sky. No other aircraft appeared on the horizon to challenge him; nothing blipped on his radar screen.

He would have enjoyed the serenity if he hadn't once again caught some conflicting thoughts running through his head. What lay ahead? Danger? Success? Failure? Death? Usually before undertaking such a mission, Hunter would set his extraordinary consciousness in one direction and then carry on through. But something was different this time, though he couldn't put his finger on it. His normally orderly thinking process was scattered; random thoughts and notions seemed to be bubbling up from inside his psyche, yet not in a form which he could understand. It was a very disturbing sensation — one that left him feeling like he was not entirely in control of his destiny. And for a person like Hunter, that was a very frightening prospect indeed.

Suddenly, the radar that was built into Hunter's brain started humming. The magical sixth sense that he simply called *the feeling,* told him something was wrong. Somewhere.

He was about to click his radio microphone to call back to the train when Catfish radioed up to him instead.

"Get to Dodge City ASAP, Hawk," he heard his friend say with the chilling tone of *déjà vu.* "The Wrecking Crew just fell into one hell of a mess . . ."

Chapter 13

Unlike the quiet, but grisly, reception in Topeka, the F-4X Super Phantoms of the Ace Wrecking Company were welcomed to old Dodge City the old-fashioned way: with a storm of gunfire.

Sent ahead to recon the airport near the city, Crunch and Elvis Q had just spotted the outline of the field on the horizon when the sky was suddenly filled with Sparrow air-to-air missiles.

"Where the hell did they come from?" Crunch had yelled over to Elvis, nimbly dodging the lead rocket.

"Beats me," Elvis called back, noting that his radar screen had suddenly filled up with a bunch of nasty blips. "There must be a low-altitude combat patrol in the area."

Elvis's guess was correct. A swarm of deadly F-104 Starfighter jets rose to challenge the Super Phantoms as they approached from the east. The Starfighters, agile supersonic fighters favored by many of the continent's air pirate gangs, had been flying at barely five hundred feet to avoid any radar interception until the last possible moment.

The United American pilots had no choice but to meet the first wave of rising air pirates head-on. Using a combination of practiced flying skills and Sidewinder missiles, the two Super Phantoms quickly managed to send a pair of F-104's tumbling down in flames. But then several others immediately took their places, with a radar indication of many more racing to join the fight.

Crunch quickly appraised the situation and then radioed

his partner. "I think we've crashed a very big party here," he said arming two more Sidewinders.

"If you're suggesting a strategic retreat, I'm with you, boss," Elvis replied, counting as many as eighteen Starfighters in the vicinity. "Maybe we can lead some of these guys back in the direction of the train, call Hawk and even the odds a little."

Crunch paused long enough to dodge a pair of F-104's that were zeroing in on him, nose guns blazing. "Makes sense to me, partner," he replied finally.

As Crunch relayed their plan back to the train via the radio scrambler, the two Super Phantoms turned away from Dodge City and headed east again. Six of the F-104's followed them in hot pursuit.

"I just hope these guys don't figure out what's going on," Crunch muttered to himself.

Meanwhile, Hunter was racing westward.

He keyed in on the Wreckers' last known position, and within minutes he saw the specks of the two Super Phantoms barreling eastward, with six Starfighters practically on their tails. Hunter knew that if they had so desired, the skilled Wreckers could have easily lost the trailing F-104's. But Crunch and Elvis had managed to stay just far enough ahead to keep their pursuers interested.

"Never a dull moment," Hunter thought as he put the Harrier into a screaming dive.

Crunch had just started to get anxious when he saw the familiar outline of the jumpjet flash down in front of him.

"It's the sheriff!" he called over to Elvis, as the Super Phantoms quickly peeled off and let the Wingman do his thing. "And not a second too soon, pardner."

Hunter pulled out of his steep dive and pointed the nose of the Harrier directly at the lead F-104. One blast from his twin Aden cannons and the enemy plane disintegrated in a ball of fire and smoke. Hunter's attack was so sudden and unexpected that one of the trailing jets plowed right into his leader's debris, ingesting burning, smoking parts into his jet intakes. Within two seconds, he too was spinning out of control.

While Hunter pulled up from his swift and deadly attack, Crunch and Elvis looped their F-4's beneath the remaining four Starfighters and quickly had two of them in their sights. A pair of Sidewinders later, two more '104's were spiraling downward. Now only two enemy aircraft remained. Their desperate pilots tried to outmaneuver the United Americans — but there was nowhere to hide in the crystal clear sky. A perfectly aimed cannon shot from Hunter sent one of the Starfighters plunging to a fiery grave; another Sidewinder shot from Crunch took care of number six.

"I suppose that's another bottle of Scotch we owe you," Crunch radioed over to Hunter as the F-4's and the Harrier formed up.

"That one was on the house," Hunter deadpanned.

"But we're not done yet," Crunch told him. "Those Starfighter drivers have a lot of buddies waiting for them back in Dodge City. Looked to us like there were at least another two dozen flying around the airport there."

"That's quite a fleet for just one gang of air pirates," Hunter observed. "Could be an alliance of some kind."

"Maybe," Crunch agreed. "Though I imagine they probably wind up fighting each other as much as anyone else. In fact, they're probably all screwed up back there right now, wondering who we were and what the hell is going on."

"Well, they're sitting right in our path, so we've got to deal with them sooner or later," Hunter said as the three jets turned back toward the Topeka airport. "And I'd prefer to do it sooner."

Two hours later, they were airborne again.

Flying low to avoid radar, their wings flush with a gaggle of ordnance, the three pilots were returning to the Dodge City airport, intent on launching a preemptive air strike. The purpose of the surprise, hit-and-run mission was to keep the air pirates off balance as well as gauge the size and disposition of their air force.

But it was Hunter and the Wreckers who were to be surprised.

They met no opposition going in—no Starfighters, no AA fire, not so much as a beep on their SAM detection equipment. And then, when they reached the target twenty minutes later, they were amazed to find the airport was deserted.

"They sure cleared out quick," Elvis said, not quite believing what they were seeing.

"They sure did," Hunter replied. "Almost *too* quick."

Chapter 14

The Hind helicopter eased onto the mile-long, dirt runway and settled down in a swirl of red dust and sand.

Duke Devillian, his pudgy body moist with excitement, climbed out of the chopper even before its huge rotor blades had stopped turning. The Skinhead pilot felt a jolt of glee run through him for an instant when it appeared Devillian might actually walk right into one of the twirling razor-edge blades, his perception screwed up by his hideously crossed eyes.

But no such luck — the terrorists leader ducked at the last possible moment, then scrambled on his hands and knees until he was out of danger.

"You would have been eaten alive by ants if that had hit me," Devillian screamed, pointing first at the rotor blade, and then at the Skinhead, all the while not quite sure himself how he could have made good on the threat.

The 'Head simply gave him the finger, then proceeded to shut down the Hind's main systems. He had been practically chained to Devillian for the past forty-eight hours as the man insisted on flying all over the southwest plains, looking for innocent victims to kill. Now the Skinhead pilot was just happy the long trip was over, knowing that Devillian would have to look for his daily dose of blood and mayhem somewhere else.

Devillian quickly regained his composure and walked like a king across the unique expanse of land that housed his secret Fortress of the Burning Cross.

Selecting the bizarre location for his base was a stroke of strategic genius for the cross-eyed madman. He had turned the place into a natural riddle: It was almost impossible to find, yet it stood out like a sore thumb from the surrounding landscape. It was laughably vulnerable from all sides, yet no enemy could approach it from any direction—either by land or by air, day or night—without being spotted while they were still miles away.

Best of all, the place looked deserted—yet it housed hundreds of weapons, a dozen barracks, a mess hall, a small power generation plant, two fuel dumps and two airstrips long enough to handle any jet fighter. To protect it all, dozens of SAM nests lay hidden in its perimeters, holding enough missiles to shoot down an entire air force and still have some to spare.

But the gem of his secret encampment was Devillian's heavily guarded, "invisible" mansion that sprawled over nearly three acres of the northern side of the base. Separated from the rest of the military installation by a series of security barriers, the mansion contained Devillian's personal living quarters, as well as the customed-designed Combat Command Center, which was the electronic brains for the Burning Cross.

This control center was actually a huge war room filled with state-of-the-art communications equipment. One entire wall of this room featured an immense control panel that electronically linked everything from the defensive installations ringing the base to the dozens of Burning Cross outposts set up in remote locations throughout the Badlands. From this one room, Devillian could send orders and receive information from anywhere in his organization's rapidly growing domain.

Devillian had two favorite spots in the twenty-room phantom mansion: One was the War Room; the other was his Play Pen.

The Play Pen was a lust chamber that contained, among other things, a giant sauna and whirlpool, a huge video screen, a forty-foot-long, marble-topped bar, several massage tables and a massive waterbed. The ceiling and most of the walls of the huge room were covered with large mirrors; the remaining wall featured a bizarre catalog of sexual restraining devices.

It was here that Devillian headed as soon as he climbed out of the Hind. Despite the period of stimulation provided by gunning down scores of helpless Indians over the past two days, the long trip from Football City had left him tired and just a little tense.

But he knew exactly how to take care of that.

As he entered the Play Pen, he immediately yanked a long velvet cord dangling from the ceiling, sounding a bell in another corner of the house. Less than a minute later, two young women — a young, busty brunette and an older, slimmer, very pretty blonde — entered the room. Both were wearing sheer silk robes that did nothing to hide the alluring contours of their bodies.

"It's been a long two days, girls," Devillian told them crudely. "And I'm aching all over. So get to work."

The two girls helped Devillian undress. He stretched out on the massage table, and for the next several minutes, their nimble fingers roamed all over his white, pudgy body.

Finally he sat up.

"Make drinks," he said to the blonde. Then he turned to the brunette and barked, "And you, help me put in a movie."

The blond girl, whose name was Desiree, scampered to the bar to make cocktails, while Diamond, the brunette, accompanied Devillian to a long, low sofa situated in front of the video screen. Devillian opened a large cabinet at one end of the sofa, revealing several shelves filled with hundreds of his homicidal pornographic videos.

"Get out three-oh-three," he commanded. "And make it quick."

Diamond's heart sank as she pulled out #303. She knew it featured women making love to each other in a variety of sadistic ways. She also knew the effect it would have on Devillian. After watching it for only a few minutes, he would order Desiree and her to perform the same perverted acts on each other. She hated it, but she had no choice. She was one of Devillian's many love slaves, young girls bought on the Southwest's free-wheeling white slavery market. She knew that the only escape from Devillian's lair was by death.

By the time Desiree returned with the drinks, Devillian already had started the movie.

He ordered the blonde to sit at his feet and lick his toes, while he forced his hand inside Diamond's robe and roughly began fondling her lovely breasts. As the action on the screen grew more heated, Devillian's excitement rapidly mounted. A snap of his fingers ordered Desiree to produce a large vial of crack cocaine, and soon Devillian was forcing both women to inhale the drug, all the while taking many long, greedy drags himself.

Of the two, he liked young Diamond the best.

"You do what I tell you, when I tell you," he said, pulling the teenager up by her hair. "Right?"

She stifled a cry and nodded her head. "Yes . . ." she said.

Devillian laughed cruelly and shoved the crack pipe into her mouth. Then he looked up at Desiree. At twenty-two, the blonde was much older than Diamond, and more in tune to Devillian's perverted ways of living. He stared into her eyes for a long moment, watching her pupils turn glassy as the cocaine smoke did its work. Then he winked at her. She smiled seductively and winked back. Both knew what lay ahead for Diamond.

The video played on for another ten minutes before Devillian could wait no longer. He roughly stripped Diamond's robe off and threw her back on the sofa, spreading her thighs wide apart. Putting his hand on the back of Desiree's head, he pretended to force her toward the other girl, at the same time putting one of her hands down to his own expanded crotch.

"You know what to do, you bitch," he whispered, closing his eyes and thinking back to all the helpless victims he had killed over the past two days. "Now do it right."

That evening, refreshed and revived, Devillian met in the War Room with the High Command he had assembled over the past few weeks for the Knights of the Burning Cross.

It was a motley crew.

Major Heck of the Twisted Cross was there as was Studs Mallox, a huge beast of a man with a totally bald head who recently had seized control of the turbulent Skinhead F-4 squadron by garroting and then disemboweling their previous commander.

Next to Mallox sat a dozen other disreputable-looking types who were in charge of the major units of Badlands bandits and air pirates that made up the Burning Cross.

Two people stood out in this latter group: a Mexican named Jorge Juarez and his sister, Juanita. Jorge was one of the fattest people Devillian had ever seen. Rolls of flab spilled over his gunbelt onto the chairs on either side of him. His eyes were mere slits in his bloated, malevolent face. A black, greasy mustache drooped from either side of his sneering mouth. Various scars and pimples rounded out the man's totally repugnant appearance.

This is one truly disgusting human being, Devillian thought.

But also a very powerful one. Jorge had managed to pull together an army of bandits, renegades, escaped felons, war criminals and other misfits from all over Mexico and turn them into the nastiest, cruelest gang of cutthroats doing business in post-war America, second only to the Skinheads in total savagery.

At first, Devillian had serious reservations about inviting Juarez to join his organization. As a rule, he regarded Mexicans as barely a half-step above blacks. But several of his confidants in the Burning Cross convinced him that Juarez was a master of spreading terror and creating chaos. In other words, he was someone who could be an invaluable ally for a while—until he became expendable.

But there was another reason Devillian decided to let Juarez into the group: the man's sister, Juanita.

Ordinarily, Devillian preferred young, white women. Juanita, of course, had reasonably dark skin. But she also

76

was one of the most beautiful and downright sexy women Devillian had ever seen.

As obese and repulsive as Jorge was, he faded into the woodwork when his sister was in the same room. Her job within the Cross was to sign up mercenaries for the cause, and in this regard, Devillian knew she would be an unbeatable recruiter. Her dark hair swirled around a face that was both angelic and inviting; her black eyes glistened with promise. In stark contrast to her brother's mountains of loose flesh, every inch of Juanita's body was tight-skinned and smooth. She was slender, yet she had remarkably large and perfectly formed breasts, rising like beautiful mountains from a landscape created in a desert paradise. Her legs and thighs were long and lean. She moved like a jaguar in heat.

And the Colt .45 pistols strapped to each shapely hip always sent a thrill through Devillian's loins.

Someday, somehow he would have her, Devillian promised himself. That is, if he could get by those damn pistols.

The terrorist leader forced himself to stop staring at this bewitching creature long enough to call the meeting to order.

"Gentlemen . . . and lady," he said, smiling hopefully at Juanita and getting absolutely no response. "Since we last gathered, a lot has happened within our organization. As you already know, Major Heck and his men have officially joined our cause. We welcome their expertise and valor.

Devillian paused for dramatic effect.

"What you may not know," he continued, "is that Major Heck and his men were responsible for destroying the Modern Pioneers' train that so foolishly attempted to travel through our territory, trying to reach Los Angeles."

Devillian's news brought a round of congratulations for Major Heck.

"Well done, *amigo*," Jorge Juarez burped in what amounted to a show of comradeship on his part. His sister gave Heck a half-smile, and the Nazi thought he detected a hint of interest in her dark eyes. Or so he hoped.

Devillian continued. "But we can't dwell too long on that

77

success. Another train is trying to make the same trip. And this train is much bigger and more heavily armed."

"Do you know who's behind this one?" grunted Mallox.

"The United Americans themselves," Devillian replied with a smile. "There's no doubt about it. I saw the train myself in Football City. And our spies tell me that Hawk Hunter was in town at the same time."

An invisible ripple of tension went through the room at the mention of Hunter's name. As if on cue, each of the terrorists—the Nazi Heck included—shifted nervously in his seat. Only Juanita seemed unaffected. In fact, Devillian thought he saw a strange, bemused look flicker briefly across her lovely face. But she said nothing.

"With Hunter and his people involved, I'm sure you'll all agree that we have to take this latest train very, very seriously," Devillian said, expertly holding back his real feelings.

"Bullsheet," Juarez rumbled, his voice filled with gas and mock courage. "We *weel* crush him like a snake!"

"Don't kid yourself," Devillian told him. "Hunter is a very dangerous man, and this train is carrying a lot of weapons."

The nervousness of the group went up another notch until Devillian smiled and said, "But, on the other hand, my friends, this is *exactly* what we've been waiting for."

He then outlined the first part of a plan that he promised would culminate in the eventual destruction of the train. However, this first phase involved little more than a series of sneak attacks, each one designed to stall the train—not destroy it outright.

When he finished, there was one question on everyone's lips.

"Why not just bomb the tracks in front of the fucking thing," Studs Mallox piped up, "and then blast the shit out of the train itself?"

"He's right, Herr Devillian," Heck said. "With the firepower we have, we could probably destroy this train in two, possibly three attacks, no matter how many weapons they have. My Skull and Crossbone battalion would be happy to lead the first assault."

Devillian was smiling and shaking his head at the same time. "You're missing the point here," he said. "If we destroy the train right away, we will be losing a golden opportunity to advance the cause of the Burning Cross."

"How so?" Heck asked.

Devillian closed his eyes and saw dead bodies. "Because, if we attack now," he went on, "all we do is kill the men on the train, and instantly, they become martyrs. But if we wait for the right moment and the right place, then we can kill not only the men on the train, but also the spirit of every do-gooder on both coasts."

"I still don't understand," Juanita said, speaking for the first time.

"We play like the spider," Devillian replied. "We lure them farther along. Hitting them hard, but selectively. And then, just when the whole country is rooting for them to succeed in this grand adventure—*boom!*—we destroy them, utterly and without compromise.

"The effect will be devastating to the American population once they see how easily the Burning Cross snuffed out their heroes. And following this glorious show battle, it will be *our* names on everyone's lips. *We* will emerge as the new power in this country."

"But how can you be certain the country will know about this so-called show battle?" Heck asked. "We can't leave such a crucial victory to the mercy of conjecture and rumor."

"I agree!" Devillian shouted. "And I have already taken steps, my friends, to make sure this battle will be seen by literally millions of people. *Millions* of witnesses who will come away with no doubts about who won or the power of the Burning Cross.

"But to accomplish all this, we must stick to my plan."

Suitably, if temporarily awed, the majority around the table nodded their agreement.

Devillian smiled again and involuntarily rolled his twisted eyes. "Already the plan is working," he told them. "Some of our advance groups made contact with the airborne elements of the train's defensive forces."

"And they snuffed them?" Mallox the Skinhead asked.

"No, no!" Devillian replied with a mixture of confidence and frustration. He knew the doltish Skinheads would have trouble understanding his intricate scheme. "Per my orders, they simply clashed with them and retreated."

One of the minor bandit leaders — a man named Mink — chose to speak up at this point. *Whaddaya talking about?* he asked crudely. "You let these United American pussys kick ass on our guys? On purpose?"

"You just don't understand," Devillian told him calmly. "The United Americans don't even know we exist. By letting them think they are making progress on this trip of theirs, we will lure them in deeper and deeper."

"Still sounds like a fairy way to fight," Mink said. "And that means you must be a fairy, too — "

Just what Mink was expecting from his ill-timed outburst would always remain a mystery. A nod from Devillian to one of his nearby bodyguards produced the flash of a knifeblade. Two seconds later, Mink's throat was slit from ear to ear.

"Now, my friends," Devillian continued, his pants instantly sopping wet. "Are there any other questions?"

Chapter 15

Dodge City

The *Freedom Express* pulled into Dodge later that evening, running right on schedule.

Hunter, Crunch and Elvis were sitting in one of the coach cars, drinking beer and trying to relax as they told Catfish of the mysterious behavior of the Starfighters and the resulting unopposed occupation of the airport. While they spoke, the long process of disconnecting the three heavily armored railway cars that would make up the Dodge City mini-fort had begun.

"So those bandits just high-tailed it out of there, eh?" Catfish asked for not the first time.

"Not your typical air pirate *modus operandi,* is it?" Hunter replied worriedly. When low-lifes like air pirates went against their normal operating procedures—swarm tactics sometimes fought to the last man—bells went off in his head. He immediately began to think trouble.

"Could be they're just laying back," Crunch said. "Maybe they'll hit us tonight and try to reclaim the airport."

"Maybe," Hunter said. "Maybe not."

"Fitz already called Jones with the news," Catfish said, opening four more beers and passing them around. "He's making arrangements to borrow a dozen F-5's and crews from the Free Canadians. They will be out here tomorrow. It's only temporary, but it should keep the air pirates away from our fort."

While the others nodded in agreement, Hunter just pulled his chin in worry.

"That's a good move," he said. "But I've got a feeling that those Starfighters aren't coming back. And dammit, that bothers me."

After another hour of conversation, the weary men turned in for the evening.

Hunter fell asleep almost immediately, though he tossed and turned most of the time. Usually his sleep was deep and peaceful, but again tonight his head was filled with strange voices. Still he did not feel the commotion around two AM when the three mini-fort railway cars were finally disconnected from the rear of the train and pushed onto a side spur at the old Amtrak station.

Thus, the new Dodge City was born.

This done, the *Freedom Express* started up again and, while most on board slept, slowly moved out of town.

The next stop was a small settlement named Cimarron, located in the northeast corner of New Mexico. This was going to be one of the most dangerous sites on the entire route for establishing a new settlement. Not only was Cimarron right on the edge of the heart of the southern Badlands, it was less than a hundred miles north of Santa Fe.

Once an attractive and prosperous city, Santa Fe had become a symbol of all that was wrong with the southern Bads. A boiling pot of vice and corruption, it drew bandits, murderers, criminals, black marketeers and other disreputable types from all over the West. Prostitution, drug dealing, gunrunning, white slavery and terrorism were in such vogue, the place made the anarchic cities of west Texas look like vacation resorts.

During the dark early morning hours, the *Express* made its way steadily across western Kansas and into the tip of the Oklahoma panhandle. A night patrol by Crunch and Elvis found nothing unforeseen coming toward the train from any direction.

But then suddenly, just before dawn, Hunter found himself sitting straight up in his bed, wide awake in a flash.

"Something's wrong . . ." an inner voice called to him.

He was strapping into the Harrier less than a minute later.

Skinhead Commander Studs Mallox spotted the train from twenty-five miles out at twenty-five thousand feet.

At this height, the *Freedom Express* looked like a great silver serpent, slithering through the foothills of Oklahoma. Already he could see the two patrolling Phantom jets circling above the train, a sure indication that his strike force had been detected.

No matter, he thought. In fact, that was the whole idea.

Studs barked out a series of orders to his five accompanying F-4's and the pair of creaky, radio-controlled B-57 Canberra bombers they were escorting.

"You know what to do," he commanded after each of his airplanes had assumed its attack profile. "Don't anyone screw up, or I'll personally fry his ass in butter."

The lumbering remote-controlled B-57's dropped down to a perilously low three hundred fifty feet and roared over the set of tracks toward the approaching train. In the meantime, Studs ordered three of his F-4's to engage the trio of aircraft — one of them a jumpjet — that was coming right toward them.

"Just keep 'em busy," Studs told the other F-4 Skinheads. "That's all. . . ."

Hunter sent the Harrier roaring through the formation of oncoming Phantoms, twisting and turning to avoid the cannon fire that suddenly filled the air. He zeroed in on the lead F-4, unleashed a Sidewinder and immediately put the Harrier into a steep climb to escape the flying debris from the resulting explosion.

Per their hastily devised plan, Crunch and Elvis dove and plunged right into the path of the Canberra bombers, knowing the bigger jets could cause more damage to the train than the smaller Phantoms. The Wreckers combined to send both B-57's crashing to the tracks—and did so with surprising ease. Meanwhile, Hunter had circled around for another pass and destroyed a Skinhead Phantom that had doubled back to try and protect the bombers.

Although the B-57's now lay burning on the trackbed about a mile in front of the train, the four surviving Phantoms clustered together and continued the attack. Hunter radioed back to Catfish with a warning, and the major assured him the train's crew members were at their battle stations.

The first two Phantoms came in low over the locomotives, raining cannon fire—but no missiles—onto the Dash-8's as well as the lead cars. One of the locomotives took a direct hit, its turbo-engine exploding in a tremendous flash.

A second later, the enemy Phantoms were greeted with a solid wall of firepower from the train's anti-aircraft batteries. At the same time, Hunter, Crunch and Elvis attacked the Phantoms from above with deadly, coordinated dives as the enemy F-4's were pulling up from their bomb runs. One enemy plane was instantly destroyed.

But the battle had raged for barely a minute when, quite suddenly, the three surviving Phantoms turned and fled.

Again, our attackers run, thought Hunter. It was a pattern that kept repeating with mysterious frequency.

He resisted an urge to pursue the retreating Phantoms, deciding instead to turn back and check on the damage to the *Freedom Express*. The train had come to a complete halt by this time, and circling overhead, he could see at least one locomotive was badly crippled and that flames were shooting from several cars.

Soldiers from the train were already fighting the fires and within minutes had the situation under control. Hunter quickly set the Harrier down on its landing car and joined Catfish and Fitzgerald, who were inspecting the damage. At the same time, the Wreckers headed for Dodge to refuel.

"It's bad, but I don't think it will slow us down that much," Fitzgerald told Hunter.

"That locomotive is done for, though," Catfish said, pointing to Engine Number 5. "Too bad it's right in the middle of all the others. We'll just have to drag it along with us for a while."

"At least the train is a little lighter than when we started," Fitz noted, referring to the cars that had been dropped off in Topeka and Dodge City. "And after tonight, it'll be more so—that is, if we make it to Cimarron."

At that point, the two Cobra Brothers pilots appeared. They had just checked out the wreckage of the F-4's downed nearby.

"Are you ready for this?" Crockett asked. "Those F-4's were being driven by Skinheads."

"That's all we need," Fitz said. "First air pirates, and now leftover Nazis."

Hunter instantly felt his worries multiply by a factor of two. Running up against the brutal Skinheads was bad enough. But there was something else: He knew the crazy Nazi pilots had a reputation of never retreating. They would usually fight on until the last man was dead.

So why did they give up and run? he wondered again.

At the controls of one of the fleeing Phantoms was Studs Mallox, and he was feeling very pissed-off.

It was the first time in his life that he and his gang had ever left a fight before it had been settled. Doing so was against their very nature.

But Devillian had been adamant; so much so, Mallox could still hear the cross-eyed leader's words in his ears: "Sting 'em, but that's all."

Mallox hated taking orders from a weasel like Devillian. But they had agreed to play it his way—for the time being, at least.

"Besides, it ain't *that* bad," Studs told himself, removing his oxygen mask and lighting up his crack pipe. "It's not like we *really* lost."

Chapter 16

The sun was just going down in a blaze of desert glory when Hunter lifted off in the Harrier and turned south.

He had spent the rest of the daylight hours helping the repair crews fix the damage to the train. The tally for the strangely limited Skinhead air attack was the one locomotive and a few shot-up storage cars.

However, they were all surprised to learn that the two B-57's that had crashed on the tracks about a mile in front of the train had not only been radio-controlled, but they had also been carrying hundreds of small mines in their bomb bays, which had scattered in every direction at the time of impact.

Now, what would have been a fairly routine track-clearing operation had turned into a delicate, hazardous and time-consuming task. Catfish had estimated the train would be dangerously stalled for at least two days.

On first glance, it might have appeared to an outside observer that the attacks on the train had been random and sporadic—potentially serious, yet just the kind of opposition the United Americans had expected to encounter and overcome during the trip.

But for Hunter, too many things just didn't add up: The lightning quick destruction at Topeka was well executed, yet no victorious troops had taken possession of the prize. The unusually large concentration of Starfighters at Dodge could have seriously damaged the train had they chosen to attack, yet instead, they mysteriously deserted their airbase. The six Skinhead Phantoms could have easily been carrying bombs that would have severely damaged the train, yet they chose only to strafe it with cannon fire.

Most important, the two remote-control B-57's could have been laden with high explosives, enough to blow a quarter-mile-wide hole in the tracks. But their bomb bays were filled only with bothersome mines.

He knew that no commander in his right mind would attempt to stop a train with mines. Nor was it wise to launch an attack as halfhearted as the one the night before — not unless the goal was something other than total destruction of the target.

And strange as it seemed, that's exactly what Hunter had come to suspect.

He was airborne only twenty minutes when the lights of Santa Fe loomed on the horizon. Bright, garish with a sickly tone of pink to them, the lights seemed to perfectly fit the description of the city itself.

Yet it was here he felt he had to go — not just to play a hunch, but to see if he could sniff out some solid evidence that would make his suspicions a little less fantastic. He knew that in many cases, truth was found only after searching through a pit of lies.

And Santa Fe was a pit.

He had no intention of landing the Harrier at the city's airport and leaving it there, unguarded, while he prowled the untamed city in search of information. Instead, he had to find an area that was properly secluded, yet still offered enough open space to accommodate the jumpjet.

Using a pair of NightVision infra-red goggles, he spotted an outcropping of large rocks about a mile north of the city. Putting the Harrier into its vertical descent mode, he eased it down into a small, flat area completely surrounded by the high boulders. Then he skillfully maneuvered the versatile aircraft even closer to the rocks, finally managing to get most of it underneath a huge, overhanging ledge.

Satisfied that the plane was nearly impossible to spot — particularly since no one in his right mind would be looking for an airplane out here, anyway — Hunter set off on

87

foot for the edge of town, his trusty M-16 slung over his shoulder.

His adventure *within* an adventure had begun.

He jogged the mile toward the lights and soon entered a particularly rough area known as West Santa Fe, which was actually on the outskirts of the main city itself.

As he walked through the streets, he saw that some of the roadways were brightly lit, while others were dim. So, too, on some streets, most of the houses seemed deserted. On others, they were overcrowded with signs of humanity.

At the end of a particularly gloomy street, Hunter turned the corner and almost ran into two men and a woman who were staggering along, trying to hold each other up.

"Watch where the fuck you're going," slurred one of the men as the trio lurched past.

When he looked up from the brief encounter, Hunter was astonished at what he saw. The street in front of him was absolutely filled with people—all of them dressed similar to him: shabby fatigues, longish hair, three-to-five-day growth of beard, some kind of weapon slung over the shoulder and a slightly bleary look to the eye.

He knew right away that these people were all of one profession.

"Jeesuz," he whispered. "It looks like a mercenary convention."

He donned a pair of almost clear sunglasses, thereby cutting down on the chances that someone would recognize him. Then he made his way into the crowd.

His first impression of a mercenary's reunion wasn't too far off. As he walked the crowded streets, he saw that dozens of storefront recruiting offices lined every block. Some had signs advertising work for trench troops, sappers, guards, recondos and rocketeers. Others wanted tank drivers, truck drivers, combat engineers, even cooks. He was simply amazed by it all. He had seen similar mercenary marketplaces in Algiers, but he never imagined such a thing was going on right in America.

And this too made him suspicious. There was only one

reason the mercs had flooded to West Santa Fe — the promise of a lot of work to be found.

He turned onto a particularly loud and raunchy-looking boulevard, one that had many rag joints squeezed into both sides. Loud music spilled out of dozens of broken windows. Small groups of young women roamed the sidewalks, brazenly approaching men and even couples, trying to sell their rather obvious talents. It was the same scene up and down the street.

"How much gold do you have on you?" one streetwalker asked Hunter, seductively grabbing his arm.

He looked at the girl's makeup-plastered face and guessed that a very pretty sixteen-year-old girl was underneath the hideous, bright violet eyeshadow and lipstick. He resisted the impulse to suggest that she should take a bath and try to salvage what was left of her youth.

"I thought the first one was free?" he replied.

The girl laughed at him. "You may be better looking than most of these bums," she said, pointing to the streetful of mercs, "but a girl's still got to make some money."

"So do I," he said. "And quick."

He produced a single gold coin. "This is yours if you can tell me something all these other guys don't know."

She understood right away.

Taking the coin and putting it down the front of her ultra-tight halter top, the girl pointed toward a bar across the street.

"Go over to that place, the Happy Apache, and ask the bartender there," she suggested. "He knows everything that's going down in this town."

Hunter thanked her and made his way across the crowded street, wondering if the world would ever again be a place where kids could grow up without losing their innocence by the time they hit the age of ten.

He pushed through the swinging doors of the Happy Apache, and his nostrils were immediately invaded by a wave of stale beer and cheap perfume. Loud and very bad piano music came from one corner of the large, crowded barroom; a woman was playfully stripping off her clothes in another.

"My kind of place," he mused.

To no surprise, he saw the saloon was lousy with mercenaries. A long bar filled one side of the room, and he made his way through the human traffic jam in that direction.

The only empty stool was next to a man who had passed out, his head lying in a puddle of spilled beer on the bar. As Hunter was claiming the vacant seat, the bartender grabbed the drunk by his hair, yanked his head up and wiped up the beer with a filthy-looking rag. Then he let go, allowing the drunk's head to fall back to the bar with a resounding *crack!*

The barkeep—a short, fat man with a straggly yellow beard streaked with gray—then turned his attention to Hunter.

"I don't serve strangers," he said, eyeing him suspiciously. "And I ain't never seen you before."

"So?"

"So get the fuck out of here."

Hunter dropped a handful of gold coins onto the damp bar.

"Just cut the crap and give me a goddamn beer," he said with intended harshness.

The bartender looked at the coins and smiled; up until recently, real gold had been a rarity in these parts. He filled a cloudy, cracked glass with a weak-looking yellow liquid and plunked it down in front of Hunter.

"That'll be a half a bag of gold," he said.

Hunter laughed in his face. "Sure thing, skinny," he replied with a smirk, tossing two coins toward the chunky man.

"Hey, nobody says you have to drink here, wise ass," the bartender rumbled, reluctantly picking up the sticky coins.

Hunter took a swig of the so-called beer. It was about as tasty as week-old dish water.

"I was told you'd know if there was any 'special' work available around here," he said.

The bartender seemed to laugh and scowl at the same time. "And who the fuck told you that?"

"Your daughter," Hunter shot back. "She just proposi-
tioned me outside."

The bartender's face turned six shades of red.

"You must be tired of living, pal," he told Hunter, reaching for a Bowie knife in his belt buckle.

A split-second later, the man was staring down the barrel
of Hunter's M-16.

"So," Hunter continued calmly, "should I assume you
don't know of any 'good' jobs?"

"I didn't say that," the fat man replied nervously as the
rifle touched his nose. "I . . . I just haven't decided if it's
worth it to tell you."

Hunter lowered the gun and pushed three more coins
across the sticky bar.

The bartender quickly scooped them up. "OK, what
kind of work you looking for?"

"I'm a merc," Hunter said. "And a guy told me there was
big doin's down this way."

Now the bartender really laughed. "Well, get in line, asshole," he said. "That's the same bullshit story I've heard
from every one of these guys."

"Is that so?" Hunter asked. "Well, any of these popheads
bragging about being able to drive a B-52?"

"You're a bomber pilot?"

"I can be if the price is right," Hunter told him.

The man stared hard at Hunter for several seconds, and
Hunter stared right back.

"Wait right here," the bartender finally said.

Hunter unconsciously took another sip of the revolting
beer and wound up spitting it out on the floor. Wiping his
mouth, he scanned the barroom again. It was a market-
place of drugs and sex. Men huddled over tables, openly
exchanging money and bags of white powder; scantily
dressed women of all ages draped themselves over every
merc who showed the slightest interest.

A moment later, Hunter felt a tug on his trousers. He
was surprised to see a midget had eased up beside him.

"I hear you're looking for action," the little guy
squeaked.

91

"Not with your sister, I'm not," Hunter replied.

The midget smiled, as if it were a joke. "Is it true you can fly heavy stuff?" he asked, his thin voice turning serious.

"Depends," Hunter replied.

The midget smiled again. "Good answer," he said. "Come with me."

Instantly Hunter's sixth sense started flashing. All of his instincts were telling him the dwarf would lead him to some valuable information. Knowing he had to start somewhere, Hunter followed the man—all three feet of him—through the crowd and out of the bar.

"Many of these mercs are just *bullsheet* artists," the midget said as they walked along. "But if you truly are a bomber pilot—or any kind of pilot—I know people who will want to talk to you."

"And supposing I'm not," Hunter asked.

"Then my brother will slit your throat for lying to me," the midget replied nonchalantly.

They went down the crowded street for about a hundred yards, then the midget suddenly turned into a dark alley. He pointed to a gray, two-story dilapidated house halfway down the court.

"Go there," he said in his crackling, squeaky voice. "Up the stairs. Say Carlo sent you."

The midget held out his hand expectantly. Hunter dropped two gold coins into it, and the little man vanished around the corner.

Hunter approached the house cautiously, noting that the alley seemed to be the only quiet place for blocks around. The first floor of the gray house was dark, but there was a light in an upstairs window. He carefully eased open the front door with his gun barrel and found himself in a dark hallway. His keen eyesight picked out the shape of a staircase on the far wall.

He mounted the stairs, each squeaking step signaling his ascent. The upstairs hallway was dimly lit, revealing several doors. One was open, and a huge silhouette was outlined there.

"Who are you?" a voice called out.

"Carlo sent me," Hunter responded. "I'm a bomber pilot—looking for work."

Hunter's eyes nearly popped out of their sockets when the man behind the voice stepped out into the hallway. He was at least seven feet tall and five hundred pounds or more—a certifiable giant.

"My brother Carlo sent you?" the giant asked. "Then come here. And *geeve* me your gun."

"No chance, big boy," Hunter replied smartly.

The Mexican monster looked like he wanted to eat Hunter for a snack. He reached out to grab him, but Hunter was quicker. His trusty stiletto jackknife was suddenly poised at the giant's ample throat.

Just then a woman's voice called out: "Bring him in here, Manuel."

The giant obediently led Hunter into the room. The only light was a small lamp on a table next to a sofa facing the door.

From the shadows in one corner came the woman's voice again.

"Come over here," she said.

Hunter walked toward the voice, and the woman rose to meet him.

She was wearing a black shirt with the top three buttons open to reveal several inches of very inviting cleavage. Her shapely hips and legs were packed into black jeans. Hunter's eyes roamed appreciatively over her enticing form and came to rest on her enormous pearl-handled Colt .45s.

"Nice guns," he said suggestively.

"Thank you," she cooed. "My name is Juanita Juarez."

Right away Hunter's sixth sense started flashing again, telling him two things: He was definitely on the right track, and the woman was extremely dangerous.

"You are really a bomber pilot?" she asked, her hand lightly touching his.

"Yes, ma'am," Hunter answered. "And I'm a damn good one. I've fought on four continents, and I'm ready for more."

Juanita's dark eyes locked with his. There was something

about this man, he could hear her thinking. Something different. She took a long look at his lean frame, his muscular shoulders, his longish, dark blond hair. Even the rumpled clothes and unshaven chin did little to conceal his innate good looks.

"Manuel, leave us," she commanded.

"But my lady—" the giant began to protest.

"I said *leave us!*" the woman sneered at him.

Manuel meekly left the room, a spot of blood leaking out from his chin.

Juanita gestured toward the sofa. "Let's talk. Tell me about yourself."

For the next ten minutes, Hunter told the Mexican beauty every conceivable lie that he could think of, all revolving around his supposed bomber pilot-for-hire career.

When he finished, he couldn't tell if she believed him or not. Oddly, it appeared as if she really didn't care.

"OK, you pass part one," she said, her jet black eyes glowing like a cat's. Then she stood up in front of Hunter, unbuckled her gun belts and dropped the huge weapons on the floor. "Now for part two. . . ."

As Hunter watched in growing disbelief, Juanita slowly loosened the few remaining buttons on her black shirt and let it slip easily off. Then she deftly unsnapped her bra, letting her lovely, round, erect-nippled breasts spring free. Next, she removed her jeans, sliding them seductively down her brown, perfectly shaped legs. As Hunter's eyes drank in her overwhelming sexuality, she eased out of her black panties and stood before him totally naked.

It was the most unabashed display of wantonness that Hunter had ever witnessed.

She lowered herself onto Hunter's lap, pushing her heat against him. "Screw me until I can't move," she whispered, ". . . and you've got a job."

Now, once again, the tormented conflicting emotions streaked through Hunter's brain at supersonic speeds. Of course he wanted her . . . any man with a pulse would. But he certainly couldn't allow passion to totally distort his sense of self-preservation.

Besides, he was on an intelligence mission. Therefore, his situation called for a plan.

He slipped the strap of his M-16 off his shoulder and laid the weapon on the floor next to the sofa, still within easy reach. Juanita quickly unbuttoned his shirt, allowing her breasts to press soft and warm against his bare chest.

He stood back from her and looked deeply into her eyes. She began to speak—but suddenly couldn't. All she could do was look back at him, her eyes magically drawn to his.

This done, he placed his hands on her bare breasts and began making counter-clockwise circles with his fingers, never taking his eyes off hers. She gasped once, her dark pupils still unblinking, and then she began to softly moan. Gradually he tightened his grip until he held both her nipples between his fingers.

Then he squeezed.

Within seconds, a sweet perspiration covered Juanita's body, glistening in the soft light of the room. Her eyes teared up with ecstasy, and yet they were still frozen in his mesmerizing glare. She felt her muscles go limp; waves of pleasure of a kind she'd never experienced were rippling up and down her body. Soon she felt as if her entire being was about to explode—a second later, it did. Suddenly she was in the throes of what seemed like a never-ending orgasm.

Although her eyes were still open, her mind began to fog over. In the midst of her incredible pleasure, it seemed like the strange person was asking her questions: Who? What? Where? How many?

Who is this man? she found herself wondering in the midst of the almost-violent perpetual climax. *How can he do this to me?*

After twenty minutes or so, Hunter's fingers were getting tired.

But the discomfort in his digits was nothing compared to the troubling ache in his mind. He had been able to extract a wealth of information from her—all of it bad news for him and the men on the *Freedom Express*.

Instinctively he knew when he'd reached the limit with her. Taking a deep breath, he squeezed her nipples a little harder. A second later, she was asleep.

Hunter gently eased her down to the sofa, then quietly slipped back into his shirt. He peeked out into the hallway. Manuel the Giant was also sound asleep, slumped in a chair tipped against the wall.

Never one to press his luck, Hunter silently slipped away.

Chapter 17

The sun was just rising when the A-37 Dragonfly appeared over the small airfield.

The diminutive, two-seat jet circled the field once, then came in for a bumpy, dusty landing. All the while, a pair of Football City Air Force F-20 Tigersharks watched from high above. It was their job to make sure the A-37 — and the valuable man behind its controls — landed safely and unopposed.

Once the Dragonfly was down, the F-20 pilots received a message.

"Thanks for the company, boys," General Dave Jones told them as he shut down the A-37's engines. "I can take it from here."

Jones watched as the two super-sophisticated F-20's circled once and then roared off to the east, heading back for Football City. Once they were gone, a pleasant sense of serenity came over him. The bleak, yet magnificent desolation of the desert looked like another planet compared to the stale-air stuffiness of his office back in Washington.

"Been too damn much ass-sitting for an old war horse like me," he whispered to himself. "It's about time I got out and about."

He taxied toward a small, dilapidated hangar at the edge of the landing strip. Beside the building, looking even more threatening than usual in the early morning shadows, was a Cobra attack helicopter. Standing next to the chopper was Captain Jesse Tyler.

"Welcome to the Wild West, General," Tyler greeted him. "I just wish it were under better circumstances."

The two old friends shook hands warmly, then pushed the A-37 into the hangar. That done, they immediately climbed into the Cobra.

"Hawk's information must be damned urgent if he insisted that I come all the way out here—alone yet," Jones said.

"From the little I know, sir," Tyler said gloomily, "I'm afraid your trip was absolutely necessary."

Moments later, Tyler had the big warbird airborne and heading eastward toward Cimarron, where the *Freedom Express* had arrived earlier that day.

The message Hunter had sent to Jones around midnight simply stated that he had information critical to the survival of the *Freedom Express*. The information was so sensitive that Hunter did not want to risk transmitting it over the United Americans' communications net, despite the usually reliable scramblers, which garbled any message heard by anyone not equipped with a compatible set.

The sun was nearly up when they spotted the flickering lights of the train. Tyler overflew its entire length once, and Jones could see dozens of men busily repairing the cars that had been damaged in the Skinhead air raid as well as the scattered wreckage of the enemy F-4's and remote-control B-57's downed during the battle.

Catfish and Fitzgerald met the chopper as it settled onto its landing car, greeting the general as the small wiry officer emerged from the aircraft's front seat.

There were grim handshakes all around, and then the small group retired to the Control car, where they were joined by the other members of the train's command team, including JT and Ben Wa.

Once inside, Jones saw that Hunter was sitting at the very end of a long table, his facial expression a mask of pain and worry.

The men took their seats, and a bottle of Scotch quickly appeared.

"First of all, how extensive was the damage to the train?"

Jones asked, doling out a handful of paper cups.

"Most of it can be fixed," Catfish responded. "We're patching it up here, and we can continue the most important repairs en route. The worst part is losing that locomotive. We'll just have to dump it at the next juncture."

Jones took a long, slow sip of Scotch. "And it was definitely Skinheads who attacked you?"

"For sure," Hunter replied grimly, politely but firmly refusing a cup of liquor.

"Well this *does* sound serious," Jones said, not remembering a single time he'd seen Hunter pass up a comradely drink. "So let's have it, Hawk."

Hunter took a low, long deep breath.

"General, there's no way I can make this easy," he began, his voice absolutely sober, his mind trying to put into words all of the information he'd been able to coax out of Juanita Juarez. "But I've uncovered information that suggests that this entire venture — the train and our own lives — are in grave danger."

"So what else is new?" JT wisecracked. "We've been fighting ever since we left Football City. But we've been kicking ass each time, and that's what counts."

"This is no time for jokes, JT," Hunter said stonily. "These skirmishes we've already experienced are nothing compared to what is waiting down the tracks."

"And that is?" Jones asked.

"More than ten divisions of enemy troops," Hunter replied, his news dropping on the Control car like a bomb.

"What?" Fitz was the first to cry. "You're talking about one hundred and fifty *thousand* troops."

"It's true," Hunter continued. "I have evidence that an enemy alliance has recently formed right here in the southern Badlands itself. One man has rallied the remnants of the Twisted Cross, the Skinheads, and an assortment of air pirates, bandits, mercenaries and terrorists into a massive one-hundred-and-fifty-thousand-man army."

Even a battle-hard veteran like Jones was stunned.

"Do we know exactly who is behind this super army, Hawk?"

"A gunrunner by the name of Devillian," Hunter replied. "Duke Devillian."

The name stung his tongue every time he said it. Immediately his mind flashed back to the last night they'd spent in Football City. Devillian was the man who had made Louie St. Louie so nervous.

"And along with his army," Hunter went on, "this guy is stamping out an ideology to go with it."

"Which is?" Wa asked.

"Pure racism," the Wingman replied, spitting out the last word. "Devillian was a Klansman before the Big War, which explains his love affair with the surviving Canal Nazis. Now it appears that he's built a kind of Super KKK. In fact, he's calling his new organization the Knights of the Burning Cross."

"That explains the flag of a cross in flames at the Topeka airport," Catfish said grimly.

"It gets even worse," Hunter went on. "This secret force may be equipped with weapons more sophisticated than anything we've faced since the Circle War."

A series of low, troubled whistles echoed throughout the railway car.

"And we're driving ourselves right into the thick of it?" Ben Wa asked gloomily.

Hunter nodded grimly. "They not only know we're here," he confirmed. "They're the ones who have been stinging us."

At this point, everyone who was drinking refilled his Scotch cup.

Although tempted, Hunter once again refused. He rubbed his tired eyes, pushed back his long hair and then continued.

"Those Starfighters at Dodge," he said. "They didn't run away. They were ordered to retreat. Same with those Skinheads. These attacks were feints—diversions under the guise of isolated actions. They've been sucking us in. Trying to make us think they were just scattered elements and that we could just roll right through."

"Incredible," several people said at once.

"I hate to ask you this, Hawk," Jones said, slowly. "But are you certain that all this information is accurate?"

Hunter looked up at him and solemnly nodded. "Solid," he said, the look in his eyes alone confirming it for most people in the room.

"There's more," he went on. "It was part of this new super army that attacked the first train. We were only half right when we said that the first train was sent crashing into that station in LA to send us a message. Actually, these guys were laying out the bait."

"And we fell for it like a bunch of Boy Scouts," JT said disgustedly.

No one spoke for two long minutes. Finally Jones turned to Catfish. "Can we turn the train around, Major?" he asked.

Catfish sadly nodded. "There's an old Conrail roundabout on the other side of Eagle Rock, sir. It would take us the better part of two days to do it, but it can be done."

"Then, from what I've just heard," Jones said, "I believe that as powerful and armored as this train may be, it seems suicidal to continue in the face of numbers and equipment this super army apparently has at its disposal."

Everyone in the room was absolutely stunned at the announcement.

"Wait a minute . . ." Hunter said. Just then, he felt an odd sensation run through him. Suddenly someone else's words were on his lips. *"It is best to confront an enemy directly,"* he heard himself say. *"Then surprise will be an ally in victory."*

Everyone turned and looked at him strangely.

"What the hell did you say?" JT asked.

Even Hunter himself wasn't sure.

"I mean . . . we've got to remember we've still got an important mission to perform," he recovered, a little shakily. "And if we let this new gang get to us now, it will only get harder to reclaim the territory when we try it the next time."

Another absolute silence descended on the room.

"Are you actually advocating that we continue?" Jones

asked him incredulously.

Even Hunter himself wasn't too sure. The strange voice that had suddenly gurgled up from inside him had him briefly questioning his own sanity.

Still, he pressed on: "Look, we've been in tough spots before. And we've always gotten out of them by thinking it through. By innovating. By using our strengths and shoring up our weaknesses. All our success has been based on that very principle. We can't change it now."

There was another minute of gruesome silence as everyone took a third drink from the rapidly dwindling bottle of Scotch.

Finally Jones broke the spell.

"Hawk, I'm prepared to order that we scrub this mission," he said. "So if you have any ideas, better spill them now."

Hunter thought again about the strange words he'd just unconsciously uttered.

"General, I think we all realize that mounting a good, standby defense for a constantly moving train is next to impossible," he said. "At least against these kinds of odds and on such short notice."

"So?" Jones asked.

"So, as the old saying goes, the best defense is a good offense. If a moving train is difficult to defend, then I say we lay out a careful plan and then go on the attack instead."

Everyone in the room once again turned toward Hunter, astonishment on their faces.

"Good Lord, Hawker," Fitz blurted out. "How? According to your information, this nut has got ten divisions hiding out there, waiting for us."

"When they are unprepared, it is the time to attack," Hunter's other voice proclaimed. *"Only when they don't expect it should you make your move."*

Hunter's odd pronouncements were stunning everyone in the room—himself included. Only Ben Wa seemed to catch on.

"But how do we do that, Hawk?" Wa asked calmly.

102

"Devillian's guys could be spread out anywhere between here and LA. We're talking about thousands of square miles, a lot of it pretty rough territory, easy to hide in."

"Hell, you can't hide an army forever," Hunter replied. "What we need is more solid intelligence."

"I think what we also need is to keep this train moving," Tyler said. "Whether we are backing up or going forward, we've got to keep rolling, or we will be an even easier target."

"You're right," Hunter said. "But we do have one element we can work in our favor. That is time."

"How so?" Jones asked.

"Because Devillian is playing a game here," Hunter said. "These feints—by the Starfighters, by the Skinheads—they're part of some master plan he's cooking up. They have to be, because, let's face it, if he wanted to destroy us, he would have tried it by now. Or if he simply wanted to stop us, he would have at least blasted holes in the tracks in front of us. Instead, he dropped a bunch of mines."

"Well, what's he waiting for?" JT asked.

On this, Hunter wasn't sure. The woman Juanita had been very vague on two points: Devillian's timing and the location of his headquarters. He had tried in vain to get at least a hint of information on these subjects from her, but she had resisted.

"I don't know," Hunter said. "Maybe he doesn't even know the answer himself at this point."

"But there's another big question remaining as well," Fitz said. "That is, do they know we are on to them?"

Hunter shook his head. "As of now, they don't," he said with assurance. Just before releasing Juanita from her spell and putting her to sleep, Hunter had given her a strong hypnotic suggestion that would wipe out most of her memory of his visit. "This means we have at least one more advantage on them, and some maneuvering room to figure out how we can get out of this."

"But Hawk, you're talking about a very, very long shot," Tyler said sympathetically.

"It's better than turning the train around," Hunter

103

countered.

Once again, a nervous silence prevailed.

Finally Jones cleared his throat. In the end it was his decision to make.

"Well, it's against my better judgement," he said. "But you make a good point about fighting this guy now and not later. And you've been right before—though not this, well, eloquently. So, OK, proceed to Eagle Rock. Do your follow-up intelligence work and see what can be found out. But I've got to put a deadline on this. If nothing turns up by the time you reach Eagle Rock, then we've got to turn this train around and go back out the way we came. Understood?"

Hunter nodded, as did the others.

Jones then turned to Catfish. "How long do you need to clear the tracks up ahead, Major?" he asked.

"Another twenty-four hours maximum, sir," the man answered.

"That's all the time we'll need," Hunter said quickly.

Chapter 18

A chorus of coyote calls greeted the full moon as it rose big and orange over the New Mexico desert.

The campfire crackled and snapped, sending showers of sparks up into the night sky, where they took their places among the stars. The sweet smell of mesquite smoke was everywhere.

"So that's the story," Hunter was saying, pouring himself another cup of coffee from the pot placed next to the roaring fire. "She was one fine lady, with a huge set of guns."

The other men around the campfire—Fitzgerald, Cobra Brothers Tyler and Crockett and Captain Crunch—laughed at the joke. It was a rare humorous moment in an otherwise humorless day.

He had finally told them about his unusual interrogation of Juanita—but only because it had to do with the urgent missions that now faced them. For although he had established that Devillian's lieutenants—most notably Juanita— were using West Santa Fe as a massive recruitment post, he still had no idea where the super terrorist's headquarters was located.

This alone told him something: It was only under the fear of death that Juanita had held the secret location so tightly that it couldn't be extracted under his all-persuasive spell. And yet finding out where the viper Devillian lay was the key to planning any further action against the man.

Hunter took another sip of coffee.

"We've got two critical pieces of information missing,"

he said, reviewing the very reason why they were sitting at the remote location. "The location of his HQ and the time frame in which he intends on attacking us for real."

"We're really walking a fine line here in deciding which is the more important, Hawker," Fitz said.

"Well, look at it this way," Hunter replied. "There ain't much between here and LA except mountains and desert."

"Well, if we let him, he'll spring a trap on us somewhere," Crockett growled. "It all depends if we're stupid enough to walk into it."

Fitz let out a long sigh. "In the old days," he said, "we'd hunt this bastard down and carpet bomb him."

Hunter nodded glumly. "Things aren't that simple anymore, Mike," he said. "Right now, getting this train to LA is the most important thing in my mind, and even a squadron of B-52's might not help at this point. Plus I'd like to believe that we've moved beyond the point of devastating whole sections of our own country."

"We'll be back to doing it if this guy isn't stopped," Fitz replied.

"Getting more information on him is the key," Hunter said once again. "And that's why we're all here. Everyone know what they're doing?"

He looked up at his friends and saw them all nodding.

The four other men had arrived at the desert meeting via the Cobra gunships, one of the choppers carrying a steamer trunk full of various uniforms and disguises. Now Fitz and Tyler would commandeer that Cobra and fly on to West Santa Fe, while Hunter tried to follow his instincts and search the nearby territory for any sign of the mysterious Burning Cross. Crockett and Crunch would stand by in case Fitz and Tyler needed help quick.

They discussed some last-minute aspects of the plan and then broke camp.

"One last thing, Hawker," Fitz said as they began to douse the fire. "We'll need descriptions of the people you want us to interrogate in West Santa Fe."

For only the second time that day, Hunter actually smiled.

"Believe me," he said. "Recognizing these two guys will be easy."

Chapter 19

Santa Fe
The next morning

The bartender's arm was nearly breaking under the weight of the food tray.

He had just spent the last two hours frying what amounted to an entire side of beef, along with three gallons of chili, several pounds of grilled hot peppers and two spaghetti pots filled with refried beans on the side. And although he'd prepared this somewhat questionable feast every day, it never seemed to get any easier.

Grabbing a jug of tequila from under his bar, he finally made his way over to the saloon's corner table, setting the huge tray down with a slam.

"Eets about time," Manuel the Giant grunted, grabbing the first chunk of meat with his bare hands.

"Pay first," the bartender bravely told him, daring to actually prevent the meat from being sucked into the man's cavernous mouth.

Manuel literally threw a half bag of gold chips at the bartender, who wisely retreated without another word. Within five minutes, half the huge meal—which was actually the giant's breakfast—was already gone.

Not overly blessed with much peripheral vision, Manuel wasn't quite sure when the two men had sat down at the table next to him.

"Kinda hungry, aren't you, big fella?" he heard a voice ask.

Looking up from a handful of red peppers, Manuel comprehended the pair of men for the first time. They were dressed in a style of black military uniform he'd never seen before. Bored, he sent a long, low belch their way, and then continued eating.

"How would you like to make five bags of gold, big guy?" one of the men asked him.

"Leave me alone," Manuel replied, washing down a mouthful of beans with a long slug of the combustible tequila.

"OK, ten bags," the smaller of the two men continued. "Gold coins, not chips."

"Get out of here before I *keel* you both," Manuel growled as he attacked his chili in earnest.

"Final offer, twenty bags," the man persisted. "And all you have to do is get laid."

Manuel looked up from his chili. "Get laid?" he asked, two rivers of red sauce pouring out from the corners of his mouth and onto his massive, unshaven chin.

"That's right," the smaller man said in a rapid-fire, slightly accented delivery. "You know, sink the putz? Hide the salami?"

"Fuck girl?" Manuel asked.

The two men at the table looked at each other and shook their heads.

"Yeah, and you can cook her and eat her afterward," the taller of the pair said.

"What mean?" the giant demanded, now turning away from his food and toward the men.

They produced an elaborate-looking video camera. "We're in the movie business," the small man said. "The *dirty* movie business. We heard that there was a lot of it around in these parts; so we're making a film right here in town, and we need a leading man, like you."

"Fuck girl in movie?" Manuel asked. "What name?"

"It's called *Freaks and Chicks,*" the man told him. "We already got the girls and another actor. All we need is a strong silent type like you."

"Thirty bags," Manuel said, with sudden, surprising authoritativeness. "Up front. Plus you buy me lunch. You buy me tequila. And *then* we talk percentage, points and distribution allowances."

Mike Fitzgerald looked at Tyler and rolled his eyes.

"It's a deal," he told the giant.

Carlo the Midget knew he'd been tricked just as soon as he heard his brother Manuel's footsteps lumbering up the stairs of the hotel.

He looked at the two partially clad young hookers who were lounging on the bed nearby and, quickly determining that they knew less about all this than he, jumped down off his chair and headed for the dingy hotel room's only window. Lifting the dirty curtain, he found the window was barred.

The door opened, and Manuel and the two men in black uniforms walked in.

"Carlo!" Manuel bellowed. "You are in movie, too?"

"Manuel, my brother," Carlo cried back. *"Thees* is a trick."

They were in the room and the door was locked by this time. It took Manuel a few seconds to realize that no movie would be made here today—at least not one called *Freaks and Chicks.*

When it finally sank in, he spun around, intent on crushing the throats of the two men who had lured him here. Instead, he found himself staring down the barrel of a M-6 grenade launcher.

"Relax, Manuel," Fitz told him, forcing the giant to sit on the edge of the bed. "All we want is a little chat."

"No, Manuel!" Carlo shouted, jumping from the bed to the floor and back again like a monkey. "Don't tell them *anything.*"

"Keep yer yap shut!" Fitz shouted at the midget, simultaneously taking the grenade launcher from Tyler. "Or the big guy gets a gut full of shrapnel."

Tyler pulled a small bag from his trouser pocket and retrieved a syringe with an extra-long needle. Within seconds he'd loaded it up with a massive quantity of sodium pento-thal—enough truth serum to get an elephant blabbing.

But when he turned around and gave the needle a test squeeze, Manuel the Giant took one look at the syringe and passed out, hitting the floor with an earth-shaking *thump!*

The hookers thought it was hysterical, but Fitz and Tyler didn't know whether to laugh or cry.

"You-know-who is going to pay for this," Tyler said, half-angrily referring to Hunter. "Giants. Dwarfs. Teenage hookers. He owes me at least a case of bourbon."

"Me too," Fitz said, turning his attention to Carlo.

It took the both of them to wrestle the midget to the floor and inject him with the truth drug, although in a quantity substantially less than they'd prepared for the giant.

Once this was done, the midget went out like a light. The two men then easily moved him from the floor to the bed.

After setting up the video camera and adjusting its tripod and built-in light meter, Tyler propped the dwarf up on several pillows and faced him toward the camera. Then he slapped the midget once across the face.

"Can you hear me, Carlo?" he asked.

The midget's eyelids barely flickered.

He slapped him again. *"Can you hear me?"*

"Yes," came the squeaky reply.

Tyler then turned to Fitz and said, "OK, roll it."

"Rolling," Fitzgerald replied, adding, "Carlo the Midget, take one."

"OK, Carlo," Tyler said, consulting a small notebook. "Tell me everything you know about the Knights of the Burning Cross. . . ."

Chapter 20

Hunter was flying west and feeling lousy.

Before his current state of disillusionment had taken hold, he had planned to cover as much territory as he could, looking for something — anything! — that might give him a clue as to the location of Devillian's main encampment.

But in his heart it just felt as if he were wandering aimlessly. Flying low above the arid New Mexico desert, he was doing little more than scaring the desert animals and kicking up a lot of dust.

"What's the point of all this?" he asked himself for at least the hundredth time.

Was he nuts, talking in these crazy proverbs and actually advocating that the *Freedom Express* continue on its trip westward? With one hundred and fifty thousand enemy soldiers standing in their path? Armed with God-knows-what? What was the matter with him? Had the bartender back in Santa Fe been right when he said, "You must be tired of living?"

Pride. That was probably the reason, he knew. He was too damn proud to see the train turned around. Too damn proud to see what had been his idea turn into what would be perceived as a defeat.

His pride was hurt because another of his big time adventures had gone awry. He had boldly blown into Santa Fe thinking that only he could get the needed information. Only he could identify the villain's hideout. Only he could play the big hero and save the world again.

112

What a bunch of bullshit! he thought.

Did he really think that he — and his pride — could actually defeat this overwhelming force? The train trip had seemed like such a good idea when they first started out: Just move across the country and show all those scumbags in the Badlands who's boss.

Had he really failed so miserably to expect the unexpected?

What had it gotten him so far? One blown-up locomotive and a completely freaky trip to Santa Fe during which he played with a strange woman's tits and mind. *Some hero!*

Back to the comic books, Hawk, he thought to himself bitterly.

He was flying only a few hundred feet off the ground, half-heartedly keeping an eye on terrain ahead and below. An hour before, the mountains and forests around Santa Fe to his left had given way to great stretches of arid scrubland. Now just ahead, he saw a cluster of small mesas rising out of the desert.

Maybe it's just fate, he thought gloomily. His strange dreams. His conflicting emotions. His less-than-focused instincts. The weird voices that were regurgitating up against his will.

Maybe it's just time to hang up the old flight helmet and check into the rubber room.

Suddenly he felt a familiar tingling along his spine. An instant later, the radar screen confirmed what he already knew. There were two other aircraft in the vicinity.

Then he spotted them, five miles ahead and slightly to his south. They appeared to be attacking something on the ground. In a burst of pure instinct, Hunter pushed the Harrier at top speed toward them.

As he approached, he saw that the two jets were Dassault-Breguet Mirage III's. And there was something else he recognized: On the tail of each plane was the same insignia that had been on the flag in Topeka . . . the sign of the Knights of the Burning Cross.

"Someone up there must like me," he murmured, arming his weapons.

In a matter of seconds, he was close enough to see what the two jets were attacking. He could hardly believe his eyes. They seemed to be chasing a single horseback rider across the desert, firing their cannons at him . . . and intentionally missing him! Although the rider was using much skill to weave his horse in a zigzag pattern across the open desert and thus make himself a very elusive target, it was quite obvious that the jet pilots were merely toying with their victim.

This changed a heartbeat later. The attackers suddenly spotted Hunter and hurriedly turned in his direction, their cannons blazing. Hunter avoided their fire by putting the Harrier into a sudden dive. He had been flying so low to begin with, he had very little airspace to work with. But it was enough.

When he was about fifty feet off the ground, he jerked the nose of the Harrier up into a hover, then looped around behind the two Burning Cross airplanes, both of which had overshot him by this time. As one started to turn back in his direction, the Wingman fired a Sidewinder that hit the Mirage dead center, nearly cutting it in half with a tremendous explosion.

The remaining aircraft obviously wanted no part of Hunter and turned to flee. Hunter knew that the Mirage was nearly three times as fast as his Harrier, so he didn't set out in pursuit. Instead, he fired one long burst from his Aden cannons, just enough to wing the tail end of the Mirage's port wing fuel tank. Then he took a careful reading of the enemy airplane's escape route. It was dead south.

Once the slightly damaged Mirage had disappeared over the horizon, Hunter swung the Harrier back toward the spot where he had last seen the fleeing horseman. The man and horse were standing near the base of a small butte, apparently unharmed. The tingling of Hunter's sixth sense went to work again; something deep down inside was telling him that he should meet this man.

In this part of the desolate country, Hunter was guessing that the lone horseman was an Indian. He also wondered if the man had ever seen an airplane drop straight down out of the sky and land vertically, as he was doing now, kicking up a

114

great amount of dust and making an ear-splitting racket.

Maybe this guy has never even *seen* any airplane up close before, Hunter thought, finally settling down and shutting off the airplane's main switches.

As Hunter climbed out of the cockpit, the rider approached. Whoever the man was, Hunter was sure he was friendly — and therefore he didn't even bother to reach for his trusty M-16. Instead, he wondered if they would be able to speak the same language.

The man pulled his horse up about ten feet from the still-smoking jumpjet. He rode tall in the saddle, with jet black hair pulled back from his face. His high cheekbones and chiseled features indicated to Hunter that his hunch about the rider being an Indian was correct, as did his clothes, which looked like they came from Hollywood central casting.

The men just stared at Hunter and his airplane, his mouth open, but apparently too in awe to speak.

Hunter resisted the urge to raise his right hand and say, "How!" Instead he called out, "Can you speak English?"

The man still said nothing.

"Spanish?"

Still nothing.

"French?"

Just when Hunter thought that verbal communication would be impossible, the man shook his head and started to laugh.

"My God, an AV-8BE Harrier?" he said in succinct English, his eyes darting up and down the jumpjet's fuselage in wonder. "Please excuse me. I just never thought I'd ever really see one."

Duped again, Hunter thought.

The man dismounted and met Hunter as he climbed down from the cockpit. He greeted him with a long handshake.

"That was mighty impressive flying up there, my friend," the Indian said. "And you certainly couldn't have come along at a better time for me."

"Glad I was able to help," Hunter replied, somehow recognizing the man's voice. He was obviously very well educated.

"It didn't look like a very fair fight."

"My name is Michael Crossbow," the Indian said slowly, allowing a puzzled look to come over him. "Have we met before?"

"It would be a hell of a coincidence if we did," Hunter told him, sweeping his arms to indicate the utter desolation of their present position.

Suddenly a look of recognition came over the Indian's face. "But you're Hawk Hunter, aren't you?"

Immediately Hunter went on guard; with the way his normally aligned instincts were skewing these days, he wasn't about to take any chances.

"What makes you ask?"

The Indian laughed, letting out a kind of friendly war whoop. "Because, if you are Hawk Hunter," he said, "then you and I went to the same college."

Hunter stared at the lean, handsome man standing before him in disbelief. "You went to MIT?"

"Graduated three years after the famous Hawk Hunter," the man replied. "Copped a degree in advanced aeronautics and used your thesis to study for my final exams. I graduated with honors because of you."

Hunter was dumfounded. The cosmos was really working overtime today.

Crossbow took a few moments to admire Hunter's aircraft.

"Great airplane," he said finally. "But I thought you flew an F-16."

"There's a good reason for the Harrier," Hunter said.

Although his instincts were now bombarding him with the message that this man could be trusted, he wanted to learn more about him before revealing any more information. "But first tell me something: How is it that an honor student from MIT winds up getting chased by two fighters across the middle of the New Mexico desert?"

Crossbow spied a small outcropping of rock nearby.

"Let's get under some shade, and I'll tell you all about it," he said.

Both men were carrying water, and in a simple, spontaneous ceremony, they drank from one another's canteens.

Then Crossbow quickly filled in Hunter on his life since he had left MIT, explaining how he came back from the war to find his Shawnee tribe nearly destroyed by the nuclear attack on the midsection of the country.

"I've spent the last several years just trying to help my friends survive," he said. "Step by step, we had managed to rebuild the life of the tribe. I thought we were going to make it. But now . . . I just don't know anymore."

He told Hunter of the recent series of aerial attacks, usually by Hind helicopters, that had wiped out many of the remaining members of his clan. "And the few who are left are terrified," Crossbow said.

"Where are they now?" Hunter asked.

"They're still up in Oklahoma, hiding in the hills near our old village," Crossbow answered. "I decided that the only hope we had — and I know this is a long shot — was for me to hunt down whoever was terrorizing us. So I've been on the trail for several days now, but obviously they found me before I found them."

"But why are these people doing this to you and your people?" Hunter asked. "Certainly they don't believe that guys on horses pose a threat to Hind gunships and Mirage jet fighters."

Crossbow lowered his head. "They do it for sport," he said, almost embarrassed. "Whoever they are, they believe the Indian is more an animal than a man. We have heard from other tribes, and this is how we know it is so. They have hunted others down like a man would hunt a deer or a buffalo. They have killed them and skinned them and left their bodies to rot . . . and I have taken it upon myself to find who is responsible and stop him. Or die trying."

Hunter looked into the Indian's clear, direct eyes and made his decision. On this his instincts were correct: Crossbow was a man he *could* trust, a man who would be a valuable ally.

"I know who you're looking for," said the Wingman. "And I'm looking for him, too."

117

Chapter 21

Near Cimarron, New Mexico

Captain Jesse Tyler eased the Cobra gunship down toward the *Freedom Express*, hovered over its special landing car for a few seconds and then set the aircraft down to a perfect landing.

It was early the next morning, and he and Fitzgerald were exhausted as they climbed out of the chopper, still wearing their fake German SS uniforms.

"First thing I'm going to do is have a stiff drink," Tyler said as he helped the railway crew secure the Cobra to the stationary platform.

"First thing *I'm* going to do is get the hell out of this goosestepper's uniform," Fitz replied.

Ten minutes later, wearing their usual fatigues and each sipping a morning pick-me-up of orange juice and vodka, Fitz and Tyler met Catfish in the Control car. Under Fitzgerald's arm was the videotape containing the drug-induced interrogation of Manuel the Giant and his brother, Carlo the Midget.

"Good God," Catfish remarked after seeing the video images of Carlo and Manuel for the first time. "Talk about misbehaving genes."

"Yeah, it's a regular carnival side-show down there," Tyler replied. "And these guys are the good-looking ones."

They watched the videotape in silence, Catfish taking a few notes along the way. However it was soon clear that the

118

interrogation was less than a complete success.

"Nothing on the location of Devillian's headquarters?" Catfish asked somewhat gloomily.

Fitz and Tyler both shook their heads.

"Anytime we'd ask them, they got brain cramps," Tyler said. "Just like hypnosis, people under sodium pentothal usually won't reveal something their subconscious knows will cause them harm."

"So they must all believe that they'll be killed if they reveal where the hell this place is," Catfish concluded.

"The little guy *did* say something in Spanish the first time we asked him," Fitz said. "We caught him off guard, and he started mumbling something."

Catfish rewound the tape to the spot.

"There it is, hear him?" Fitz said.

Catfish replayed the segment several times.

"What the hell is he saying there?" he asked, watching the ghostly figure of the drugged-up midget repeat over and over.

"Sounds like: *'la caza de last est rell laz,'* " Fitz said, attempting to mix a murky Spanish with his Irish brogue. "Whatever the hell that means."

" 'House of something or other,' maybe?" Tyler offered.

Both Catfish and Fitz shrugged. "There's got to be someone on this train who speaks Spanish," Catfish said, making a note. "I'll check the duty roster."

Catfish then made arrangements to have the entire tape transcribed and radioed via the scramblers to Jones, who had just arrived back in Washington.

This done, they discussed the situation with the train itself.

"The tracks will be completely cleared within an hour," Catfish told them after checking with his work crew chief. "Believe me, getting those mines deactivated was a bitch. There were more than three hundred of them just on the tracks alone."

At that moment, the Control car's intercom crackled.

"Harrier coming in," came the crisp, static-free message. "Platform crew to your stations."

"So our clean-up hitter returns," Catfish said. "Maybe he's found something."

It was with great surprise that Catfish, Fitz and Tyler saw not one, but two figures emerge from the Harrier.

At first they wondered just how Hunter had been able to accomplish this, especially with the extra seat on the Harrier being taken up by the multitude of equipment he'd transferred over from his F-16XL. They began to catch on when they spied some of the F-16's equipment strapped to the hard-points under the Harrier's wings. Still, it had been a tight fit for the two men.

"Pick up a hitchhiker, Hawk?" Fitz yelled to the pilot as he and his passenger climbed down from the jumpjet.

"More like a tour guide," Hunter replied, quickly introducing Crossbow to the others. "And I'll save the discussion on meaningful coincidences for later. First tell me, how'd you guys do?"

Fitz gave Hunter the lukewarm report as the group headed for the Control car.

"Everyone seems very convinced that they'll go belly up if they breathe a word of where Devillian's HQ is located," Fitz told him.

Hunter was momentarily disheartened. "If we don't hit the jackpot on this soon, Jones will have us backing up all the way to Football City," he said.

"Well, your friends Mutt and Jeff *did* say something in Spanish," Fitz said. "We've got to get it translated, but it sounds like *'la caza day lez est rellas.'* "

"La Casa de las Estrellas?" Crossbow suddenly asked.

"Could be," Fitz replied.

The Indian closed his eyes and said, "The House of the Stars."

"Do you know what it means, Michael?" Hunter asked.

Eyes still closed, Crossbow smiled slightly. "Yes," he said. "I think I might."

Chapter 22

Duke Devillian leaned back and thought of his aunt Thelma while the young girl between his legs went to work.

"You're getting better at this, aren't you, bitch?" he asked the girl harshly, her only reply coming as a series of muffled slurps and gurgles.

Devillian's aunt Thelma had been run over by a truck years before. It was a nasty, particularly bloody accident that Devillian happened to witness as a young boy of five. Thelma had been his favorite aunt ever since.

Devillian was about to climax when the phone next to his thronelike chair started buzzing.

"I'll kill whoever is on the other end," he swore, his stiffened excitement instantly petering out.

The girl between his legs was confused. She looked up at him as if to say: What happened? Angrily, he kicked her away from him.

"Get out of here, you ugly bitch!" he screamed.

The girl stood up and fled the room in tears.

"And if that happens again, honey, I'll feed you to the Skins," Devillian called after her in a familiar rage of sexual frustration.

Finally he answered the buzzing phone.

"What the fuck is it?" he screamed, pulling his pants up. "I left orders that this phone should not be used unless it's an emergency."

The voice on the other end, that of Devillian's top communications officer, was terror-stricken.

"The men from Rome are here, sir."

Instantly, Devillian's mood changed. "Are you sure?" he asked, checking the time.

"Yes, sir," replied the voice, gaining some strength. "They just arrived with ten helicopters full of equipment."

Devillian was positively delirious with excitement. He quickly hung up the phone, picked up his Polaroid instant camera and went out the front door of the Play Pen. Grabbing one of the six guards always on station outside, he proceeded to walk down the corridor until he reached the top communication officer's small office.

He kicked open the door, and then pointed to the man who had just called him on the phone.

"Shoot him," Devillian commanded the guard.

The soldier unquestioningly raised his rifle and shot the terrorized man right between the eyes.

Devillian smiled as he snapped a picture of the still-twitching body. Ten seconds later, the photo appeared, and ten seconds after that, Devillian felt the lower part of his body go pleasantly moist and numb. Mission accomplished, he thought. His climax had simply been delayed.

He then pointed to the messy corpse.

"Now clean that up," he said to the guard.

Ten minutes later, he received the trio of "Family" men from empirical Rome, Italy.

"You have brought everything?" he asked them.

"Everything and more," one of the men boasted. "We were able to get into the best warehouses in Rome, Naples and Florence. Then, as an extra favor for you, we stopped in Cannes, France and raided two more."

"Ten helicopters full," one of the other men said.

"You will be very pleased at what we can do for you," the third chimed in. "We have the best equipment of its type in the world."

"You'd better," Devillian snarled back at them.

Chapter 23

It was somewhere around noon when the *Freedom Express* lurched forward and started moving down the tracks once again.

For everyone on board, the sensation of motion came as a great relief. They had been stalled on the tracks for more than a day and a half, a two-mile-long sitting duck just waiting for any enemy who had the gumption to launch a major attack against them. Now that they were moving again, they all knew they presented a much more formidable target.

A scrambled report back to Jones in Washington informed the general they were under way. His reply message confirmed that they had his permission to continue at least to the next mini-fort drop-off point, which was the small town of Eagle Rock, New Mexico.

Barely a crossroads on the edge of a small lake of the same name, Eagle Rock had always been considered a very important junction in the train's journey. From this point on, the tracks left the flat desert terrain and began a long twisting passage through the Sange De Cristo Mountains. The switchover from desert to mountain terrain meant that should the train continue, it would be faced with at least a half day of continuous climbing, thus slowing its speed. Plus, the mountains would also give an enemy an infinite number of hiding places from which to attack the train.

Hunter was able to catch a few hours of troubled, fitful sleep, and by six PM, he was back in the Control car, pouring over a map of the American southwest with Crossbow, Catfish and Fitz.

"House of the Stars is what my ancient Shawnee ancestors used to call heaven," Crossbow explained to them. "Actually, I suppose it was more like a Mount Olympus to them."

"A place where the gods resided?" Fitz asked.

"Exactly," the Indian confirmed. "It was where the Sun and the Moon lived, and the whole universe spun around it. The myths say it was a great city that just floated in the air. It was up so high that it looked like it touched the stars. That's how it got its name. My grandfather told me about it, and as a kid all I could imagine was this great village just hovering in the sky. I used to have dreams about it. Of course, these legends went back hundreds, even thousands of years. More recently, say from 1900 on, my people assumed it was all just a fable—and not an actual place."

"Civilization kills another myth," Hunter murmured.

"Yeah, that's right," Crossbow replied. "But get this: I can remember, when I was a teenager, a team of anthropologists came to visit our tribe. They were asking us what we knew about *La Casa de las Estrellas*. Our chief at the time was a stubborn old goat; he wouldn't let anyone talk to them until they told him why they wanted all this information. Finally they gave in and told him that House of the Stars might not be just part of a legend. They said they knew where it was."

"Fascinating," Fitz said.

"Not to our chief," Crossbow declared. "He became very angry and threw them right off the reservation."

"But why?" Hunter asked. "You would think he would have been pleased."

"He wasn't—for two reasons," Crossbow said. "First, he hated the fact that the white man was tampering with the Indian gods."

"And second?" Catfish asked.

"Well, he didn't like it when they told him the House of the Stars wasn't anywhere near where our people originated."

"Wasn't in Shawnee Territory?" Fitz asked.

"Worse, it wasn't even in the United States," Crossbow said. "In fact, they claimed it was down in Mexico."

Bad news arrived a few moments later with the buzzing of the Control car's phone.

Catfish took the message and wearily hung up, by now very tired of his role of bearing unpleasant tidings.

124

"JT and Ben just called in," he reported. "They flew out of Dodge this morning, looking for serviceable airfields that we could use along the way."

"And?" Hunter asked.

"And they report that every abandoned field between here and LA has been sabotaged. Blown up. Destroyed."

"By the Burning Cross?" Crossbow asked.

"That would be my good guess," Catfish replied.

"Those fucking bigoted bastards," Fitz groaned. "So they *are* intent on nipping us to death."

"What about JT and Ben?" Hunter asked.

"They're flying on to LA," Catfish said. "They'll contact Jones, and maybe he can get some long-range aircraft out there fast. Then they'll have to cover us as best as they can from there."

"With only the entire Rocky Mountains in the way," Fitz said disgustedly. "They've nearly succeeded in completely isolating us."

Hunter found himself simply shaking his head over the latest news. He couldn't help thinking that a noose was slowly tightening around their necks.

Chapter 24

Late the next day

Hunter and Crossbow had spent the entire day flying back and forth along the old Mexico-Arizona border looking for something that was supposed to be invisible.

After consulting every map of northern Mexico available to them, Crossbow could only make an educated guess as to where the location of the mythical *Casa de las Estrellas* might be. He remembered the anthropologists mentioning something about the Ring of Fire, and there was a section of northern Mexico close by the Arizona border that went by that name. However, even in the pre-war days, this part of Mexico had been utterly deserted; these days it might as well have been on the moon.

Their first notion was to look for some kind of mountain base. To an ancient Shawnee, a tall mountain might appear to reach up to the stars. But the few mountains in the Ring of Fire area were all sharply peaked, barren and extremely uninhabitable. Giving up on this tactic, they checked out several hidden valleys and canyons — places *surrounded* by high mountains. But again they came up empty. Finally they just found themselves sweeping back and forth across the desolate area, hoping they'd get lucky.

They didn't — at least not right away.

It was getting dark by the time they'd taken off from the train after their third refueling stop. Hunter planned to return to the search area, set the airplane down for the night and resume the search in the morning.

They found a wide-open stretch of scrubland, one that featured a rare tree in its midst, and set down next to it. Both men were tired and frustrated; so after a quick supper and a couple cups of wine, they turned in—Crossbow sleeping under the protective cover of the tree, Hunter bedding down atop the Harrier wing itself.

Despite the long day, the Wingman found sleep was still hard to come by. Many things were troubling him—not the least of which was the prospect of the whole *Freedom Express* mission going down the drain. If more information on Devillian and his army could not be found, then he knew Jones would order the train turned around when it reached the junction of Eagle Rock within the next twenty-four hours.

So a clock was running, and it was almost as if Hunter could feel every second painfully ticking away.

On top of all this, his own psyche continued to act somewhat unruly. It felt like his mind was beating to a very strange vibe, but he couldn't put his finger on what was causing it. Odd thoughts kept bubbling up from deep down in his gray matter and shooting up through his mouth without stopping first in his consciousness.

The overall result—a less than infallible trust in his normally right-on instincts—was somewhat frightening.

He finally drifted off to sleep and immediately plunged into a very strange dream.

He was all alone, out in the desert. It was the middle of the day—high noon, in fact—and the sun was beating down on him without mercy. High above—improbably more than one hundred miles up in the sky—a large airplane was circling. In one moment it looked like an airliner, in another like a vulture. And someone in that airplane was laughing at him.

Then in an instant the day turned into night. Suddenly, he was looking up at the stars and imagining that a group of them had formed into a huge city—an enormous constellation connected by thin streams of red light.

A second later, he was wide awake.

"Airplanes," he murmured, sitting straight up on the wing and feeling his sixth sense clicking back on track. "Right near

127

by. . . ."

He scanned the moonless clear sky, and moments later his extraordinary vision detected the silhouettes of two fighters passing about fifteen miles to their south. Just then he saw something else in the southern sky. A bright flash of red — like a laser beam — shot out toward the two airplanes and stayed on for less than a second.

But it was visible long enough for Hunter to figure out its purpose.

"Wake up, Michael," he yelled to Crossbow as he jumped down from the wing. "We're going for a ride."

Sometimes the hardest things to look for turn out to be the easy things to find.

Hunter had been sure the laser beam was being used as a directional device — a beacon flashed only momentarily which would direct pilots to their base from hundreds of miles away.

Once the Harrier was aloft, he steered in the direction of the millisecond flashes and wound up about one hundred miles south of the territory where they'd been searching earlier in the day.

Now, an hour later, they were down again, both men convinced they were close to finding Devillian's headquarters.

"We were probably fooled just like my ancestors," Crossbow said as he and Hunter peered out at the desert through NightScope glasses. "I'm sure they searched for the House of the Stars on top of every mountain they could find. It probably never occurred to them that it was really on top of something like that."

Hunter could only nod in agreement. Finally things were beginning to add up.

Off in the distance was not an enormous, Mount Olympus type mountain. Rather it was an enormous, mushroom-shaped mesa. It was surrounded by nothing but desert; not a single rise or hill of any consequence broke the horizon for 360 degrees around.

The mesa's strange shape was the key. Its crown was ringed

with what looked like a necklace of sharp rock formations. This meant that anyone looking up toward its summit would be led to believe the top was jagged and inhospitable.

But Hunter had the feeling this was not the case.

"All this will make sense if that thing is really flat on top," Hunter said.

"Only one way to find out without being spotted," Crossbow replied.

Packing only the essentials of guns, ammunition and water, the two men set out across the pitch-black desert, heading for the mysteriously shaped mesa.

Twenty minutes later, they found another piece of confirming evidence along the way.

It was the wreckage of a Mirage III. A quick inspection convinced Hunter that it was the same airplane he'd damaged in the dogfight just before he'd first met Crossbow.

"It ran out of gas," Hunter said, pointing to the plane's perforated fuel tanks. "The question is, was it only a few miles short of landing?"

They continued walking. Twice more they saw airplanes following the quick flashes of red light toward the enormous mesa, then *disappearing* just beyond it.

"Amazing," Hunter breathed.

"Frightening," Crossbow replied.

They were about halfway to their goal when another giant, yet near-invisible beam of red light suddenly swept across the desert floor, falling just short of their position.

"A different laser," Hunter whispered as they both hit the ground. "This one's like a big burglar alarm. Break the beam and bells go off."

"Damn . . . whoever's on top of that thing can cover every square mile in the area," Crossbow said.

"We're going to have to dodge it somehow," Hunter said.

Crossbow stared ahead into the night. "Some cactus over there," he said, pointing. "A few boulders over there."

Hunter was reading his mind.

They lay in wait until the next sweep of light passed by them. Then, like two running backs trying to dodge a squad of linebackers, they dashed from cactus to boulders to more

129

cactus to a gulley and back up to some more cactus, all the time trying to keep one step ahead — or behind — of the powerful, sweeping beam of laser light.

Gradually, they zigzagged their way the final three miles to the base of the towering mesa.

Chapter 25

Burning Cross Master Sergeant Hans Swek was fuming mad.

As officer of the watch, it was his responsibility to make sure all of his sentries stayed awake and alert until sunrise. It was a job that demanded *he* also stay awake and alert, and this he usually did via a handful of amphetamines.

But tonight was different. He had foolishly bargained away his nightly dose of speed to another sergeant. In return the man had promised him one of Devillian's best young girls to do any and all of Swek's bidding.

The pre-arranged time had been nine o'clock; the place, a rocky area known as the Spine.

Now it was close to eleven, and there was still no girl.

Swek had already plotted his revenge. It would be a simple matter of bribing another sergeant to kill the double-crosser sometime soon. Twenty speed pills would practically guarantee it was done in a slow and painful manner. Another few pills would insure the body would never be found. *Then,* Swek would bribe someone else—someone he could trust—to get him one of Devillian's girls.

But now his main worry was staying awake. He'd never made it through night duty before without a bellyful of uppers, and he wasn't looking forward to going cold turkey right now—especially in a place so goddamn spooky as this.

Swek didn't even want to think about some of the stories he'd heard since arriving at this place: the Indian ghosts they said you could see moving around on top, visions that always seemed to pop up around midnight. Swek would have passed it all off as hogwash if it hadn't been for the fact that six of his soldiers had already mysteriously disappeared in just the last

131

month alone.

He stopped to light a cigarette. He was sweating and jittery and letting his imagination get the best of him.

Maybe if I just took it easy for a while, he thought.

The next thing he knew, he was looking directly into the eyes of an Indian.

He had looked up from lighting his smoke, when he saw the man standing right on the edge of the mesa's lip; so close, at first it appeared as if the figure was floating in the air.

He was dressed just like the hundreds of Indians Swek had seen on TV back in Germany when he was a kid: long braids, leather pants and boots, bright-patterned body shirt.

Yet it appeared as if he'd suddenly materialized out of the ethers. Swek immediately wet his trousers, so sure that he was face to face with a ghost.

"Are . . . are you *real?*" he blurted out, taking several seconds before thinking to raise his gun at this apparition.

That delay cost him his life.

The Indian was real enough to grab Swek's rifle barrel and give it a tremendous yank, sending it and Swek hurtling off the mesa and into the dark abyss below.

All the way to the bottom, the terrified man's screams echoed eerily across the vast desert. They ended with a sharp *thump!*

Hunter and Crossbow pulled themselves onto the mesa top and hugged the ground, both men thankful they'd survived the torturous, back-breaking climb. Luckily, Crossbow had proved to be somewhat of a mountain-climbing expert. He had practically coached Hunter up the entire way, showing him footholds and ledges, telling him to avoid grabbing any vegetation growing out of the side of the rock.

Now they were on top and waiting. But no other sounds reached their ears. It seemed the ill-fated rifleman had been the only guard in the area.

Slowly, they rose, looked around and were astounded.

"What the hell is going on?" Crossbow whispered urgently. "There's *nothing* up here."

At first, Hunter had to agree. The top of the mesa *did* look completely empty. It was as if they had actually scaled the

132

wrong mountain. Squinting through the darkness, he could see nothing but various rock formations, the clusters of large boulders that gave the optical illusion that the entire mesa top was jagged.

But then he was able to turn up his extraordinary vision a couple notches, and slowly, things began to take shape.

"Christ," he whispered. "It's not empty; it's all camouflaged."

He pointed to several rocky shapes about one hundred feet away. By concentrating, they could gradually detect the edges of a huge sand-colored net that was covering what were actually several long, low buildings.

"Barracks," Hunter whispered. "See them?"

Crossbow squinted some more, but then started nodding his head.

Hunter pointed to a taller rock formation. "Radar set," he said. "Hear the tone?"

Crossbow was nodding even more quickly now.

"Over there," he said, pointing to more sandy clumps nearby. "Missiles . . . they look like SAMs."

"Great sun," Crossbow exclaimed. "There are hundreds of them."

Despite their somewhat precarious position, Hunter still had to shake his head in admiration for Devillian. Not only were there more SAM sites than he'd seen in such a concentrated area before, there were also gun platforms, hangars, fuel dumps, ammo houses, radar dishes and a myriad of other military equipment on top of the mesa—all of it masterfully camouflaged. He'd never seen such a convincing deception. Between the unnatural coverings and the mesa's geographical isolation, Devillian had managed to build a nearly invisible base; even from directly overhead, the place would have looked deserted.

They took a few minutes to study the lay-out, absolutely staggered by the amount of weaponry on top of the mesa.

"There must be a central command post here somewhere," Hunter told Crossbow.

They circled the barracks area and continued across the giant plateau, avoiding the sentries at every turn. Coming over

133

the top of a low ridge, they found themselves approaching the edge of a dimly lit airfield. They ducked behind a couple of nearby rocks and once again surveyed the scene before them.

First they saw the outlines to two rough, but serviceable, runways. It was what was on the far side of these landing strips that made Hunter's spirits take a nose dive. Under low rows of masterful camouflage sat a fleet of at least thirty airplanes: Soviet Floggers, a few Skinhead Phantoms, some Mirages, a single Voodoo and several varieties of MiGs. There was also at least a squadron of Hind attack helicopters, as well as a dozen or so cargo choppers. All in all it was a deadly hodgepodge of aircraft.

"There's enough firepower sitting on top of this place to take over half the country," Crossbow whispered.

"Imagine what it could do to the train," Hunter replied gloomily.

Sergeant Josef Karls was worried.

His bloodstream was pumping massive quantities of amphetamines through his system, yet he was hardly enjoying the buzz. Plus the handcuffed girl he was dragging along beside him was getting to be a real pain in the ass.

Karls was supposed to meet his superior, Master Sergeant Swek, more than two hours ago. He had traded the girl to Swek in return for the speed that was now coursing through his system. But Swek was not at the rendezvous point, nor was he anywhere on the mesa's perimeter.

The girl struggled wearily as Karls dragged her back over to the rocky edge of the cliff known as the Spine, the spot where Swek was supposed to meet them two hours before. She was one of Devillian's favorites, but that wasn't why Karls was worried. The big boss didn't mind his troops screwing around with his bevy of women — just as long as they videotaped it and provided a copy to him the next day.

No, it was Swek himself that had Karls concerned. The man was known around camp as a hothead — someone who wouldn't think twice about retaliating just because Karls was late in bringing this bargain bitch to the meeting spot.

They reached the Spine, and still no Swek. His body ripping with speed now, Karls figured he couldn't let the whole night be a waste.

To this end, he roughly shoved the girl to the ground.

"Whether it's me or him," he told her. "There's not much difference."

With one massive swat, he ripped off the front of her robe, exposing her breasts. She was young and firm, just how Karls liked his women.

"You look good, bitch," he said cruelly. "But can you blow a horn?"

He started to undo his belt buckle, closing his eyes, in anxious anticipation of the moment. When he opened them, he was startled to see a man in a fighter pilot's helmet standing between him and the girl.

One terrifying instant later, Karls was screaming at the top of his lungs as he plunged off the edge of the mesa and down to the desert floor below.

The girl began to scream herself, but moving like a cat, Hunter was able to put his hand over her mouth before she could raise a sound.

"I'm not here to hurt you," he said to her. "Believe me."

He looked directly into her beautiful eyes and detected something. Was it fear? Or was there a glimmer of hope there?

The girl stared back at this stranger; neither the lightning bolt decoration on his helmet nor his somewhat disheveled appearance could disguise something burning down deep. His eyes . . . they were like no other. She saw daring and bravery there, but also kindness.

Take a chance, her instinct seemed to be saying.

Slowly, he lifted his hand from her mouth.

"What's your name?" he asked.

"Diamond," she replied softly.

Hunter covered her over with the remains of her flimsy silk garment.

"Are you a prisoner here?" he asked.

"I'm a slave," the girl answered with a whimper.

"To whom?" Hunter asked, his voice betraying a note of anger.

135

"A man named Devillian," she replied tearfully. "I have to do whatever he wants."

"Not anymore you don't," Hunter declared boldly.

Just then Crossbow appeared out of the shadows.

"She's coming with us," Hunter told him, his tone indicating that any argument would probably be fruitless.

"It'll be tough going down the same way we came up," the Indian whispered.

"No matter," Hunter said. "I'll carry her down if I have to. If we all make it, she can give us more information about this place than we can ever gather here ourselves. Now let's go."

Chapter 26

Aboard the Freedom Express

"Ouch!"

"You've got to hold still if you want me to do this properly."

Hunter shifted uncomfortably in the chair. He knew Fitz was right, but at the moment it felt like his back was on fire.

It was early the next morning, and they were in the Control car. The Irishman—being the jack-of-all-trades that he was—was applying a healthy dose of old-fashioned Witch Hazel to the two long series of scratches that extended the entire length of Hunter's back.

"Tell us again, Hawker," Fitz said as he dabbed more of the stinging liquid to the wounds, "how didya get so mangled."

"I already *told* you," Hunter snapped. "I had to carry that girl down the mountain on my back, and the only way she was able to hang on was to dig her nails into me."

"Oh, that's right," Fitz deadpanned. "It's just that these wounds look so, well, familiar. I remember a girl back in Cork. She had fingernails like switchblades. Aye, one night with her and me back looked just like yours."

Standing off to one side were Catfish and Tyler, both having to hold their hands over their mouths to keep from laughing.

"Very funny," Hunter said.

Actually, getting off the mesa with the beautiful, extremely frightened Diamond clawing at his back had been the relatively easy part of their escape.

It was crowding a trio into the Harrier jumpjet that had proved the most difficult. Even the zigzagged scamper back to the aircraft had been a breeze compared to the brain teaser Hunter had to unravel in order to carry three people in a cockpit barely designed for two.

In the end he had solved it—quite painfully as it turned out—by lashing still more of his F-16's avionics to the under side of the Harrier's wing, thus opening just enough room in the cockpit for Diamond to squeeze between Crossbow's legs. Then, by purging half his fuel, Hunter was able to lighten the overall weight of the aircraft enough to make it back to the train.

And after all that, all his friends could do was joke that the scratches on his back looked more like the results of a night of passion, than a harrowing escape.

Once all the Witch Hazel was applied and his shirt was back on, Hunter good-naturedly let his friends' jokes ride. Diamond was already proving very valuable to them. She hadn't been aboard the train more than an hour when she had drawn in exacting detail the entire layout of Devillian's mesa fortress. She had also told the United Americans something they'd suspected all along: While the mesa was the super terrorist's main base, the majority of the Burning Cross troops—they being the collection of bandit gangs allied under Devillian's banner—were scattered throughout the American Southwest, ready to move into battle positions at their leader's first order.

This new information was being poured over even as Hunter, Fitz, Crossbow and Diamond were eating breakfast. A scrambled report was sent to Jones. The general's confirmation message also contained an unexpected piece of information: The news of the *Freedom Express*'s cross-country journey was on the lips of every concerned American citizen from New England to LA. The publicity of the train's mission—whipped up by the country's rapidly reemerging electronic media—was so widespread that huge spontaneous demonstrations of public support had popped up in Washington, LA and even in the heart of heartless New York City.

With the news of the train's widespread publicity came the

additional pressure for it to succeed. The train trip had quickly turned into a crusade — a cause in which every freedom-loving person on the continent now had a stake.

For Hunter and his friends to fail now would mean disaster.

These were the thoughts the Wingman carried to bed with him shortly afterward.

He would have preferred to continue working in the Control car, but Catfish took one look at him and had literally ordered him to sleep, threatening to take it all the way to Jones if Hunter didn't comply.

With only a token protest, Hunter retired to his quarters.

It took all of ten seconds for him to drift off, for a change the sleep he needed so desperately coming to him with relative ease. But about half an hour later, he became vaguely aware of something warm and soft next to him.

Diamond pressed her ripe body tightly against his and whispered into his ear: "Don't move. I know you're exhausted. Let me do the work." And expertly, she began to caress him.

Still asleep, Hunter spoke a single word: "Dominique?"

Diamond stopped her gentle stroking. "Dominique?" she asked, her voice sounding softly distant. "Is that someone special in your life? If it is, then just pretend that's who I am . . . I'm Dominique. It's all right."

Hunter was only half awake now. But he was able to look directly into Diamond's beautiful, adoring eyes.

"Thank you," he said gently.

Then he pulled her into his arms.

Chapter 27

La Casa de las Estrellas

Duke Devillian was in a rage.

He had been in a good mood when he landed back at his headquarters, having just returned from a successful recruiting trip to the old city of San Antonio. Two more bandit gangs had signed on with the Burning Cross, and negotiations were under way with a third.

Then, he found out his mesa fortress had been penetrated.

The news came in the form of a report concerning the two bodies found at the foot of the cliff. At first, his soldiers thought that the two dead sergeants had fallen to their deaths accidently or had even jumped. After all, six soldiers had already died in the past month, although never two in one night.

The unlikely double-suicide theory was ruled out when evidence of a small avalanche was discovered near the body of Sergeant Swek. From there, Devillian's soldiers found several pieces of ripped clothing hanging from the jagged rocks leading up to the northern face of the mesa. When two series of footprints were discovered on the mesa's top — one made by a person wearing flight boots, the other by someone wearing soleless leather shoes — Devillian's men knew their perimeter had been compromised.

Devillian ordered the immediate execution of all twelve guards on duty that night, an exhibition that he made sure everyone on the mountaintop witnessed. He took care to film the entire proceeding himself, watching the carnage several times before being satisfied. Then he ordered an investigation as to how someone had been able to climb up the sheer rock face and what they had seen once they reached the top.

But for him, the worst news was yet to come.

When Devillian finally retired to his adobe mansion, he planned to relieve all of his anger and frustration by losing himself in a sex carnival with the girl named Diamond.

Uncharacteristically, he had found himself thinking about her while he'd been in San Antonio. Not that he was falling in love with her or anything; the Duke was absolutely devoid of any remotely human feelings such as love and affection. No—he had thought only about the ways he could use her sexually. He had more than sixty women at his disposal, ready to feed his every perverted whim. But Diamond was different. She was so young, so beautiful. He had bought her a trunk of clothes while in San Antonio—cheerleader outfits, high school clothes, bikinis, even a Sunday-School-type dress—and all the way back, he had fantasized how she would look wearing these clothes and how he would use her with other women to satisfy his twisted libido.

Unlocking the huge Play Pen, he had every intention of starting this sex party immediately. But when he called Diamond's quarters, she didn't respond. Mystified, he called the captain of his security patrol, a beast of a man named Bruno.

"She's not in her room," Devillian said as the huge, hairy man reported to him. "Find her and bring her to me. *Now.*"

Bruno departed and didn't return for nearly an hour— sixty minutes during which Devillian became so furious, white foam actually started to form at the edges of his mouth.

When Bruno reappeared, he was out of breath and crestfallen.

"Well, where is the little slut?" Devillian demanded of him.

Although he was a full head taller than Devillian and outweighed him by seventy-five pounds, Bruno was intimidated by the smaller man's savage temper.

So Bruno swallowed hard before answering. "We've looked everywhere, sir," he stuttered. "I'm afraid . . . no one knows where she is."

"*What?*" Devillian exploded. "Are you saying she jumped?"

"No, sir," Bruno replied, gulping hard again. "We

141

checked. There are no bodies below."

"So?" Devillian asked, spitting the foam from between his teeth. "Where is she?"

"I believe she's escaped, sir," Bruno said, knowing he was speaking the last few words of his life.

Devillian's face turned deep crimson.

"Escaped," he said in a frightening whisper.

Bruno tried to say something, but couldn't. All he could do was shrug and slowly nod his head.

"Do you want me to believe that you can't even keep track of one little broad?" Devillian screamed, his crossed eyes rolling with rage.

Bruno unconsciously started backing toward the door.

"It must have something to do with what happened last night," he croaked. "Whoever got in here and killed the guards must have taken the girl."

"That's obvious," Devillian continued to whisper crazily. "And somebody's going to pay." Then an entirely new crazed look came into his hard, twisted eyes. "And I know who."

Before Bruno could flee from the room, Devillian jerked his revolver from its holster and fired. The first bullet plowed into Bruno's huge chest, and as he started to fall, the second bullet crashed into the middle of his skull. That shot slammed the man backward against the wall. As he slid slowly down the wall, leaving a broad trail of blood, Devillian fired three more times. Bruno slumped to the floor, the blood spurting from five holes in his body.

The shots brought two more guards running to the room. They stopped, gaping in horror, when they saw the gory mess that had been Bruno, then looked up to see that Devillian was taking Polaroids of the body.

Chapter 28

Eagle Rock, New Mexico

The *Freedom Express* rolled into the small town of Eagle Rock, New Mexico at dawn the next day.

The place was barely a pinpoint on the map; even before the Big War it was home to only fifteen hundred people. Here the tracks led from the desert terrain to the forested mountains of the Sangre de Cristo Mountains. There was also a set of track turn-offs just outside of the town which could be used to switch the train's locomotives from its front to its rear and thus enable the *Freedom Express* to reverse direction and retreat back to the East.

It would be up to Jones whether this would happen or not.

But Eagle Rock was special in another way—this one totally unexpected: It was the first town where citizens had actually come out to greet the arrival of the train.

It was the Cobra Brothers who first saw them. Scouting ahead of the train as usual, they had just overflown the small town when they spotted the first indications of a crowd forming in the town square shortly before dawn. Not surprisingly, the Cobra pilots first suspected the people below were getting ready to attack the train. In all of the towns the *Express* had passed through so far, not so much as a single person had been waiting when the train rolled in.

But after arming their weapons and making two intimidating low-altitude passes above the small settlement, the Cobra pilots were surprised to see the people below waving back at

143

them enthusiastically. Instead of weapons, they were armed with signs containing messages for greeting the train. There was even a small brass band on hand.

So, an hour later, the train arrived at Eagle Rock to a small ceremony. The Cobras had landed beforehand and radioed back that the train could expect an entirely friendly stop. Thus informed, Catfish had his troops turn out in their best uniforms. A number of American flags and banners were broken out and displayed on the locomotives, the gun cars, the missile platforms and the troop cars.

The out-of-tune but lively brass band was playing when the train finally pulled into the town's tiny station. A crowd of about one thousand people — men, women and children, all of them hearty stock — cheered and sang *America the Beautiful* as the official delegation of Catfish and Fitzgerald climbed down off the train and was greeted by the town's mayor.

A brief ceremony followed during which the mayor gave a hand-sewn flag of Eagle Rock's Town Seal to Catfish, who promised to display it on the *Express*'s lead locomotive. Then work began on detaching the three-car mini-fort to be left at the small town, Catfish diplomatically asking the mayor's permission before giving the order to disconnect the trio of railway cars. While this went on, the citizens walked up and down the train, passing home-cooked cakes and pies to the soldiers on board.

The entire ceremony lifted the spirits of everyone on the train, bearing witness to Jones' report that news of the train and its mission had spread throughout the entire country, and into the uncivilized Badlands as well.

Yet, the men on board were holding on to a dire secret: Eagle Rock could possibly be the end of the line for the *Freedom Express*.

Hawk Hunter watched the proceedings from behind the drawn curtains of the Control car.

He would have liked to take part in the celebration, but he knew it was much more important for him to write a lengthy report on his visit to Devillian's headquarters.

It turned out to be a sobering task. Using Diamond's descriptions as well as his own memory to sketch Devillian's defensive lay-out, Hunter realized that any attack on the mesa fortress would be a costly proposition, in both lives and equipment. A land approach was, of course, impossible. A helicopter assault would be spotted from miles away, and even an air strike would run into the mesa's incredible wall of SAMs and AA fire, not to mention thirty or so enemy jet fighters.

Even a long-range missile strike would be chancy. Devillian had so many radar dishes spinning on top of the mesa, Hunter was sure at least a few of them were dedicated to close-in defense. He also knew a weapon such as an anti-radiation missile would have a tough time penetrating the electronic counter-measures shield around the plateau. Plus, such sophisticated weapons were in short supply.

What was more, recent UA intelligence revealed that a squadron of Burning Cross aircraft had been deployed to the Santa Fe airport, and that many of its small tanker and cargo aircraft had moved there as well. Hunter was certain this was a direct result of his penetrating Devillian's inner layer. With his headquarters compromised, Devillian was no doubt expecting some kind of an attack on the mesa. By deploying some of his fighters and cargo-carriers to Santa Fe, he was simply buying some insurance. First of all, his vital fuel and supplies would be safe. And second, if the mesa *was* hit, the planes at Santa Fe would be called on to attack the attackers.

Hunter was a ball of nerves by the time he finished the first draft of the report. All of their efforts in locating and reconning the goddamn mesa had been for the purpose of devising a plan on how to attack the place.

But now, that seemed like an impossible mission. No matter how he looked at it, it appeared as if Devillian was holding all the aces.

The *Freedom Express* moved out of Eagle Rock around noon, again to a big ceremony given by the residents.

It had been decided long before that the train would stay in the town only as long as it had to. This was necessary in case Devillian's legions decided to attack the train while it was in station. The resulting battle from such an action would undoubtedly cause many civilian casualties and probably destroy the town in the process.

So as soon as the three-car mini-fort was disconnected, Catfish ordered the *Express* to move ten miles up the track.

The short trip west deposited the *Freedom Express* right at the foot of the Sangre de Cristo Mountains. Here they would again wait for a decision from Jones on whether to continue or not.

The Pentagon

It was getting to be late afternoon back in Washington.

General Jones sat alone in his office, drinking cold black coffee and trying to decide the fate of the *Freedom Express*.

He knew there were many reasons why he should not let the train continue. There were no illusions that no matter how heavily armed it was, the train could not defeat ten divisions of Devillian's troops, not to mention his warplanes and helicopters. The report he'd just received from Hunter detailing the madman's mesa-top headquarters only underscored this fact.

But he had a new twist to consider — a very troublesome one.

This complication was that so many citizens across the country were now rooting for the *Freedom Express* to succeed. With this glare of publicity the stakes had been raised. Jones was convinced that Devillian was very aware of the notoriety that the *Freedom Express*'s mission was getting. Thus the battlelines for another struggle — that for the hearts and minds of America's citizens — were being drawn, and again, it seemed like the United Americans were playing right into the hands of the super terrorist. For just as they had undertaken the mission to bring law and order to the southern Badlands and therefore cement the legitimacy of their democratic government for the entire country, Jones knew that Devillian wanted the mission to fail and thus ruin those very chances.

This meant that whatever the outcome was, it would have to be high-profile and unambiguous. And this was what weighed on Jones' mind as he wrestled with his decision. To turn back would undoubtedly save many lives, but also it meant backing down to Devillian. To continue was to invite a back-breaking, morale-busting defeat, one that could quite possibly lead to a wholesale slaughter, and maybe the collapse of the entire United American government.

Jones took a long, sad gulp of his ice-cold coffee in an effort to wash down the gloomy prospects. But it was no use: He knew that as a Commander-in-Chief, he should have ordered the train to return to Football City at the first discovery of Devillian's massive hidden power structure. The real reason he hadn't was Hunter's appeal for time.

But now the general felt that time was close to running out.

Chapter 29

The train had just shut down at its new location ten miles outside of Eagle Rock when Catfish ran into the Control car.

"You guys have got to see this" was all he said to Hunter and Fitz before beckoning them to follow him.

They ran out of the car and up to the front of the train. Once there, they were astonished to see that several hundred bronze-skinned horsemen were blocking the tracks ahead of them.

"Now, who the hell is this?" Fitz cried.

"I'm not sure," Catfish replied. "Indians of some kind, I would guess."

Hunter had to agree. The band of horsemen looked like something right out of a western movie. They were dressed in authentic Indian garb, and their faces were smeared with war paint. The only difference between them and their ancestors was that many of these warriors were armed with high-powered rifles and automatic weapons as well as bows and arrows.

Quickly the call went back for Michael Crossbow, and a strange stand-off ensued which amounted to a staring contest between the Indians on one side and Catfish, Hunter, Fitz and about fifty Football City Rangers on the other. However, unbeknownst to the mounted Indians, several squads of Catfish's elite Airborne troops were making their way through the forests on both sides of the track, a maneuver which would quietly encircle the newcomers.

The strange, silent impasse continued for a few more minutes until Michael Crossbow came running up the tracks.

Quickly reading the situation, he stared at the colors being worn by the horsemen. At this point Hunter saw a very worried look come over his friend.

"Anyone say anything yet?" Crossbow asked.

"Nope," Fitz replied, never once breaking his gaze. "We've just been staring at these guys, and they're staring back."

Hunter turned to Crossbow. "Recognize them?" he inquired.

Crossbow continued studying the mounted army carefully.

"Yes, I'm afraid so," he finally said. "They're Piutes—and that means they are tough motherfuckers. I think the one in front is a chief named Bad River. His tribe is about the only one left in the southwest that still has enough manpower to mount a threat against anybody."

"Are they as unfriendly as they look?" Hunter said.

"Probably more so," Crossbow replied. "We'd better talk to them and see what they want."

At that moment, Fitz heard two, seemingly innocuous clicks of static come from his walkie-talkie. Actually, it was a message.

"Airborne guys are in place," he whispered to Hunter. "First sign of trouble, you guys hit the ground and stay the hell down."

Hunter nodded, at the same time hoping it wouldn't come to such drastic measures.

He and Crossbow slowly approached the tall, grim-looking rider that Michael had identified as Chief Bad River. Hunter half-expected the two Indians to start conversing in some strange tongue, but both spoke perfect English.

"Greetings, Bad River," Crossbow called. "I am Michael of the Oklahoma Shawnee Plains tribe. Our grandfathers were friends."

Bad River didn't say a word or move a muscle.

Crossbow raised his voice. "What are you doing here, my friend?"

"I could ask the same of you" came Bad River's sudden, deep-voiced reply. "You are a Shawnee. Why are you with these blacks and whites?"

"They are friends," Crossbow explained. "I am helping them get their train across the Badlands. In return, they will help my people against our common enemy."

Bad River looked at Hunter and the other United Americans.

"Are they not with the people who have been bombing us, killing our people and destroying our villages?" he asked.

Crossbow shook his head. "No—those are the people we are trying to defeat. We want to drive them from the Badlands and make this area safe again. Like before the war."

For a long time, Bad River continued to stare at the small group behind Hunter and Crossbow. Finally, he dismounted and slowly walked forward. Out of the corner of his eye, Hunter could see the well-hidden faces of the Airborne troops lying in wait on both sides of the track.

Bad River reached Crossbow and stood no more than a few inches away from him.

"Our tribes have not always been friends," he said sternly. "But in these times, when there are few men to be trusted, I am forced to greet you like a brother."

"And I you," Crossbow replied.

Bad River gestured to Hunter and his group. "If you say these people are fighting our enemy, then I must believe you."

"It is an honor to have your trust," Crossbow answered correctly.

On that, the two Indians shook hands.

Crossbow motioned for Catfish and Fitz to come forward, and introduced them along with Hunter as the three men in charge of the train.

The men exchanged curt nods.

"We wish you no harm," Bad River said. "It is the devils who attack us with their airplanes that we seek."

"We are after them, too," Hunter said. "Perhaps you can help us. We can always—"

Suddenly Hunter stopped talking. He turned and quickly scanned the southern horizon.

"Aircraft coming," he said, almost to himself.

The other men turned to look in that direction. At first, they could see nothing. Then came a low, rumbling sound, followed by six dark specks in the sky. The specks rapidly grew into a half dozen F-4 Phantoms, bearing down on the train.

Pandemonium broke loose on the ground. The Piute warriors scattered, as did the United American soldiers. Hunter was already running top speed down the tracks toward his Harrier car when the first pair of Phantoms roared over.

Alerted at the very last possible second by the train's fairly sophisticated radar system, a half dozen of the *Express*'s anti-aircraft crews were ready for the F-4's. As the six jets streaked over in three staggered pairs, the AA gun crews commenced firing. First only a few scattered pops could be heard—but

150

within seconds, a cacophony of gunfire filled the air, combined with the distinctive *whoosh!* of small SAMs being launched. The Phantoms were flying so low over the train that some of the Airborne soldiers hidden in the woods were firing at them with their various infantry weapons.

Yet, the Phantoms did not return the fire, nor did they drop any bombs. Instead they flew through the near-solid wall of lead and SAMs, careening back and forth and surviving the heavy AA fire. All the while their nose cannons were silent, their wings full of undropped ordnance. Just as quickly as they came, they turned and disappeared over the eastern horizon.

Nevertheless, Hunter was firing up his Harrier by this time, determined to give chase.

Major Stef Drews was the United American Airborne officer in charge of the mini-fort so recently installed in Eagle Rock, New Mexico.

He had just finished a long meeting with the town's mayor and several of its leading citizens when his second-in-command rushed into the center car of the fort.

"Sir!" he shouted. "We just heard from the train. They say an enemy air strike is heading our way."

Drews couldn't believe it. Why would the attackers bypass the train and head for the small town? After all, the small fort was an unlikely target when compared to a prize like the two-mile-long train. Yet even before he could tell the mayor and the others to take cover, the first pair of Phantom jets roared over the small town.

Drews' men went to work with such courage and efficiency he made a mental note to officially commend them afterward. No sooner had the Phantoms appeared than his twelve-man SAM team deployed and began keying in on the enemy F-4's. All the while, the citizens of Eagle Rock — they having been so deliriously happy at the arrival of the *Freedom Express* just hours before — were running for their lives.

Drews himself was at one of the SAM sites when the Phantoms turned and came back over the town. His men got off a solid first shot with their Stinger missile; it exploded just off the wing of the first high-speed, zigzagging jet, causing damage to its tail section.

Still, the F-4 pressed on, dumping two cannisters of napalm on the small row of buildings next to the rail station. A sudden explosion of flame engulfed the structures with terrifying proficiency. Another F-4 roared in, two black teardrops of jellied gasoline falling from its wings. These hit the Town Hall and church, immediately enveloping them in a blossom of deadly orange fire.

A second pair of Phantoms appeared. Two SAMs were immediately launched, both of which hit the lead F-4 head-on. The instantly crippled airplane never wavered from its course however; it continued over the town, dropped its payload then smashed into a row of houses next to the tracks.

The destroyed F-4's wingman flew low over the fort itself, then dropped what appeared to be a large iron bomb on the tracks beyond it. The bomb exploded with such violence the entire town shuddered as if it had been hit by an earthquake. The UA soldiers watched in horror as a mini-mushroom cloud rose from the site — the trademark of an authentic, and very rare, blockbuster bomb.

At the same moment, the third pair of Phantoms streaked over, and they too unleashed heavy bombs, not on the town or the fort, but on the tracks to the east.

"God damn it," Drews whispered as he tried to interpret the enemy pilot's odd strategy. "What the hell are they doing?"

Nearly half of Eagle Rock was burning when Hunter roared onto the scene.

Without a moment's hesitation, he sent a Sidewinder missile streaking into the ass end of a nearby Phantom, causing an explosion that destroyed both the enemy airplane as well as the one behind it. At the same moment, the troops on the ground downed an F-4 just as it was dropping its payload on the already devastated trackbed.

That left but two Phantoms, both of which had already dropped their bombs. As one, they turned and started to flee, when suddenly six *more* Phantoms appeared just over the horizon. Sensing them before seeing them, Hunter quickly vectored the Harrier into a sudden hover, turned a tight 360 degrees, then shot off in the direction of the approaching F-4's.

Hunter took on the first two enemy planes, firing Sidewinders at both with uncanny accuracy. He immediately broke left as the now-flaming Phantoms streaked by before plunging to earth.

Another Phantom had overshot the pair of doomed F-4's and was dropping its massive blockbuster bomb farther down the tracks. As the Phantom completed its bombing run and started to climb, Hunter's Harrier suddenly appeared in its path. A missile from the jumpjet ripped into the belly of the F-4, tearing the aircraft apart.

As Hunter started to turn the Harrier back toward the town, he spotted a pair of Phantoms maneuvering directly behind him.

Two solid streams of cannon fire passed over his head as he instantly applied his vector thrusts to braking. The lead F-4 flashed over him a second later, the look of astonishment on the pilot's face clearly evident as the plane streaked by. One of Hunter's Sidewinders followed close behind, smashing into the F-4's hot exhaust and obliterating the plane in midair.

Hunter then put the Harrier into a dive, pulling it out of the line of fire from the trailing Phantom. Suddenly, there was a huge flash, and this F-4 too disappeared. Hunter swung around to see a friendly trail of smoke coming from one of Drews' SAM crews.

By now, the surviving enemy planes had dropped their bombs and had retreated to the south. A half dozen had been shot down, but at least six others had made it to their target.

Now, Hunter overflew the section of track just east of Eagle Rock where the enemy pilots had dropped the blockbuster bombs. Where a half-mile-long stretch of perfectly straight track once lay, now were five enormous craters, some of them more than a football field in width. Not even a few strands of twisted metal remained; everything in and around the craters had turned to dust. The well-aimed blockbusters had destroyed the trackbed and the nearby turn-arounds beyond any hope of repair.

As he turned back toward the train, Hunter quickly surmised the reason why the enemy pilots had bombed the tracks in *back* of the *Freedom Express* and not in front of it.

"Those bastards don't *want* us to turn back," he whispered bitterly.

Chapter 30

Hunter and the others spent the rest of the afternoon helping the survivors of Eagle Rock bury their dead.

The *Freedom Express* was somberly backed up into the town where its troops were deployed in recovery and burial details. Even Chief Bad River and his warriors joined in the task that was so grim, some of the Football City Rangers had to forcibly restrain the grieving families from entering the devastated areas where their loved ones had been killed.

Hunter felt horrible about the tragedy that had befallen the small town — everyone on the train did. No amount of rationalizing could erase the fact that Eagle Rock probably wouldn't have been caught up in the terror bombing had the *Freedom Express* not been close by.

A brief memorial service was held at sunset, with an Airborne trooper tearfully blowing taps. Then, leaving behind an additional battalion of troops to reenforce the mini-fort, the train painfully slipped away into the night.

Once it had reached its former position ten miles west of the town, Catfish ordered the *Freedom Express* to halt once again.

It took about an hour to secure the train, and as soon as this was done, a gloomy meeting began in the Control car.

"We're fucking trapped" was how Fitz so succinctly put it. "We can never return the way we came now, and the only alternate track routes are hundreds of miles west of here."

No one argued his point; those were the facts. With one swift blow, Devillian had once again changed the equation. With their all-important route of escape now cut off, most around the table figured there were only two realistic options left: They could fight their way to a track turn-off located just inside of Arizona, then travel north to the border of Colorado

154

and *then* retreat to the east. Or, they could abandon the train where it sat and hope Jones could muster up enough transport — preferably large troop-carrying helicopters — to lift out all of those on board.

Either way, it would be like admitting defeat.

Catfish left to radio Jones and brief him on their situation. As he was going out, Chief Bad River was ushered in.

"We fight the common enemy," the Piute leader proclaimed. "And my men are good warriors. Some of them will stay with you. If you are attacked, they will fight to the death."

The weary United Americans were grateful for the help, knowing however that it would do little in altering their grim predicament.

"And how about you, Bad River?" asked Crossbow. "Where will you be?"

"I will take the rest of my men and ride into the mountains," the chief said. "You will not see us . . . but we will be there if you need us. And we will let you know when danger is near."

Fitz gave Bad River a customized walkie-talkie that would allow the chief to communicate with the train. Then, leaving twenty-five of his braves behind, the chief took the rest of his men and disappeared into the nearby mountains.

Chapter 31

At 0500 the next morning, Jones ordered that the *Freedom Express* be abandoned.

His message, sent via scrambled telex, didn't carry any weighty discussion as to why he'd decided as he did. After the massive attack on Eagle Rock, no lengthy explanation was needed.

It was Catfish who volunteered to deliver the bad news to Hunter. Although his friend wasn't due to report to duty until 0600, the train commander knew Hunter would want to hear of Jones' decision immediately.

Pausing outside Hunter's quarters, Catfish placed his ear against the cabin door. He figured the pilot was either asleep or possibly "involved" with Diamond. Either way, Catfish knew he'd probably be disturbing him.

So it was with mild surprise that he opened the cabin door to find Hunter lying awake on his bunk, his face clearly showing the past few days of worry. Catfish slowly entered the room, trying not to stare too long at the beautiful Diamond, who was still asleep and quite naked on the bunk next to the door.

"Sorry, Hawk, am I bugging you?" Catfish asked.

"No, Cat," Hunter said, looking up at him only for a moment. "I'm just trying to think of something that can get us out of this mess —"

"Hawk," Catfish interrupted, "it's over."

"What do you mean?" Hunter asked, not really wanting to know the answer.

Catfish took a deep breath. "Jones just killed the operation," he said finally. "We're to abandon the train here and walk back to Eagle Rock. He's sending every available chopper unit to carry us out, figures it'll take about two, maybe three days."

156

Hunter stared up at Catfish, an extremely painful look in his eyes.

"No," he said in an urgent whisper. "We can't turn back now."

"We have to," Catfish said. "Jones is sure that Devillian's troops are all over the hills of Arizona. Some of them are even as far east as the track turn-off. They're just waiting for us, Hawk. We'd be fools to walk into such a situation."

"But we can't let this bastard win," Hunter replied. "If we turn tail now, we might just as well hand him all of the Bads on a silver platter."

"He just about owns it anyway," Catfish said somberly. "Look — you know if it were up to me, damn, I'd keep on going 'til we couldn't go anymore. That's how much I believe in this. But Jones is looking at it from another perspective. Ultimately he's the guy responsible for every person on this train. He simply doesn't want to see us all get killed."

"But what about the train itself?" Hunter said, tossing away the notebook in which he'd been scribbling ideas. "We just can't leave it here, with all these weapons. Devillian will have it stripped down in a matter of days."

Catfish nodded somberly. "I know," he said. "And that's the most painful part of all."

That night, Hunter fell into a fitful, nightmare-ridden sleep.

His dreams were filled with the burning faces of the people of Eagle Rock being napalmed as their small brass band played on. Hundreds of the distinctive-colored Burning Cross F-4's filled the sky, and despite his best efforts, he could not shoot down a single one. Everytime he fired a Sidewinder, it would dematerialize into vapor long before reaching its target. Anytime he pulled the trigger for his Aden nose gun, streams of blood would come out instead of cannon shells. Even the Harrier was beyond his control in the nightmare. When he wanted to go forward, he would invariably wind up going backward. When he wanted to go up, he would go down and vice versa. Finally, he wound up completely upside down and streaking straight up, giving him a terrifying, diminishing view of the small town being eaten up by flames, all

157

to the bleats of an out-of-tune tuba.

He shook himself out of the disturbing dream and got up to throw cold water on his face. Sleeping peacefully on a bunk in the opposite corner of his quarters was Diamond. He was tempted to crawl in bed with her; maybe that would ease the dread left over by the dream.

But in the next instant he knew it would only be a brief respite, and Band-Aid approaches would do him no good now.

Instead he lay on top of his bunk and simply tried to think — about the *Freedom Express* and the current grave situation; about the fate of the country; about his own complicated life.

But try as he might, he could not prevent the other voice from creeping into his stream of thought. Once again, he did not recognize it; it was like someone trying to communicate with him from some great beyond, and the words were being broken up by some kind of cosmic interference.

At first he tried to fight off the strange sensation, but ultimately found it impossible. Finally, after all his fighting, he gave in. He cleared his mind of all its usual defenses and let the message come to him.

Difficult missions should be prepared for while they are still easy; do great things while they are still small.

Hunter felt a shudder run through him from head to toe. This time the voice sounded so close — so real — that he opened his eyes thinking someone had crept up beside him and had whispered in his ear. But no one was there.

Where the enemy is prepared, avoid him; strike at his weakest point.

Again, Hunter was chilled to the spine. He could hear the voice so clearly, he imagined he felt a hot breath beside his ear.

When appropriate, make them chase you; go slow when it bothers them.

Once again, Hunter began to question his sanity. For a third time he opened his eyes, convinced that he would find someone standing next to him.

But no one was there. The voice — so loud, so clear — had come from deep within.

Chapter 32

Two days later

The all-black Boeing 707 leveled off at forty thousand feet and turned due north, half of its dozen F-4 Phantom escorts leading the way, the other half trailing close behind.

Inside the old airliner's luxurious main cabin, Duke Devillian was lighting a huge water pipe filled with crack cocaine.

"It's hard to believe things can get better than this," he said, his twisted eyes instantly turning bloodshot with the first long puff. "But they will."

Sitting across the long, curved couch from him was the lovely Juanita Juarez and her gross brother, Jorge. Both were drinking champagne from the bottle. Next to them was Major Heck, wearing a Twisted Cross dress uniform and popping amphetamine pills like they were candy. Scattered throughout the rest of the plane and indulging in a cornucopia of drugs and liquor were two dozen other gang leaders, the top dogs of the unholy alliance that was Duke Devillian's Burning Cross.

Only Heck seemed nervous.

"One surface-to-air missile and this plane could be destroyed," he said to Devillian. "And all of us would die."

Devillian laughed at him. "So what?"

"So, everything we've been working for would be lost," the Nazi replied, his eyes going narrow.

Devillian laughed again. "Then what difference would it make?" he asked, taking another long drag on the crack pipe. "None of this will matter if we're all dead."

Heck popped two more pills and crudely washed them

down with a swig from Juanita's champagne bottle. He hated such existential blather.

"What's your problem, Major," Juanita asked him, grabbing the champagne back. "Where's your Nazi Iron Will we hear so much about?"

"Will is one thing," Heck said, anxiously twisting around to look out the plane's window. "Stupidity is quite another."

"Relax, *mein Fuehrer*," Devillian needled him. "We've got twelve escort fighters around us and more radar equipment on board than three squadrons' worth of jets. Besides, who do we have to worry about? Not the United Americans. Their shoulder-launched missiles do not fly this high, nor do they have any high-performance jets in the area. We would see them from a hundred miles away if they did. Besides, they have other things on their minds."

Devillian smiled at this last statement, although his present excitement was as intense as he thought it would be.

"Alas, our adventure with the United Americans ended too soon," he said, just a tad wistfully. "I would have thought they'd put up a better fight."

He turned to his guests and let out a great chuckle.

"But I overestimated them," he said. "And now they are retreating, as you will all soon see for yourselves."

At that moment, the copilot of the aircraft stuck his head into the cabin.

"We are about thirty minutes from the coordinate, sir," the man said through a thick South African accent.

"Let me know when we are ten minutes out," Devillian snapped at the man. "And lock that door behind you."

The copilot did as told. Devillian then picked up a red phone next to his seat.

"OK, send them in."

The door at the opposite end of the cabin opened, and four young women were pushed in by two burly Skinhead guards.

"I have arranged a little entertainment to go along with our tour," Devillian said.

He clapped his hands, and the Skinheads nudged the girls toward the long couch. Each one was dressed differently: One was wearing a Sunday dress, another a tiny bikini, another a Catholic school uniform, and the fourth, a cheerleader's uniform.

"The first choice is yours, Major Heck," Devillian said, turning toward the Nazi officer.

The man was slightly taken aback. "Here? Now?" he stuttered.

"Yes, yes!" Devillian roared, his eyes twirling crazily. "I bought these young beauties in Dallas especially for this—the occasion of our greatest triumph! So, all of you, take your pick."

Juanita's brother Jorge needed no further prompting. He immediately grabbed the girl in the Sunday dress. Roughly forcing her to the ground, he yanked up her skirt and crudely entered her. Devillian grabbed the cheerleader and mimicked the Mexican bandit's rude behavior. Being only slightly more modest, Heck took another two pills, then pulled the girl in the bikini into a corner and forced her to perform fellatio on him.

This left only Juanita and the schoolgirl.

Devillian lifted his head from his lecherous activity just as Juanita pulled the young girl down onto the couch next to her. Instantly the Mexican beauty was all over the girl, ripping her blouse open and kissing her small breasts.

Devillian was instantly delirious. His plan to see if Juanita would take on a female had succeeded beyond his wildest dreams. He let out a howl as he tried to climax, completely ignoring the girl underneath him, instead watching as Juanita worked over her innocent victim.

"Ten minutes, sir," the South African copilot yelled from behind the locked cabin door.

"Thanks for nothing," Devillian screamed back.

In this short time, Devillian's temperament had turned around 180 degrees. The terrorist was puffing madly on the crack pipe—but nothing he could do would restore the stamina he'd just lost, as usual, in mid-thrust.

"OK, party's over," he yelled at the three others, who were still being serviced by the somewhat depleted young girls. "We're coming up on the coordinate."

The pair of Skinhead guards appeared out of nowhere and grabbed the four girls—one of them right out from

161

underneath Jorge. Even Juanita was disappointed to see her sex object go. She had forced the girl between her legs and was letting the orgasmic waves wash over her when Devillian so crudely brought the activities to a halt.

"I would like her again," Juanita told Devillian matter-of-factly as the girls were marched out of the cabin. "She looks so much like Diamond."

The comment caused something to snap inside Devillian's already distracted brain. Try as he might, he just couldn't stop thinking about Diamond. Now the ache of lust lost was added to his usual sexual frustration.

He knew there was only one solution: "Someone's going to have to die," he whispered to himself.

Five minutes later, Devillian and the others had their noses pressed up against the cabin's windows, watching with delight the rather pathetic scene below them.

They were cruising right over the *Freedom Express*. The train was dead in its tracks, ten miles west of Eagle Rock, right where its forward progress was halted two days before. Streaming back those ten miles were two long lines of United American soldiers—retreating to Eagle Rock.

A minute later, the 707 was coming up on the small town itself, and the observers could plainly see that an elaborate, though hasty, evacuation was taking place below. In a large field just outside of the town, literally hundreds of helicopters of all shapes and sizes were shuttling in and taking off, their holds filled to capacity with United American troopers.

"It is like Dunkirk!" Major Heck screamed in joy, referring to the inglorious evacuation of Allied troops from France during the Nazi *blitzkrieg* of 1940. "So they *are* running from us."

Devillian was laughing again. "You are seeing the end of the United American Army," he said, pressing a video camera up against the cabin window and still secretly wishing that his victory had been more bloody. "Those comic book heroes have finally seen their day."

Two Burning Cross F-4's were lazily sweeping up and down the evacuation plain, weaving in and out of the choppers. Even from thirty thousand feet, it was apparent to the people in the 707 that the F-4's were simply harassing the helicopters and the troops on the ground and not firing their cannons with any regularity.

"You do not shoot at the enemy?" Jorge asked.

"Why should we?" Devillian asked. "I could have fifty jet fighters picking those choppers out of the sky like quails if I wanted to. But I don't."

"But why?" Juanita wanted to know.

Devillian smiled slyly, turning the video camera on her lovely breasts for a brief moment. Maybe she was coming around to him.

"Because each one of those men is more valuable to me alive than dead, my dear," he answered. "Each one of them will return to their homes and tell everyone they know about how enormous a failure this whole *Freedom Express* nonsense has been.

"They will be interviewed by the press. They will be the subject of endless debate. They will get drunk and wail about their sorrows in barrooms. They will have fights with their loved ones. Families will split apart; children will suffer. Best of all, those soldiers will forever hate the blacks, and the Jews, and the Papists, and the Indians and all of the other non-white scum who got them into this position in the first place.

"They are an army in disgrace, and they will no longer consider themselves as true men. And they will go to their graves knowing that the Burning Cross was responsible.

"Now I ask you, my friends, is there any better way to spread our message than that?"

Chapter 33

Eagle Rock, two days later

"It is with great honor that we accept this mission," Major Heck told the five hundred blackened faces before him. "Herr Devillian has chosen us to take possession of the ultimate prize of war."

Heck paused for effect, staring into the eyes of the men of the Twisted Cross's most elite shock unit, the Skull and Crossbone battalion.

It was barely dawn, and the men had just finished a field breakfast. They had been airlifted into Eagle Rock during the night, landing in the same field where the United Americans had evacuated forty-eight hours before.

On a hill nearby, a large cross was burning.

"You men know your orders," Heck went on. "We will take possession of the train and drive it to Arizona, where it will pass in glory by our many strongholds there. Once we reach the hills of San Bernardino, we will strip off any useful weaponry. Then, just as before, we will send this train crashing down into Los Angeles, a further message that the Burning Cross is in control of this part of the country—territory that rightly belongs to it!"

There was a great cheer from the troops, their enthusiasm stoked by the amphetamine pills their medics had generously distributed with the morning chow.

Heck snapped into a ramrod posture and raised his right arm in salute.

"*Heil* Devillian!" he screamed.

"*Heil* Devillian!" the soldiers screamed back. "*Heil Hitler!*"

It took the Skull and Crossbone Battalion just a little over an hour to reach the *Freedom Express,* the last mists of the New Mexico dawn burning off as the first elements came up on the tail end of the train.

Within minutes, the unit's advance scouts were clamoring all over the end cars, sweeping through the mile-long series of empty mini-forts with giddy abandon. Inside they found much ammunition and many cases of TNT, brought along by the United Americans no doubt, for track clearing operations.

By this time, the main elements of the elite battalion had split in two and were walking up on either end of the train. Some of the men were grumbling that the battalion's advance scouts—known among the regular soldiers as "The Forty Thieves"—were getting the lion's share of the booty. Still the Twisted Cross troops were in high spirits. They were practically sprinting by the long section of mini-fort cars, determined to get to the weapons cars. This was where the *real* souvenirs would be found.

The dash to the front of the train nearly turned into a disorderly race before the battalion commanders shouted at their troops to slow down and *walk.* This order hit home quickly, and the soldiers returned to their standard single-line advancements. Thus, it was an orderly troop that marched up toward the midsection of the train, where the mini-fort cars gave way to the weapons carriers, the first of which was the mighty howitzer, Big Dick.

Meanwhile, the scouts inside the train had already reached the midpoint. It was Heck's second-in-command, a Captain Ruzz, who symbolically swung open the door at the front of the first mini-fort and stared with smug delight at the railway car carrying Big Dick.

"Behold the spoils of war," he said, turning to his two dozen souvenir-laden scouts and pointing back toward the enormous howitzer. "And remember this moment well. Just as our forefathers touched the waters of the Atlantic after only a few days of *blitzkrieg,* we now claim this prize, for ourselves and for our children."

Ruzz's scouts would have appreciated their leader's visionary prose more if they hadn't been so anxious about the exact position of the gigantic howitzer's gun barrel.

It was pointing directly at them.

It was Heck himself who first saw the mighty flash.

Walking at the head of the column advancing on the train's southern side, he saw the monstrous tongue of flame roar out of the barrel of the howitzer and simply obliterate the first twenty mini-fort cars in its wake. Oddly, the sound of the explosion didn't reach Heck for a long second or two, but when it did, it was powerful enough to knock him to his knees.

"Take cover!" someone screamed as six of the railway cars shot straight up in the air, carrying long trails of flame and smoke and debris with them. Suddenly it seemed as if the whole world had caught on fire.

Heck was already hugging the ground, biting his tongue in an effort not to go into shock. A full quarter mile of the second half of the train had simply vanished into the frightening conflagration set off by the howitzer's shot. In seconds, a rain of murderous shrapnel and debris began falling all around Heck and his troops, killing and injuring scores of the prone, confused soldiers.

Heck's brain could not believe what had just happened. At first he thought some kind of terrible accident had taken place. But then he heard more explosions. Twisting around to look back through the hell that had erupted on the tracks, he saw each of the remaining mini-fort cars blowing up in precise succession, likely an orderly detonation of a string of enormous firecrackers. Anyone within twenty feet of either side of each car was instantly blown to bits, adding to the carnage already created by the monster blast from the howitzer.

Still, Heck searched his consciousness for some kind of rational explanation. But the horror was only fifteen seconds old when he finally came to the dire conclusion that the railway cars had all been elaborately booby-trapped and that his elite Skull and Crossbone battalion had blundered into an incredible ambush.

His fears were confirmed as he peered through the smoke and flames and death at the titanic howitzer. He could see men in distinct blue-camouflage uniforms—the colors of the accursed United Americans—rapidly reloading the gun.

"*No!*" Heck screamed just a millisecond before the enormous howitzer fired again.

The second shot only blew apart what little remained from the first. Still, it added to the confusion and the terror of the moment.

Heck felt like he was floating on a sea of blood. His brain was pulsating, and his tongue had gone thick. He closed his eyes and imagined that he was suddenly floating above the earth, which was hanging motionless in space. Then suddenly with the crack of a mighty thunderbolt, the huge globe began spinning again.

He managed to shake himself out of the terrifying hallucination only to be hit on the forehead by a chunk of flaming metal an instant later. As he passed into true unconsciousness, he lifted his head one more time to see that the front half of the *Freedom Express* was slowly pulling away. . . .

Chapter 34

Santa Fe Airport

Bull Sheehan was feeling lucky.

"This is the life," he murmured, taking a healthy slug from his bottle of beer. "I must have been crazy knocking myself out all those years."

Sheehan, a ground-attack pilot-for-hire, had spent the previous two years fighting in Central America for whatever side was paying the most. The hours had been tough; but the money had been good, and his base of operations in Costa Rica—now known simply as Big Banana—had been a trading post for everything from drugs to white slaves to X-rated videos.

Everything changed however when the United Americans stomped the Twisted Cross in Panama. After that, most of the air mercenary work dried up. A few months later, Sheehan decided it was time to get into a new line of work.

He had been gunrunning for only four months when he met the representative from the Burning Cross one night in the waiting room of a cathouse. The man was drunk and loudmouthed, but not so much that Sheehan wasn't able to arrange a meeting with him the following day. It was in the midst of this hangover-plagued get-together that Sheehan was given his first assignment by the Burning Cross: locate and buy as many of the rare blockbuster bombs as he could get his hands on.

The job took him all the way to the enormous weapons markets of Algiers in North Africa. Using the bottomless sack of gold from his employers, Sheehan had made arrangements with a South African cartel to buy ten dozen of the extremely destructive, high explosive weapons. Like any other customer, Sheehan wanted to see some of the bombs in action, and once he was satisfied, he shipped the first dozen to the Burning Cross for their approval.

As he later understood it, the Burning Cross had used this first shipment of bombs in an attack up in northern New Mexico. Just what the fight was all about, Sheehan didn't know—or care. He'd received the OK to buy the remaining 108 blockbusters, and left Algiers in a rented Ilyushin I1-76 cargo jet, its belly full of the rare weapons.

That had been two days ago. Now Sheehan was sitting at a poker table in Santa Fe Airport's largest barroom, losing his shirt and not caring a whit. Locked in the strongbox between his feet was his payment from the Burning Cross for a job well-done. It was more than eighty pounds of gold—so much bullion that he had taken to wondering if he would ever have to work again.

His daydreams were interrupted when he realized he was in the process of casually losing still another pot to the four bloodsuckers sitting around the poker table. They were a motley collection—no different from all the other air pirates, bandits and highwaymen who had been drawn to the airport like flies to garbage in hopes of getting in on the Burning Cross's largesse.

"Big doing up in the hills," an air pirate appropriately named Shithead kept saying over and over. "They'll need some air cover soon."

"Who will?" a scummy highwayman named The Scratch asked. "You keep jabbering away about this, but you never provide any details."

"The Burning Cross, you idiot," Shithead replied, trying but failing to sound properly conspiratorial. "I'm telling you, they are bombing the living shit out of those

169

United American heroes."

"The guys who have the train?" Scratch asked.

"The guys who *had* the train," Shithead corrected him, at the same time shuffling the cards and dealing out a hand of Jacks-or-Better. "They bugged out two nights ago. Left without a fight, the pansies. Now the word is that Devillian's going to get all his guys together and attack LA. If he does, he'll be offering top dollar for guys like us, and I want to be in on that."

Sheehan had just leaned back in his chair to admire the absolutely lousy hand he was holding. Another hour with these assholes and I'll go nuts, he thought.

But in the next moment, he knew he wouldn't have to wait that long. Shortly after completing the deal with the Burning Cross, he had bought himself a small T-38 trainer jet. It was being readied for flight at that moment, and quick check of the time told him he had barely a half hour to go before he could take delivery and get the hell out of Santa Fe forever.

"I call," Shithead declared after everyone had finished betting.

Sheehan drunkenly laid down nothing more than a pair of threes.

"I lost again," he said with a laugh.

Each of the four other men at the table eyed him suspiciously.

"What the hell are you so happy about?" The Scratch asked him. "You haven't won a hand in two hours."

"Can't help it, I guess," Sheehan responded, downing a shot of bad whiskey. "Just not my lucky day."

"You don't seem too upset," Shithead told him. "Must be a reason, unless you just like losing."

"Maybe I just don't give a fuck," Sheehan told him, kicking the strongbox between his legs for luck. "And maybe I just completed the biggest deal of my life."

Suddenly Shithead's ears perked up. "You doing some work for the Burning Cross?" he asked.

"Maybe" was Sheehan's coy reply.

170

"Big money?"

"Maybe," Sheehan repeated.

Shithead let out a whoop that attracted the attention of just about everyone in the bar.

"So it's true," he said, banging the table with his fist. "The Cross is paying big bucks to everyone."

"Yeh, but you've got to have a brain to get hired on," Sheehan snapped back at him, effectively silencing the big mouth air pirate.

"How'd you do it, Cowboy," asked the third man at the table, a drug runner named Twix. "Kill somebody?"

"Nothing that messy," Sheehan boasted. He then went on to describe his adventure in Algiers, taking note not to mention that his grandiose payment was sitting at his feet.

"There's plenty for everyone" is how Sheehan ended his story. "You've just got to know what they want."

Three hands later, Shithead and The Scratch cashed out. A minute later, Twix bought a hooker who just happened by, and he too was soon gone.

This left only Sheehan and the fourth man, a small, dark character who had spoken not a word during the entire card game.

"So tell me, Mr. Sheehan," the man said through a thick Irish brogue, lighting up an enormous cigar. "Just where were you able to store all those blockbusters?"

An hour later, Bull Sheehan was sitting in the cockpit of his T-38, literally chewing his lip in nervousness, waiting to get clearance to take off.

"You've always been too greedy," he whispered to himself. "Someday it's going to catch up with you."

He fervently hoped today was not that day. Stored behind the cockpit seat was his trunk full of Burning Cross gold. Sitting in the sack between him and his parachute was an additional forty pounds of bullion, the result of a quick and very dangerous transaction he'd

171

made with the last man at the card table.

All the guy wanted to know was where in the complex of hangars and bunkers that made up the Santa Fe Airport did the Burning Cross store the 108 blockbuster bombs.

Sheehan had haggled the price up from twenty pounds to forty pounds of gold in less than a minute—astronomical figures that had blinded him to the foolishness of the deal. If the Burning Cross ever found out that he had pinpointed the storage bunker on the west side of the field as the resting place of the blockbusters, he was certain that a squad of Skinheads would be dispatched to track him down and kill him—slowly.

"Damn that fucking Mick!" he grumbled, as he heard another two airplanes get clearance before him. "I should never have listened to him."

The fourth man had been all too persuasive—and forty pounds of gold was hard to turn down.

Still, Sheehan continued to curse him, even though he would never find out the temptor's real name was Mike Fitzgerald.

Sheehan finally got his clearance and executed the quickest take-off of his life.

It was just in time as it turned out. No sooner was he aloft and turning south when his early-warning radar started flashing.

Looking out to the northeast, he could see at least a dozen specks of light heading right for him. Before he knew it, the specks turned into aircraft: two F-4's, two F-5's, several old F-105 Thunderchiefs and a handful of hot-shit F-20 Tigersharks. Leading the pack was a AV-8BE Harrier jumpjet.

Even before Sheehan had a chance to alter his course, the jets were peeling off and screaming in on the airport. He watched in a mixture of fascination and horror as the Tigersharks strafed row after row of fighter planes and cargo jets, all of them belonging to the Burning Cross. One of the first airplanes to go up was the black Boeing 707 that Sheehan knew belonged to the Burning Cross's top dog himself.

Meanwhile, the F-4's and F-5's were firing barrages of air-to-ground missiles into the airport's most important structures, such as the control tower and main terminals. As this was happening, he could see the antique F-105 "Thuds" flying low over the airport's runways, their underbelly weapons dispensers crackling as they deposited thousands of asphalt-cratering bomblets up and down the landing strips.

Just where the airport's air defense crews were all this time Sheehan didn't know. However, he wouldn't have been surprised to learn that Mike Fitzgerald had paid them off too.

Meanwhile, the Harrier was doing slow orbit of the base. Suddenly it went into a screeching dive and, at about five hundred feet, released a large, pencil-shaped missile.

Sheehan watched as the missile went through a series of wild gyrations, weaving back and forth in such a way that he knew it was most likely being guided to its target by a laser aimed by someone on the ground.

When he saw the missile do one final twist and streak toward the bunker containing the blockbusters, he realized his worst fears had come true. Undoubtedly, the man who he'd sold his soul to for forty pounds of gold had shot a laser designator at the bunker, and the skill of the Harrier pilot was enough to deliver the missile on target.

Sheehan couldn't bear to watch as the missile slammed into the bunker. He had turned the T-38 around and was now fleeing west as fast as its rather smallish engine would carry him. Still, despite his speed and altitude, the airplane was buffeted by the enormous shock wave resulting from the 108 blockbusters igniting at once.

He dared only one more look over his shoulder before he set out for the Fiji Islands or someplace equally distant. The glance produced a vision he'd never forget: All that was left of the Santa Fe Airport was one big, smoking hole in the ground.

Chapter 35

Few places on the post-war world were as isolated as Port Desemboque, Mexico.

Located on the north western edge of the Mexican mainland, the city looked out on to the Gulf of California and the Baja beyond. No more than two thousand people lived there, and just about all of them worked on or around the docking facilities that provided the settlement's total flow of income.

In the pre-war years, the harbor was known as a major shrimp fishing center. Since the war, the boats tying up there had tended to carry more lethal loads: drugs and guns, as well as fuel, food and basic supplies. Most of this larder came from the fairly prosperous countries and kingdoms of South America.

Despite this change in imports—or actually, *because* of it—the small seaport did well in the post-war world. Its location close to the border of America helped—it was only one hundred miles south of the Arizona border—as did its less than honest harbormasters, who controlled every pound of cargo that went in and out, skimming a profit from each one.

Still, the attitude in the city had always been seriously laid back. No one had to work very hard to get fed, clothed, and to put some gold in his pocket. Plus the typical post-war vices—drugs, hookers and guns—were always in ready supply. The city leaders never had to worry about such things as security, because no one had any reason to attack them. In fact, the local bandit gangs actually served as the police force for the port city, and they had ruthlessly pursued their assignment to keep the place free of anyone who would attempt to screw up a good thing.

All of this changed in one day.

A man named Duke Devillian visited the small port city one morning. Arriving completely unannounced, he and his entourage met with the harbormasters, seeking to lease the city's entire waterfront. The harbormasters initially agreed, but when a dispute arose concerning their skim-off percentage in the deal, Devillian pulled out an Uzi submachine gun and shot them all.

From that point on, the people in the port of Desemboque worked exclusively for the Burning Cross.

Little changed in the ensuing months. Few people worked very hard, the bandits were still the police force, and if anything, the flow of cargo — from guns to food — had picked up. The only real difference was that every pound that came into the port was earmarked for Devillian, specifically for his Burning Cross headquarters. Thus, the route plied by Devillian's helicopters between Desemboque and the Ring of Fire area was the major lifeline for the isolated mesa fortress.

Desemboque was *so* relaxed that the city's only SAM installation hadn't been serviced in two years.

Its owners felt there was no need. But now, on this fateful day, just six hours after the devastating attack on Santa Fe Airport, they would discover how mistaken they had been.

They heard the jets before they saw them. There were six in all: Two A-7E Strikefighters had roared in from the east and linked up with four bomb-laden A-10 Thunderbolts that had appeared out of the northwest. The half dozen jets buzzed the port for five minutes, flying low and loud, their engines emitting screeches terrifying enough to drive everyone away from the docks.

The port facilities thus cleared, the jets went to work.

The four Thunderbolts lined up in a single file and one by one screamed down and methodically unloaded their ordnance—cluster bombs, mostly—on both the dockworks and the dozens of storage facilities lining the harbor. Once each A-10 had dumped its bomb load, it returned to strafe any target of opportunity with its enormous GAU 8/A Avenger 30mm cannon. All the while, the two Strikefighters circled overhead, ready to deal with any return fire.

There was none.

When the six attackers finally regrouped and roared off to the north ten minutes later, more than three-quarters of the port of Desemboque was in flames.

Chapter 36

La Casa de las Estrellas

Duke Devillian couldn't remember the last time he'd felt so good.

He was sitting in the middle of the Play Pen, perched on a high-backed director's chair. An enormous bowl of crack cocaine sat on the table in front of him; a case of chilled champagne was to his left. Juanita Juarez was there, gulping the bubbly as usual and rummaging through Devillian's videotape collection. Four young girls were there too, and at the moment, Devillian was directing them in a scene.

One of his Roman visitors was manning the video camera; another was handling the lights. Two of the girls in front of him were playing out a seduction scene Devillian had scripted just minutes before.

"Have you ever been with another girl?" the older of the two "actresses," she being dressed like a schoolteacher, asked the other right on cue.

"No," the other one answered, her outfit being the Catholic school uniform left over from Devillian's airborne orgy two days before. "I've always been afraid."

"Don't worry," the schoolteacher said, slowing moving her hand down the younger girl's blouse and caressing one of her small, sweet breasts. "Take these pills, and then the lesson will begin."

Suddenly there was a commotion at the front door of the Play Pen.

"Cut!" Devillian screamed.

He turned to the two men who had just barged in. They were officers of his communications squad.

"Are you crazy?" Devillian shrieked at them. "I'm going to have you both cut up into bacon!"

Both men gulped simultaneously.

"We are extremely sorry, sir," one of them stuttered. "But we've been getting some pretty way-out messages that you should know about."

Juanita stopped perusing the videotape file. "What kinds of messages?" she asked.

"Bad news," the other communications officer croaked. "From all over."

Devillian clapped his hands once, and everyone but Juanita and the two communications men fled from the room.

The cross-eyed terrorist leader hastily sucked on a bowl of crack and chugged half a bottle of champagne at the same time. His incredibly good mood—most of it the result of Juanita accepting his invitation to watch him direct the two girls in action—was now completely dissipated. He felt that such a rare excitement would never return to him, and this made him especially furious.

Finally he gave the signal for the two communications officers to go ahead.

"First of all," one began, reading from a telex sheet, "the Skull and Crossbone battalion has been nearly wiped out."

Devillian's face drained of color. "What the hell are you talking about?"

"We just got a message from Major Heck," the man continued. "He was hurt real bad, and it took him almost a half day to get through to us on the radio. It seems that train was booby-trapped. When he and his guys moved up to take possession, half of it just blew up on them. He says that more than eighty percent of

179

the unit was killed."

Devillian took a long, desperate draw on his crack pipe.

"Damn, did they get pictures?" he wanted to know.

The communications officers looked at him strangely for just a moment, then one of them hastily replied: "He didn't say, boss."

"Go on," Devillian ordered them.

"Well, after the half of the train blew up, the other half took off."

Devillian nearly spit out his mouthful of champagne.

"What do you mean it took off?" he demanded. "That train was abandoned two days ago."

"Apparently not, sir," one of the men replied. "The first half—the one carrying all of the weapons cars—pulled out right after the Skull and Crossbones guys got blasted."

"Those *fucking* comic book heroes!" Devillian sputtered. "Those goddamn flag-waving sons-of-bitches."

"They tricked you," Juanita said with a cruel smile.

Devillian fought the temptation to shoot her on the spot. Not now, he thought. Maybe later.

"Major Heck is being airlifted back in a medivac chopper," one of the officers said. "He'll be here within the hour."

"I don't give a fuck about him," Devillian seethed. "Is that it?"

"No, boss," one of the officers replied. "There's more. A lot more. . . ."

The men took the next five minutes detailing the devastating sneak attack on Santa Fe Airport. The more they talked, the harder Devillian sucked on his crack pipe.

"It's just a big hole in the ground" was how they ended the report. "Nothing left at all. The 707 is gone, as well as a lot of our supply planes and some fighters."

180

"Christ, did someone nuke the place?" Devillian asked angrily.

"Not quite," replied one of the officers. "The only thing we can figure is that the United Americans somehow found out where we were storing the blockbusters and they hit it with a guided munitions missile."

The other communications man took a deep breath. "One of our guys who survived said he saw a jumpjet launch a missile just before the place went up."

Devillian was beyond words by this time. He nearly passed out from rage when the two men told him about the similarly devastating strike on Port Desemboque just an hour before.

"These United Americans do not give up so easily," Juanita said to the terrorist leader.

The man did not answer her. Instead he just closed his eyes and lowered his head.

"It appears as if they fooled you completely," Juanita pressed on, enjoying herself. "The abandonment of the train was obviously a ruse. And now these attacks on our major installations. When the people of America get wind of all this, it will be us that look like the fools, not them."

Again, Devillian could not answer. He just slumped over in his chair, spilling a bottle of champagne in the process.

"I think . . . you all better leave . . . now," he said in a voice so weak, Juanita and the two communications officers barely heard it. "Please. . . ."

They slowly backed out of the room, Juanita not quite knowing what to do. Devillian looked absolutely pathetic, so much so, she heard herself whispering: "This is the end of him."

She was sure her intuition was correct as she closed the huge doors of the Play Pen behind her.

In her last glimpse of Devillian, she saw that he had picked up a revolver next to his chair, unloaded five of its six bullets and then put the gun to his head.

Now, with her ear pressed up close to the door, she could hear only the man's labored breathing and a faint, disturbing *click!*

Chapter 37

Kansas

Catfish Johnson pulled another burr out of his backside and cursed.

"Goddamn things will cut you up like a knife," he muttered, flicking the sharp piece of grass away from him. "Between these frigging things and the smell of all this horseshit, I'm losing my enthusiasm."

He was sitting next to a small campfire, hidden underneath an outcrop of rock in a blind canyon about twenty-five miles west of Dodge City. Twelve of his 1st Airborne troopers were lounging next to the fire, which was doing only an adequate job of warding off the night chill. A larger fire would have helped—but they couldn't risk attracting any more undue attention. As it was, there werc morc than one hundred paltry campfires such as this one within a five-mile radius.

Just then, twelve more of his troopers walked into the small camp. None of the men were wearing their standard Airborne uniforms; instead they were dressed as cowboys. Slowly, they climbed out of these outfits and, in a ritual that Catfish had seen many times already, exchanged them with another dozen troopers.

Within five minutes, the squad of twelve new cowboys was marching out of the camp, with the men who'd given them the clothes getting into their usual uniforms and taking their places around the fire.

"How are the horses doing?" Catfish asked Captain Drews—the same officer who had briefly commanded the mini-fort at Eagle Rock before it was abandoned—

as he settled down next to the fire.

"Everything's fine," Drews answered, warming his hands. "The count is right: nine hundred and seventy-four. The hay is holding up OK, and I doubt if that watering hole is going to run dry anytime soon."

"How about the fence?"

"Also, OK," Drews answered. "We strapped up a piece near the south gate. It was just old, falling apart. The boys fixed it up real good though."

Catfish caught himself unconsciously taking a deep breath of night air. As usual, it practically caught in his throat.

"Goddamn, I knew horses smelled bad," he said, "but not *this* bad."

"Some people like that smell, Major," Drews kidded him. "Some people like stepping in the horseshit, too. They say it's good for you."

"I'm sure they do," Catfish replied. "But not me — I'm a city person."

Drews poured himself a cup of coffee and leaned back to relax.

"Look at it this way, sir," he said. "We're babysitting the smallest herd. Imagine the guys up near Abilene. They're sitting on top of *three thousand* of these gigsters. Can you imagine how that must smell?"

"Can't be any worse than this," Catfish replied.

The night passed, and Catfish spent the time going over his duties for the following day.

They were expecting two air drops. One was a shipment of saddles which were being parachuted in by the Free Canadian Air Force just before dawn. The other was their daily food drop, also courtesy of the Canadians.

Catfish had to shake his head at the enormity of this new, rather bizarre mission he and the 1st Airborne had taken on. Just the logistics alone of keeping nearly ten thousand men — the better part of a whole division—fed and hidden in the wilds of Kansas were staggering. Flying all the stuff in from Free Canada only made the whole thing even more complicated.

But he knew it had to be done this way.

As the hours crawled on toward midnight, Catfish also found time to catch up on his field reports. More than three battalions of the 1st Airborne Division were hidden in the camps in his immediate area. Despite being deployed undercover—if, in fact, ten thousand soldiers could ever really be put undercover—there were still the day-to-day things to attend to, like strength reports, sick call and so on. Even back in his office in Washington he'd never had to wade through so much paperwork.

However, despite his current situation—and the one-in-a-million long-shot operation that they were slowly preparing for—Catfish only had two real worries on his mind. The first concerned his family: They had undoubtedly heard that the United Americans had abandoned the *Freedom Express* and that the 1st Airborne had ingloriously retreated from Eagle Rock in the face of overwhelming opposition from Devillian's white supremacist armies.

As such, Catfish knew that his family was probably expecting him to arrive home at anytime now, defeated but still alive. Trouble was, he didn't know whether he'd ever make it home again.

His second worry was of a more immediate concern: Within the next couple of days, he would have to learn how to ride a horse. He was not looking forward to that experience at all.

"I hope you know what you're doing, Hawk," he whispered into the night. "Wherever you are. . . ."

Chapter 38

Aboard the Freedom Express

Hunter sneezed once, hard.

"It's too strong," he said to himself. "Damn stuff is clogging my nostrils."

He reached over to the cup of water next to his chair and threw half of it on the incense that was burning in a makeshift urn nearby.

But the spray of water only increased the amount of pungent smoke drifting around the dark cabin.

"It's all right, Hawk," Diamond called over to him. "I think you are getting use to it."

The train was moving slowly—painfully so. He could feel every jolt and bump, every quake and quiver as it sluggishly wound its way through the Sangre de Cristo Mountains.

It had been like this for nearly a day and a half.

He closed his eyes and returned to his meditation.

If you must attack an enemy far away, create the illusion that you are only going a short distance.

"I understand that," he whispered.

But if the enemy is nearby, trick him into thinking that you are going a long way.

"That is clear too."

He had finally stopped questioning the strange intonations in his head; finally stopped worrying about where they came from or why. For many reasons, his concern for his own sanity was secondary right now.

He had more important things to do.

It had been the voices that convinced him that the *Freedom Express* should carry on—though explaining his elaborate plan to Jones and the others had been one of the most difficult things he had ever done. Something was happening to him, he tried to tell them. Something deep inside. If they just followed his advice—as he received it from deep in his psyche—there was a chance the train, or some part of it, would reach LA.

But they had to trust in his instinct more than they had ever done before.

Predictably, JT had been the hardest to convince. He thought the whole thing smacked of the New Age channeling craze of years back—supernatural voices coming through human mediums. Hunter tried to explain to his friend that it was nothing like that, but the sometimes hotheaded pilot remained unconvinced. And at times, Hunter wasn't entirely sure his friend was not right.

Fitz, Crunch and the Cobra Brothers didn't know what to think that day after Jones had cancelled the mission when, during a completely bizarre meeting, Hunter spelled out his strange plan to them. They had seen him in action before—had seen his gambles pay off. But it was a little too much for them to watch as Hunter sat, eyes closed, deep in a trance, spewing out ancient-sounding adages on military strategy and tactics while a stick of homemade incense burned nearby. Even Michael Crossbow, he being a student of myths and legends, was baffled by it all, especially when Hunter suggested that he become a ghost and go on a very dangerous solo mission.

Oddly, only Ben Wa seemed to fully understand. Before he "abandoned" the train with the others, he had urged Hunter to go with the strange feelings.

"I don't know what's happening to you," the Oriental

fighter pilot had told him. "But sometimes, I feel it happening inside of me, too."

It was Catfish who proved to be the biggest surprise. When Hunter told him that an intricate part of his strategy involved his proud 1st Airborne retreating, he thought the former NFL player would have cried foul.

But he didn't. Instead he listened carefully to Hunter's grandiose plan—the strange advice from beyond included—and then simply said, "OK, we'll do it."

This had left only two hundred people remaining on the train—volunteers all. In addition to Hunter, Diamond, Fitz, the Cobra Brothers, the rest were Football City Special Forces Rangers, and 25 of Bad Rivers Piutes, probably the toughest, most versatile troops in the world. These soldiers had taken over manning the various weapons on the mile-long train, as well as all aspects of the train's movement.

It boosted everyone's spirits enormously that the first elements of Hunter's strangely inspired plan went off so smoothly. The advice he'd received pertaining to them—*Attack where they don't expect it*—had boded well. Turning Devillian's arrogance back on him, Hunter deduced that the racist leader assumed the United Americans were finished after the retreat from Eagle Rock. Or, if he was expecting a counter-attack at all, he would expect it would be launched against the mesa fortress. Using the mysterious voices as a guide, Hunter suggested the United Americans hit the white supremacist where he wasn't looking. That beautifully simple bit of advice turned into the air strikes on Santa Fe and Port Desemboque.

The second half of his subconscious message—*Move when your enemy thinks you cannot*—resulted in the more elaborate booby-trapping of the second half of the train. The egomaniacal Devillian had made the over-confident mistake of prematurely sending his best troops in to claim the *Freedom Express*.

By conservative estimates, only about forty of five hundred enemy soldiers had survived.

There hadn't been any action against the train since Hunter orchestrated these bold moves.

It was almost as if Devillian had instituted a kind of unilateral ceasefire. Some on the train even went so far as to suggest that the terrorist leader might be all through, that the surprise attacks on Santa Fe, on Desemboque and against the Skull and Crossbone battalion had been enough to shatter the madman's dishonorable alliance of bandit gangs and mercenaries.

But Hunter didn't believe this for a moment.

All he had to do was close his eyes, and he knew that the larger battles lay ahead. Though stung, Devillian's army was still a very formidable force. As many as one hundred fifty thousand enemy troops were waiting along the tracks up ahead, and it was only a matter of time before the train would have to deal with them.

Once again it had fallen to Hunter to figure out how to accomplish an impossible mission for his country. And to do so, he knew he had to pull out all the stops, even if it meant taking on a totally weird persona and listening to voices in his head that could be announcing nothing more than the onset of insanity.

He sneezed again, but resisted the temptation to spill more water on the incense.

It was only through many hours of intense concentration that the voice was able to come through—and then only in spurts. But Hunter had found that certain changes in the atmosphere of his cabin helped ease the messages to the surface.

Therefore his chair now rested high atop a table at one end of his cabin; he had moved it there after receiving the message: *In times of emergency, a leader must climb up to a high place and throw away the*

189

ladder.

The cabin was also very dark, the only light being provided by the two dozen candles Diamond had found on board. Now as the young girl walked through this shimmering, flickering illumination, she looked absolutely beautiful. Holding a piece of straw to a large red candle that was burning nearby, she used the flame to relight the stick of incense.

Hunter had no idea why the combination of the incense and the candle light, plus his high perch, somehow helped the messages from beyond to come through. But other elements were necessary too: Having only Diamond in the room with him helped enormously. Intuitively she knew that she was somehow caught up in all this, too.

To this end, she had taken some silklike material that a woman had passed to her back during the Eagle Rock celebration and sewed a long, Oriental-style gown for herself as well as a similarly styled tunic for him. Although he felt like some kind of mandarin, the soft feel of the material next to his skin seem to aid in the channeling process.

And so did Diamond's symbolic breast feedings.

"It is time again," she would say to him about once an hour.

He wouldn't speak; rather he would just watch as she undid the front of her gown revealing two of the loveliest breasts he'd ever seen. Gently, she would place one of them up to his mouth, and he would softly suck on the nipple. Then she would withdraw it and repeat the act with the other breast. No words were ever spoken. But the ceremonial suckle never seemed to fail to uncap yet another stream of wisdom from the mysterious well in his soul.

The intense meditation continued, Hunter sitting perfectly still, trying to summon the voice, take its advice and then incorporate it into the grand strategy that still

190

only existed in his mind.

So, he barely heard the knock on the door.

"Fitz is here," Diamond told him.

Despite the time needed for his meditations, Hunter tried to meet with someone from the outside—usually Fitz or the Cobras—at least once every few hours.

He sneezed a third time.

"Let him in," he said.

Mike Fitzgerald slipped into the room, immediately squinting to adjust his eyes to the low, flickering light.

"How's it going?" Hunter asked him as he climbed down off his perch.

Fitz shook his head. "Damn spooky," he replied, rubbing the incense smoke from his eyes. "Nothing is happening, and I don't like it. It's making me nervous."

The Irishman then took a long look around the room.

"Of course, not so nervous as all this," he added.

Hunter shrugged self-consciously. "I don't understand it completely myself, Mike," he told him. "All I know is that something is compelling me to act this way, and this feeling gets stronger by the hour."

"I can't argue with your success so far," Fitzgerald replied. "I just wish this place didn't look so much like a church."

"What's the latest on our situation?" Hunter asked, as they sat down on the floor.

"Nothing much," Fitz replied, gratefully accepting a glass of ice water from Diamond. "As you suggested, we're going as slow as we can without burning up the engines. Everything is functioning well, and we're cutting down on all unnecessary power sources. We've still got plenty of fuel, but it can never hurt to conserve a little."

"I agree," Hunter replied. "Anything new from the Airborne guys?"

"Not really," Fitz said, habitually reaching for a cigar

then thinking better of it. "Jones told me over the scramble phone earlier that they're getting their airdrops regularly. Our old pal Major Frost is taking care of all that from the Canadian side. They should be getting their first bunch of saddles today, in fact. I guess it won't be long after that when they'll be ready for the next order."

"I've been, well, *meditating* on that for the past few hours" was all Hunter had to say on the subject. "How about the high altitude recon flights. Have they picked up anything on the tracks up ahead?"

"Nothing major," Fitz told him. "They did a big heat sweep last night—you know—with the infra-red gizmo that can detect movements on the ground by keying in on heat? Went right across the northern edge of Arizona. Found pockets here and there—but nothing that would indicate a heavy concentration of troops."

"And what do you think about all this?" Hunter asked him.

Fitz could only shrug.

"Devillian hasn't made a peep since we hit him," the Irishman said, taking off his green beret and running his hands through his thinning hair. "We don't see any signs of large enemy movements up ahead. All of our escape route junctions are still clear; we could pick any one of a dozen track lanes to follow, either north, or south. And there are at least five that would turn us around and point us back to Football City. So, who knows? Maybe Devillian is finished. Or maybe he'll crawl back into his hole and stay hidden for a while and we can all breathe a little easier. After all, we got the last shot in, so maybe turning back now wouldn't be such a big deal."

"Once the heart and soul is committed, it is too late to turn back," Hunter said in a voice that alarmed even a hardcore like Fitz.

Hunter closed his eyes and sat very still for five long

192

minutes.

"Devillian will begin to deploy his major formations within thirty-six hours," he said finally. "He is planning his final attack right now."

Fitz was astonished. It was almost as if he were talking to an entirely different person.

"Are you sure, Hawk?" was all he could ask. "Once we get over these mountains and into Arizona itself, there won't be many places they can attack us from concealed positions. That terrain out there is pretty flat — most of it anyway."

"This is why we must prepare to be attacked while we are still in these hills," Hunter replied. "But these will not be the major actions — rather they will be designed to weaken us. Therefore, we must ward off these smaller attacks as economically as possible. We must not deplete our strength swatting at flies."

Fitz took a long look at his friend. Not only had Hunter's voice changed, but it seemed like his features had also been transformed somehow as well. His hair appeared to have grown several inches in just a few days, yet his stubble beard remained the same. But strangest of all, the corners of his eyes seemed to have become slightly slanted.

This overload of scary mysticism was nearly too much for Fitzie's Old Sod sensibilities. Still, Hunter was his closest friend, and he had stuck by him in strange times before.

"Well, our boys are ready for anything," Fitz finally told him. "Just give us the word and we'll do it. We've just got to remember that it will be hard to fight anyone off with us moving so slowly."

"I know," Hunter said, rubbing his weary forehead and hearing his own voice return to normal. "But there is a reason why we are down to just a crawl. We can't let them know our true capability."

Fitz nodded and gave Hunter a fatherly pat on the

back.

"How are you holding up, Hawker?" Fitz asked him sincerely. "I don't pretend to understand any of this, but I can tell it's quite a burden to carry."

Hunter nodded wearily and sneezed again.

"It's just something that has to be done, Mike" was all he said.

Chapter 39

Juanita took a deep breath and knocked once on the Play Pen's massive oak doors.

There was no reply.

She turned to the squad of sentries behind her and nodded.

"Break it down," she said calmly.

It was a big decision. No one had seen or heard from Devillian in nearly twenty-four hours — not since he'd received the news about the devastating attacks on Santa Fe, Port Desemboque and the near-annihilation of the Skull and Crossbones battalion.

Predictably, things had ground to a halt on top of the mesa. Many believed Devillian was dead — shot by his own hand shortly after hearing all the bad news. Others theorized that he was simply wounded inside the vast sin chamber, or perhaps unconscious from too much crack and liquor.

Still, despite these fears, none of the officers at the Burning Cross headquarters had enough gumption to break into the Play Pen and find out. They knew from past incidents that should Devillian still be alive, he would most likely shoot the first, second, and even third person to walk into the room, for little or no reason at all.

Only Juanita had had the guts to agree to go in to the room first, and then only after the soldiers broke the door down for her.

Now two guards walked up and smashed the door with their heavy axes. It took only about a half dozen blows to spring the bulletproof lock. Once this snapped, the soldiers retreated. Juanita on the other hand kicked the door open with her high-heeled black boot and calmly walked inside.

To her utter astonishment, Devillian was sitting on the huge couch, a large box of popcorn in his hand, watching a movie on his giant TV screen and listening to the audio through a pair of headphones. In one corner, the terrorist leader's popcorn popper had overheated and had filled the room with a haze of sickly salty smoke.

Yet, despite the damage and commotion caused by the broken door, the cross-eyed white supremacist hardly winced when he saw Juanita standing before him.

"You look beautiful today," he said, glaring at her after freezing the frame on the TV screen.

"We were concerned," Juanita replied, noting by the frozen TV frame that Devillian had been watching a cowboys-and-Indians movie. "We thought you were . . . despondent."

Devillian laughed as he took off his headphones completely. "You thought I was dead," he told her bluntly. "I'll bet suicide was the theory, wasn't it?"

She didn't answer him.

"I guess I shouldn't be too surprised," he continued. "However, I've spent this time very constructively. Do you remember, my sweet, that at the first meeting of our command officers I mentioned that my grand design was actually in two phases?"

Juanita nodded. "Yes, the first phase was to draw the train into our territory," she said. "To hit it only marginally—*sting it*—as you called it."

"Very good," Devillian replied with a leer. He then pointed to a bulging notebook next to the couch. "In

196

there, my beauty, is the blueprint for the second phase," he bragged. "It is my auteur theory, you might say. I have finally completed the details of my plan for final defeat of the United Americans."

"I admire your enthusiasm," she told him. "We have lost two major points of supply and almost five hundred of our best troops. Anyone else would have considered what has happened to us in the past few days to be very dire."

Devillian began laughing hysterically.

"When will you realize that I'm not like anyone else, my dear?" he asked her, his voice affecting a strange, childlike tone. "In fact, I am authentically happy that those events happened."

"But why?"

"Because, my dearest," he continued. "Now our ultimate goal can be fulfilled. Don't you see? The United Americans are continuing this foolish adventure of theirs, even though many of their troops have left the train. If I was despondent over anything, it was the fact that three days ago, it had appeared like they have given up before I could complete the second bold stroke of my plan."

"But I do not understand why you are so happy that the train continues," Juanita said. "To my mind, we should have hit it—*destroyed* it—as soon as we learned about their surprise attacks on us. Now, I'm sure the word has spread across the country that the train is still moving west, and that can only make the citizens root for these United Americans even more than before."

"That's exactly my point, my lovely," Devillian replied. "The people in this country will be even more enamored with these fools than before. And for us, that's *perfect*. Because this increased adoration will be like a monkey on the backs of the people who stayed with the train. With every mile west they go, they will have that many people rooting for them. And that means when we finally *crush* them, we will have the undivided attention of everyone. *Everyone!* That is the essence of the second phase of my plan."

Juanita was authentically confused now, but this did nothing to stop Devillian from continuing his speech.

"What I am saying," he continued, "is that we will have our audience! Millions will see our grand finale. It will be an event on the order of the greatest production ever undertaken."

Suddenly, Devillian's momentary gleeful appearance gave way to a worse-than-usual scowl.

"These United Americans probably think they're playing tough," he said, gritting his teeth. "Well, we'll see just how tough they are when I start to cut them with a thousand knives. I will *bleed* them — slowly. Then, when they get to precisely the right point, I will crush them once and for all!"

"But what if they are simply heading for the next track turnaround?" Juanita asked him. "There are many they could try for. Perhaps this is all just a way for them to salvage the valuable weapons on the train and escape."

Devillian looked at her and for the thousandth time fantasized what it would be like to ravage her.

"My dearest, our first phase was so successful in drawing the train into our territory that I promise you it will have no choice but to keep moving west," he said. "In fact, I guarantee it will go right where we want it to."

Juanita cocked her head to one side as if to say that Devillian's boast was impossible to fulfill.

"You doubt me?" he asked her. "Then just watch." He reached down and pushed his intercom button. "Get me the commander of the Skinhead squadron," he barked into the microphone.

Three seconds went by, and then a gruff voice came

on the line.

"Mallox here. . . . What do you want?"

Devillian's harsh voice turned to an authentic growl. "I want you to launch every one of your aircraft immediately and bomb every railroad junction that the train could use in order to turn back," he commanded. "The only track route I want still intact by the end of the day is the Amtrak southern tier track — the one that the train is riding on now. Do you understand?"

They could hear Mallox start to swear. "Why don't we just go and blast the shit out of that fucking train like we should have done days ago?" he asked.

"No!" Devillian screamed back at him. "That train will be destroyed only when I give the order to do so! Now, do you understand the mission I just gave you?"

"Sure, I do." came the Skinhead commander's less than enthusiastic reply. "But you realize this is going to take a big bite out of our fuel reserves."

"Fuck the fuel!" Devillian screamed. "Just do what I tell you!"

With that, he pushed the intercom's OFF button, effectively hanging up on the man. Then he pushed it on again and reached one of his bodyguards.

"I want every one of those hoodlums from Rome up here, right now," he screamed at the man. "And tell them I want an entire inventory list of their stuff — lights, cameras, everything."

Devillian released the intercom button, took another toke of crack and turned back to the beautiful Juanita.

"The show, my dear, is just about to begin."

Part Two
Ten Miles to Hell

Chapter 40

Studs Mallox nearly burned himself trying to light his crack pipe while at the same time keeping his F-4 Phantom level.

The leader of the Burning Cross's Skinhead squadron was bored — *very* bored — and even the insane pleasure of smoking dope in the cockpit while flying a high-performance jet fighter was beginning to get dull.

"Damn, I hate this hanging-around crap," he said to himself. "I want to shoot something. *Kill* something. . . ."

However, the only thing Mallox was able to shoot was the camera sticking underneath the nose of his F-4; his only ammunition was its special brand of high-speed recon film. His mission was to keep constant track of the *Freedom Express* as it snaked its way through the Sangre de Cristo mountains. It was a long, laborious piece-of-shit job that Devillian had typically thrown on the Skinheads once all the nearby railroad junctions had been destroyed.

"Why the hell does he give *us* these babysitting duties?" Mallox asked himself after taking one last quick drag on his crack pipe and readjusting his oxygen mask. "He's got all those pansie air pirates just sitting around jerking off. God knows what would happen if they ever had to actually *shoot* at somebody."

In the same instant, he knew why Devillian had ordered the 'Heads to keep an eye on the train. For the most part, the air pirates' planes were older than the Skinhead F-4's. They weren't as efficient and therefore used more fuel. And right now, fuel was getting in short supply on top of the fortress.

Still, Mallox and his men lived under a solemn pact to kill something—*anything*—once a day. It had been several days since anything like that had happened—the attack on Eagle Rock had been their last offensive action—and his troops were getting restless.

Mallox just hated dealing with it all. The pay was good, but even that was starting to lose its appeal on his men. Gone were the glory days of the Twisted Cross. During that time, his superiors *insisted* that the Skinhead squadron draw blood every day, just to keep up the veneer of terror in the skies of Central America. Now he and his guys were nothing more than a bunch of photographers, taking snapshots of the mile-long train as it moved through the hills at less than ten miles per hour.

His radio crackled once, and then he heard the repulsively sissy voice of one of Devillian's communication officers come on the line.

"Recon Two-Four, this is base—time for the quarter-hour report."

"Big fucking deal," was how Mallox answered. "The fucking train is about two and a half miles from where it was the last time I talked to you, asshole."

"Any weapons displayed?" the comm officer asked, going down the usual list of questions that constituted the fifteen-minute reports Devillian had insisted on.

"No, you fucking jerk," Mallox replied. "They ain't so much as showed a pop-gun."

"No warning tones, no SAM radar emissions detected?"

"I just told you no, shithead," Mallox grumbled.

"Have they launched their choppers or the jump-jet?"

"Jesus Christ—*no!*"

"Have they significantly altered their speed in any way?"

"Fuck you, I'm hanging up!" Mallox shouted, switching off his radio and ending the transmission.

He put his F-4 into another, long and lazy sweep and brought it high over the train once again. It was still another two hours before his relief was due on station.

"Man, am I getting sick of this," he said, lighting his pipe again.

Five thousand feet below, Hawk Hunter shivered as he felt another message spring up from his psyche. *Divide them. Destroy their alliances.*

Chapter 41

Antonio Anthony Antonioni was sweating bullets.

He had never been so hot—not in Rome, not in Naples, not even in Tripoli. And all that crap about the heat in the American desert being bearable because it was "not the heat, but the humidity" was total bullshit. Hot was hot, and Antonio Anthony Antonioni—Tony Three to his friends—was, at the moment, *very fucking hot*.

He sat down under the sliver of shade provided by an outcrop of rock and cursed himself for ever leaving Rome.

Back there, he and his men were practically kings, their every whim and fancy granted by the puppet government that served as the seat of the New Holy Roman Empire. Just like the old one, this rekindling of glories past was hardly holy, or Roman, and only an idiot would consider it an empire. Rather, the fiefdom barely stretched south from Rome to the end of the Italian peninsula. And in truth, it was run by Sicilians. And not one of them had been to church in years.

Still, Tony Three and his men had had a good thing going back there. Broads, booze and "booga sugar" had all been in ample supply. All they had to do was control production and distribution of the hundreds of X-rated videos that were being made in the south of Italy every month. The post-war dirty movies were the New Holy Roman Empire's chief export in trade—and it was a very profitable business. Buying jerk-off films didn't go out of style just because the planet was turned on its ear by World War III. If anything, they had increased in popularity.

But somewhere along the way, Tony Three had gotten bored. He had felt the need to strike out—not so much to make more money, but to see another part of the world. So when he heard that some guy named Devillian was looking for people of his skill and acumen, Tony Three and his boys simply hijacked a jumbo jet, filled it with the very latest in stolen movie-making equipment from Italy and Cannes, France and headed for New Mexico. Once there, they cut a lucrative deal with Devillian's underlings—a ten-picture agreement, which would have included at least three bombastic X-rated extravaganzas directed by Devillian himself. Their pockets filled with Burning Cross gold, they put the jumbo in storage, bought ten Chinook helicopters and moved the stuff to Devillian's mesa fortress.

Things started to go wrong shortly after their arrival.

First of all, Devillian turned out to be a total fruitcake. In the Roman parlance, he was a *gootz*, meaning an idiot, or in this case, a man with power and money but absolutely no fucking brains or class. Rather than reveling in the pleasures of making young tit films, Devillian insisted on bizarre elaborations that De Mille or even Fellini himself would have scoffed at. It didn't take long for Tony Three and his boys to realize that despite his bluster, Devillian didn't know dick-shit about making a good porno.

Then this whole thing with the train popped up—and it was something that Tony Three and his boys hadn't expected. Nor could they understand it all. If you wanted to go from the east coast of America to the west coast, why take a train? Wasn't it easier just to hijack an airplane?

Things got worse when Devillian insisted that the

207

Romans' Chinooks be made available to carry his troops here and there. Then their jumbo jet got blown up in the air strike that obliterated Santa Fe Airport.

Since then, they had found themselves to be little more than prisoners of the cross-eyed madman. And that's why Tony Three was now sweating buckets in the middle of the Grand Canyon.

"Finally got one of the generators working, boss." One of his boys, a guy named Rico, climbed up the rock formation to tell him.

"Thank God," Tony Three replied. "Will it pump out enough juice to run the tools?"

Rico just shrugged. "I hope so," he said. "Or at least enough for us to get one of the other generators working. If we bust ass, we can probably have juice to the whole set-up in two days."

Tony Three wiped his forehead with his already-soaking rag.

"Well, if we do it that quick, Devillian will be happier than a pig in shit," he said.

"I know," Rico answered. "The question is, how long will the diesel fuel hold out? Once we flick on those big lights, them generators are going to start drinking the stuff nonstop."

Tony Three thought for a second, then turned and studied the broiling landscape before him.

They were approximately three miles south of the southernmost rim of the Grand Canyon. Directly below him were two sets of railroad tracks that ran straight for a full ten miles, the only section of track that did so for such a distance anywhere within one hundred miles of them. At the beginning of the stretch, about three miles to the east, was a bridge that crossed the Desert Point View River. The tracks ran through a small forest right after this bridge and then broke out into the straightaway that was bordered on both sides with various hills, cliffs and outcrops of rocks. Off to the west at the end of the uncurving railbed, there was a sharp hill that was steep enough to roll a train all the way into Las Vegas itself.

"Rico, take a look at them ledges," Tony Three said, thinking he'd found the solution to his fuel problem. "How about we put some big reflectors up there? That way, we can cut down on using some of the lights, and maybe the generators won't go dry on us."

"It's worth a try," Rico said, shading his eyes to view the cliffs. "If we can get a good f-stop reading, and protect against camera flash, it should work. That is, if we got enough sun when the train finally gets here. If not, we'll have to stop down a couple notches and throw on the auxiliary lights."

Tony Three spat in disgust. "That asshole Devillian will just have to live with it," he said. "Fucking jerk that he is. We come to make porn flicks, and he has us in the middle of Gone with the fucking Wind."

Chapter 42

The Mexican bandit nicknamed Sin Dientes — literally "No Teeth" — couldn't believe his good fortune.

In the sack on his back there was more gold than he had seen in his life — fifty pounds, in coins and in chips. Best of all, most of it belonged to him.

All he had to do was attack a train.

The money — as well as his orders — had come straight from Devillian himself. The cross-eyed terrorist had hired Sin Dientes and the hundred-man bandit gang that bore his name to set up an ambush in the vicinity of Arroyo Honda, the pass that ran through the Sangre de Cristo Mountains near the Rio Grande Gorge, approximately thirty miles west of Eagle Rock. Train tracks passed hard by the gorge itself, and a dense forest bordered the other side of the railway bed.

Their orders said that the *Freedom Express* would soon be passing through and Sin Dientes should attack it.

"But do not disable it or blow up the tracks," Devillian had told him. "Or I will personally make you bleed to death. Kill as many men on board as you can, but let the survivors continue on their way."

Sin Dientes did not question the strange orders, nor the fact that Devillian had provided him with several video cameras on which to record the bloody action. The leader of the Burning Cross had signed up the bandit gang just a week before, and already Sin Dientes knew the penalty for challenging the man's slightest whim. If Devillian wanted the bandit gang to simply sting the train, then Sin Dientes and his men would do just that.

It had been two days since the bumpy helicopter ride from Sin Dientes' hideout near Palomas, Mexico to the place called Arroyo Honda.

Devillian had provided ten big Chinook helicopters for the airlift, as well as new rifles and plenty of ammunition for his men. However, the pilots of the choppers—Roman Empire gangsters who seemed bewildered that they would be making such a flight—got lost several times on the way. What was worse, the holds on their helicopters were already filled with big black boxes and huge lights and other strange things, so much so that No Teeth and his men could barely squeeze aboard. Finally, Devillian had to dispatch two F-4's to guide the dangerously overloaded Chinooks to the correct coordinate. After all that, unloading the Sin Dientes gang and their meager equipment proved easy.

No Teeth carried the gold himself. There was not one of his men that he could completely trust, and just watching over the treasure would be as hard as attacking the train itself. Still, each man knew he was in for at least a quarter of a pound of the stuff, and that was more than most of them had been able to rob and/or steal in the past three years. They also knew that if they failed, Devillian would send the Skinheads to hunt them down—and there was no fate worse than that. In fact, they had spotted at least three Skinhead F-4's flying over their position just in the past few hours alone, and even a cutthroat like No Teeth got nervous with people like the Skinheads circling above him, like so many vultures waiting to rip into the carcass of some still-squirming prey.

No Teeth had taken a full day to examine the terrain around Arroyo Honda, starting soon after the Chinooks had departed for the Grand Canyon. He

211

found the place exactly as Devillian had described it — a long sloping hill next to the Rio Grande Gorge that the train would have to slow down and climb before proceeding over a bridge that spanned the Rio itself.

The bandit leader finally decided to position his men in clumps of twos and threes along the edge of the thick forest that skirted the railway bed. Most of the men were equipped with either a brand new AK-47 assault rifle or an M-16 with an M203 grenade launcher attached. A half dozen were manning flame-throwers, and three would be shooting the videotape. There would be no use of heavier weapons, and the men launching the grenades were ordered not to shoot at the wheels of the railway cars, although most of these were thought to be protected with armor-plating anyway.

Once his men were dug in and the ambush was set, No Teeth sat and counted his gold again. Around midnight, he'd heard from Devillian's communications officers that the train was expected to pass through Arroyo Honda sometime before dusk the next evening.

That gave No Teeth enough time to count his gold at least ten more times.

Chapter 43

La Casa de las Estrellas

"When is it my turn, boss?"

Studs Mallox spun around and confronted the whining man.

"You ain't going to get a turn, you pansie," he told the transgressor, a less-than-dedicated Skinhead named Ant. "We decided to cut you out."

Mallox turned back to the matter at hand. He was sitting in his barracks headquarters, it being a heavily camouflaged building on the far end of the fortress mesa. Sixteen of his men were there; two others had pulled night duty flying over the train.

The entertainment for the evening was a gang bang of two of Devillian's pretty young love slaves. The girls were already there—tied up and ready to be violated. They'd been properly pumped full of speed and crack and were now unwittingly titillating the Skinheads with their authentic whimpering. Mallox had just drawn lots for the order of penetration when one of his group—the man named Ant—realized he was being left out.

"But what the hell did I do to deserve this?" Ant foolishly demanded of Mallox.

The evil squadron commander smiled and took a toke of crack. "You just fucked up one too many times, Ant," he said. "We don't want a candy-ass like you in here anymore."

"That's right!" one of the other 'Heads screamed.

"Fairy!" yelled another.

"Pansie!"

"You prissy fuck!"

Ant started sweating at this point—and with good reason. After belonging to the Skinhead squadron for nearly a year, he knew that deep down the 'Heads were really just a bunch of cowards—*dangerous* cowards. They were only brave when they were together and the odds were overwhelmingly in their favor. It was a total group-think situation with them. When frustration set in—like of late after having spent the last two days doing little more than flying over that stupid fucking train and bombing railroad tracks—their release valve was to gang up on one member, usually with fatal results.

And they had just picked Ant on which to work out their infantile unfulfillments.

"Why me, Studs?" he asked in a jittery voice. "I've been doing OK."

Mallox laughed. "You're right, Ant, you *have* been doing OK," he replied. "But I guess the guys and me just don't like you anymore."

"What are you going to do to me, Studs?" Ant foolishly asked.

"Stomp him!" someone yelled.

"Yeah! Stomp the shit out of him!"

Suddenly the room was filled with the bloodcurdling cries of *"Stomp! Stomp! Stomp!"*

Mallox smiled again as the terrified Ant backed into a corner of the barracks.

"The jury has spoken, Ant," he said, standing over the cowering man. "See you in hell."

With that, Mallox delivered a mighty blow to Ant's forehead, cracking the man's skull with his heavy hobnail boot. Ant reeled backward, hit the wall and fell facedown on the barracks floor.

In an instant, the rest of the Skinheads rushed toward his twitching body and began viciously kicking him with their boots, all the while screaming: *"Stomp him! Stomp him!"*

It took the screaming Ant three long minutes to die.

Mallox considered it a stroke of genius to have the two love slaves clean up the blood and waste and cranial matter that had once been Ant.

Killing their colleague was just the tonic the 'Heads needed to keep their edge. Fucking the girls after they'd been covered in blood would serve to raise their killing lust even higher.

But even Mallox had his limits; he didn't want to ravage the women with a stiff in the room. So, after dutifully taking photos of the body to give to Devillian later, Mallox had the corpse wrapped in a plastic sheet and tied with twine.

Then he selected a 'Head named White Smoke to help him carry the body outside and to the edge of the mesa, where they would unceremoniously dump it over.

"Don't do a thing until I get back," he told his drooling legion while he roughly fondled one of the terrified girls before heading out the door with White Smoke. "Remember, I'm always the first one in and the last one out."

It was a fairly cool, moonlit night.

Mallox had White Smoke do all of the heavy lifting of course, leaving the man to drag Ant's body alone while he strolled ahead to the dumping spot, admiring the broad expanse of stars above him.

Studs was proud of the Skinheads' little corner of the fortress, it being well away from the other Burning Cross units. At his insistence, Devillian had even built a separate runway and parking strip for the 'Heads' Phantom jets. Knowing the Skinheads' reputation as human vomit was well-deserved, the rest of the Burning Cross members were more than happy with the mesa-top's segregated living arrangements.

Mallox reached the edge of the mesa and waited impatiently as White Smoke dragged the damp corpse across the landing strip and passed the row of F-4's.

215

Finally he reached the place where the 'Heads dumped all of their snuffs.

"Must be getting pretty crowded down there," White Smoke said, peering over the mesa to the ravine below. "Kind of smelly, too."

"Are you kidding?" Mallox told him. "Those bodies don't stay down there very long. Either some big cat eats 'em up or the bugs get them. You're history in a matter of days."

"What a way to go," White Smoke replied.

Mallox resisted the temptation to push the man over the side, just for the hell of it. He would have done it—he was in that kind of a mood—but at the same time he knew it was foolish to lose a perfectly adequate pilot.

"C'mon, let's get this over with," Mallox told the man. "We got some young pussy waiting for us back there."

White Smoke was about to lift the body up and over some edge rocks when suddenly both men heard a strange noise—kind of a *whoosh-thump!*

It was dark, and at first they could not see what had caused the odd sound.

"What the fuck was that?" Mallox asked, instinctively reaching for his sidearm.

Suddenly White Smoke grabbed hold of his arm. "Jessuz, Studs—look!"

Mallox looked down at the corpse and was astonished to see an arrow was now embedded in its throat.

"Where the fuck did that come from?" White Smoke asked.

An instant later, they heard the noise again.

Whoosh-thump!

This time, they looked down to see another arrow had pierced the body bag in the stomach region.

"Shit, Studs, those stories are true!"

Even a big, bad brave guy like Studs was nervous now. The Burning Cross fortress had been rife with

216

rumors that some kind of a ghost was running around on top of the mesa, fucking with the equipment, starting little fires and scaring the shit out of the midnight-to-dawn guards. About a half dozen regular Burning Cross soldiers had sworn they'd seen the spirit in the past few days, but the Skinheads had always just attributed the sightings to the fact that the rest of the soldiers on top of the mesa were just pansie-asses.

Until now, that was.

"Shut up," Mallox told White Smoke, trying to calm his own nerves by talking brave. "There's nothing up here."

Whoosh-thump!

Mallox spun around to see the shaft of a third arrow suddenly embedded in White Smoke's throat.

Neither of them could believe it. There was no blood—yet. But White Smoke's face had drained completely of color in a half-second.

"Is it bad?" he gurgled to Mallox before tumbling backward.

Studs began to panic. Instantly he kicked White Smoke's still-twitching form over the side of the mesa, pushing over Ant's stiffening corpse for good measure. Then he hit the ground and covered his head with his hands, petrified that he would be on the receiving end of the next deadly arrow.

What seemed to Studs like an hour passed—it was really only a few seconds—before he became aware of a figure standing over him. Too terrified to even open his eyes and look up, he began crying, certain that a painful death awaited him. In a second, his mind flashed over the scores of people he had killed. Bloody and decaying faces, they were all laughing at him.

He felt the cold edge of an extremely sharp knife slowly slide under his throat. Every time he would whimper, the knife would slice a little deeper into his Adam's apple. Finally he heard someone say to him: "Get up."

Studs slowly rolled over, his eyes still closed and crying. One mighty hand lifted him up to his feet, the knife at his throat never moving an iota.

Finally, he had no choice. He opened his eyes and found himself staring into those of an Indian.

Chapter 44

Hawk Hunter only stopped writing long enough to splash a handful of cold water onto his face.

He could not even smell the incense now; in fact, the cabin didn't even look that smoky anymore. However, Diamond still looked beautiful—even more so.

Her beauty was the only bright spot in his increasingly darkened consciousness. His prediction that Devillian was very much alive and preparing for battle had proved all too true. He had just gotten a report from Jones that Burning Cross fighter-bombers had destroyed all the track junctions to the north and south of them, meaning that if the train was to keep moving, it could only move on tracks Devillian deigned to keep open for it.

Plus, the madman's recon planes were now keeping the train under hourly surveillance.

But like buzzards, Hunter knew they would not attack the train—and for the moment, he would not attack them.

He had picked up pen and paper about three hours before and, for the first hour, drew nothing but squares and triangles. By letting his hand move where it wanted, his sheets of paper would quickly become filled with intricate patterns using only those two shapes: squares inside of the squares, triangles within triangles. Soon, he began drawing the triangles inside of squares and vice versa. Then hundreds of tiny triangles inside of one huge square.

He knew what an unbeliever would call it: automatic writing. The supposed written link with the spirit world. But Hunter knew better. The seemingly endless drawing actually had a meaning, one connected to the flow of information from his psyche. His continual mining of this strange wellspring had simply taken on another manifestation.

At the beginning of the third hour, he began writing down the phrases that were now coming to him with renewed regularity.

When you traverse mountains, forests, steep defiles or any route difficult to travel, this is called bad ground.

When the way is narrow and a small enemy force can strike at you even though your numbers are greater, this is called surrounded ground.

When you will survive if you fight quickly and perish if you do not, this is called dying ground.

By the fourth hour, his hand was stiff and getting numb from writing. But he knew the words of wisdom were just a trigger. They were telling him of things to come. He was certain they would be attacked soon.

"Diamond?" he called out into the smoky room. "Please ask Fitz to come here."

Chapter 45

Over the Sangre de Cristo Mountains

The Skinhead pilot known as Duzz checked the time, then called back to the mesa.

"This is Black Flight Two with the quarterly time report," he told the Burning Cross communications officer on the other end of the radio. "The train is still moving very slowly. I estimate no more than ten to twelve miles per hour. It is presently climbing an incline, approximately twenty miles west of Arroyo Honda, and approaching the Rio Grande Gorge, which is marked at Red Area Two on my map. You got all that?"

"Affirmative" came the reply. "Any weapons display?"

"No" was the reply from Duzz.

"Any warning tones or radar emissions?"

"No."

"Any aircraft launched from the train?"

"No."

"Roger Black Flight Two, stay on station. . . . Out."

Duzz clicked off his radio and put the F-4 into yet another of the endless sweeping orbits needed to keep the train in sight.

"This is a drag," he whispered. "A real *fucking* drag."

Duzz was more on edge than usual. This was the day after a strange night on the mesa. First of all, the anticipated gang bang never happened because Studs never returned from getting rid of Ant's stompified body. White Smoke never reappeared either—but that made little difference to 'Heads waiting to pounce on their intended female victims. Studs' last word to them

221

was not to commence until he got back. When he didn't, most of the 'Heads simply passed out or eventually went to sleep.

They awoke to find Studs had still not turned up, but this wasn't all that unusual. Their leader had been summoned to Devillian's mansion at odd hours before, and Studs was not the type to send a note back to his worried brood.

Still, it *was* peculiar that the man still hadn't appeared by the time Duzz lifted off just after two in the afternoon. When he flew out over the mesa, he saw the search parties were just starting to organize on the ground below.

Duzz once again looped back over the train, snapping another roll of pictures as he went.

It had reached the top of the hill and was now slowly going into a long curve which would eventually bring it out onto a straightaway that ran close to the Rio Grande Gorge. Duzz checked his map again, wondering why this particular section was marked as Red Area Two.

He got his answer a minute later.

His radio crackled to life with a message from the communications officer that Devillian himself wanted to speak to Duzz.

"I hired a bunch of wetbacks to suckerpunch the train," the terrorist leader said, his distinctive high-pitched twang coming through loud and clear over the F-4's radio. "They're going to hit it just before it crosses over the Rio Grande Gorge. I want you to make sure those greaseballs don't destroy any of the railcars or fuck up the track in front of them. Their orders are to only kill people on the train—not snuff it out completely. They are only supposed to be using small arms fire and nothing else. Do you understand?"

"Sure I do," Duzz replied.

"Now, if those refried beanheads *do* fuck up and wreck that train, then I want you to first call me directly. Then I want you to strafe those assholes until I

222

can send out your whole goddamn squadron to plaster the bastards. Get it?"

"I get it," Duzz replied.

"All right," Devillian said. "Now keep your eyes open. Those Mexicans should be opening up on the train any minute now."

The bandit No Teeth had just finished relieving himself when he heard the first sounds of the approaching train.

"At last," he whispered, pulling up his pants. He was getting sick of waiting in the woods, battling off legions of bugs and jumping from fright every time a small animal scampered past. "We do the job, we get even more gold."

The sounds of the train—a kind of dull roar—were mixed with the high-pitched scream of the Burning Cross jet fighter that had been circling the area since early afternoon. No Teeth knew that the plane's pilot probably had two functions: to keep an eye on the train and to keep an eye on No Teeth and his gang. All the more reason that the bandit leader wanted the job to go exactly how Devillian had ordered.

He made his way back to his gang's positions, enthusiastic that he couldn't hear them.

They must be learning, he thought, silently praising his men for having the smarts to keep quiet as their target approached. Usually he couldn't stop his men from jabbering for more than ten seconds.

The train was only about a half mile away by now, and No Teeth was having trouble moving fast through the dense forest. It would be embarrassing if he missed the opening shots of the attack just because he had gone too deep into the woods to take a dump.

Suddenly he saw that the train had picked up speed and was now closing in on the ambush site at about twenty-five miles per hour. No problem, he thought, finally coming upon the first of his gang's firing positions. They could still fuck up the train sufficiently, no matter what its speed may be.

He jumped into the firing hole and whispered to his two men to get ready. When he didn't even hear a grunt in reply, he turned toward the man beside him and saw that his throat had been slit from ear-to-ear.

No Teeth almost screamed, not so much at the horror of it, but at the surprise. He pushed the man, knocking him over to reveal his firing partner also had most of his throat hanging onto his chest.

The Mexican bandit leader jumped straight up out of the hole and belly-crawled to the next firing position. But here too he found his men were dead; one had even had his heart cut right out from his body and stuffed into his mouth. The other was inexplicably covered with ants.

Verging on complete panic, No Teeth scampered from hole to hole and found nothing but death in each one. All the while the train was approaching, and now, as it passed by, unharmed, he saw a single face staring back out at him from a car window. The man had longish hair and a short beard. He was wearing a blue tunic, and his eyes were slanted in a very strange way.

The train roared past — one full mile long. The extraordinary collection of military might on the railway cars seemed to mock him as they clicked and clacked on by. In less than a minute, No Teeth found himself staring at the enormous howitzer on the tail end of the train as it passed over the Rio Grande Gorge Bridge and disappeared around a bend in the mountain.

"This is like a bad dream," he murmured.

He dropped his bag of gold and hurriedly checked each one of the gang's firing positions, hoping, *praying,* to find someone still alive. But he could not; every one of his ninety-nine men were dead, most of them butchered beyond recognition.

What had happened? How could his entire force be killed so quickly, so silently in the few minutes that he had taken to answer Nature's call?

224

Oddly he soon found a graphic answer to these questions.

Coming upon the last firing position, he stumbled across one of the men who had been tapped to video-tape the planned ambush. The viewfinder in the camera was still flickering, and with trembling hands No Teeth first pushed the Rewind button, then the Play button. Then he watched in horror through the viewfinder's preview screen as the last seconds of his unit's life played before his eyes.

The videotape man had obviously clicked the camera on at the first sound of the train. Then, swinging it to his left, he was able to focus in on the firing positions nearest to his own. Suddenly, out of the corner of the frame, a dark-skinned man appeared. With one swift motion, he reached into the firing hole closest to him and slashed the throats of both bandits. The camera started to jiggle at this point, the video man obviously stunned at what he had just captured on tape. With alarming speed, more dark-skinned men appeared. In one swift motion, they jumped into the firing holes, slaughtered the bandits and crawled back out again. The man holding the videotape then caught the image of one man coming straight for him. It was probably from sheer fright that the man kept the camera rolling even as his killer silently approached, a huge Bowie knife in hand. One, then two mighty thrusts later, the camera fell sideways. Its lens was partially splattered with blood, but not enough so as to miss the man with the knife as he slipped away out of the hole and out of the frame.

No Teeth let the camera drop from his hands, absolutely horrified at what he'd seen. The killers were Indians, he was sure of it. In fact, he recognized the colors on the silent men with the knives. They were Piutes, the most dangerous tribe in these parts, and he imagined that the woods nearby must be swarming with them.

And suddenly, No Teeth realized that he was alone.

"Base . . . this is Black Flight Two . . . come in."

Duzz put his F-4 into a sharp turn and came over the train again, knowing that something was definitely wrong.

"Go ahead, Black Flight" came the response.

"The ambush on the train did not happen," Duzz reported. "Repeat . . . train was not attacked at Rio Grande Gorge."

There was a burst of static, and then the voice of Devillian himself filled Duzz's headphones.

"What the fuck are you telling me?" the terrorist screamed at him through a storm of static.

"I'm telling you that the train just ran through Red Area Two without a shot being fired at it," Duzz replied. "It picked up speed, crossed the bridge and is now heading down into Tres Piedras Pass. It should be in the San Juan Mountains inside a half hour."

There was nothing but silence on the other end of his headphones, but Duzz could almost *feel* Devillian's rage burning through the radio waves.

"OK, baldy," the man said after a while. "Here's what I want you to do. . . ."

Twenty minutes later, Duzz was nearly whistling. He had armed his cannon as well as the two guided munitions bombs that hung beneath his wings.

With considerable ease, he swooped down on the bridge crossing the Rio Grande Gorge and sent first one, then the second missile into its support girders. Two mighty explosions later, the span was falling into the rapid waters of the Rio Grande, thus insuring that the train was again cut off from any means of reverse-gear retreat.

This done, Duzz turned back and screeched down along the track straightaway where the train was supposed to have been attacked. On his first pass, he saw what he believed to be about fifty occupied gun positions. Oddly, the men inside them didn't move a whit as

226

he roared past, but this made no difference to him now. He didn't care why the bandits had chosen not to shoot at the train. The order from the top man himself was to "fuck up the bean-eaters" for failing in their mission.

Duzz turned and came in on the positions again, this time opening up with his powerful nose cannon. He felt exhilarated as he watched his cannon shells rip into the bandits' gun holes, their flimsy camouflage being shredded by his awesome barrage.

It was the beginning of his third stafing run when he saw a single man leap onto the tracks. He was carrying what looked to be a heavy bag on his shoulder. But as Duzz bore down on him, the man dropped the bag and started waving wildly, almost as if he was pleading for the airplane to stop shooting.

"Not a chance," Duzz whispered as he pulled the trigger and cut the man to pieces.

Chapter 46

When Studs Mallox woke up, he was naked and shivering.

He also had no idea where he was or how he got there. The bump on his forehead was sore and bleeding slightly, and he felt as if he'd been injected with some kind of drug. The frightening sight of the Indian was still blazed upon his mind, as were foggy visions of being carried down the sheer side of the mesa, trundled over the desert and finally thrown aboard a helicopter.

Now he was in a bare, windowless room, surrounded by three men wearing masks.

"Surprised, Mr. Mallox?" one of the men asked him gruffly, as the trio moved closer to the bunk. "Surprised that you are still alive?"

"Who . . . are you?" Mallox stuttered, trying his best to cover up his genitalia with his hands. "Where am I?"

"You're on your deathbed," one of the other men said. "What part do you want to go first?"

Mallox almost fainted. He saw that all three men were holding machetes.

"What do you want?" he asked, gagging on the words. "Money? I can give you lots of money."

The three men laughed.

"It's not a question of gold," the third man, the smallest of the three, said with a vague accent. "It's a question of your actions in the past. The people you've killed. The women you've brutalized. The lives you've ruined. You see, you can consider us your Grim Reapers. You've just committed too many sins."

"But I was just following orders," Mallox pleaded. "I

have commanders. They *told* me to do the things I've done."

"Where have I heard all this before?" one of the men asked.

Then, in a lightning swift movement, he hacked down on the bunk with his machete, ripping the dirty mattress just two inches from Mallox's foot.

"It's the truth!" Mallox screamed. "I've never been a commander myself. I was always under orders. . . . You want names? I'll give you names of all my officers. Some of them are still around. You can go get them. I'll even *help* you find them."

The three men laughed again. "So much for the famous Iron Will," the man with the accent said. "This guy is caving in like a scared pup." He walked forward and placed the machete directly over Mallox's privates. "You actually have two choices," he said, lowering the huge blade closer to the Skinhead's groin. "We kill you now. Slow, painful, just like you've killed so many, but something that will be over in a few hours. Or, we kill you a piece at a time. And you pick the piece."

At that moment, the hooded man poked the tip of the machete into Mallox's pubic region, opening up a small but bloody gash.

"Make your decision, you Nazi scum," the man said harshly. "Our way? Or your way?"

Mallox was terrified beyond tears. He tried to whimper out some plea for forgiveness, but found his voice would not come out. He looked down at his hands, now bloody from his wound, and nearly vomited.

The men only laughed at his panicky state. One of them produced a Polaroid camera and started taking snapshots.

Finally, another hooded man entered the room, carrying a small satchel.

"Here it is," he told the trio, handing them the bag and then departing.

One of the men looked inside the bag and laughed again.

"Just your style, Curley," he said, throwing the bag at Studs. The Skinhead looked inside and saw the bag contained a garishly pink dress.

"That's for you, Studs," the man who threw him the dress said. "Now put it on."

Studs was so terrified, he did as told.

By the time he had climbed into the mumu-type dress, the three men were practically rolling on the floor with laughter.

Thoroughly humiliated, Studs was then made to pose in several positions as the hooded men took about a dozen snapshots and then convulsed with laughter after looking at each one just thirty seconds later. In fact, the men kept on laughing even after they'd run out of instant film.

"This could be a whole new career for you, cutie," one of them taunted. "Wait 'til the boys back in your squadron see these."

Just then, the whole room started shaking, causing Studs to jump with fright. A rumbling noise filled his ears, nearly deafening at first, then quickly dropping to a rhythmic pulse. Then a new sound, a regular click-clacking, found its way into the room.

It took Mallox several more seconds to figure out that he was on a moving train.

Chapter 47

Near Dodge City, Kansas

Catfish Johnson thought he was finally getting the hang of it.

Throughout his military career, he had been called on to do strange and varied tasks. In the pre-war years, he had been a Marine DI. During the war he had fought in Turkey with the late, great hero, Captain Bull Dozer. After the war and the imposition of the New Order, he had helped Dozer run the famous 7th Cavalry. Then, after Dozer's death, he had turned the 900-man 7th into the 10,000-man United American 1st Airborne Division.

But not once in all that time had he been called upon to ride a horse.

Still, here he was, sitting tall in the saddle, atop a huge Appaloosa, gun in hand, cowboy hat in place.

"This isn't as bad as I thought," he said to Captain Drews, who, being a cowpoke from way back, had just finished several minutes of spontaneous trick riding.

"You just got to move as he moves, that's all," Drews said.

Catfish adjusted his backside in the saddle again and for the first time was able to look up and fully appreciate the scene before him.

It was about an hour before dawn, and the air was absolutely still. He was on the edge of a bluff overlooking the airport located just outside Dodge City. Sitting side-by-side on the end of the airport's largest, recently elongated runway were four gigantic C-5 Galaxy cargo jets, each one bearing the emblem of the Free Canadian

Air Force.

The Galaxy was the largest airplane ever built in the Free World. Its hold was so cavernous, it could carry more than a quarter of a million pounds of cargo. Yet, Catfish was sure that no C-5 had ever been called on to carry as strange a cargo as what was being loaded into these four particular airplanes at that moment.

"Lord, I wish Captain Dozer were alive to see this," Catfish said, as he watched the four separate lines of horses and riders move slowly up the ramps and into the huge airplanes. "Old Bull finally got himself a *real* cavalry."

Chapter 48

Santa Fe

Juanita Juarez was frightened for the first time in her life.

It had been a strange twenty-four hours.

The trouble had started early that morning when Studs Mallox — the human slug himself — was first reported missing. She was there when Devillian got the word, and at the time, he calmly ordered the fortress to be searched. When this proved fruitless, several squads of Burning Cross guards repelled down to the desert floor where they found the half-eaten bodies of two Skinheads — Ant and White Smoke — but no sign of Studs.

This news served only to inflame the already rampant rumor that someone — or *something* — was running around the mesa top, scaring some people, killing others and making at least two disappear completely. But Juanita didn't believe in ghosts; so she just ignored these tattles, at the same time being happily amazed at how skittish the men around her were acting.

Then came the odd report from the Sangre de Cristo Mountains. Devillian himself had bragged to her how he'd hired the toughest bunch of Mexican bandits in all of the southwest to "put the hurt on the train." These bandits — the well-known Sin Dientes — had a reputation even worse than that of her brother Jorge's various gangs. They had been paid a fortune in gold to be the first bandit group to sting the train as it passed through the narrow trackbed next to Rio Grande Gorge.

233

Yet, for some reason, the attack never came off.

A pair of Hind gunships were dispatched to the location, and their pilots found all the bandits dead, most with their throats slashed. The Skinhead pilot that Devillian had ordered to strafe the bandits after they'd failed in their mission had for the most part expended his ammunition shooting at dead bodies.

Things got worse by mid-afternoon when it was discovered that a large part of the fortress food supply was infested with maggots. Although it appeared like a faulty switch on the mess hall's refrigerator was to blame, Devillian insisted that it was in fact sabotaged and, in a fit of rage, executed all of the fortress's cooks.

With the night came even more bad news. A supply train of helicopters flying in what supplies were left in the ruins of the bombed port of Desemboque had been attacked over the Sierra de la Madres, about one hundred miles away, by two jet fighters of unknown origin. All eight of the helicopters were lost.

The tension was relieved somewhat an hour later when Devillian made several quick deals with a syndicate of black market suppliers located in El Paso to truck in supplies overland to the mesa. A three-week supply of food, water and diesel fuel would come first; ammunition, liquor, drugs and other necessities would be trucked in the next day. At the moment the plan was to stockpile the stuff at the bottom of the mesa then lift it up to the base using one or two of the fortress's six working Hind copters.

Still, supplying the mesa by this overland route would not come close to replenishing the most critically short commodity—aviation fuel. For that, Devillian had to make a separate deal with an old PEMEX refinery located near La Pesca on the Gulf Coast. The price was double what the Burning Cross had been paying for the aviation fuel via Port Desemboque.

Plus, the tenuous supply lines were not attached to an endless spigot. Because these commodities were in demand everywhere, Devillian's new suppliers could only sell him enough material to keep the mesa operating for two weeks at the most. Then they would have to shut him off.

But at this point, Juanita knew Devillian didn't care about what was going on inside the fortress. His total consuming passion was this new grand design of his — this massive production that he was planning in order to make the eventual destruction of the United Americans' train a well-recorded and highly publicized historical event.

But to her mind, it was all total madness.

She had begun to settle down around nine that evening, drinking a bottle of champagne herself and splitting a huge chunk of crack with Jorge. He and his lieutenants were scheduled to leave for the Grand Canyon the following day, and so their routine intoxication turned into a going-away party.

Devillian was the spontaneous host, and he rewarded Jorge and the six officers of his entourage with their pick of the harem of love slaves. It was mildly amusing for Juanita to watch her brother attempt to get it on with two screaming teenage girls, but she sobered when Devillian insisted on sitting very close to her. She quickly shut him down, grabbed one of the girls for herself and insisted that she be flown back to her house in West Santa Fe.

Although aviation fuel was in short supply, Devillian bowed to her demands and had her and the love slave taken to Santa Fe by one of the Hinds.

Once there, Juanita drank another bottle of champagne and then ravaged the young beauty. But oddly, she quickly tired of this also, and soon sent the whimpering girl on her way, out into the cruel night.

Shortly afterward, she found the box.

It was the strangest thing. She had left her house to go to the nearby bar to get one last bottle of champagne. When she returned, there was a small box sitting in the center of her bed. Inside the box was a photo of Studs Mallox — wearing a dress.

This was when she began to get scared. She despised Mallox, but she also knew that he was a tough number to bring down, never mind get into a mumu. Anyone who was able to do that could only be tougher.

235

Plus, she knew the photo had been left as some kind of a warning for her—though it was a strange one.

She loaded her two enormous guns immediately and locked the doors and windows of her place. Another few gulps of champagne served to settle her down somewhat, but not enough to prevent her from dousing all the lights in the place.

She longed for Manuel, the seven-foot giant who used to sit by her door whenever she was in town, screening the potential mercs for the Burning Cross and aptly scaring away anyone else who might have designs on her. But Manuel was no longer in West Santa Fe—she had heard that he and his midget brother, Carlo, were on their way to Italy to make movies.

The night passed slowly, Juanita climbing into a small, black tight bikini in order to cool off, and eventually wishing she hadn't dismissed the young love slave so quickly.

Then there was a knock on her door. She quickly retrieved both of her enormous guns, then walked carefully to the door.

"Who is it?" she asked, both pistols up and ready.

"I'm the one who delivered the photo," said the somewhat familiar voice in reply.

She drew the hammers to her guns back in unison.

"What do you want?"

This question was met with only silence.

"Why are you doing this to me?"

Again, silence.

"Do you know I could have you killed in a second?"

Still, nothing.

Juanita raised her pistols heart-high and slowly opened the door.

The figure on the other side was dressed in all black. He was wearing a heavy overcoat, with the collar turned up and a black fedora pulled low over his eyes, so much so that she couldn't see his face. She raised her guns to shoot, but in one lightning move, the visitor knocked them both away.

Only then did he raise his head so that she could see his features.

"You?" she blurted out.

"Yeah—me," Hawk Hunter replied.

Chapter 49

Near Petaca, New Mexico

The bulky, awkward Transsail C. 160 cargo plane had been circling the small field for thirty minutes, its pilots cautiously waiting for the first rays of sunlight to break through the early morning gloom.

Finally, low on fuel and anxious to get on with their mission, the pilots decided to go in using what little pre-dawn light was available to them.

"Get ready back there!" the pilot yelled into his intercom microphone, alerting his flight crew in the rear of the ship. "This one's for real."

The plane circled the tiny clearing once more, then went into a shallow dive.

"Christ, here he comes," grumbled the commander of the South African mercenary unit as he and his men watched from the ground. "Let's see if they can get it right this time."

"Everybody down!" the unit's second-in-command yelled to the group's fifty specialist soldiers.

Without further prompting, every man in the unit — known by the perversely romantic title "Tongue of Fire" — lay facedown in the small grove of trees next to the field and covered their heads. They knew the next fifteen seconds would be very dangerous, and hearing the sputtering engines on the approaching cargo plane only underscored that danger.

The C. 160 was only about twenty-five feet off the ground now and heading a little shakily toward a large *X* that had been marked in the field with flour by the Afrikaners. The airplane was not trying to land — rather it was attempting a low-altitude cargo drop. Two large pallets of supplies for the Tongue of Fire sat in the rear of the plane's hold, a tangle of wires, ropes and huge rubber bands just barely holding them in place. Squeezed in between the pallets, three members of the aircrew waited nervously for the word to kick the cargo out the door.

"God, don't fuck this up," the unit commander muttered as he too lay flat out on the ground and covered his head.

The Transsail came down to about fifteen feet when one of its engines began to stall. The plane's pilot quickly applied throttle, and the engine coughed back to life. Trouble was his aircrew was pushing first one, then the other of the pallets out the back of the airplane at the same moment.

The combination of actions caused both pallets to hit the ground much harder than intended. Each one kicking up as much dust as a small bomb, the cargo loads slammed into the rocky desert ground and immediately split open, scattering their contents all over the field.

At the same time, the plane's pilot yanked back on the control column and put the aging aircraft into a dangerously near-vertical climb. Despite the drastic maneuver, the airplane just nicked the tailplane of another Transsail—the one that lay burning and charred at the end of the clearing.

"Well at least they didn't crash," the Afrikaner commander said sarcastically as he watched the airplane climb unsteadily to about five thousand feet, then immediately turn south, the very first rays of the dawn glinting off its nearest wing. "They'll probably ask Devillian for a raise."

The Tongue of Fire had been hiding in the very inhospitable forests of the South San Juan Mountains for more than a week. When they were first hired by the Burning Cross to attack but not destroy the *Freedom Express*, the Afrikaners had been under the impression that they would be airlifted in and out the same day. But the events in Eagle Rock—first the United Americans' evacuation and then the destruction of the Skull and Crossbones battalion—had caused them to stay in the field for eight long days.

Trouble was, the unit had only brought along enough

equipment for thirty-six hours; so they had to be resupplied by air by the Burning Cross. The resupply effort was a tricky operation from the word go, as the wreckage of the Transsail at the end of the field clearly attested. This was not helped by the especially volatile cargo the Tongue needed to stay effective—that was, gasoline.

True to its name, the Tongue of Fire was a flamethrowing outfit. Their profession was strategic and tactical burning—of buildings, military equipment, people, whatever. Their speciality was rooting out hard-core cases from caves, mountains and deeply dug fortifications, and their reputation of ruthless efficiency was well-deserved.

But they had never been called on to attack a train before.

"OK, guys," the second-in-command yelled. "Let's pick up all the salvageable stuff on the chop-chop. *Hustle!*"

Immediately, the troopers jumped up and took to the field. In a minute they were sorting out the usable goods from the ones that were damaged in the drop.

"Tell me again," the unit commander said. "How much are we getting paid for putting up with all this crap?"

"Not nearly enough," the second-in-command replied bitterly.

The officers walked out to the field and did a quick count. Seven of the gasoline barrels dropped by the airplane had burst open upon impact. That left eleven relatively intact.

"Some of the barrels are leaking," a sergeant reported to them. "But we can draw the gas out before they drain away."

"Well, get to it," the unit commander ordered.

Due to the nature of their work, the Tongue almost literally drank gasoline. Their flamethrowers were custom-designed jobs that mixed the petrol with a gelatin base that created a kind of highly fluid napalm. Anyone or anything on the receiving end of a "tongue blast" would be covered with a fiery jelly substance that would stick to anything: wood, concrete, metal or skin. And because of its congealed gasoline property, the flames took minutes, sometimes hours to completely burn themselves out.

But the eight days in the desert had drained them of some

of their already critically small supply. Gasoline was not easy to keep in the field; some just naturally evaporated, some went bad, and some was just simply spilled. Plus the daily necessity of testing their thirty-five separate weapons burned up about two barrels alone per day.

Now, with the drop, they were up to twenty barrels, just one barrel over the prescribed amount needed for a successful operation.

Also retrieved from the scattered remains was a pouch containing the unit's up-to-date orders from the Burning Cross.

The orders, which ran more than twenty pages long, contained the latest updates on the train's extremely slow progress, as well as various charts and graphs with which the Tongue commander could determine the train's ETA in their area.

As always, the missive ended with a warning from Devillian himself: "Do this job right or I'll make sure you never burn a damn thing again."

This was one threat that the Tongue commander took seriously. He had heard of Devillian even before he'd gotten the call from the Burning Cross to transit over from Pretoria not a month before. But the Afrikaner was also confident that there'd be no screw-ups. The gasoline jelly dispensed by their weapons was perfect for stinging the train. His plan was to concentrate on lighting up the last third of the train cars as they passed by. Then the men on the train would have no choice but to cut those cars loose.

This way, the train would be severely crippled from the loss of thirty percent of its defensive weaponry, yet still able to continue on to its deadly rendezvous with Devillian's main force.

"Then maybe we can get the hell out of here," the fastidious Tongue commander told his second-in-command after reviewing the new orders. "I haven't gone this long without a bath since college."

Chapter 50

La Casa de las Estrellas

The Burning Cross communications officer didn't know what to do.

He had just received a bit of good news — something that was running in critically short supply on top of the mesa lately, along with everything else. The Transsail crew had completed their mission and the Tongue of Fire unit was now resupplied for at least the next forty-eight hours.

The communication officer's dilemma was whether to wake Devillian with the news or not. It was just six AM, and he had to figure the Burning Cross leader was still sleeping — or, more accurately, still unconscious. Waking the cross-eyed terrorist was a dangerous proposition. The officer knew that on one hand, the boss shot people for rousing him too early. On the other, he'd also shot a number of people for delivering news *too* late. Such were the pitfalls of serving close to the top of the Burning Cross power structure.

The communications officer remained undecided during most of the long walk toward Devillian's Play Pen. He was about two thirds of the way there when he hit upon a compromise strategy. He would simply put his ear to the lust nest's door and knock only at the first sign of life inside.

So it was with great surprise that the officer found the doors to the Play Pen open and a groggy, yet noisy party still inside.

The man gulped when he first saw Devillian. The white supremacist leader was lying on his huge bed, drunkenly orchestrating a bevy of confused, naked beauties as they halfheartedly flagellated him.

On the floor next to the bed was the massive frame of the bandit Jorge Juarez, naked from the waist down and laying in a multi-colored pool of unidentifiable liquid. The recently returned Major Heck, he being bandaged on the head and shoulder, was sitting in one corner of the huge room, babbling incoherently as he tried to stick the needle of a morphine-filled syringe into his arm, two unconscious naked girls at his feet.

All the while, an extremely sickening video of newsreel footage depicting the horrors of the World War II Nazi war camp Treblinka was playing unwatched on the enormous TV screen in the far corner. The room itself smelt of vomit.

The officer had no choice but to give Devillian the message now. Holding his breath, he saluted and handed the communiqué to the cross-eyed man. Devillian started gurgling as he tried to focus on the neatly typed-out words, all the while enduring the less-than-satisfactory flogging.

It took a full two minutes before he caught the gist of the news.

"This is great!" he proclaimed, so loudly even the gross mass that was Jorge Juarez stirred slightly. "Leave it to those South Afrikaners to prove to me that you shouldn't give a critical job to a bunch of darkies."

Heartened that Devillian seemed pleased at the news, the communications officer was still trembling with anxiety. Devillian had been known to kill people on an early morning, get-the-day-off-to-the-right-start whim before, and the man knew that if he saw the terrorist reach for his trusted Polaroid instant camera, his life was soon to come to an end.

So the communications officer was amazed when Devillian promptly jumped up from the bed and swallowed a handful of speed tablets instead.

Then he turned to him and said, "You've just been promoted. Be in the War Room in one hour."

* * *

It was actually an hour and ten minutes later when Devillian finally entered the crowded War Room.

The communications officer was sitting in the front row when the terrorist leader swaggered in, resplendent in his jet black Nazi-style uniform. He was followed by a phalanx of guards who had been pressed into service as an unlikely squad of cooks. Two of them were wheeling a cart that contained a large, six-tiered cake. Except for the lack of a wax bride and groom figure on top, the cake would have been appropriate for an enormous wedding reception.

"Today is a new beginning for the Burning Cross," Devillian said. "Today, we commence feeding from the fruits of our new power. Today, we begin pulling the strings that will make the people in this country stand up and take notice of us."

The last thing that the twenty other people in attendance—representatives from the various bandit gangs, air pirate groups and other mercenary units in the employ of the Burning Cross—thought they'd hear at the early morning meeting was a sugar-coated pep talk. Instead, most had been under the impression that the terrorist leader was going to address the alarmingly critical supply shortage. The last they had heard, an overland convoy was to reach the mesa by that afternoon. Yet essential items such as diesel fuel, food and water were in such low supply that the replenishment would be sucked up immediately, thus doing nothing to relieve the base of the shortage problem.

Making a bad situation worse was the fact that Devillian had ordered most of what precious supplies they had left to a secret location somewhere in northern Arizona, the purpose of which the terrorist leader had yet to reveal to them. Until now. . . .

"The final die has been cast," Devillian said, strangely sounding as if he were reading from a movie script. "Here is the layout for the triumph of our will."

Turning on the War Room's huge electronic map, Devillian indicated the Tongue of Fire's current position on the

244

west side of the San Juan Mountains.

"Going along with our plan of harassing the guys on the train, I've got a unit of South Africans sitting here on a bend in the track near a shit hole named Petaca," Devillian explained. "They've just been resupplied, and when the train passes by them, they're gonna burn them."

There was a spontaneous cheer from those assembled.

Devillian then indicated an area in the northwest corner of New Mexico. "When they reach this point, we'll send up a bunch of Hinds to pop them. This will keep them thinking while they pass into Arizona territory."

There was another cheer.

"Then," Devillian continued, pointing to the area around the southern rim of the Grand Canyon, "they'll reach this area, where most of our forces are deployed. At this point, gentlemen, we stop toying with them and let them have it with both barrels."

Now the room erupted in an explosion of cheering and whistles. Finally, they were actually going to destroy the accursed train.

Only the newly promoted communications officer raised his hand.

"Why there, sir?" he asked, somewhat naively. "If we are going to destroy them, why don't we do it sooner? Closer?"

Devillian turned from pale to red back to pale in a matter of seconds. Possibly the only thing that saved the communications officer's life was that the Burning Cross leader had recognized that he'd just promoted the man minutes before and that he was entitled to just one stupid question.

"Because," Devillian began, "when we finally annihilate these assholes on the train, I intend to make it a historic battle. I want to see the bodies fly, burn, be crushed, the very life sucked out of them. But, more importantly, I want every person in this whole damn country to see all that as well. Consider it a live news event — history instantly in the making."

"But why there?" the man persisted.

Devillian routinely reached for his pistol. "Because, that's the farthest point that we can still beam TV transmissions back to LA, of course," he answered somewhat enigmatically.

With that he fatally shot the man in the neck.

There was another, less than spontaneous round of applause, and then Devillian called the meeting to a close by asking, "Does anyone have a camera with them?"

Chapter 51

Mike Fitzgerald was getting nervous.

He was standing under the stairway of the dilapidated gray house that sat in the alley off the main drag in West Santa Fe. His trusty Uzi was in one hand, its safety off. A flash grenade was in his other, the pin just a hairbreadth away from being disengaged. He was also carrying a .440 Magnum under his coat, and a back-up 9mm machine pistol in his boot.

Still he wondered if he could really hold off the number of people he envisioned being roused by the racket going on up in the second-floor apartment.

It wasn't screaming, per se. Quite the opposite in fact. Instead it was the very loud, passionate sound of a woman moaning — and doing it so loudly that Fitz could actually feel its strident tone vibrating the hair on the back of his head. And as the chorus of delight was growing progressively in volume over the past twenty minutes, Fitz could only conclude that it soon would be loud enough to start attracting attention.

And that's when he'd be forced to break out his weapons.

"Jessuz, Hawker," he whispered, bringing the Uzi up a little closer to his chest as another even louder wail of undeniable pleasure echoed through the dingy alley. "What are ye doing to the poor girl up there?"

"I can't take any more of this," Juanita was saying, her erotic pleasure zones becoming overloaded. "I just can't. . . ."

Hunter felt the same way — but for different reasons. His

247

fingers were almost numb from carefully squeezing Juanita's lovely nipples.

He'd been at it for what seemed to be hours now. It hadn't taken very long for Juanita to remove her clothes for him after he'd first appeared. On first sight of him the amnestic hypnotic suggestion he'd given her during their first meeting had quickly evaporated. However he had thought the real convincer would have been when he told her that Studs Mallox was now a prisoner and that she too would be kidnapped if she didn't cooperate; after all, that was the whole idea of leaving her the picture of Studs in his mumu. But at that point she didn't even care. Even when he revealed to her who he was, her only concern was for him to put her back into the orgasmic trance. Clearly she needed this kind of fulfillment as much as he wanted the intelligence on Devillian.

And so slowly he had drawn the information out of her — how Devillian intended to finally attack the train and where.

But as the interrogation went on, the problem was that he was apparently doing his job too well; Juanita's moans of delight were getting louder by the minute.

Five more minutes went by until Fitz — his anxiety getting the best of him — finally bounded up the stairs and banged on the door.

"You got crowds at both ends of the alley," he yelled in to Hunter. "Time to wrap it up."

Hunter was out of the door a few seconds later, Fitz just catching a glimpse of the topless, happily unconscious Juanita as she lay on the apartment's couch.

"Did you get what we want?" Fitz asked him.

"I did," Hunter replied, feeling only a mild pang of concern that he didn't have time to reinstitute the hypnotic suggestion that Juanita forget everything that had just happened to her. "And you probably won't believe it when I tell you — "

"Save it for the long walk back to the chopper," the Irishman said. "First we've got to figure a way out of here."

One glance down the stairway told them that a crowd of

twenty-five or so armed men was now moving down the alley, the strange wailing coming from the gray house indicating that something was amiss. A look out the window of the second-story porch gave Hunter and Fitz a good view of the smaller, but no less meaner crowd that was coming down the opposite end of the court.

"She must be quite popular," Fitz said dryly.

"All these guys are either her boyfriends or her brothers," Hunter observed.

They broke through a skylight and climbed up to the roof only to find that no other adjoining rooftops were within jumping distance.

Back down into the hallway, they briefly discussed their options.

"Flash or crash?" Hunter asked.

"Flash," Fitz confirmed.

By this time, the two approaching gangs were only about twenty feet apart and getting very close to the stairway that led up to Juanita's place. Suddenly they were startled to see two men leap from the stairway to the ground right between them.

"On three," the shorter of the two men said. "One . . . *two—*"

He never said three. Instead, the men in the two gangs were suddenly blinded by a tremendous flash. Instantly, everyone went to the ground and raised their weapons.

But by the time the flashsmoke finally dissipated and their collective eyesight returned, they saw that the two strange men had disappeared.

Chapter 52

The Skinhead pilot named Duzz couldn't believe his ears; it was as if he were hearing a voice from the dead.

"Just do what the fuck I tell you," the man claiming to be Studs Mallox told him via Duzz's F-4 cockpit radio. "Go to the fucking coordinate and land that fucking airplane on the south side of the fucking interstate."

Duzz didn't know what to do. It sounded like Studs—the cadence, the obscenities, everything—but the message to land on a nearby long-deserted highway was truly bizarre.

"Studs, if this is you," Duzz began, "you know that if Devillian caught me doing an unauthorized landing, he'd cook my crogies."

"I'll slice them up raw if you don't do what I tell you!" came the definitely Studs-like reply.

Duzz checked his present position. He was just thirty miles southwest of the San Juan Mountains, heading back to the mesa after having tracked the train for the past three hours as it moved incredibly slowly through the hills. He then checked his critical fuel supply and estimated that he could theoretically set down and take off and still have enough gas left over to return to the mesa. But it would be close.

He decided to buzz the location and four minutes later was flying over the empty highway. He circled down and eventually did see a figure that *looked* like Studs, waving to him from an overpass.

"Get your fucking ass down here!" Duzz's radio crackled again. "Or I'll hunt you down."

Duzz was convinced now. He turned again and set the F-4 down to a bumpy but successful landing.

250

Five minutes later, he was face to face with Studs in the flesh.

"Jeesuz, boss, we thought you had bought it somehow," Duzz said, only now realizing that Studs was wearing a dress. "What happened to you, and what the hell is with this broad's outfit?"

Studs' face was already red—now it grew redder. He resisted the urge to smack Duzz in the face.

"Fuck you," he said instead, unconsciously straightening the hem on the mumu. "These assholes made me wear it."

Duzz looked up to see that both he and his airplane were surrounded by about a dozen heavily armed soldiers who had appeared as if out of thin air. What was worse, Duzz could tell right away from their distinctive uniforms that they were members of the famous Football City Special Forces Rangers.

"What the hell is going on here, Studs?" Duzz asked.

This time Studs did hit him—once—with an open palm upside the head.

"What the fuck do you think is going on?" Studs yelled at him. "You've just been captured, you idiot."

Duzz was blindfolded and taken to a helicopter of some kind. After a twenty-minute ride, he was astonished to find himself sitting inside one of the cars of the *Freedom Express*.

"How the hell did these guys get a chopper off the train?" he asked incredulously. "We've been watching them night and day."

"You dumb fuck," Studs scolded him. "They were able to fly them off inside of one of the mountain pass tunnels. Then they waited until you jerks moved on and went from there. They've been doing it all day!"

It took a few moments for that concept to sink into Duzz's head.

"Just listen up," Studs told him, still nervously fussing with his dress. "I want you to go back to the base and tell all the guys to get the hell off that mesa . . . and I mean *now*."

"What!?"

"You heard me," Studs told him. "We're pulling out. I've

251

cancelled our contract with the fuckhead Devillian."

"Does he know that?" Duzz asked, still not quite believing what was happening to him.

"He will when you guys take off!" Studs yelled, reeling back to slap Duzz a second time.

Duzz looked at the five other men standing in the windowless room. All of them were wearing hoods.

"Studs, you know how our guys are," Duzz said. "They'll think I've gone around the fucking bend if I go back and tell them that you say to bug out. They all think you're dead."

"Well I'm not, shithead, am I?" Studs yelled at him. "They had some Indian snatch me when I went out to dump Ant. I yelled like crazy when I was fighting this guy off, but you pansies must have been too busy to hear me."

Duzz just kept shaking his head. "This is too much, Studs," he said. "You gotta tell me what the hell is going down."

"I told you, we're cancelling on Devillian," Studs retorted. "We've just been hired by another employer."

"Who?" Duzz asked absolutely astounded by this point. "Not these guys."

"Yeah, these guys," Studs said flippantly. "They're going to pay us just to get the hell out of the fight."

"Pay us? To give up?" Duzz had never heard of such a thing before. "How much?"

Studs threw a left hook that caught the man on the shoulder. "Will you knock that shit off?" he demanded. "They're paying us by not *killing* me, you dinkshit. Now go back and tell the guys to pull out. Head for Mexico City — form up there. Wait until this mess is over. These guys say they'll release me then. I'll join up with you, and we'll figure out what to do from there."

"It might be pretty hard all of us just flying off like that, Studs," Duzz replied. "The gas situation on that mushroom top is getting pretty low."

"I don't give a fuck," Studs told him. "Fill everyone up the night before from our own supply. Mexico City is just a dick hair over eleven hundred miles from the mesa. If you guys go slow and don't fuck around, you'll make it on one full tank plus the drops.

Duzz was still having a hard time taking it all in.

"OK," he said finally. "Let's say I go back and we get enough gas; how the fuck am I going to make the guys believe that I talked to you? That you are still alive?"

Now Studs' face really flushed red—but not so much from anger as from embarrassment.

"These heroes already thought of that," he said, angrily glancing toward the five hooded men.

He reached inside his dress pocket and pulled out a handful of Polaroid photos.

"Show 'em these," he said, flipping the pictures to Duzz. "They'll believe you then."

Duzz picked up the photos. All of them were of the same shot—Studs woodenly posing in his mumu.

Chapter 53

"Got a light?"

The South African flamethrower unit's second-in-command reached down for his Zippo and lit his commander's cigarette.

"Won't be long now," he said, lighting a butt of his own.

They both scanned their unit's positions for the hundredth time, each man satisfied that at last they were actually going to get to do their job and then get the hell out of the brutal desert woods environment.

They had set up their troops along a bend in the tracks that measured just over a half mile. In all the unit had thirty-five flamethrowers, most of them one-man set-ups, though a few of the bigger models required two-man teams. The fueling process was rather simple. One barrel of gasoline and a half barrel of gelatin mix could supply two flamethrowers. The gas and the jello were pumped in via separate hoses that stretched 125 feet behind each fire team. When the two elements mixed inside the combustor of the flamethrower itself, the long deadly stream of sticky flame was born.

The unit's officers had to take special precautions in preparation for attacking the train. Never before had their men deployed in positions actually facing each other. Therefore, the spacing of the flamethrower locations had to be such that one team's tongue of fire wouldn't somehow jump over the train and across the tracks and envelope a team on the other side. Moreover, the fire teams had to be placed behind rocks and not scrub trees or bushes; when the fire started flowing, no one wanted to be around anything combustible.

"We look all set then, sir," the second-in-command said. "Should I have the men suit up?"

The commander checked his watch. "I would," he told the man. "If Devillian's calculations are right, the train will be here within two hours."

High above and laying flat out on a small butte about a half mile away, a Piute scout named Green Feather watched through binoculars as the men of the Tongue of Fire climbed into their bulky fire-proof suits and helmets.

After taking a careful note of their number and dispersement, the Indian slipped back down the butte to the desert floor. Then, retrieving his swift horse, he quickly rode away.

It was two and a half hours later when the commander of Tongue of Fire heard the crackle of his walkie-talkie coming to life.

"I can hear the train, sir" came the report from the unit's advance scout who was positioned about a mile up the tracks. "It sounds like it's coming down off the mountain right now."

"Good work," he radioed back to the man. "Can you estimate how far away it is from your position?"

There was another burst of static, then the scout replied: "Hard to say at this moment, sir. I can see the smoke from its engines over the tops of the trees up here, and it's getting louder with every second."

The unit commander quickly checked his watch. He figured the train would pass by sometime within the next five minutes. He yelled the warning to his second-in-command, who in turn shouted the message down the line.

Then the commander called back to his scout. "I want you to keep talking to me until you actually see the train!" he yelled into the walkie-talkie.

Oddly, there was no reply.

"Did you hear me, man?" the commander called. Nothing.

The commander tried two more times, banging the walkie-talkie and thinking that either his instrument or that of the scout's had suddenly gone bad.

Still, all he heard was static.

Odd, he thought, tossing the walkie-talkie away from him.

Four and one half minutes later, the men of the Tongue of Fire heard the train themselves.

"Here it comes!" several people yelled at once, noting the black smoke that appeared above the trees that separated them from the opposite side of the bend.

"Battle positions!" the second-in-command hollered. "First unit get ready!"

The first unit was comprised of three flamethrower teams that had been positioned at the very edge of the long curve where the unit intended to attack the train. These men would be the first to not only see the train but also to fire on it.

The unit commander checked his watch once again, then stared up into the sky. It was almost high noon — the hottest time of the day. Perfect for starting a fire.

"There it is!" someone yelled.

The unit commander turned and saw the distinctive yellow guardrail of the first locomotive as it slowly made its way around the bend.

"Let's go to work!" he shouted back to his troops.

But no sooner were the words out of his mouth when he realized that something was wrong. Desperately wrong.

His first teams were already unleashing their streams of flame at the locomotive, but as the engine cleared the bend, everyone could see that it wasn't the entire train that was approaching. Rather it was just the single locomotive.

"What in bloody hell is going on?" the commander yelled.

Suddenly he thought back to the scout whose walkie-talkie had screwed up at the last critical moment. Maybe it hadn't been the radio at all.

Confused, the flamethrower teams along the line nevertheless hit the lone locomotive with all they had — much more than what was called for in the original plan. Within seconds the huge engine was engulfed in the broiling, sticky flame. It barreled past the fire teams like a huge rolling house afire, the noise of the flames alone being near deafening. Finally, it tumbled off the tracks and into a gulley below.

But suddenly the unit commander was aware of another noise, this one coming from high above him.

He looked up and was terrified to see that while their attention had been drawn to the single locomotive, a jumpjet had managed to maneuver right above their position.

And now it was starting to descend.

The Aden gun pod carries a powerful 25mm cannon, capable of firing at an astounding rate of fifty shells *a second*.

What's more, the shells themselves were capable of great destructive power due to their iron sheeting and their long, slender length. More suited to piercing metal, one cannon shell could literally cause a man to explode if it hit him full in the chest or abdomen.

The Harrier jumpjet that had suddenly appeared in the midst of the Tongue of Fire teams carried two Aden guns. Stunned by the jumpjet's sudden appearance, the flamethrower teams were ironically frozen to their spots. They were not equipped with SAM weapons; few of them even had rifles. So they could do little else but watch in horror as the Harrier went into a hover only about twenty-five feet above them. The plane's pilot expertly dipped its nose, at the same time putting the jet into a tight, quick 360 degree turn.

That's when its Aden cannons opened up.

Because of the velocity at which a 25mm cannon shell traveled, they tended to ignite anything they hit, due to the tremendous friction upon impact. The massive barrage of cannon shells that rained down on the hapless fire teams seemed to almost seek out the barrels of gasoline, the fuel-clogged hoses and the flamethrowers themselves as targets.

Suddenly it was as if the earth had opened up and let a little piece of hell poke through its surface. There were flames and explosions everywhere within the radius of the Harrier's deadly circle. The conflagration became so intense that the flamethrower teams' fire-resistant suits burned up like tissue paper. Men screamed as they watched their own skin melt away from them. Others tried to flee, but they couldn't escape the instantaneous firestorm the Harrier's cannon shells had created. Still others simply let the flame roll over them, succumbing to the fire that they had so many times created as an instrument of death.

"My God, what have I done?" the Tongue of Fire commander cried out as the flames engulfed him. In the eternal instant before death, a strange truth came to him: White or black, all men die the same way. Therefore, they all must *live* the same way, too. . . .

When the rest of the *Freedom Express* rolled through the area ten minutes later, the ground on either side of the half-mile curve was still smoking. All that remained of the Tongue of Fire soldiers was a scattering of bones and pools of sticky burned skin.

The train quickly passed by the instant graveyard and continued its journey west.

Chapter 54

Michael Crossbow hadn't eaten in more than two days. Yet, his stomach felt full and he had no thirst. His reflexes, if anything, were sharper than before, and his eyesight was nearly as good now at night, as it was during the day.

Such were the ways of a ghost.

He had been atop the mesa fortress for almost thirty-six hours, returning the same way he and Hunter had first come, that was, hand-over-hand up the formation's craggy northern side. Hiding out on top of the plateau had been fairly easy; the Burning Cross soldiers used the jagged collection of rocks on the mesa's north end—the place called the Spines—as a sort of garbage dump, and Crossbow had found numerous places to hide out during the day in amongst the junk.

He spent this time observing what he could of the enemy's activities. Then, once the night fell, he crawled out of the trash and resumed his one-man haunting of the mesa top.

For the most part his dangerous mission to disrupt the Burning Cross from within was working very well. The fact that many of Devillian's men believed the mesa to be spooked in the first place had turned out to be an unexpected plus for him. Anytime a mysterious fire broke out, or a sentry was found missing, the superstitious/drug-paranoid Burning Cross soldiers tended to blame the mesa's ghost, and not a saboteur hiding out in their midst.

Ruining the fort's food supply had served as a major disruption for the enemy. Contaminating their water supply had also resulted in many sick enemy soldiers over the past three days.

But facilitating the kidnapping of Studs Mallox had been Crossbow's greatest task so far—though he had had some help. A troop of Bad River's Piutes had been moved several days before to positions near the mesa itself, completing the grueling trek to the Ring of Fire desert on horseback in an unbelievably short amount of time. Their mission was to attack any resupply effort attempting to reach the mesa overland, and already they had destroyed one convoy and had driven another away. These braves had proved very helpful in spiriting the Skinhead leader far enough away from the mesa to the place where he was picked up by one of the Cobra Brothers.

Yet, Crossbow had run up against two factors he could do nothing about: One was trying to assassinate Devillian himself—a job that was virtually impossible due to the fact that the cross-eyed white supremacy leader very rarely emerged from his heavily guarded mansion headquarters. The second disappointment had to do with the mesa top's anti-aircraft defenses. Try as he might, Crossbow could not locate a central point from which the fortress's multitude of SAMs and AA guns were controlled. Destruction of such an elusive target—perhaps a fire control house or a computer bank—would have made a United American air strike on the Burning Cross base a less-than-suicidal possibility.

But eventually the Shawnee determined that there was no central point; the South African technicians who had set up the air-defense system had wisely diversified the fire controls and feeder lines for the dozens of SAM sites, making the whole kaboodle virtually invulnerable to sabotage and thereby thwarting any chance of a successful air raid.

Still, Crossbow *was* working on one last critical job: the neutralizing of the Skinhead's F-4 Squadron. Two of the most important components of this task—the kidnapping of Mallox and the subsequent meeting between him and his lieutenant, Duzz—had already been accomplished.

Now, on this night, Crossbow had to deliver the crucial third strike.

It was to his advantage that the Skinheads occupied an

isolated corner of the vast mesa top themselves. The fact that they were despised by their Burning Cross allies almost as much as by their enemies worked in Crossbow's favor. Once the sun went down, none of Devillian's other troops dared to go near the Skinhead camp for fear they would be snatched and stomped to death by a group of bored Nazis. Even the mesa's well-equipped sentry force steered clear of the area. And because the Skinheads saw absolutely no reason to deploy guards themselves, Crossbow had little problem moving through the shadows and gaining access to the barbed wire enclosure.

Once inside, he headed for the squadron's small fuel dump and was not surprised to see that unlike the perimeter of the camp, it was buzzing with Skinheads. Due to Hunter's strategy of striking at the mesa top's supply lines as opposed to the mesa itself, aviation gas was becoming more valuable than food or drugs on top of the mesa, and the Skinheads were protecting their juice like gold. But unlike Devillian and his command staff, Crossbow knew the 'Heads were keeping a close eye on their JP-8 in order to make good on Mallox's secret instructions to abandon the mesa and fly to Mexico City and thus gain his release.

Now, as he watched from the shadows, Crossbow could see the Skinheads were playing their part exactly according to the script, convinced no doubt that anyone who got Studs Mallox to dress up in a mumu meant business. One by one, their F-4's were being pushed to the fuel dump to have their tanks filled. The terms of Mallox's release hinged on the fact that the Skinhead squadron would have to be in Mexico City by noon the next day. This meant the entire twelve-plane unit would have to start preparations to launch from the mesa shortly after dawn to make the eleven hundred-mile journey south in time and do so either without letting Devillian on to what was happening, or ignoring the terrorist leader once he learned the 'Heads were bugging out.

How the Nazi pilots handled Devillian was not Crossbow's concern; everything from doing nothing to an all-out battle within the Burning Cross was possible. Right now, all

261

the Shawnee had to concentrate on was the 'Heads fuel supply.

He watched the refueling operation for two hours, not moving, barely even breathing. By silent calculations, he determined that it took nine and a half minutes to push a Phantom into position, another twenty to fill its tanks and then another nine to get it out of the way. Yet he knew that the procedure would have to be repeated again the next morning—though in quicker intervals. The warming time for a cold F-4 engine was a half hour and used up as much as a fifth of a tank of fuel. This meant that when the F-4's were started up for real at daybreak their tanks would have to be refilled for the flight to Mexico City.

And it was this necessary topping-off procedure that played right into Crossbow's plans.

As was typical of operations like this one, the Skinheads were more concerned about getting the job done quickly rather than doing it securely. Therefore, the guards surrounding the 'Head fuel dump were not walking the line or even guarding anything. In fact, they were pitching in to push the F-4's into position next to the large fuel pump, and then pushing them out of the way when the fueling was complete. What they should have been guarding—the small semi-elevated fuel storage tank and the nine-inch fuel hose that ran from it to the fuel pump—was virtually ignored.

Instinctively knowing when to move, Crossbow made his way to the back of the fuel tank and ducked underneath one of its support bars. Working in the nearly pitch-black conditions, he withdrew a small rubber tube he'd been carrying very gingerly ever since arriving on the mesa top. The tube contained a highly concentrated amount of a rare chemical called titanium oxide. Just where Hunter had dug up the stuff, Crossbow had no idea. But being an MIT grad with a minor in chemistry, the Shawnee knew what the titanium oxide—TO for short—could do when mixed with jet fuel.

Moving slowly and carefully, he retrieved a syringe from his utility belt and expertly filled it with the TO. Then he found a weakened spot in the nine-inch fuel hose and injected the chemical into it. Once this was done, he refilled the syringe and repeated the procedure. It took him twelve injections to use up the titanium oxide, coincidently one injection per Skinhead airplane.

Once the TO was expended, he buried the syringe and the tube and slowly moved out from under the fuel tank and back to his original position near the refueling operation.

Here he sat for the next two hours, watching the Skinheads huff and puff the F-4's in and out of position.

Then, with the first indication of dawn, he stole away out of the Skinhead camp and back to his hiding place in the Spines.

Chapter 55

It was around nine the next morning when Hunter drank his first can of beer in three days.

It had followed a plate of powdered scrambled eggs and rock-hard toast, not surprisingly easing its way down his throat with smooth abandon.

"Been awhile since I had beer with breakfast," he said to Fitz, who was quickly polishing off a lager of his own. "Then again, it's been awhile since I had a breakfast."

Sucking down a victory beer seemed appropriate for Hunter. For the first time in what seemed like years, his head was fairly clear. He knew that his side trip to West Santa Fe as well as his successful action against the enemy flamethrowing unit had worked to bring him back to reality, so to speak. He no longer felt odd leaving the incense-laced cabin. He had begun to recognize the voice coming from his lips to be his own. And just as something deep inside of him had told him to listen to the voices and use them for what they were worth, now something was telling him the period of channeling was over.

Now was the time to use the knowledge he'd received.

What had caused it all — or where the strange voices had come from — he still had no idea. But he was never without the small notebook that he had used to take down all of the adages. In fact, it had taken its place among his other articles of honor, inside his left breast pocket, wrapped within the small American flag he always carried with him, right next to the faded photograph of the lovely Dominique.

And although everything inside the notebook was committed to his memory, he still studied the writings in every spare moment he had.

The bad news was those moments were getting few and far between.

The train had successfully foiled the two ambushes Devillian had arranged—and they owed a debt of gratitude to Bad River and his Piutes on both accounts. Without their help, the *Freedom Express* would have been in a lot worse shape than it was at present.

Juanita's information said that Devillian had stationed the bulk of his troops and their weapons along a ten-mile stretch of track just south of the Grand Canyon. The comparison to that of running a murderous gauntlet was inescapable. And strangely enough, somewhere back in his psyche, Hunter had always had the feeling it would come to this—one gigantic battle in which the last one standing wins.

After draining the last sip of the somewhat-symbolic beer, he, Fitz and the Cobras gathered around their planning table, examining the terrain that lay ahead of them. They were gradually passing out of the forested mountains and back into the northern New Mexico desert landscape again. The change in topography helped in one respect: The wide-open spaces reduced the chance of further surprise ambushes. Except for the occasional mountain pass, the train would be traveling through almost absolutely flat country.

Once they'd scoped out their hoped-for progress for the day, the four men turned to the task of attempting to interpret the bits of intelligence that were coming to them over the scramblers from Washington.

During the night, JT and Ben had led yet another raid out of LA against Port Desemboque. According to their preliminary damage report, the harbor would not have to be attacked again. Not only were its docking facilities near totally destroyed, but on the last mission, they had sown several strings of high-impact mines along the harbor mouth, effectively sealing off what remained of the port from the open water of the Gulf of California.

Fitz read the next item of business, this one concerning

the recent movement of the 1st Airborne. A short report from Catfish said the troops — and their horses — had reached the highly secret second location. Now, with the new information from Juanita on hand, Hunter prepared a message that would instruct the airborne cavalry to deploy to its third and last location.

"This is where the hard part begins for those guys," Hunter said. "We will have wasted a lot of time and effort if we tell them to be at the right place at the wrong time."

Finally the subject of the Skinhead Squadron came up, and this too was discussed only in the briefest terms.

"We'll know by noon whether this gamble has paid off," Hunter told them. "And then we've got to find some kind of a medal to pin on Mike Crossbow."

"Amen to that," Fitz said. "How he can stay hidden up on that mesa all this time is spooky."

"It's that Indian know-how," Hunter said. "Sometimes I wish I had a little of it myself."

Just then, the scrambler started churning out a new message. And even before he read it, Hunter's sixth sense was telling him it was *really* bad news.

Fitz retrieved the scroll of teletype, read it quickly and swore. "Oh, God, I don't believe this."

"What is it?" Tyler asked.

Fitzgerald read the message again and then turned to Hunter.

"I hate to have to be the one to tell you this, Hawker," he said. "But someone has stolen your F-16."

It was true.

A scrambled phone call to Jones sadly confirmed that the hangar at Andrews AFB where Hunter had left his F-16XL after transferring its avionics to the Harrier had been broken into and the precious jet stolen.

"I'm afraid I can't add much more than the initial report, Hawk," the general told him over the scramble phone. "It happened two days ago. The morning guards reported for duty and found your airplane gone and two sentries missing. It's like they vanished into thin air."

Hunter still could not quite believe the news.

266

"Just like that?" he asked. "It must have been an inside job."

"We don't think so," Jones replied. "The DC militia has always been top-notch, so there's no real reason to suspect they'd change now. As far as we can tell, the thieves kidnapped the guards when they took the airplane."

"But how did they get it out of there?" Hunter asked. "They certainly didn't fly it out."

"No, not exactly," Jones answered. "We think they actually used a flatbed truck with a mobile crane. A vehicle like that was spotted near the base just before dawn that day. Then later on, a cargo plane pilot coming in from Toronto reported that he saw a Sky Crane chopper hauling something heavy about a hundred miles north of Bethesda. It was painted in wild colors—green and blue stripes, like a lumber carrier—and it was carrying something wrapped in white tarp. The cargo pilot says the shape could have been that of a small jet. This pilot just assumed it was one of our copters until he heard about your plane being clipped."

Hunter was simply stunned. "It must have been a pretty elaborate operation if they had a Sky Crane," he said, referring to the massive heavy-lift helicopter. "I mean, I haven't seen more than two of those birds in five years. They're pretty rare items."

"I agree," Jones replied. "And we're doing everything we can to track it down. I've got every guy I can spare out there looking for it. I can't promise anything, but we'll try like hell to find it."

"Thanks, General," Hunter said, his now all-too-familiar voice choking up slightly. "I'll appreciate anything you can do."

The rest of the day passed by with an eerie serenity. The train was traveling at the slowest possible speed again, heading out of New Mexico and into Arizona.

And with every mile it got closer to the impending clash with Devillian.

There had been a piece of good news around noon. Scouts from the detachment of Bad River's troop that was keeping the mesa under twenty-four-hour-a-day surveil-

267

lance radioed in that they'd seen twelve F-4's take off from the mesa top around mid-morning with no indication of hostile fire coming from the reluctant allies left back on the fortress itself. Hunter replied that the Piutes should get a message to Crossbow that now that his mission was done, it was time for him to leave the mesa top for good.

The Wingman spent the rest of the day busying himself with duties on the train, trying his best not to think about what had happened to his F-16. It was only when night had fallen and he had a few moments that the real shock of his loss began to set in.

He had climbed up on top of his railway car and let the breeze from the slow-moving train cool him. The moon was rising fast, its glow lighting up the desert with a warm orange shine. Yet he was in no mood to appreciate the landscape's undeniable beauty.

His period of denial slowly dissipating, he felt the pain of such a huge part of his life being ripped away. It both enraged and saddened him that something so important and precious to him as his F-16 was now in the hands of thieves. And for what purpose? Would the perpetrators ask for a ransom? If they did, he would pay it, get the aircraft back and then hunt them down like dogs. Actually he knew this was just wishful thinking; he should be so lucky that the whole business was just a case of plane-napping. Maybe the thieves would cut the plane up, or sell it, or simply destroy it. He tried his best to shake these thoughts away; they were just too painful for his soul to bear.

Now looking down at the Harrier, lashed as it was to the platform car in front of him, he felt a little comfort that the brains of the F-16—the avionics and so on—were safe aboard the jumpjet. But it was a cold reprieve; the F-16 was more than just a bunch of gizmos attached to a fuselage and wing and powered by an engine. It was greater than the sum of its parts. It was an entity unto itself.

It was part of him.

His melancholy was broken by the sound of someone climbing up the ladder to the roof.

"Hawk? Are you up there?"

268

It was Diamond.

He helped her up the last few steps, and she settled down next to him.

"It's really beautiful up here," she said, snuggling closer to him. "I feel like we're a couple of hobos."

He nodded, somewhat sadly. "I wish all I had to do was ride the rails," he said.

She touched his hand lightly. "I heard about your airplane," she said. "I've never seen it, but you were talking about it in your sleep a few nights ago."

He was not surprised that he had been dreaming about the F-16—along with everything else.

"I spent a lot of time in that airplane," he said. "It's carried me just about everywhere, and I've been damn lucky with it. Now, to just have it swiped like that . . ." his voice trailed off.

She pulled even closer to him, and he put his arm around her. She was a very sweet girl, and in just the few days they'd been together, she'd put up with a lot: the attacks on the train, the crazy forty-eight hours of his out-of-this-world meditation, the uncertainty of their fate. She seemed to roll with it all though, showing an amazing ability to adapt to the strangest situations.

Through it all, she was never less than upbeat, confident, even optimistic. In a way, he felt himself falling for her.

He pulled her even closer and was about to kiss her when he felt a damnable familiar feeling run up his spine.

"*Quick,* climb down," he told her, leading her to the ladder.

"But what's the matter?"

"Trouble's coming" was all he said. "And it's coming fast."

He saw them just about a minute later.

First one speck of red light appeared on the southern horizon. Then there were two. Then three. Then a dozen.

"Hinds . . ." he heard himself whisper.

By this time, the men on board were scrambling to their battle stations—reacting to his called-out warning as well as the *Express*'s own radar systems. The train was traveling through a long, low desert valley, with no bends or curves for at least twenty miles. Nor were there any tunnels or forests in which the train could seek shelter.

Hunter was inside the warmed-up Harrier within the next minute, and airborne a minute after that. By this time, the enemy choppers had reached the train and were circling it at about three thousand feet, much like Old West movie Indians would circle a bunch of wagons. Hunter instantly banked toward the line of orbiting gunships and dove through them with his guns blazing.

One chopper immediately exploded, and another suffered serious damage from his initial barrage. But at the same time, six of the choppers dove straight for the train. Obviously the Hind pilots' battle plans were to split their force; six would provide fodder for Hunter while the other six strafed the train.

Hunter laid a Sidewinder into yet another copter when he heard Fitz's distinctive brogue come through his headphones.

"Clear the area, Hawk," the Irishman yelled. "You've got ten seconds."

Hunter quickly acknowledged the request and booted the jumpjet forward at top speed. He didn't question why Fitz had requested he break off the engagement; he already knew why.

Leveling out the Harrier at 4500 feet about two miles off the train's starboard, he began to count off "three . . . two . . . one — "

Suddenly the night sky above the train lit up like a massive Fourth of July fireworks display. Streaks of bright yellow light shot off from eight of the railway cars, entrapping the buzzing Hinds in a fiery web. Hunter forced himself to smile; at last he was seeing exactly what the train could do, or at least part of it.

He knew that in the ten seconds prior to the pyrotechnics, the train's on-board air defense systems had clicked on. Using radar and infra-red detectors to assess the threat, the computers had ordered eight of the train's sixteen SAM cars to arm, lock on to the Hinds and launch.

And launch they did.

No less than four dozen S-2 SAMs screamed up from the railway cars, in seconds obliterating the half dozen attacking Hinds, some of which suffered as many as ten direct hits. Another smaller, but more accurate barrage was launched four seconds later. This one caught the four remaining enemy choppers that were supposed to be harassing Hunter.

In a matter of twenty-two seconds, it was over. All ten Hinds were destroyed, leaving ten individual flaming wrecks on flat desert on either side of the slowly moving train.

It was a display that gave even a veteran like Hunter pause. In the previous enemy aerial attacks, the confined spaces of the mountains and forests had prevented the air-defense computers from formulating such an awesome fusillade of SAMs.

But in the wide-open spaces, the system had performed to perfection.

As the train increased speed and disappeared into the night, Hunter swept over the wrecks of the Hinds, double-checking that there were no survivors.

Then, just as he was about to head back for the train to land, his inner sense told him to proceed farther up the track instead, that something would be found there.

He had relied too long on his instincts to question them; besides, since his strange meditative period had ended, his instincts seemed to have come back in line. So, after radioing his intentions back to Fitz, he throttled up and sped ahead of the *Freedom Express*.

At a point about twenty miles from the train, his sixth sense began buzzing once again. There was something below, in the narrow pass that carried the tracks between two bare desert hills. It was not a threat; the *feeling* was telling him something different.

He put the AV-8 into a hover and set it down about fifty yards from the pass. Retrieving his M-16 and his infra-red NightScope goggles, he double-timed it to the tracks and then carefully walked into the pass itself.

Something happened here, his senses were telling him.

He slowed his pace a little as he reached the middle of the pass, scanning its sheer walls with the infra-red glasses.

He saw nothing until he turned the slight bend in the tracks.

An instant later, he found what he was looking for.

There were 24 of them in all. They were hanging from ten separate gallows, their rickety remains flowing gently in the light desert night breeze. They were skeletons rather than bodies, and each one had a dagger sticking out of its ribcage.

"So this is how far they got," he whispered. "Their nightmare ended here."

There was little sense in inspecting the corpses. He didn't need a close-up look to know that he'd just discovered the remains of the Modern Pioneers.

Chapter 56

Los Angeles

Nick "Red" Banner, LA's leading newsman, had just finished eating his dinner in his plush apartment's dining room when he heard the first air raid siren go off.

Like just about everyone else in the city, the KOAS-TV anchorman thought the alarms had gone off either by mistake or as part of some kind of a test. Unconcerned, Banner poured himself a brandy, switched his telephone back to ON and settled in front of his large screen TV, intent on watching a videotape of his broadcast earlier that day.

He had just started the replay when his phone rang. Taking a sip of brandy, he answered it in his deep, affected anchorman voice.

"Nick Banner here . . ."

"For Christ's sake, Nick!" the man's voice on the other end screamed. "Where the hell you been?"

He immediately recognized the voice of his boss, KOAS station manager, Wild Bill Austin.

"I've been right here," Banner answered quickly.

"With your goddamn phone switched off?" Austin raged. "You know that's against company policy."

"Why, yes, it was off," Banner stuttered, knowing full well that Austin was the only person who could actually fire him. "Well, actually it's been broken . . . going off and on, and—"

"Don't give me that bullshit, Banner," Austin interrupted him fiercely. "Have you taken a goddamn look out of your window?"

"I'm sorry, Bill," Banner replied. "I'm having trouble hearing you over these damn sirens. They must be testing them or something. What did you say?"

"You idiot!" Austin raged back at him. "I said take a goddamn look out of your window! You're missing the biggest story in years!"

Banner yanked on the phone's cord and slowly walked to his porch window. He lived on the 38th floor of a luxurious high-rise right in downtown LA, and as such had an expansive view of the city.

Drawing back the heavy drapes, Banner walked out onto the porch and peered out on the semi-soggy metropolis.

And instant later, he wet his pants.

"Jesus Christ!" he yelled. *"We're under attack!"*

As Banner clenched his sopping wet crotch, he watched in absolute terror as at least a dozen jet fighter-bombers screeched over the city, dropping bombs, firing missiles and strafing indiscriminately. The air raid sirens were now blaring at full pitch, and several SAMs could be seen streaking up from the outskirts of the city.

"Banner! *Banner!*" Austin was screaming from the other end of the phone. But Big Red was not in any condition to speak coherently.

He had just barely gotten over the shock of the crash of the Modern Pioneers train several weeks before and now this!

"Who . . . what . . ." he babbled into the phone.

"Spoken like a true journalist!" Austin roared. "We don't know who in Christ they are! But I want you to get your ass down to this station right now. We've got to go on the air with this, and you got to do it!"

"But . . . how . . . when . . ."

At this point, Banner was even having problems spitting out syllables. A whole newscast might be out of the question.

Suddenly one of the raiding jets flashed right over his building, emitting a terrifying shriek and rocking the high-rise like an earthquake.

The next moment, Banner found himself on the floor of

his living room, praying that (A) he wouldn't die and (B) his body functions wouldn't commit open revolt.

But the only answer to his prayers was the sound of even louder sirens, more screaming jet engines and more bombs going off.

Then, amongst the racket, he heard someone pounding on his door.

Thinking it was some kind of rescue team, Banner leapt to open it, stained pants and all.

Total incontinence hit when he found three heavily armed men in Nazi uniforms waiting on the other side.

"You're coming with us," one of the men said before slugging Red in the temple, knocking him cold.

All the while Austin was screaming from the other end of the now-abandoned phone. "Banner? *Banner!* Are you still there?"

Captain Crunch O'Malley of the Ace Wrecking Company landed his F-4X Super Phantom at the main base of the Republic of California's Air Force, not quite believing his eyes.

Part of the air base—formerly known as LAX—was in flames, and there were at least three burning jet fighters on its auxiliary runway. He taxied around one wreck, nothing through the flames and smoke that it was an F-101 Voodoo, and pulled up to a stop in front of his assigned hangar. His partner, Captain Elvis Q, was waiting for him there.

"What the hell happened?" was Crunch's first question.

"Air raid," Elvis replied in his authentic Southern drawl. "They hit us right after seven; snuck up on us real good. Came in over the ocean. Voodoos mostly. A bunch of them launched a few Mavericks to keep us busy here, while another bunch bombed the city itself."

"Christ, who were they?" Crunch asked, removing his helmet and rubbing his neck from his long flight.

"Still checking," Elvis replied.

The air raid was just another bit of strangeness for the Wreckers. Although the distances involved had kept him and Elvis out of the direct action around the train as of late, they had been doing nightly recon missions over Arizona and western New Mexico, trying to spot any Burning Cross troop concentrations.

"Did the city's air defenses work?" Crunch wanted to know. "Did anyone scramble to meet them?"

Elvis nodded. "It was a quick hit-and-run attack," he said. "But the Coasters were able to launch a half dozen F-5's. They iced one Voodoo right over our heads. That's the one burning way out there. SAMs got the other two here, and I hear the inner city AA and SAM guys got another two. It was noisy, but overall the damage both here and in the city was very light."

Crunch rubbed his weary eyes, his brain flashing all the implications of the air raid. "You know why Devillian is pulling this crap now, don't you?" he asked Elvis.

The younger man nodded. "Sure do," he replied. "He knows that once the train is in range of the fighters here, we can escort the thing through west Arizona and make it a lot harder for him to attack it full force."

"Right," Crunch replied. "But now, with this new air raid stuff, he knows the Coasters will have to keep some of their fighters at home, just in case the Voodoos come back."

"He's not only crazy," Elvis said, as they walked toward the base's debriefing room, "he's smart, too."

"That's the worst kind of animal," Crunch told him.

Twenty minutes later, they were sitting in the debriefing room with three officers from the California Air Force.

On the TV screen in front of them, a videotape retrieved from Crunch's recon pod was just beginning.

"Everything is as it should be," Crunch said as a burst of static introduced the tape. "Just like Hawk predicted, I found twelve holes in the ground just north of Chihuahua."

The tape's static cleared up and quickly became focused. It depicted first, the vast reaches of the Mexican desert near Sierra del Nido from a height of forty-two thousand feet, and then after a long zoom-in, the mountainous area north of the mostly abandoned city of Chihuahua.

"There's the first one," Crunch said. "See it?"

Elvis squinted and soon saw a light stream of smoke rising from the desert floor.

"And the second," Crunch went on. "And the third. . . ."

By this time the other officers saw the columns of smoke as well.

"Twelve F-4's took off from the mesa," Crunch said. "Twelve auger in three hundred and fifty miles due south."

"Well, he was right again," Elvis said, picking up the rest of the smoke columns. "If this were peacetime, our old buddy Hawk could be rich just from gambling."

They slowed the tape and zoomed in closer on the dozen spirals of smoke, all that was left of the Skinhead squadron.

It was the titanium oxide that had done the job. The weird little chemical had effectively turned the twelve F-4's into time bombs, just waiting for the right moment to go off. When mixed with JP-8 jet fuel, TO added just enough instability to the volatile mix to begin a break-down of the fuel's molecules. Working mostly on the kerosenelike base of JP-8, just a touch of the TO turned the jet fuel into a completely new mixture, one that actually raised the temperature of fuel proportionally until it quite literally blew itself up. Not only that, but the time of the reaction could be determined right down to the last minute.

"It must have been quite a shock to them when their airplanes just started going up around them," Elvis said. "Well, at least we won't have to worry about them anymore."

"Yeah, those boneheads really fell for it," Crunch said. "When it came right down to it, they were more concerned with saving their own asses than anything else. But I would have felt a whole lot better about it if this air raid thing had never happened."

Elvis nodded glumly. "Kind of changes the whole equation, doesn't it?"

Chapter 57

It was close to six AM when word reached the *Freedom Express* that LA had been bombed that previous evening.

The crew of the train had just completed a sobering ceremony next to the freshly dug graves of the two dozen Modern Pioneers, when a series of messages came over the scrambler telex.

The first message detailed the air raid, its damage, the number of raiders shot down and a preliminary report that the Voodoos were owned by a notorious southern air pirate band run by a former drug-running pilot named Riggs.

The second communiqué reported Crunch's discovery of the destroyed Skinhead squadron.

"Will we ever catch a break on this one?" Fitz asked, as he read the reports over for the third time. "No sooner do we get rid of those Skinhead bums than a new bunch takes their place."

Hunter too was momentarily disheartened. With the Skinheads gone and many of Devillian's Mirages and Soviet aircraft destroyed in the Santa Fe air strike, he had hoped that the Burning Cross's air support would be at a minimum once the train reached the Grand Canyon.

But now it appeared that this would not be the case.

"The only bright spot is that these air pirates are probably undertrained as compared to the Skinheads," he said. "If they've thrown in with Devillian — which it appears that they have — they might be a little easier to handle when the time comes. But not much."

"Devillian's got to be hopping mad over the fact that the Skins deserted him," Cobra Brother Jesse Tyler said.

278

"He probably doesn't even realize that we just did him the favor of icing the bastards."

"That appears to be true," Fitz said, reading a new report as it clicked over the telex. "This is from Bad River's guys down near the mesa. They say that Devillian's own chopper was spotted leaving the place early this morning. He had an escort of Hinds with him, and fighter contrails were also spotted overhead."

"If past performance is any indication, Devillian's probably on board," Tyler said. "They're so short of fuel I can't imagine anyone just taking the SOB's personal gunship up for just a joyride."

Hunter nodded gloomily. "He's making his move."

Chapter 58

Red Banner was terrified.

He'd been beaten and chained by the three men in Nazi uniforms. Yet the worst torture of all for him was the frightening helicopter ride he had been forced to endure shortly after his abduction. Following the flight he'd taken the day the Modern Pioneers train crashed into the LA Amtrak station, Banner had an addendum written into his contract at KOAS-TV that he would never have to fly while on duty again. Being the station's senior on-air man, the management agreed, and Banner was positive that he would never leave *terra firma* again.

But his mysterious kidnappers had changed that.

After being spirited away from his high-rise, his abductors, practically oblivious to the air raid going on all around them, pummeled him for several minutes and then threw him into the trunk of a car. Roaring off into the night, they drove at break-neck speed for more than three hours.

When they finally stopped and pulled him out, it was close to midnight. They were in an isolated canyon that might have been near Topanga, but Banner had been too frightened to even get his bearings. At this point, he was clubbed briefly with what looked to be pool sticks.

He was then thrown into a sack, and minutes later he heard the dreadful sound of the helicopter approaching. Through a pinhole in the bag, he saw that the aircraft was a cleverly disguised version of a regular LA militia chopper. Banner vomited heavily at this point, so certain that the strange men in Nazi uniforms were about to drop him into the Pacific Ocean.

Instead, he stayed sick for the next five hours as the helicopter made its way south and east, setting down frequently in order to dodge the Coaster militia's air patrols.

When the chopper finally reached its destination and Banner was unleashed from the bag, it was morning, and he was standing on the edge of the Grand Canyon.

He vomited once again, his condition hardly being helped by the several swift kicks to the stomach he received courtesy of the man dressed in the very ornate Nazi uniform. Then he was blindfolded, dragged up a hill for about an eighth of a mile and at some point thrown into a small pool of water, which though muddy, did serve to wash away the more disgusting stains from his clothes.

Still blindfolded, he then was force marched for about fifteen minutes. When his captors finally removed the cloth from his eyes, he was astonished to see that he was in the middle of what looked like a cross between a military encampment and a movie set.

Some sort of a lecture was going on not far away, and his guards eventually kicked him in that direction. They met a tall, blond, very German-looking man who was covered in bandages about his head and shoulders.

One of the men addressed this man as Major Heck.

"This is the newsman," the other told Heck. "He threw up the entire way here."

The Nazi officer looked at Banner and sneered. "Typical," he said.

"What . . . what do you want with me?" Banner was surprised to hear himself ask.

The Nazi officer smiled, though obviously it pained him to do so.

"You are a guest of the Burning Cross," he told Banner with fake politeness. "You are a newsman, and we are about to create one of the biggest news events of all time. We want you to report it."

"But I'm not a *reporter*," Banner replied weakly, thinking he might have suddenly found a loophole out of his predicament. "I've never taken a journalism course in my entire life."

Heck looked at him angrily. "You are on TV reporting the news, no?" he asked.

"*Reading* the news," Banner corrected him. "I've never actually written a news story. I don't even know how to type!"

Heck turned to the three kidnappers. "Did we get the right man?"

As one, the three men nodded. "Yes, sir," one said. "This is the guy that Devillian showed us on the tape. He's supposed to be the most watched newsman in LA."

Heck turned back to Banner. "This is true?" he asked, fingering his sidearm. "If not, you die here."

Banner recognized the man's pistol as a .45 automatic and quickly changed his tune.

"It *is* true," Banner assured him. "More people watch me than any of those other guys combined. I even pull better ratings than our weatherman."

The boast was completely lost on Heck.

"You are here to report a story," he said through gritted teeth to Banner. "We have a camera crew for you, and a satellite dish which will feed pictures back to your station in LA."

Banner began stumbling around for the right words.

"I don't know what you guys have in mind," he said, once again eyeing the elaborate camp. "But have you cleared all this with KOAS? I mean, they won't run just *anything.*"

Heck slapped him once, hard across the cheek.

"We are about to make history here!" he screamed at Banner. "Believe me, they will not only put it all on the air, they will show the movie once it is finished."

The slap had knocked Banner nearly unconscious. Still, he somehow was able to cough out one last question.

"You mean you guys are making a movie, too?" he croaked.

On the other side of the encampment, Duke Devillian

adjusted his fiery red beret and then snapped his leather horse whip.

"This is it," he told himself out loud. "This is the first day of the rest of my life."

Two quick tokes from his crack pipe and he bounded out of the circus-size tent that served as his temporary headquarters and onto a wooden stage that had been erected at the edge of one of the canyon walls.

Before him was an audience of about fifty men—officers of the Burning Cross as well as representatives from the various mercenary groups that made up the bulk of his army.

They gave him a polite round of applause, and then he spoke:

"As you all know, today we are about to embark on our greatest adventure," he began, virtually repeating the speech given to practically the same audience back at the mesa a few days before. "And it is an opportunity given to us by those preposterous heroes who even as we speak are heading this way on that train of theirs.

"Today, gentlemen, we are going to change the path of this country. We are going to finally put an end to all this mamby-pamby talk about the mixing of the races, the love of all men, that all men were created equal. After tomorrow, there won't be a single person left in this country who doesn't know what the Burning Cross stands for."

With a drug-induced flair, Devillian dramatically pulled back the curtain that was hiding a large easel in the center of the stage.

"Tomorrow . . ." she intoned, "we begin the new era of a pure, all-white America!"

Written across the top of the large white pad being held by the easel were the words *"Ten Miles to Hell,* a Duke Devillian/Burning Cross Production."

Devillian cleared his throat and began strutting up and down the stage.

"It is time for a review, gentlemen," he said. "Our plan is to fight a battle here along the southern rim of the canyon that will be viewed by a large number of citizens of this country. Just like the politicians in the pre-war days, we must adhere to the fact that TV and the filmed image are what make people pay attention—*actions,* not words, are what make people take notice.

"And that's what our production tomorrow will have: Action! Also adventure, realism, thrills and chills. In short, we will create the world's largest action, adventure, splatter/slasher/snuff film of all time. And of course our production will have a moral—which is, that White is right.

"This creation will be our tool. Anyone who sees it—just like anyone who saw *Triumph of the Will*—will be convinced that we *are* right, that *we* are the future of this country. That we are the power! And they will accept this, whether it takes one viewing or a hundred viewings!"

By this time, most of the people in the audience were convinced that Devillian had finally gone off the deep end.

Not only was the man repeating parts of the same old speeches he'd been peppering them with for days, but even the crudest air pirate leaders saw that the cross-eyed terrorist was swinging in and out of reality, one second imagining himself to be some kind of Hollywood mogul, the next the commander of the dangerously large entity called the Burning Cross. Not a few of them were wishing they were someplace else.

But they had little choice but to sit and listen. They were a captive audience in all respects, a fact driven home by the large number of Devillian's personal bodyguards surrounding the small open-air stage. It was also well known that with the defection of the Skinheads, Devillian was even more inclined to turn his wrath against any ally who showed less than dedicated enthusiasm.

The supremacist leader turned back to the easel and indicated a large map of a nearby section of the Grand Canyon rim that had been drawn in multi-colored crayons.

"Now, as you all know by now, all of our troops have been deployed along this ten-mile stretch of track," he

284

continued. "The United Americans' train has no choice but to pass through here, and we'll have every weapons system in our combined arsenals waiting for it. For those bleeding hearts, this stretch of track will truly be *Ten Miles to Hell*.

"Along with a myriad of gun posts and so on, we have stationed literally dozens of movie cameras as well as video machines. These will insure that every second of action is captured for posterity. Every moment of the fighting will be recorded on film and on video.

"Now, the video portion of the battle will be immediately beamed up to a working satellite and directed to the largest TV station in LA. They will have no other choice but to put it on the air because their citizens have been following the progress of this wretched train for days, wondering if it will make it to the West Coast. Well, gentlemen, it won't—and we will have a fully documented video broadcast as evidence as to why this insane *Freedom Express* mission failed. We have even retained the services of one of LA's best-known newsmen, and he will be describing the action for the large viewing audience out on the coast.

"We will also be filming the action in wide-screen 35-millimeter, courtesy of our friends from the New Holy Roman Empire. You can see that they've been working very hard up here setting up their lights and cameras and so on. Later on, when our Roman friends develop and edit this film, we will distribute it to anyone and everyone who wants a copy, so that you can see once again the defeat of these United American dreamers. I predict here and now it will be one of the most-watched films of all time.

"So that once again, gentlemen, is our plan."

There was an eerie silence as the officers in the audience tried to make some sense out of this, just one of a series of Devillian's strange performances. Were they discussing a battle or a movie? No one was quite sure.

Suddenly one of the bodyguards began clapping. Then another joined in, and another and another. Soon the audience of officers was clapping too, harder and harder so as not to upset their leader.

When the somewhat reluctant applause finally died down, a number of Burning Cross lieutenants made their way through the audience, distributing small booklets marked "Shooting Schedule." Inside the book were instructions for each unit of the Burning Cross and how they would play their roles during the production.

"In conclusion . . ." Devillian yelled in order to regain the attention of his audience, "we are looking for everyone to play their part when the time comes. We expect the train to pass through here as fast as it can. But the way we have laid out our gun posts and so on, our intent will be to gradually slow it down, thereby creating the tension as well as the momentum that every great production of this type must have.

"We estimate that by the time the train reaches the last few miles of the ten-mile stretch, it will be so battered and damaged that we will then be able to apply the *coup de grace,* so to speak. This is why the majority of our fixed cameras will be located around Mile Six through Mile Ten.

"I can also tell you that we have a number of surprises cooked up—as contingencies arise—plus a secret grand finale that you won't want to miss."

This pronouncement was met with only scattered applause and a barrage of baffled stares.

"Now, I do want to make a very special introduction at this point," Devillian said, feeling that he was losing the audience ever so slightly. "I want to call someone up on stage here with me. Someone who has contributed mightily to this effort.

"Let's have a big round of applause for Major Heck of the late, great Twisted Cross!"

Despite his injuries and bandages, Heck ran up to the stage with the enthusiasm of a game show contestant.

Joining Devillian at center stage, Heck saluted and bowed, bathed in the loud, bodyguard-directed applause.

Devillian laughed and, putting his arm around the German, asked the audience: "He's a heck of a guy, isn't he?"

Few people got the joke, but they clapped anyway, ever wary of the dozens of bodyguards' guns that were close to being leveled at them.

Devillian went on: "I just want to say that Major Heck here has been given a very special place in the production tomorrow. He will be in charge of the opening sequence, which every buff knows is the most important part of any production.

"I would also like to say to him and to you, Good luck and don't screw it up."

There was yet another round of enforced applause. Then Devillian took one long bow and yelled:

"We begin shooting at daybreak tomorrow!"

Chapter 59

Juanita Juarez awoke with a start.

For a moment she didn't know where she was. The dilapidated ceiling above her was cracked and peeling, and the bed smelled of mildew and dust. It was raining outside—hard and cold—and through the yellow-stained window next to her bed she could see the runny outlines of pine trees swaying in a heavy wind.

It was late afternoon, and she had just had a dream in which she was a movie star who became fabulously wealthy and famous only to be shot by one of her admiring fans. The weird twist was the actual shooting was filmed before a large audience who seemed to enjoy it each time a bullet hit her—in slow motion, appropriately enough.

It was slowly coming back to her now. Her middle-of-the-night flight from Santa Fe, just one step ahead of Devillian's men—or so she supposed. It had been that man who caused it all—that mysterious stranger who claimed he was Hawk Hunter. She didn't know whether she believed that or not; all she *did* know was that he had the power to put her into a sexual trance so deep, she would have revealed anything and everything to him just upon his request. That hot night in her apartment, she had told him the most dangerous thing of all: what she knew about Devillian's plans for the train.

Spilling the information was akin to putting a death sentence on her own head. She knew that eventually she would have to pay for it, thus her decision to flee Santa Fe and go north, bound for a place she wasn't sure even existed—but knowing that if it did, she would be safe, at least temporarily.

Someone stirred beside her; it was the pilot. She didn't even know his name, but that didn't matter. He was serving his purpose, which was getting her out of Santa Fe and eventually up into Free Canada, all in return for unlimited sex.

That was fine with Juanita. She didn't mind playing the harlot in exchange for a good chance of escape.

The pilot woke up, and he too seemed to have trouble remembering where he was. He turned and saw her, and this was the trigger back to daytime reality.

"How much farther is it?" she asked, pulling up the coarse army blanket to her breasts, modestly covering them.

"To the border? About another day and a half," he replied. "We still have to keep up our front by flying low and slow, like the lumber jocks do. Once we reach Free Canada, I figure another day, that is if you are sure where the hell this place is we're going."

"Just get me in the general area," Juanita said. "I'll find it."

"You're the boss," the pilot replied with a lecherous smile.

"Then, we must leave soon," she told him.

He yawned and stretched and looked out of the stained window of the small, dusty mountain cabin.

"We ain't going nowhere in this weather," he said. "Not for a while anyway." He reached over and pulled the blanket away from her naked body. "Besides, I always get paid in advance."

She didn't fight it. She simply laid back and let him have his way with her. It was over fairly quickly; coincidently, the rain outside stopped at just about the same time.

They rose, and Juanita lit the old stove and heated up the pot of leftover coffee. The pilot, still wearing a wide grin, embraced her like a newlywed husband would his wife on their first day back from the honeymoon, but Juanita quickly brushed him aside.

289

"Get your machine ready for take-off," she ordered. "I want to leave as soon as possible."

The pilot just laughed and put on his jacket. "OK — like I said, you're the boss," he replied. "And I mean that as a compliment. I actually like this arrangement. It sure beats the assholes I was working for a few days ago. They had plenty of money, but I was looking over my shoulder every second, thinking some fighter plane was about to burn my ass."

"You were carrying some precious cargo then, too?" she asked him, more out of boredom than anything else.

"Just something wrapped up in a big white canvas tarp," he said, zipping up his jacket. "Never did find out what it was, and I wasn't about to ask any questions. But as soon as I dropped it off, I just wanted to get as far away from DC and the Northeast as possible. That's how I happened to go to Santa Fe — heard that people in my line of work could make some, well, 'profitable arrangements' down that way. And I guess I heard right."

With that, he squeezed her buttocks once more, walked out the door, and headed for the huge blue and green Sky Crane helicopter that was parked in a field nearby.

Chapter 60

The *Freedom Express* crossed the border from New Mexico into Arizona with anti-climactic ease.

Roaring along miles-long, straight-as-arrow stretches of track, the train passed through the territories of De Chelly, Black Mesa and Hopi without incident. However, the relative smoothness of the train's dash west was contrasted by the bits of information that flowed from the train's scramble telex with disturbing frequency.

Hunter and Fitz had been monitoring the communiqués from Washington throughout the afternoon and into the night. First came the follow-up report on the LA air raid. The LA militia was able to confirm the Voodoos were part of a pirate gang linked to the Burning Cross. At the same time, the militia had informed Jones that they would have to station two squadrons of their F-5's around the city to protect against further raids. This meant that only twelve of the LA fighters would be available to fly cover for the *Freedom Express* once it passed into their operating range, which was an invisible point located at about the halfway point of Arizona.

Hunter knew the decision to keep two thirds of the Coasters' fighters in LA was a sound and logical one, but that didn't make it any less painful to accept that the air cover the train had been counting on for the climactic trip through Arizona would be cut drastically. This was especially true since another communiqué had told them that the information Hunter had received from his second visit with Juanita—that the Burning Cross's major build-up was being planned for a ten-mile stretch on the southern rim of the Grand Canyon—was proving quite true. High-flying, infra-red-equipped recon planes flying out of LA and Dodge City confirmed that the massive Burning Cross troop concentration that had eluded them for so long had finally appeared in the area at the south of the canyon, beginning on the morning before. Apparently the enemy troops had been streaming into the area for the past week, in groups too small to register on the infra-red, heat-detecting devices being carried by the recon planes. But now that the train was approaching the area, and all other routes to the north, south and east of them had been destroyed, there was no point in concealing the massive enemy build-up any further. In fact, in the words of one of the recon pilots, there were so many enemy troops located in the area, it was almost like they were "flaunting it."

"All this way," Hunter sighed, "just for us to meet them along a ten-mile stretch of track."

"It does seem a bit ridiculous," Fitz agreed. "If we can arrange a miracle and somehow make it through them, then we win. But if they stop us—they'll be so powerful, it will be impossible to prevent them from taking over the whole country if they want to."

"And I'm sure they do," Hunter replied.

Fitz poured them both a cup of coffee and added a generous splash of bourbon to each.

"We've been through many a critical situation," he said a bit wistfully. "But I can't shake the fact that we may have jumped into this one without looking."

"I disagree," Hunter said, sipping his liquor-laced java. "If we hadn't confronted Devillian now, it would have been worse as the months went on. He would have gathered more strength, more mercenaries. He would be even stronger than he is now. Then it would be a near impossibility to get rid of him.

"No, Mike—maybe I'm being foolish, but I see this trip as something that we were meant to do. Win or lose, it's like we're holding the magic sword that has the opportunity to slay the beast with one thrust. The heart of this twisted bastard's way of thinking is lying out there waiting for us. All we have to do is get through that stretch, and he'll fall apart like a house of cards."

Fitz smiled for the first time in what felt like years.

"I admire your optimism, Hawker," he said. "The question is, can we do it?"

Another hour passed, and by midnight they were deep into Arizona, passing by the area known as Moenkopi.

Suddenly their scramble radio started beeping, presaging a report from the Cobra Brothers, who were flying lookout about twenty miles ahead of the train.

"Stop now!" was the urgent message from Captain Tyler. "You won't believe what's waiting for us up ahead."

A half hour later, Hunter and Fitz landed the Harrier next to the two Cobra gunships which were parked atop a high butte just south of a place called Tuba City.

The train had stopped about fifteen miles from this point on the suggestion of Tyler. Now, as Hunter and Fitz climbed out of the jumpjet, they could see why Tyler had urged them to halt so quickly.

Gazing down into a small valley in front of them, Hunter could see the tracks stretched in a straight line for at least twenty-five miles, and to the casual observer, it appeared that nothing was wrong up ahead. But then, on Tyler's direction, he studied the tracks through his NightScope glasses. What he saw simultaneously baffled and even amused him.

"I can't believe this," he said. "Either we're all seeing things or Devillian is off his rocker more than we think."

Lined up along a mile stretch of the straightaway was a series of red brick walls.

"He is nuts," Fitz declared, getting an eyeful through his own night goggles. "I've heard of blocking the tracks with trees or boulders or blowing them with explosives. But building—let's see I count thirty-six—*brick* walls? What's the point of that?"

Hunter studied the obstructions closely. "I think we're looking at something that's more than meets the eye," he said, somewhat mysteriously.

Then he turned to Tyler and said, "Let's go down and take a closer look."

It was a brief trip down off the butte to the first wall.

Hunter and Tyler landed about fifty yards away from the barrier and carefully climbed out of the Cobra, their weapons drawn. Meanwhile, Fitz and Crockett kept watch in the other Cobra which was circling overhead.

The first thing Hunter saw were wires. They were running every which way alongside the tracks, stretching from the first brick wall off into the desert. He fingered the first set he could get a hold of and saw that they were actually of different types and gauges. One was a thick co-axial cable, which could be used to transmit TV signals; another was typical silver-gold speaker wire, a heftier version of what would be used on a home stereo unit. Still another was a simple outdoor electrical cable which presumably would carry power to what was actually running the other two.

Finally they slowly approached the first wall itself. It was well-constructed—or so it appeared from a distance of about twenty feet in the darkness. Each brick was bright red with the mortar between being of even brighter white, almost a luminescent pearl in color.

For a brick wall, it looked perfect—too perfect.

Hunter stepped up close to it, and like the famous monkey in the movie *2001*, he touched the brick with his ungloved fingers.

"Just like I thought," he said, turning to Tyler.

The Cobra captain mimicked Hunter's action, running his fingers along the bricks.

"I'll be damned" was all he could say.

Hunter then drew back his fist and punched the wall with all his might, an action that seemed likely to break his hand.

But it didn't. Instead, like an optical illusion, a section of the wall collapsed into dust and paper. In reality, the wall was nothing more than an elaborate-looking movie prop.

"This is very strange," Tyler said with appropriate

understatement.

They called up to Cobra Two, and soon Fitz and Crockett were also standing next to the ersatz wall.

"What the hell is the point of this?" Fitz asked, punching out a piece of the wall himself.

Hunter followed the band of wires that led underneath the track past the wall and into the desert. They ended in a cemented-over hole about twenty feet off to the left of the track.

"These wires are some kind of trigger device I would think," he said. "But what they do exactly, I can't imagine. Unless . . ."

With that he walked back about fifteen paces, and then, to the amazement of the other three, took a running start and crashed into the fake wall.

Suddenly it was as if a bomb had gone off. No sooner had Hunter broken through the paper mache barrier—causing it to collapse in a great cloud of smoke—than the immediate area was rocked by the roar of an explosion.

Or actually what sounded like an explosion.

Instinctively all four men hit the ground. Yet just as they did, they realized their reaction was not necessary. The sound hadn't been caused by an explosion at all. Rather the force of Hunter hitting the wall had triggered a hidden recording device which in turn blasted out a sound effect of an enormous explosion. Combined with the fake smoke that burst from the paper wall when Hunter crashed through it, the overall effect of a brick wall exploding looked and sounded very convincing.

"God, can this get any weirder?" Tyler exclaimed.

"Don't ask," Hunter replied.

"What is this all about?" Crockett asked. "Fake walls. Smoke bombs. Sound effects? . . ."

"I think it's just what it appears to be," Hunter said. "It's all for the benefit of a camera—or many cameras. There are probably a bunch of them hidden out in the desert—ready to take movies when we come barreling through here."

"So what now?" Fitz asked. "Obviously this isn't meant to stop us."

"Hell, we call up the train and break through it," Hunter said. "We know that Devillian is caught up in this weirdo film-making thing. So screw it. Let him get his jollies. We've got more important things to do than figure out just what the hell this all means."

As they walked back to the choppers, Tyler put the whole thing into perspective.

"God, they even have *us* playing a part in all this," he said.

No more than thirty minutes later, the *Freedom Express* screamed down the straightaway and burst through the line of fake walls, triggering row after row of smoke bombs, sound effects and hidden video cameras, which recorded the entire event.

Fifty miles away, Duke Devillian was sitting in his enormous headquarters tent, one young girl's head between his legs, another at his toes, a huge crack pipe in one hand, and a massive bottle of champagne in the other. Before him was a large video screen on which he was watching the telecast of the *Freedom Express* bursting through the line of fake walls.

"Stupendous!" he screamed as the walls disintegrated in a cloud of fire and smoke. Combined with the realistic sound effects, it was all very convincing. Even the normally sedate Tony Three, sitting nearby, was bowled over by the footage.

"It's so fucking symbolic I could just about crap my pants," the Roman cried out. "I can't wait to see what they do when they reach the Desert Point View Bridge. If your Nazi go-boy Heck doesn't fuck it up, it should give us some great stuff for the opening credits."

Devillian swigged his champagne, drunkenly letting most of it dribble down his unwashed face.

"Props now," he said, forcing the girl between his legs closer to the action. "Real stuff later."

Chapter 61

Near Desert Point View Bridge, Arizona

Major Heck wished he'd brought along at least a dozen amphetamine tablets; as it was, he'd only been able to scrounge three speed pills since midnight.

So he'd been drinking coffee, gulping down the only buzz-producing alternative left to him, as he watched the Burning Cross's sapper unit wire the Desert View Point Bridge with Devillian's own brand of explosives. It was three hours before the dawn of the day that Devillian had guaranteed all of them would change the history of the world.

"History!" Heck grumbled, as he finished his fourth cup of coffee and quickly drew another. "Nothing more than the distillation of rumor."

Still, he knew at this point, he had no choice but to follow Devillian's wishes. The only reason the numerically superior Burning Cross had let the train come so far without destroying it completely was to allow it to reach this point—the entrance to the southern rim of the Grand Canyon. From here it would be a simple matter of disposing of the train and all aboard via Devillian's carefully orchestrated production.

Trouble was, Heck hated movies.

"Done," the young lieutenant told him after climbing up the small hill next to the bridge where Heck had been monitoring their task.

Heck let out a long low breath and threw away the remainder of his coffee. He was glad to hear the six-hour effort to wire the bridge was nearing an end.

"Is it all checked and grounded?" Heck asked.

"It is all checked, grounded and *re*-checked," the young officer replied. "The sensors are all set. Just as soon as the first locomotive trips the electric eye — well, that's when it all goes."

Heck was tempted to bum a speed pill from the man, but thought better of it. Instead he told him, "Do you realize that if all that stuff doesn't go off at exactly the right moment, Devillian will have us all ground up as meat for his dogs."

The man gulped loudly. "I do, sir," the man replied slowly. "And while I'm confident in our job, I believe I'll go down there and check it all once again."

Throughout the night, more of Devillian's soldiers moved into positions near Desert Point View Bridge.

Heck knew with the dawn less than three hours away — and the arrival of the train possibly just an hour beyond that — he would be wise to check on the progress of their deployment.

For the most part, these particular troops were drawn from the Burning Cross's mountain units. Experts in setting up ambushes, the troops had established positions in the rocks on both sides of the tracks just beyond the bridge.

Heck walked by most of these positions, checking those he could see with the aid of a flashlight. A typical gun post was made up of four men. Two were armed with high-powered infra-red/telescopic-aided rifles, the third was in charge of a small mortar complete with a dozen illuminating rounds.

The fourth man squeezed into the gun position was, in most cases, a cameraman.

It took Heck thirty minutes in all to check the majority of the positions, stopping at each one and offering several words of praiseless advice such as "Don't fuck this up or Devillian will do an autopsy on

298

you—while you're still alive."

At the end of this inspection, Heck returned to his own position and poured out yet another cup of coffee, unaware that just twenty-five yards away, two Piute scouts were watching his every move.

It was three AM when the radio console inside the Control car started to buzz.

The railway was crowded with officers of the Football City Rangers, as well as Hunter, Fitz, the newly returned Crossbow and Jesse Tyler of the Cobra Brothers. They had just gotten a report from Crockett in the other Cobra that two of Devillian's warplanes had bombed the trackbed twenty miles back, further sealing off the train from any possible reverse-gear escape route.

Tyler answered the radio on the second buzz. It was Bad River himself on the other end of the line. Tyler took a quick message, then thanked the chief and hung up.

"More bad news," he announced to the others. "A couple Piute scouts just called Bad River to tell him that the Desert Point View Bridge has been wired."

"Damn . . ." Fitz said softly. "Are they really going to blow that bridge and trap us here on this side?"

"Either that or blow the bridge while we're going across," Tyler said. "Either way, we're screwed."

Hunter thought it over for a few moments then said, "This doesn't make sense. Why would he go through all the bullshit we know he's up to in the canyon, just to ice this one bridge and bring it all to a grinding halt—*before* the fact?"

It seemed as if it was a question with no answer.

"What can we do?" Crossbow asked. "With the track blown twenty miles back, we have no choice but to go forward."

"Well, we have one other option," Hunter said

quickly.

"Which is?" Fitz asked.

Hunter shrugged. "Go in and see what they've attached under that bridge."

Even the battle-hardened Fitzgerald immediately started shaking his head. "You've got to figure that the troops who planted the charges are keeping a close eye on it, Hawker," Fitz said. "It will be impossible to get anywhere near that span."

Hunter closed his eyes and thought a moment. Then he turned to Fitz and asked, "If we maintain this speed, how long before we reach the bridge?"

Fitz consulted a series of maps, then replied, "I'd say just before dawn—three hours from now at the very most."

"That should give us enough time, I think," Hunter said.

"Enough time for what?"

"To reach the bridge and find out what they're up to," Hunter answered matter-of-factly.

"But how?" Fitz asked. "Your airplane or a chopper would draw too much attention if you landed anywhere near the bridge. And approaching on foot is risky, because I'm sure Devillian has both sides of the river heavily guarded there. Not to mention that we don't have enough time to get there on foot."

"So there's only one way left," Hunter said, grabbing his crash helmet.

"I'm almost afraid to ask this," Fitz said. "But if it isn't by air or by ground, then what is it?"

Hunter just shrugged again. "By water, of course," he said.

The Little Colorado River was running fast—*too* fast—when Hunter and Fitz reached its banks less than an hour later.

They had hoped the river would be just like the

hundreds of peaceful meandering streams they'd passed in this part of the country—only bigger.

They were wrong.

One look told them the rapids in the river were treacherous.

"Always wanted to go white-water rafting," Hunter whispered sarcastically. "But this is ridiculous."

"Aye, and it will be damn cold if we have to go in," Fitz said.

Yet they both knew it was too late to turn back now.

They were traveling light, as per necessity. Being dropped by one of the Cobras a quarter mile away, they had to double-time it to the riverbank, carrying only one weapon apiece, plus an air pump and a folded rubber raft.

"Can this little dinghy take rushing water like this?" Fitz asked, concerned the rubber raft would explode with the water roaring by them so rapidly.

"I don't know," Hunter answered truthfully. "I didn't have time to read the directions."

It took about five minutes to inflate the raft, and another pair to assemble the enclosed oars, climb aboard and cast off.

In seconds they were traveling at high speed down the river, the rapids bouncing them up and down like a broken amusement ride. Instantly both men were soaked head to toe.

"*Jeesuz!*" Hunter yelled over the roar of rapids. "Shift this thing down into second gear will you?"

Fitz was trying to employ one of the oars to steer the dinghy toward the bridge, which was coming up on them very quickly. Yet both of them knew they were going much too fast to stop under the bridge—unless they collided with one of its supports, and that would mean disaster.

Yet Hunter knew that there was a chance they wouldn't have to stop. He had two theories on what was wired to the underside of the bridge. Proving

Theory Number One would involve stopping under the bridge—but at their present velocity that looked like an impossibility. Proving Number Two would be more of a gamble, but at that moment, it was the only option left.

"Hold it as steady as you can," he yelled back to Fitz, as the bridge loomed just an eighth of a mile in front of them.

"What are you going to do?" Fitz yelled ahead, getting a mouthful of water in the process.

Hunter didn't have time to answer. He knew that all he could do was attempt to snatch one of the packages as they sped past in the raft.

He stood up in the front of the boat and tried his best to see under the span. He squinted, adjusting his extraordinary eyesight while still trying to maintain his balance.

He pulled up his M-16 in his left hand just as they roared underneath the bridge. Then, in one swift motion, he was able to snag one of the many packages attached to the support beams with the snout of the rifle. Before they knew it, they were on the other side of the bridge and moving even more quickly due to the sudden narrowness of the river.

They proceeded to be propelled down the river and around a wide bend. Then, finally at that point, the river widened again and became more shallow, leading them to a relatively peaceful pool. Within a minute, they were drifting slowly to the shore.

Hunter was the first to jump onto the shore, reaching out to help Fitz do the same. Then, retrieving their weapons and the package from the raft, they punctured the dinghy with their knives and set it free, watching it sink in seconds.

"Any ancient proverbial sayings for that little adventure?" Fitz asked Hunter, already shivering in his soaked uniform.

"I'll get back to you on that," Hunter said, sitting

302

down on the small sandy beach and examining the satchel charge. "All right!" he yelled less than a half minute later. "I figured Devillian would do something screwy like this."

He turned to his friend, who was taking a nip of brandy from a small flask in an attempt to warm up, and pointed to the handful of words inked across the package's canvas outer lining.

"Glory be," Fitz said, passing the flask to Hunter. "This gets stranger and stranger."

Hunter took a huge swig of the brandy and then packed up the satchel and his rifle.

"We've got to get to that rendezvous point toot sweet," Hunter told Fitz. "Not only do we have to make sure the train goes across that bridge, we have to make sure it goes across at *full speed.*"

Chapter 62

One hour later

"Hit the deck!" shouted the Burning Cross soldier, getting ready to push down on the handle of the detonator. "It's going off in one minute."

The sun was just popping up over the eastern hills when the *Freedom Express* rumbled around the bend and onto the approach to the bridge. From his vantage point, Heck could see that all of the windows and openings on the railway cars were shuttered and locked, but he didn't have time to wonder how this would affect their impending action against the train.

He grabbed his walkie-talkie and pushed its ON button.

"Gun positions, ready?" he barked into it.

The inquiry was received with a quick sound off of the twenty-two gun nests on either side of the tracks.

"Mortar teams?"

This was answered by another twenty-two yeas.

"Cameras?" Heck heard himself yelling, feeling foolish as he did so.

The answer came back as twenty-two mumbled OKs.

"Thirty seconds!" the detonation officer yelled.

"Start cameras!" Heck yelled into his walkie-talkie.

But no sooner had he given the order than Heck knew something was wrong.

It was standard railway operating practice to slow a train's speed down to two-thirds whenever crossing a bridge or similar structure. Yet now, as Heck watched the approaching *Express* through his spyglasses, he realized the train was *increasing* its speed.

"Ten seconds!"

This is going all wrong, Heck thought, rapidly beginning to panic. He knew if the train didn't go across the bridge at a relatively slow speed, the whole operation at Desert Point View would be a bust.

"Five seconds!"

Heck didn't know what to do. They had to activate the charges, but. . . .

"Three . . . two . . . one . . . *now!"*

Suddenly the entire bridge was lit up in an incredible flash—so bright it turned the misty dawn into high noon. A half second later, there was the noise of an incredible explosion, so loud, it caused several large rocks to topple down the side of the small hill where Heck was located.

But the bridge did not crumble, collapse and go down with the speeding train on top. Rather it stayed completely intact—as it was supposed to. This was because the packages were not real explosives—as Hunter had found out shortly before.

Rather they had been flash explosions—fake bombs from a Hollywood special effects department. And just like the fake brick walls earlier, the noise of the "explosion" had actually been a loud recording, blared out over a large speaker at the pinnacle of Heck's hill.

The original plan had been two-fold. First, detonate the incredible flashes for the benefit of Devillian's camera crews and the loud boom for the necessary sound effect. At the same time, it was hoped the men driving the train would think the bridge was wired with *real* bombs, causing them to instinctively jam on the brakes which would, in turn, allow the men in the hills to fire on them with relative ease, their special targets being the train's many SAM cars.

But for some reason, the men on the train hadn't fallen for the hoax. The mile-long collection of locomotives and shuttered weapons cars roared through the false explosions and across the span at top speed, giving the gunmen in the hills a mere few seconds to open fire instead of the half minute or so that Heck had originally hoped to have it in his sights.

Within twenty seconds, the last of the train was across the bridge and winding its way out of sight, giving the Burning Cross cameramen only a handful of seconds of usable footage.

"What the *fuck* happened?" Duke Devillian roared at Heck as the German officer emerged a little shakily from his Hind helicopter just seconds after it had touched down at the Burning Cross main observation station.

"I don't know," Heck stammered. "They must have somehow figured out we wired the bridge with fake bombs."

"Well, that's pretty fucking obvious!" Devillian screamed, a script girl patting his forehead with a wet cloth. "No wonder you guys got your asses kicked down in Panama."

"What could I do about it?" Heck asked, finally snapping out at Devillian. "Only a fucking idiot would go through the trouble of wiring a bridge with fake bombs. In fact, only a *real* fucking idiot would have let that train come this far already!"

Immediately he knew his outburst would cost him his life.

"You're right," Devillian said to him in a strangely tranquil voice. "I *am* an idiot—for thinking that you could really pull it off. You fucking Germans . . . you screwed up two wars; you couldn't even hold on to one lousy canal. Some Master Race. You're just a bunch of fuck-ups."

"Nobody talks that way to me," Heck snarled, reaching for his revolver. Before the gun could clear the holster, however, Devillian's automatic weapon was up

306

and ready. With two bullets, he calmly blew out the Nazi's heart.

Several of Heck's men were standing a few feet away and had witnessed this sudden carnage. Devillian swung his gun in their direction.

"He got what he deserved," the Burning Cross leader barked. "He told me he could do a job, and he failed. We can't have that kind of weakness in our organization. If you guys can't cut it, then you'll be right after him."

To punctuate his point, he nudged the bloody corpse with his boot, and signaled for the body to be photographed. A barrage of camera flashes later, Devillian turned and walked away, leaving the men staring at the bloody remains of their former leader.

Chapter 63

Minutes later, Devillian's own personal helicopter was touching down at the nearby Grand Canyon National Park airport.

His rage at Heck's screw-up was tempered somewhat when he saw the two rows of shiny F-101 Voodoos lined up beside the small airfield's single runway.

"Finally, someone who can do *something* right!" he screamed at no one in particular as he alighted from the chopper to be greeted by a flurry of underlings.

"Where's the squadron commander?" he yelled.

"Right here!" came the quick sharp reply.

Out from the crowd surrounding Devillian stepped a tall skinny man with a bad facial complexion.

"Colonel Billy Lee Riggs," the man said, giving the cross-eyed terrorist a halfhearted salute. "We finally meet again."

Riggs was a man that Devillian had hated for nearly ten years. A former top officer in the pre-war Imperial Knights of the Klan, Riggs and his boys would frequently do battle against the United Klans of America, the hate group to which Devillian had belonged before World War III.

In the post-war years, Riggs, a well-known air mercenary, had gathered together a dozen and a half likeminded pilots and formed what he arrogantly, yet accurately called the Ku Klux Klan Air Force, or the KKKAF.

Desperate for aircraft after the Santa Fe air strike, Devillian had been forced to deal with the man. He had struck a bargain with Riggs via the radio several days before, first paying him an exorbitant amount of money to conduct the air raid on LA and then leasing the entire outfit for the duration of the canyon battle. The KKKAF had deployed from their secret base in West Texas to the canyon field just an hour ago. It would be their job to deal with whatever aerial opposition the United Americans would garner—the assignment formerly held by the long-departed Skinheads.

"I'll tell you what I tell everyone else," Devillian said to Riggs. "Play your part right and you'll get more gold than you thought existed. Fuck it up and my pit bulls will tear you all to shreds—one at a time.

They retired to a small tent, where one of Devillian's lackeys unfurled a map.

"A bunch of Twisted Cross guys fucked up, and the train got across this bridge almost untouched," he told Riggs. "So the script is going to change a little."

Riggs actually took notes as Devillian ordered him to deploy his fighters in a kind of umbrella formation that would orbit the critical *Ten Miles to Hell* trackbed.

"Your guys have to keep the United American fly-boys busy while we hit that train from the ground," Devillian concluded, purposely neglecting to tell him that the train's SAM cars had not been attacked as planned. "Then once we've got enough footage from the ground level, you guys can start strafing what's left of the train itself. Got it?"

"Yeah, I got it," Riggs answered flippantly. "And don't worry, Duke, we won't fuck it up like your German pretty boys did."

Three minutes later, Devillian was aloft again, shuttling back to his location HQ. Flying over the approaches to the canyon, he could see the train making its way slowly through the small patches of pine trees of the Kaibab Forest that bordered the tracks before they spilled out beside the rim of the canyon itself.

Devillian grabbed the chopper's radio and contacted Jorge Juarez. The obese bandit leader not only commanded an army of mounted bandits located three miles in from the beginning of the Hell stretch, he also controlled a detachment of troops just a half mile before the Mile One post itself.

"Scratch pages one through four from your script," Devillian told the man. "The train got over the bridge without a fucking scratch. This means your men have got to be ready to hit it the fucking instant your cue happens, and it means your mounted guys are going in a lot sooner in the play. Can you clowns handle that?"

The Mexican, as usual, grunted a response. "Don't fuckin' worry about us," he replied. "We're always ready to *keek* some ass."

"You better be, you fat fucking slob," Devillian replied. "If not, I'll *keel* both you and your sister—when I find her."

Devillian's next call was to the outpost at nearby Tusayan where the squadron of Hind gunships was waiting.

"Looks like we'll need you sooner than expected," Devillian told the squadron commander, a reject from the New Order named Lt. Nicholai Kolotov. "Skip to page sixteen of the script. That's where you guys come in and strafe the train around Mile Two and a half.

"We'll be there, comrade," Kolotov responded.

Up and down the line, Devillian contacted the various unit commanders along the ten-mile stretch of Hell.

Finally, only one call remained for Devillian to make. He reached the officer in charge of his secret weapon, which was waiting at the far end of the canyon straightaway.

"The plot at the bridge went bad," Devillian told this officer. "So we're tearing up the first four pages of the script. Understand?"

"We're ready and more than willing" came the reply.

Chapter 64

The train had traveled a relatively quiet two miles since the strange incident at Desert Point View Bridge.

Hunter was now airborne and flying low and slightly ahead of the *Freedom Express* as it slowly made its way out of the dense forest and onto the trackbed that ran alongside the Grand Canyon itself.

He actually took a moment to admire the incredible beauty of the canyon. But like everything else, he didn't have the time to dwell on Nature's splendor. He knew that within minutes, the train would enter a killing zone so intense and overwhelming that anyone in his right mind would believe that not even a miracle could help it now.

Still, a low spark was smoldering in the back of Hunter's mind: *"Only those on defense can be truly invincible. It is those who attack who leave themselves open to vulnerability.*

The lull below was shortlived.

Routinely monitoring all nearby radio channels, Hunter was astonished to hear a message from the enemy come over the shortwave receiver.

It was a squeaky, high-twanging voice that screamed at the top of its owner's lungs: *"Roll 'em!"*

Only later would Hunter find out the voice belonged to Devillian himself.

Now, before the train had traveled a half mile out of the forest, a blast of fire erupted from the rock formation on the right side of the train. A small missile anti-tank rocket corkscrewed its way through the air and slammed into the side of the lead locomotive.

At the same moment, a dozen parachute flares were launched on either side of the train as well as from a wide pedestrian footbridge about a half mile ahead.

Suddenly the ever-brightening dawn sky was aburst with the surreal pink glow of the dozens of parachute flares. Then more fiery anti-tank missile streaks homed in on the train from three sides, joined by a rain of tracer rifle fire.

The running of the gauntlet had begun.

"This is it," Hunter said to himself, immediately arming all his weapons, taking care to pat the front pocket of his flight suit where he kept the meditation notebook and his small tattered American flag wrapped around a worn picture of his love, Dominique. "This is where it gets settled, once and for all."

As always, Hunter was carrying an odd assortment of munitions under the Harrier's wings.

After first speaking with Fitz in the Control car, he put the jumpjet into a quick dive, pulling up at one hundred fifty feet into a long slow, right-to-left bank. Those on the train saw first one, then two, then a half dozen retarded-flight bombs fall from the Harrier's left wing. They hit the ground with terrifying precision, scoring direct hits on four out of six enemy anti-tank positions, and severely damaging the other two.

Then without missing a beat, the jumpjet reversed direction via a 180 degree horizontal translation and mimicked the first bombing run, this time over on the other side of the tracks. Within seconds, five of the six enemy targets were utterly destroyed.

Instantly the enemy rocket and rifle barrage petered out to a few random, badly aimed shots. The train continued plunging forward at full speed through the early morning mist, all of its windows and weapons openings electronically shuttered.

"Everything OK down there?" Hunter called down to Fitz.

"So far," Fitz quickly replied, his voice fighting a

storm of interference.

"We've got a lot of company up on the overpass ahead," Hunter yelled through the static. "So stay locked up."

Captain Luis Repello was the commander of the bandits stationed on top of the overpass footbridge, and at the moment he was having a hard time calming his troops.

They had just witnessed the Harrier's incredibly brutal air strike on their comrades positions on either side of the tracks. Now they watched in confused horror as the jumpjet went into a quick hover and then shot straight up into the sky.

"Forget the airplane!" Captain Repello was screaming to his junior officers via his walkie-talkie. "Get your men ready for the train."

Somewhat reluctantly, the first wave of bridge bandits lined up on the edge of the structure, paired off in twos. Then, with commendable if not exactly rational aplomb, the bandits began leaping onto the train as it passed underneath.

"Go! *Go!*" Repello was screaming so loudly, he didn't need his walkie-talkie. "Keep them *moving.*"

In the midst of the action, Repello was surprised by the enthusiasm of his troops. It seemed as if they were all leaping onto the train at once.

Suddenly, the bandit commander was aware of a strange high-pitched noise coming from behind him—one so loud it even drowned out the roar of the mighty train streaking by underneath the bridge.

Repello turned around to see the Harrier hovering no more than fifteen feet off the opposite side of the bridge, its Aden cannons blazing away.

In an instant Repello realized that the men he saw toppling off the edge of the bridge were not enthusiastically jumping onto the train at all. Rather they were being blasted off the overpass by the jumpjet's guns.

In the last moment of his life, Repello saw the distinctive lightning bolt helmet of the pilot inside the jumpjet, who was cooly mowing down the bandit unit, and in that instant, he realized that this time he had indeed joined the wrong side.

Hunter kept his cannons spitting fire until he had eliminated most of the soldiers on the bridge.

But nearly twenty-five had managed to drop onto the tops of the cars in the speeding train. Some of them lost their balance and tumbled off to be crushed by the mighty steel wheels of the train below. But the others managed to crawl over the sides of the cars and started firing their rifles through the windows. The bulletproof glass resisted most of the onslaught, but several windows cracked under the pressure of the constant bombardment.

Now clear of the bridge, the train rolled around a sharp curve, Fitz pushing computer control buttons like mad, trying to get every ounce of speed out of the remaining Dash-8 locomotives.

Hunter jammed his throttle forward and was soon flying over the lead locomotive, matching its speed exactly. The bandits crawling on the roofs of the railway cars looked like a pack of human-size spiders. Hunter knew that he would have to help get them off, yet he didn't want to light up his cannons for fear of damaging the train.

Instead he dropped the Harrier down to a point just ten feet off the top of the train. Then deftly lowering his vertical thruster deflectors, he was able to blow off a number of bandits from the roof by brutally scorching them with his downward-pointing, red-hot jet engine exhaust blast.

Inside a half minute, the roof of the train was cleared of the enemy.

But suddenly a new threat appeared.

As the *Express* roared down onto the canyon rim itself, both Fitz and Hunter saw that the mighty train was barreling headlong toward a huge pile of rocks blocking the tracks straight ahead.

Chapter 65

A Football City Ranger combat engineer named Spreat was the chief driver of the train. Viewing the pile of boulders on his closed-circuit TV screen, he frantically radioed back to Fitzgerald in the Control car.

"Do you see what's up ahead?" he yelled. "We've got to stop!"

Both Fitz and Crossbow had already seen the blockade.

"Could they be fake?" Fitz asked Crossbow, remembering back to the line of cardboard "brick" walls and the flash bombs on the Desert Point View Bridge.

The Indian shook his head. "I don't think we've got the time to find out."

Fitz knew he was right; there *was* no time to think about the choices or the consequences. Both sides of the tracks had come alive again with small arms fire, interspersed with some increasingly heavy artillery shelling. To stop the train now was tantamount to capitulation.

Relying strictly on his instincts, Fitz called ahead to Spreat: "Any way of telling whether those might be props or not?"

"They look damn real from here!" came the instantaneous reply.

"Then what happens if we don't stop?" Fitz urgently radioed back. "What happens if we give it everything we've got and they turn out to be real?"

There was just a slight delay before the engineer replied. "Jeesuz, I don't know," Spreat called back. "I know these Dash-8's pack a lot of power, but—"

"If we stop now, we're dead," Fitz cut in. "I say, boot it—*full speed!*"

Spreat relayed the order to his computers. Within a split-second, each of the locomotives hauling the massive train received the command. The powerful engines responded, and the *Freedom Express* hurtled toward the barrier of rocks at a deadly speed.

Fitz had his face pressed up against the bulletproof window and was screaming back to Crossbow: "Keep your fingers crossed . . . they might be fakes!"

They weren't. . . .

The train hit the boulders with such force that the nose of the first locomotive was completely shattered, sending chunks of steel flying everywhere. But the train kept going, driving with relentless force against the pile of rocks. Two, three locomotives were smashed; still the *Freedom Express* drove forward. Finally the train broke through as the last of the huge rocks was blasted from the tracks.

"*Goddamn!*" Fitz yelled. "Even *I* hope they got that on film!"

Billy Lee Riggs taxied to the head of the line of F-101 Voodoos that were waiting at the Grand Canyon airport, their engines roaring.

Suddenly his radio crackled to life.

"Triple-K flight," said the voice from the speaker. "You're on."

Riggs checked the last page of his script, and then strapped on his oxygen mask.

"OK, guys," he called to the seventeen other pilots. "Just like we rehearsed it. Six flights of threes, starting at Alpha-One. Check?"

"Check!" came the chorus of replies.

"Roger," Riggs said, popping his brakes and gunning his own engines. "Alpha One, follow me."

* * *

By now the first full streaks of the sunrise were appearing in the eastern sky. The deep blackness of the canyon depths were slowly turning into murky, misty shades of gray.

Hunter's inborn radar was flashing like crazy when he saw the first six Voodoos appear out of the south. At the same moment, he heard the radio calls of the Coaster Air Force fighters approaching from the west, the very familiar voice of JT and Ben Wa being mixed in.

Turning back toward the Voodoos, he saw they were climbing up to fifteen thousand feet, much too high to begin a strafing attack on the train. Within a half minute, they had leveled off and banked into a large circular flight pattern. Hunter recognized the tactic right away as an umbrella formation.

"Red flight, this is Blue, do you copy?"

Hunter keyed in his radio mike. "This is Red flight."

"Hey, Hawk!" JT called over. "What the hell are you getting us into here? We just flew over the canyon rim, and it looks like something out of a Hollywood nightmare."

"Couldn't say it any better myself," Hunter replied. "This is one movie we won't have to wait to see."

They quickly discussed the orbiting Voodoos.

"Just waiting for us to come up and meet them," Ben Wa radioed over. "So their buddies can jump the train."

"How about we give them a 'burst," Hunter replied. "With a three-king finisher?"

Being former Thunderbird pilots, Ben and JT knew exactly what Hunter was proposing. As the flight of five Coaster F-5's dove and formed a low CAP over the train, Hunter, Ben and JT quickly formed up ten thousand feet below the circling Voodoos.

"Any idea who these guys are?" JT inquired of Hunter.

"We'll know soon enough," Hunter replied, arming

318

two of his four Sidewinders. "On three . . . one . . . two. . . ."

On the next heartbeat, the two Strikefighters and the Harrier booted their engines and zoomed up into true vertical climbs, their three airplanes forming a triad that looked like a huge dagger heading for the heart of the Voodoos' orbiting pattern.

Within seconds, they roared through the line of F-101's. Then, with exquisite split-second timing, the three airplanes turned over and came screaming down in a three-pronged dive, perfectly completing the old Thunderbird demonstration stunt known as the starburst.

The United American fighters had moved so fast, the KKK pilots didn't have time to react. Suddenly three of them were being chased by a like number of Sidewinders. Three puffs of smoke later, the sky was filled with pieces of burning, tumbling Voodoo wreckage.

Their stunt only half over, the three fighters continued their earth-shattering dive, arriving back at five thousand feet just as the first trio of reserve Voodoos were making their move toward the train.

Hunter bore in on the lead F-101, ripping a large gaping hole in its wing with two solid blasts from his Aden cannons. The Voodoo began to smoke and spin downward, its pilot punching out just a second before its wing fell off. It was only then—when Hunter got his first good look at the emblem on the F-101's busted wing—did he realize that they were fighting against the KKK Air Force.

"There's your answer, JT," Hunter said, indicating the fluttering Voodoo wing. "It's the scumbag of scumbags' air force. It had to be their airplanes that attacked LA too."

"The Klan?" JT called back. "I didn't think any of those guys were smart enough to fly."

"Me, neither," Hunter replied. "But they just made a hard job a little easier for me."

As the aerial battle continued, Hunter and his allies

dueled with the numerically superior but less-skilled force of the KKK Air Force. Although the Harrier was slower than the Voodoos, its incredible versatility, plus Hunter's extraordinary flying talents, more than evened the score. Time after time, a KKKAF pilot had Hunter in his sights, only to find that the Harrier had somehow disappeared. Seconds later, a missile would rip into the Klansman's airplane, and his last earthly thought was along the lines of "Where in the fuck did that come from?"

By now, a second wave of Coaster F-5's had arrived, but so had another nine Voodoos. Devillian's fleet of Hind helicopters was also cued, to be countered by the out-numbered but nevertheless effective Cobra Brothers. The ever-lightening sky over the Grand Canyon was now filled with flashes of gunfire, streaks of smoke, and sudden bursts of brilliant flames as airplanes exploded.

Then on Hunter's call, the United American airplanes suddenly evacuated the area. A snap second later, the roofs of four of the train's SAM railway cars clanged open, and a massive barrage of SA-2 surface-to-air missiles were launched. Four Voodoos fell victim to the SAMs, the roofs of the SAM cars clanging shut almost immediately after the missiles were away.

Far below, in the guts of the gorge, the *Freedom Express* rumbled on, assaulted on all sides by recoiless rifles, bazookas, steady waves of rifle fire, grenades and flamethrowers. All the while the Football City Rangers were pouring the fire right back, in some cases deflecting their artillery gun muzzles down to level and firing away at point-blank range. Several railway cars caught on fire—from the enemy fire as well as the close-in muzzle flashes—but the Rangers assigned to fire duty managed to douse the flames quickly.

In the midst of the hundreds of enemy soldiers firing at them, the Football City Rangers also saw dozens of cameramen, lighting technicians, and sound men. Huge, bright klieg lights would nearly blind them at every turn. Wires, ropes, cables and perches made of scaffolding were everywhere. The presence of the massive filming crew only added to the unbelievable and surreal pandemonium.

Yet in a testament to their moral values, the Rangers couldn't bring themselves to fire directly at the unarmed members of the film crew. Instead they sought to destroy their cameras, lights and sound equipment whenever possible, the TOW anti-tank missiles being the weapon of choice for this job.

Through it all, Fitz and Crossbow were everywhere—directing the fire-fighting, encouraging the soldiers, firing out of broken windows with their own M-16's whenever they had the chance—all the while staying in touch via radio with Hunter overhead.

"We've already gone a mile and a half!" Fitz yelled to Crossbow at one point.

But that still left eight and a half miles to go. . . .

"Where's that fucking script girl!" Devillian screamed as he watched the relentless and ongoing air and ground battle from his high-perched command post.

A scantily clad young blonde—she had played a role in an earlier White Power Fuck Movie—ran up, her hands full of notebooks and long sheets of paper.

"What the fuck is coming next?!" Devillian demanded of her.

She quickly consulted the appropriate script pages.

"There's gas attack scene at Mile Three," she said hurriedly. "Then the Mexican Cavalry guys come in. Their cue is a smoke bomb explosion at Mile Three and Three Quarters."

Devillian threw away his high-powered binoculars in a rage.

"It's moving too fast!" he raged. "The pacing is all fucked up now." He grabbed his radio. "Where are

321

those fucking bombers?!" he screamed so loudly that the vibration on the other end of the line nearly busted Tony Three's eardrum.

"Last report they were orbiting at thirty miles south," he told Devillian, checking his schedule sheet for the position of the four B-57 mercenary bombers.

"Well, call them and tell 'em to get their asses over here now!" Devillian screamed through the line. "They might be going on earlier."

Tony Three gladly hung up on the terrorist leader and radioed the flight commander of the bomber force.

"What do you mean, go in early?" a nasty Austrian named Shinz replied. "Those fighters will pick us off in a minute."

"Just do it," Tony Three wheezed back at the man. "Or you'll never fly again."

There was a brief burst of static, then Shinz radioed back: "OK, but we're definitely going to have a meeting on this after this is over!"

"Yeah, sure," Tony Three replied. "And I'll bring the doughnuts, asshole."

At that moment, the Harrier roared right over Tony Three's position, its Aden guns blazing away at a wildly jinking, yet already doomed KKK Voodoo.

Knowing what the United American pilots would do to the slow bombers, Tony Three immediately thought of Shinz and his pilots. "Those guys should get a new agent," he mumbled.

As their airplanes were shot from the skies by Hunter and his mates, the Burning Cross stage commanders simply called for reinforcements and wave after wave of Voodoos, as well as the few remaining mesa-top based Floggers and Mirages, joined the attack. Meanwhile, as the train passed Mile Two and A Half, huge guns of all types were hurling tons of ammunition against the walls of the train.

Yet the *Freedom Express* kept driving forward.

As he was gunning down still another Klansman, Hunter suddenly *felt* bigger planes were approaching.

"Bombers coming in," Hunter called to JT, who was flying next to him.

A few moments later, they saw the outline of four B-57's streaking in over the northern horizon about thirty miles from the on-going train battle.

"Something tells me they ain't going to be dropping mines this time," JT radioed back.

As he watched the four planes break into two formations, Hunter began to suspect what the bombers were up to. A quick check of his threat-evaluation radar confirmed this suspicion.

"They're carrying Mavericks" was all Hunter had to say to raise an alarm with JT.

"Christ, that's all we need," the other pilot groaned. The AGM-65 Maverick was a TV-guided air-launched weapon that had an unparalleled reputation for accuracy. It was especially effective in piercing protective armor like that on a tank, or a bunker — or a train.

"They're going to try to blast the armor of the weapons cars, open them up like sardine cans," JT said.

"Not if we stop them first," Hunter replied.

As Hunter pulled the Harrier away from a swarm of Voodoos and toward the bombers, he was followed not only by JT, but by two of the Coasters' F-5's who had heard their exchange. Within a few seconds, the four fighters were rushing toward the bombers at full speed.

"We can't let them get anywhere near the train," Hunter called, immediately firing a Sidewinder at the lead bomber. The B-57's pilot was surprised by the rare head-on shot; the air-to-airs were usually shot from behind unless the pilot was one of extraordinary skill. Seeing the tell-tale brown smoke coming right for him, the B-57 pilot put the two-engined bomber into a sharp bank. But it was too late; the Sidewinder caught him

323

on his right wing's leading edge, blasting a hole in the wing itself and seriously damaging his starboard engine.

The B-57 managed to struggle on long enough for its bombardier to launch two Mavericks. Then it exploded as the flames from its wings reached its topped-off fuel tanks.

Now, even though the mother ship was gone, the Mavericks headed for the train just eighteen miles away, their infra-red homing systems taking over.

Hunter immediately assessed the situation and slammed the Harrier into a near-hover.

"JT, can you guys handle those three?" he called over to his friend. "I've got to stop those Mavs."

"Go, Hawk" was the reply.

The jumpjet was heading in the opposite direction less than two seconds later.

Chapter 66

Fitz was in a state of controlled chaos when several buzzers went off at once inside the Control car.

"*Damn* . . . that's the incoming missiles warning system," he yelled out to Crossbow, punching several buttons on the threat-evaluation computer at the same time. A readout quickly informed him that two infra-red-guided Mavericks were homing in on the train, their distance only fifteen miles away.

The problem was that the train's own defensive systems — they being radar-controlled Gatling guns which destroyed incoming missiles by putting up a wall of lead that nothing could get through — were being worked ragged by the multitude of smaller TOW missiles being fired non-stop by enemy troops in the hills on either side of the tracks.

The incoming missile warning system was positively screaming by the time Fitz saw the Harrier streaking directly toward the train. Suddenly, it stopped on a dime and went into a hover about one hundred yards off to the right of the speeding train.

"Mother of God," Fitz cried, knowing at once that Hunter was placing his airplane between the Mavericks and the train. "Can he possibly get the both of them?"

Hunter was wondering the same thing as he watched the two Mavericks streak right for him, guessing correctly that their infra-red homing device would ignore the train and key in on his hot engine.

The two missiles were no more than one hundred yards away when Hunter took a deep breath, counted to three and then opened up with his Aden cannons.

Imitating the train's own close-in defense system, he filled the air with a wall of cannon shells and crossed his fingers. . . .

The first Maverick blew up not more than 150 feet from the Harrier—the second one just 30 feet away. The resulting explosions lit up the sky like a gigantic Fourth of July fireworks display; shock waves crashed into the Harrier, and it took all of Hunter's skill to keep the jumpjet from spinning into a nosedive.

"Right on, Hawk!" he heard Fitz screaming through his headphones.

"That was too close," Hunter replied under his breath.

Meanwhile, a short but deadly aerial battle had erupted between JT, the F-5's and the three remaining bombers. Through quick action and flying skill the United Americans were able to shoot down two of the B-57's and send the other one scurrying away, both its engines smoking heavily.

But now Hunter had another problem.

The actions against the bandits around the footbridge, the Voodoos and the Mavericks had depleted his ammunition. And yet the train was just barely two miles into the hellish ten-mile straightaway.

Hunter knew he had to re-arm, or be totally out of the battle at the most critical juncture.

Contacting Fitz, he told him of his predicament.

"But what can you do?" the Irishman asked. "There's not a friendly base in five hundred miles."

"I know," Hunter replied. "That's why I have no other choice."

Despite a murderous rain of rifle, rocket and cannon fire that was pelting the sides of the train non-stop, he knew his only option was to attempt to land on his platform car.

Now he would really see what this Harrier could do, he thought grimly. Landing on a small flatcar was difficult enough when the train was stopped; doing it while it was speeding through the narrow canyon bed, under heavy enemy fire would be, to say the least, challenging.

Looking down on the speeding train, he felt like he was watching some immense video game. Everything was moving by so quickly; the air was filled with bullets and rockets, most of them bouncing off the heavily armored sides of the train, but some finding targets. The smoke and missile exhaust alone was enough to obscure visibility.

However, the train crew was fighting back—and in a big way. Once every ten seconds or so, three or four of the armored railcars would suddenly lift their shutters and let loose all at once with an incredible barrage of their own, usually directed at a concentration of troops on a hillside or hiding beneath an underpass. Then just as quickly, the shutters would be closed again, only to have four more cars do the same thing farther down the line.

Directly above the train, the Cobra Brothers seemed to be everywhere—dogfighting with the pesky Hind gunships, and occasionally taking out a fixed target with their powerful nose cannons. High above it all, JT, Ben Wa and the others were still battling the KKK fighters.

And Hunter knew he had to rejoin the fight.

He located the landing car and got the Harrier in position overhead, matching the forward motion of the train. It was a tricky maneuver, and it wasn't made any easier by the hail of enemy gunfire that was suddenly directed at the aircraft. The train was rounding a bend and was soon to pass through a small grove of trees. Knowing it was now or never, Hunter slammed his thrusters into the descend mode and sent the Harrier crashing to the landing car, just as the front portion of the train passed into the small forest.

To his surprise, he found he'd landed in one piece, the grove of trees giving him the cover he needed to set down, though none too gently. A courageous team of Rangers appeared immediately. Half of them helped him secure the airplane, while the others fired their heavy weapons off both sides of the car, suppressing some of the incoming fire. Meanwhile Fitz had ordered that the weapons cars on either side of the Harrier platform open up with everything they had once the jumpjet was down.

Hunter and the Rangers quickly secured the plane and then started loading it up with what he needed: fuel, ammo and missiles.

Halfway through the operation, Fitz and Crossbow scrambled out to the platform car.

"Just got a message from the Cobras," Fitz yelled above the cacophony of gunfire hitting all around them. "They've spotted at least a battalion of cavalry up about a mile . . . looks like mounted Mexican bandits."

"The terrain flattens out right up ahead." Crossbow shouted above the din. "They might be attempting a boarding scene . . . a real one this time."

"Christ . . . that's all we need," Hunter yelled back.

"We've alerted everyone on board," Fitz told Hunter, as the pilot was once again climbing up into the Harrier. "They're expecting hand-to-hand combat within the next few minutes."

"I'll go up ahead," Hunter yelled back, just before closing the Harrier cockpit. "Maybc I can soften them up before you get there."

Then, in a flash of fire and smoke, the Harrier lifted off once again.

Chapter 67

Jorge Juarez was sitting in the back of his extra-wide jeep, eating a large salami sandwich.

"Geeve me more mustard," he ordered one of his go-boys.

A script girl appeared out of nowhere and shoved three pages of scene information under Jorge's disgustingly dirty bearded chin.

"You're on in thirty seconds," she told him.

He seemed not to notice the cue at first. But then, very gradually, he reached down into the folds of his grossly obese body and came up with a .45 Colt automatic.

"Amigos!" he spit out loudly between bites. "Get ready. . . ."

He wiped his mouth with his sleeve and struggled to get a pair of binoculars up to his eyes. A few seconds of lens adjustment went by before he spotted the train heading down into a slight gulley about a mile from his position, the Harrier jumpjet rising above it.

Jorge didn't even have the stamina to turn around and review his troops. Instead he called his second-in-command, a bandit officer named Feelth, who was positioned at the rear of the mounted column.

"Is everything ready?" he asked the man.

A quarter mile away, Feelth popped the button on his walkie-talkie and looked out on the five hundred members of the Mexican bandit cavalry. They were lined up in ten waves of fifty apiece, with no units held in reserve, per Devillian's orders.

"Si," he finally replied to Jorge. "We have the white

horses up front as you requested. Plus our best-looking riders will also go in first."

"Remind your men not to look directly at the cameras," Jorge chomped as he polished off the huge sandwich. "Any man seen looking at the cameras during the screening will be shot. Got that?"

"*Si,*" Feelth answered again.

Jorge took the first bite of another huge salami sandwich and then calmly shot his automatic twice into the air.

"First unit . . . *attack!*" he yelled only slightly louder than his loudest belch.

In an instant the first wave of bandit cavalry was off—heading down the slight rise and toward the tracks.

"Second unit . . . attack!"

Again, another wave of mounted soldiers were dispatched by his command.

Another bite of his sandwich, another order: "Third unit . . . attack!"

With that the bandit chief settled back down into the jeep's already weakening seat, his work done.

He continued stuffing his face, practically oblivious to the mounting racket of gunfire, jet engines, the roar of the locomotives, missile blasts and explosions going on all around him. When one of the KKK Voodoos was suddenly shot out of the sky by a Coaster F-5 and came crashing down no more than a half mile from his position, Jorge barely lifted an eyebrow.

So it took him about thirty seconds to realize that his third unit of cavalry had turned around and was now heading straight back toward him in total disarray.

"What is happening?" he managed to burp out before he realized that something was chasing his horse soldiers up the rise and away from the train. Using all his strength, Jorge managed to stand up in the jeep to get a better look. What he saw was the Harrier streaking right behind his rapidly retreating troops.

330

"You fuckin' yellow-bellys!" Juarez screamed at them, as they rode right past him in hordes. "Get your asses back here! You gonna let one airplane chase you away?"

For some of his men, the answer apparently was yes.

Juarez quickly ordered his driver to pull back, at the same time calling Feelth on the radio.

"Regroup your last two waves into one," he told the second-in-command. "Have half of them fire at that airplane, the other half get down to the train . . . and *hurry,* the cameras are rolling!"

The last two hundred bandits followed Feelth's quickly shouted orders. Half of them started firing at the Harrier as it swept overhead, blazing away with their rifles, hoping that a lucky shot might hit a fuel tank or another vulnerable spot on the jumpjet.

Just then, five Hind gunships appeared over the edge of the canyon and dipped down into the gulley next to the tracks taking dead aim at the Harrier. Hunter saw them coming and, in an instant, sent the AV-8BE screaming straight into their formation. Firing frantically at the ducking and diving Harrier, two of the Hind pilots succeeded only in blowing each other out of the sky. Hunter downed two more with his cannons, leaving just one gunship flying. That Hind pilot, suddenly realizing he was all alone, desperately tried to flee and ran the chopper right into the side of the canyon wall. Within seconds the flaming debris from the gunship was raining down onto the bandits below.

Meanwhile, the two hundred bandits who had actually made it to the tracks found out that the train was going much too fast for them to attempt a boarding. What was more, they realized too late that every fourth weapons car was firing back at them with Gatling guns, rockets and combined rifle fire.

The resulting slaughter was sickeningly brief. Men and animals were cut to shreds by Gatling guns firing at a rate of six hundred rounds a second.

Within a half minute, the train had passed through Mile Four checkpost and disappeared around a small, craggy mountain, leaving on the tracks behind a grotesque jumble of dying horses and massacred riders.

Jorge Juarez decided he'd seen enough.

Throwing away his sandwich, he ordered his driver to "get this jeep the fuck out of here!" The vehicle began to scramble over the rocky base of the canyon, heading for the relative safety of a nearby area of brush and overhanging boulders.

Spotting the fleeing jeep, Hunter called to Fitzgerald.

"Anyone get on board, Fitz?"

"Not a one!" came the reply. "And we're almost halfway through this."

"OK," Hunter replied. "I've got what looks to be a major officer in front of me, leaving the scene of battle. I'm going to pursue."

He put the Harrier into a 180-degree turn and shot off toward the jeep. Overtaking it quickly, he buzzed it low, letting the red-hot jetwash cover the vehicle.

In an instant, the jeep and the two men inside it spontaneously combusted—Jorge's huge mass literally exploding from the intense heat. Out of control and on fire, the jeep failed to turn away from the edge of the canyon. It went over the ledge in a spectacular blaze of fire and smoke, plunging more than a half mile down into the canyon itself.

At the same moment, Devillian and a dozen of his cameramen were also following the action from about two miles away.

"That was brilliant!" he screamed with rare authentic enthusiasm as he watched Jorge take his fiery death plunge. "That stuntman was great, whoever he was."

Devillian's rapture was quickly dissipated once he was informed of the failure of Juarez's bandits to

332

board the train.

Now, all around him, he saw evidence of his script going up in smoke. In the sky above, it was obvious the United American pilots were more than a match for Riggs' KKK Air Force. The combined efforts of the jumpjet, the Strikefighters and the Coaster F-5's had so far been successful in keeping the dwindling swarm of KKK Voodoos from reaching the *Freedom Express*.

And one look into his high-powered binoculars told him the damned train was still speeding through the canyon.

With a curse, Devillian retreated to his command tent and lit up a bowl of crack. He still had a pair of aces up his sleeve—both of which he was sure would look great up on the big screen.

And now was time to play his first one. He first ordered his personal Hind gunship to get ready to fly him to another location. Then he took another long drag from his crack pipe and placed a radio call to the officer in charge of his first secret weapon.

The conversation was brief. "I'll be there in five minutes," he told the man. "And then, you're on. . . ."

Hunter rejoined JT, Ben and the Coaster pilots as they continued to drive away enemy aircraft while at the same time strafing the concentrations of Burning Cross soldiers hidden along the train's route.

They passed through the Four and One Half Mile and entered a section of track that was elevated from the canyon rim and therefore gave the enemy no positions to fire on the train at close range. This meant for the next mile or so, the train would be relatively free from point-blank attacks.

Fitz ordered the train slowed to one third, to give Hunter the time to set down again, arm up and top off his tanks.

333

"We're almost halfway through," the Irishman said, trying hard not to sound over-confident. "And our casualties have been very light, considering. . . ."

"I know, Mike," Hunter replied. "But we've still got a long way to go."

But even Hunter couldn't imagine what Devillian had waiting for them up ahead. In the previous four and half miles, the train had been attacked by helicopter gunships, fighters, anti-tank rockets, air-to-surface missiles, mortars, flamethrowers, mounted gunmen, and thousands of regular infantry weapons. Once a mighty mass of shining metal, the train was now a string of scorched, dented and smoking cars, with nearly half of the working locomotives disabled.

But the fact that they still stayed on the track was proof of their rugged construction—and it was almost as if that mettle was flowing down through the entire train. True, the *Freedom Express* was battered—but it was not beaten.

And true, Devillian's airplanes and troops were still ahead, but nevertheless, the valiant train pushed forward on its treacherous dash through the canyon.

Hunter could almost *feel* that the *Freedom Express* had taken on a fighting personality of its own. In an instant of reflection, he knew it *was* alive—alive with the spirit that was America. The damn-the-torpedoes, full-speed-ahead locomotion that had kept the country alive throughout its travails since the big war had also kept it great in its own way. And that power came from its people, its citizens—of all colors, all religions, all walks of life. He knew that America was not about white power, or black power, or green power or polka dot power. Nor was it about one religion, one belief or one God. That kind of rationale was as foolish as saying the country should be about one baseball team, one type of haircut, one type of beer.

For it was the very fact that everyone *was* mixed in together that made the patchwork stay tight. Anyone

334

who believed different was an idiot—a very *unpatriotic* idiot at that. But then again, who else but an imbecile would put on a white sheet just so he could play with matches at night once a month? And who but a fool would dare to wave a swastika?

What was the matter with these people? Hunter would ask himself over and over. *Haven't they ever read a goddamn history book?*

And as for America's true heroes, Hunter knew they weren't hard to find. He was riding with two hundred of them right now.

The respite lasted exactly one minute and ten seconds. Then the inevitable call came in to the Control car.

It was from Cobra Brother Captain Jesse Tyler. He and his partner Bobby Crockett had flown their choppers one mile ahead of the train to reconnoiter the track.

"We've got more trouble up ahead—" the radio crackled with warning—"and you won't believe what it is."

Fitz and Hunter looked at each other, both of them sagging slightly at the bad news.

"We give up," Fitz yelled back, as if they were all involved in one long, deadly game.

"Believe it or not," Tyler replied. "There's another armored train in the canyon—and it's heading our way!"

335

Chapter 68

For the first time in his life, Red Banner felt like he really needed a drink.

Beer, Scotch, even rot-gut Badlands wine would do — anything to get his nerves settled down and his stomach turned back from inside out.

He was on top of one of the highest peaks on the southern edge of the Grand Canyon — so high, it was as bad as flying. Sharing this perch with him was a Burning Cross anti-aircraft crew, three South African video technicians, and a pair of Burning Cross guards, both of whom had Uzi machine guns leveled at his head at all times.

From this great height, Banner had witnessed the entire battle so far between the Burning Cross troops and the *Freedom Express*. From the opening shots near the forests at Desert View Point to the attempted Maverick strikes, to the Mexican cavalry attack, Banner had not only seen it all, he had narrated it. Screaming into a microphone which was hooked to the South African's equipment, he was providing a blow-by-blow description of the incredible events to go along with the video that was being picked up all along the Ten Miles of Hell.

Next to him was a huge satellite dish through which the Afrikaners were beaming both the video and his audio back to his station in Los Angeles. And there was no longer any question that KOAS-TV would broadcast the battle; he had already talked several times with the station manager, Wild Bill Austin himself. Austin assured him that the "live news report" was being watched by millions of people on the West Coast and that Banner's "reporting" would place his name up there with such journalistic greats as Murrow and Cronkite.

Trouble was, Banner was sure he'd never live to benefit from the honor.

"My God . . ." Fitz kept saying over and over. "How can there be any other trains out here?"

He and the others were still trying to make sense out of Tyler's almost unbelievable report.

"It isn't exactly an Amtrak cross-country pleasure train," Tyler had told them. "It's carrying artillery, anti-aircraft guns, SAMs—just like ours. It's completely black, from one end to the other, and it's got a bunch of cameras hanging all over it too. The only difference is that it has six locomotives in the front and six pushing it in the back."

The news had temporarily stunned the battle-weary United Americans. But Hunter quickly recovered. In an instant, his mind began racing ahead, planning for the impending encounter.

"We'll need all the aircover we can get," he told Fitz, turning to rush back to the Harrier.

"I'll keep the Cobras way up there and get JT and Ben Wa on the line," Fitz called after him.

Hunter was lifting off his platform car less than a minute later.

He rose to five thousand feet, then quickly throttled the Harrier forward. Within ten seconds, he was passing over the high west end of the canyon rim. From here he could see that after the three remaining miles of Hell, the tracks ran through a series of twists and turns, interspersed with several long straightaways, all of it on a gradual downward slope.

As he cleared the tops of the high hills, JT and Ben pulled alongside him.

"We just caught something about another train," JT radioed over. "Please tell us we're just hearing things."

" 'Fraid not, partner," Hunter told him grimly. "Take a look for yourself."

Down below, probably no more than ten miles away and coming on fast, was a long, black train slithering its way along a set of tracks running parallel to the ones being used by the *Freedom Express*.

"I can't believe this," Ben said.

"Anything's possible in the movies," Hunter reminded him.

"But what's with the two sets of locomotives?" JT asked. "Six in front, six in back . . . does that make sense?"

"It does to them," Hunter replied grimly. "They know that if we get past them in the canyon, they can just switch gears, have the pushers become the pullers and vice versa, and then chase us all the way to LA."

As the three fighters zoomed down for a closer look, they were met by a barrage of anti-aircraft fire from the black train. Hunter quickly located the source of the gunfire; three flatcars in the midsection were carrying half a dozen S-60 AA guns.

"Those are our first order of business, guys," Hunter radioed to his companions. "But we'll keep it down to cannons. If we blast that train with anything heavier, it will go off the track and screw the railbed. Then our guys won't be able to get through."

Hunter's suggestion was approved by two calls of "Roger!" Then they quickly circled behind the enemy train, and before the men on board had a chance to reposition the S-60 AA guns, Hunter was coming at them, flying just a few feet above the roof of the cars, his Adens blazing. He took out two of the guns with his first pass; JT and Ben Wa were right behind him, and they disabled two more.

Leaving the last set of S-60's to his friends, Hunter shot on ahead of the train, turned the Harrier sharply and came right back at the lead locomotive. He opened up with both cannons, tearing up the first engine and damaging the second one in line as well. But just as the *Freedom Express* originally carried a dozen locomotives, so too did this *Death Train*. Its ten remaining engines — now four in front and six in back — generated more than enough power to keep it streaking full speed ahead toward the oncoming *Freedom Express*.

Hunter took the Harrier up several thousand feet to get a better view of the overall area. From this vantage point, he could clearly see the United Americans' train approaching rapidly from the east and its nemesis coming just as fast from the west. After a brief flurry of calculations, Hunter determined that in about two minutes and sixteen seconds, the two huge trains would be parallel to each other.

"Get ready, Fitz," Hunter radioed. "We slowed them down a little, but they're still heading straight for you. Keep your engines at top speed, and whatever's left, you'd better get it loaded up and ready."

"We are going all out right now," Fitz told him. "But we've lost so many locomotives, our top speed isn't all that fast anymore. I'm afraid that the train will have quite a long time to shoot at us."

What was worse was that the two trains were already so rapidly closing in on each other that bombing the enemy cars was now too risky.

Yet Hunter knew he had to do something — anything. Maybe the *Freedom Express* could weather the first assault from the *Death Train*. But he knew the United Americans' train couldn't endure a constant pounding all the way from here to LA. It was up to him to disable the enemy train to the extent that it would not be able to pursue them.

The question was, how?

As the two armored monsters drew even closer to each other, Hunter's mind raced through a slew of options. In seconds, he came up with the plan that although risky, was also the only one most likely to succeed. One look told him that the locomotives powering the *Death Train* were similar to the Dash-8's pulling the *Freedom Express*. And, if they were like the Dash-8's, then they too were controlled by computer.

And if he was able to destroy those computers, then the brains of the black train would effectively be destroyed.

Or so he hoped. . . .

"Get ready!" Fitz yelled into the *Freedom Express*'s intercom.

Like everything else, its speakers were smoking and battered, and his voice came through like a blast of static. Yet no further call of warning was needed. Everyone on board—he, Crossbow and the surviving Football City Rangers and the few remaining Piute braves—could see the *Death Train* was now bearing down on them, its hundreds of guns loaded and ready.

But those aboard the *Freedom Express* were loaded and ready, too.

"Fire on my command!" Fitz yelled, as the black train was now no more than a quarter mile away, the distance between the two trains being halved with every second as they hurtled on toward each other.

"Good luck, guys!" Hunter yelled down to the men on the *Express*, knowing that it was up to the two trains now to determine who would win this battle.

Ten seconds later, the trains met right at the Eight Mile point. Even the enemy troops in the hills on either side of the track stopped firing as the two great trains began to pass each other. Every possible weapon on board the *Freedom Express*—all of its machine guns, artillery, rockets, even the enormous Big Dick howitzer—was firing at full blast as quickly as possi-

340

ble. If anything the barrage from the *Death Train* was even more intense.

As Hunter watched from above, the two trains looked like nothing less than two Man o' Wars passing each other, desperately blasting away almost as if they were moving in slow motion with the horror paradoxically being stretched into hours.

Finally after ten horrible seconds, the trains cleared each other just before the *Freedom Express* entered the final mile of Hell.

Hunter swooped over the American train once, his heart instantly sinking as he saw that nearly every one of its cars was now ripped apart and smoking, some of them going through massive exploding death throes. Two thirds of the remaining locomotives were now just hulks, wrapped in flames and belching incredibly thick black smoke. The fact that the train stayed on the tracks was almost a miracle in itself.

He tried radioing the Control car but was not surprised when he received no reply.

He coldly rationalized that even if everyone on board the *Freedom Express* were dead, he still had to stop the *Death Train* from backing up and hitting them again.

"JT, Ben . . . cover for me as much as you can," he said. With that he nosed the Harrier down toward the top of the black train, which had nearly stopped as it prepared to switch directions.

If only he could get down before the train reversed gears and began to pick up speed again.

"Hawk, what are you doing?" JT demanded.

But Hunter had switched off his radio. This wasn't the time to argue strategy; he knew he could blast away at the black train all day and still not stop it. He quickly scanned the rooftops of the cars on the enemy train, trying to decide where the computer controls might be housed. On the *Freedom Express*, they were in the first car after the string of locomotives,

341

but the black train had two strings of engines, one at each end.

He decided to pick the back end of the train, which soon would be the front end as the direction changed. Running through a storm of rifle and small artillery fire, he lowered the Harrier gingerly onto the roof of the car nearest the line of locomotives, and quickly scrambled out.

Once again, his instincts were correct. One entire wall of the railroad car he'd suspected was filled with a huge, mainframe computer. That was the good news; the bad news was that three men, armed with rifles, stood in front of it.

The trio was stunned that the Harrier had actually landed on the train, and their bafflement cost them their lives. In a split-second, Hunter cut them down with his M-16, turning quickly to take out two more enemy soldiers who had appeared atop the car opposite the one he'd used for the landing platform.

The fire from the hills had died down by this time as many of the Burning Cross gunners were reluctant to shoot at him for fear of damaging the black train. This lay-off in the opposing fire allowed him to climb down into the enemy train's computer car without further gunplay.

There was no one tending to the computers; like just about everything else aboard the enemy train, the Control car was totally automated. In all he guessed there were no more than twenty enemy soldiers on board.

"Machines run it," Hunter murmured. "Machines fire its guns. Machines do its killing."

Using his M-16, Hunter opened up on the banks of computers, his fiery tracer barrage destroying the heart of the evil calculator with every bullet. Like the killing of a giant beast, the *Death Train* began to slow down as its computers gave out. It took only a half dozen bursts from Hunter's gun to disable the computer systems completely.

342

"But no machine is a hero," he said aloud.

"How true, Mr. Hunter . . ." he was startled to hear a voice call out from behind him.

The Wingman swung around and found that he was staring into the sneering face of Duke Devillian.

Chapter 69

Cobra Brother Captain Bobby Crockett had just completed a strafing run on a hillside Burning Cross outpost when his pull-away maneuver brought him directly over the stalled *Death Train*.

He was astonished to see Hunter's jumpjet hanging precariously off the side of one of the enemy railway cars — its engines still running.

"What the hell is going on here?" he wondered as he pulled up and came back around. In the last few minutes of brutal, confusing combat, Crockett had lost sight of Hunter and his Harrier, which in itself was unusual as the Wingman always seemed to be everywhere at once whenever the bullets were flying.

Crockett dodged some scattered enemy fire and lowered the Cobra until it was just a few feet above the ground. Flying parallel to the train, he quickly looked through the windows of the various cars as he went along.

In the third car that he passed, he caught a glimpse of Hunter, M-16 in hand, defiantly standing before a man who was also holding a rifle.

It took only an instant for Crockett to realize his friend's dilemma. The shot-up computer car told the story as to why Hunter had landed on the *Death Train* in the first place.

Now the Wingman needed an assist to get out.

I hope this works, Crockett thought, as he turned the Cobra sharply and put a single blast of cannon fire through the roof of the wrecked computer car.

Although the stream of bullets was way above his head, Devillian dove to one side of the car. This gave Hunter all the time he needed to leap onto the staggering Burning Cross leader and jerk the weapon from his grasp.

He quickly slammed the butt of the rifle against the side of Devillian's head, knocking the man unconscious.

Suddenly the door of the railcar burst open and two Burning Cross soldiers charged into the room. Hunter, firing as he went, bolted from the door on the other side of the car, leaving one man wounded and the other gaping at the downed Devillian.

Crockett was circling over the train when Hunter emerged. With a wave to show his thanks, Hunter sprinted to the teetering Harrier, then jumped into the cockpit just as a half dozen of Devillian's soldiers appeared on the roof of the car with their weapons blazing.

But it was too little, too late. With angry frustration, the enemy soldiers watched as Hunter gunned the engines of his Harrier and lifted off the black train with a tremendous rush of noise and power.

The de-computerized black train was now dead on the tracks.

The soldiers on board, realizing what was happening, intensified their gunfire, doing their best to halt the *Freedom Express* before it got out of range. But, battered and smoking as it was, the United American train managed to limp out of range of the enemy guns, finally rolling through the last few feet of the hellish ten miles and onto the long sloping incline which would keep it moving west for miles.

Back on the black train, Devillian quickly regained

consciousness and tried desperately to assess the damage Hunter had caused to the computers. One look however told him the damage was irreversibly complete. His first secret weapon was now incapacitated.

That left him with only one more card to play. It was time to call in the extras. . . .

One of the men who heard Devillian's radio order several minutes later was Lieutenant Kolotov, the commander of the fleet of Burning Cross helicopters. He quickly ordered all of his pilots to land near several of the remaining Burning Cross troop concentrations and load as many soldiers as they could into the helicopters.

Then they set off in pursuit of the *Freedom Express*.

Once they were over the battered, rolling United Americans' train, Kolotov stunned his soldiers by commanding them to leap from the choppers onto the roof of the train. By now, battle-weary, confused and terrified by Devillian's rantings, the men didn't have the will to resist, even though most of them realized they would be committing suicide. So they jumped, and about half of them bounced off the train and fell to their deaths along the tracks.

But several dozen of them managed to hold on long enough to get their bearings. They began to crawl along the burning train until they found cars with broken windows or sides ripped apart. Climbing inside the *Freedom Express,* they began firing wildly at anything that moved, shredding the insides of several cars with their bullets.

From both ends of the train, the United American soldiers grimly moved in to trap the invaders. With Fitz in command of the men at one end and Crossbow leading a group on the other end, they caught Devillian's forces in a deadly crossfire. When the bullets ran out, hand-to-hand combat took over.

Once again, the battle was bloody, but brief. About fifteen minutes after the first of the Burning Cross soldiers had dropped onto the train, all of them were dead. About ten cars in the middle of the devastated train were filled with bleeding corpses. For miles along the down slope of tracks, the canyon railway bed was littered with the mangled bodies of dead soldiers.

Ahead of the train, some of Devillian's reserve commanders, inspired or perhaps crazed by their leader's orders, actually started piling some of their artillery pieces on the tracks. They even forced some of their men to get onto the tracks, telling them that the *Freedom Express* was moving so slowly now that they could easily jump on board.

Seeing what was going on, the Cobra Brothers dropped their powerful gunships down in front of the train's lead locomotive and led it along the next several miles of track, blasting the human barricades out of the way. The once-mighty *Freedom Express* now had only two of its original twelve locomotives pulling it. But this, in addition to the momentum gained by the train as it rolled downhill, provided enough power to plow through the few piles of artillery and other flimsy barriers that the desperate Burning Cross troops had tossed onto the tracks. A few fanatics actually tried to leap onto the front of the lead locomotive, but were immediately hurled onto the tracks and crushed underneath the huge, grinding wheels.

Leaving a path of blood and death in its wake, the *Freedom Express* finally approached the far western end of the mighty gorge.

At last, the tracks ahead looked clear.

But overhead, the remainder of Devillian's air force continued to pursue the train.

Hunter and his companions managed to keep most of the enemy aircraft at bay, but an occasional KKK

347

Voodoo would slip through and riddle another car with a new round of cannon fire.

Still, KKKAF leader Billy Lee Riggs had seen his once-formidable force of Klan pilots dwindle to about a dozen. But he wasn't through yet. During his many forays over the train, he had come to realize that the key to the brilliant aerial defense the United Americans were providing for their train centered on the amazing feats performed by the lead Harrier. Obviously, Hawk Hunter was at the controls of that aircraft.

With his final group of Voodoos behind him, Riggs decided to make one last, all-out effort to get Hunter.

That might finally break down the train's protective shield; even if it didn't, at least Riggs would have the satisfaction of gunning the world's most famous pilot out of the sky.

It was Fitzgerald who first noticed the squadron of Voodoos heading straight for Hunter's Harrier.

Trying his best to get the train's air defense radar system working inside the battered Control car, he saw twelve blips rising up about fifteen miles from the train.

Determining that they were heading right for the train, Fitz quickly radioed a warning to the United American jets.

But Hunter had already sensed the approach of the Klansman fleet. Low on missiles, he had been getting ready to land for a final re-arming. But there was no time for that now.

He would have to make the most of his two remaining Sidewinders.

JT and Ben Wa quickly came up in the rear of the enemy force and started picking off the trailing F-101's, but the first wave came straight at Hunter. And they were prepared for the Harrier's aerial escape tactics; two of the Voodoos were flying slightly higher than the Harrier, the other two were slightly low, waiting for whichever way Hunter went.

So the Wingman simply stopped the Harrier in midair.

The two Voodoos on top shot past their target before they realized what had happened. One of the two pilots underneath tried to slow down enough to get a shot but only succeeded in getting his jet rammed by an F-101 charging rapidly from the rear.

Riggs, who was flying one of the Voodoos that had taken the higher route, swore into his radio.

"That sneaky son of a bitch," he cursed through gritting teeth. Then he hit his radio SEND button. "You boys stay out here and cover me, I'm going to double back and get on his tail until I nail him good!"

Meanwhile, Hunter had used one of his two remaining missiles to good advantage, destroying one F-101 with a close-in shot and seriously damaging another with his Aden cannons. His flying buddies also had been busy, and now only Riggs and three other Voodoos were left.

While the other F-101's kept JT and Ben Wa busy, the leader of the Klansmen continued his determined assault on Hunter. Several times he had Hunter in his sights and fired, only to have the Harrier dodge out of the way. Hunter, meanwhile, was carefully maneuvering for one clear shot with his last Sidewinder.

Despite the superior speed of the Voodoo, the Wingman was totally frustrating Riggs by avoiding everything the Klansman could throw at him. And as he ducked and dived all over the sky, he slowly led Riggs closer and closer to a tiny gap in the canyon wall just ahead of the two airplanes. As Riggs fired still another cannon barrage, Hunter and the Harrier disappeared into the shadows of that narrow passageway.

Just in time, Riggs pulled the Voodoo up and over the canyon wall. Cursing, he looked below, into the darkened gap where Hunter had flown, but he couldn't see the Harrier. Frustrated, he continued flying over the area, searching.

Suddenly, from nowhere, the Harrier was right behind him. Riggs frantically tried to twist his Voodoo out of Hunter's line of fire, but the Harrier's last Sidewinder instantly crashed into his tailsection. Bellowing a final curse of hatred and fury, the Klansman panicked and started a mad scramble to eject from the flaming aircraft. But he was too late. Before he could punch out, the plunging Voodoo smashed into the side of the canyon and exploded into a roaring ball of flames.

Chapter 70

Even in his semi-deranged state of mind, Devillian slowly began to realize that the impossible was about to happen.

He was about to lose the battle.

Even the fact that most of the brutal combat was on film didn't sooth his drug-soaked brain waves.

Most of his airplanes were gone, and the Grand Canyon was filled with the bodies of his men. Even if the black train could be repaired and caught up with the *Freedom Express* again, there weren't enough soldiers left on board to have much of a chance against the battered, but determined surviving United Americans.

Slowly it dawned on Devillian that the hated Hunter and his allies had run the gamut. This time. But Duke Devillian was not going down with his army. He had launched one crusade of terror; he could do it again. He remained absolutely convinced that his twisted, unpatriotic cause — the right of "superior" white people to rule the less-capable races of the world — would triumph in the end.

But only if he was around to make it happen.

The failure of the Knights of the Burning Cross was easy to figure. Against his own instincts, he had aligned himself with Mexicans, washed-up Germans, and other assorted scum from around the globe.

Next time, he wouldn't taint the blood line of his army. Next time, it would be "true Americans" only.

But first, he had to escape from the present situation. And his best chance was with one of his few remaining allies — ironically, still another non-American — Lieutenant Kolotov, who had managed to keep a handful of his Hind gunships still aloft.

Devillian reached Kolotov by radio and ordered him back to the black train.

"You're going to fly me out of here, Beethead," Devillian told the Russian pilot.

Kolotov and his squadron of Hinds soon appeared next to the train, and Devillian climbed into the leader's chopper.

"Let's get the fuck out of here," he barked.

As the fleet of Hinds started to rise above the train, another aircraft appeared in the distance, streaking straight for the Hinds so fast that Devillian let out an involuntary bellow.

It was the Harrier. . . .

After disposing of Riggs, Hunter had returned to the heavily damaged *Freedom Express* for the last of the remaining fuel and missiles, and immediately took off again to help chase the remaining KKK aircraft from the region. It wasn't hard; once they'd realized the battle was lost, the few Klan pilots still alive typically turned yellow and fled the area.

By this time the train had emerged from the Grand Canyon and was limping toward California's Sacramento Mountains and the great expanse of the Mojave Desert—the last stretch of untamed territory separating the United Americans from Los Angeles.

Low on fuel and weapons, JT, Ben and the five Coaster F-5's nevertheless seemed to have the situation in hand above the crippled *Freedom Express*. This allowed Hunter to double back toward the black train.

His instincts were telling him that Devillian would be making a run for it, and as he approached the train, his suspicions were confirmed. As he saw the squadron of Hinds leaving the train, he knew the leader of the Knights of the Burning Cross was aboard one of those choppers.

"I should have finished you off when I had the chance," Hunter muttered under his breath.

Lieutenant Kolotov ordered his pilots to stay between Devillian's helicopter and the Harrier at all times.

"Blast him out of the sky if you can," he commanded. "But whatever you do, just don't let him get through to us."

The other Hinds formed a flying circle about Kolotov and Devillian, their guns keeping the sky filled with cannon fire and missiles. It was a moving wall of destruction that no jumpjet pilot in his right mind would even try to penetrate.

So Hunter calmly started to pick the wall apart.

One at a time, he targeted the Hinds, maneuvering underneath them, over them, always darting up and down and sideways, never giving the gunships a clear shot at his Harrier. As this macabre aerial ballet continued, the number of performers began to dwindle. The first Hind chopper went down in flames, the victim of a well-placed burst of gunfire from the Harrier. A second Hind fell, ripped in half by a Sidewinder. Then a third. Then a fourth. . . .

"Why can't they hit the son of a bitch?" Devillian screamed in Kolotov's ear.

"They're trying," the Russian shouted back. "But he's not . . . he's just not like any pilot I've ever seen. He's there one minute, gone the next. He's just impossible to stop!"

"Well, they damn well *better* stop him pretty soon," Devillian yelled, as he watched still another Hind smash into the desert below. "Can't you make this crate go any faster?"

"We're going top speed," Kolotov replied.

The buffer around Devillian continued to fall apart. Two more Hinds went down, victims of the same Sidewinder. Now only five were left, in addition to Kolotov's. Hunter fired again, and the squadron was reduced to four.

The remaining Hind pilots had seen enough of this flying demon in the magic airplane. Their desire to survive overcame their fear of Devillian, and they pulled away from the formation, heading in four different directions.

Now, Kolotov and Devillian were alone in the sky with the Wingman.

By now they were over Death Valley, in the midst of the scorching Mojave Desert. But the heat below was nothing compared to the fire-filled sky. Kolotov's nose gun threw every ounce of firepower left on board the Hind at the jumpjet and still it kept coming. Finally it pulled alongside. Devillian stared in horror as Hunter grimly nodded at him. The deadly look in his eyes told Devillian that it was all over.

And then, suddenly, the Harrier dropped out of sight.

"Where the hell did he go?" Devillian bellowed.

Kolotov had no time to answer. He sensed, rather than saw, the Sidewinder coming.

"I'm dead, *damn it!*" he correctly exclaimed.

Devillian twisted in his seat to look behind him,

and saw the rear of the Hind explode in a ball of fire. The last thing he felt was the terrible heat, and the sensation of falling through flames. . . .

Chapter 71

The *Freedom Express* ground to a halt about fourteen miles into the Mojave Desert.

Its two remaining working locomotives were spent — out of fuel, out of computer commands, out of breath. The stress put on their drive systems had finally taken its toll. Exhausted, they could go on no longer in their present condition.

"So close," Fitz said, as he wearily sat down, feeling his own body teetering on the verge of total collapse, ". . . but so damned far. . . ."

Crossbow slouched down in the seat next to him, barely paying attention to the numerous wounds he'd received in the last assault on the train.

"At least I know I'm going to heaven when I die," he said, his normally deep bass voice substantially subdued. "Because I've already done my time in hell."

More than half the Football City Rangers and Piute braves on board had been killed or wounded in the outrageously violent battle. Plus only three of the weapons cars were intact, these being located toward the front end of the train. The rest were little more than smoking hulks of metal riding on cracked and wobbly steel wheels.

Those Rangers who were able carried their wounded comrades into the relatively cool shade of the three intact forward railway cars, and then they too slumped to the floor with exhaustion. Just what would happen to them now, they had no idea. All they yearned for was ten minutes of peace.

But it was not to be. . . .

Fitz and Crossbow saw them at about the same time. Off in the distance, like a long black deadly line, a reserve division of Burning Cross infantry soldiers — Devillian's "extras" — were marching on the train.

"This is truly it," Fitz said, knowing that there weren't more than fifty workable weapons on board the train, less ammunition and not enough power in the locomotives to carry them out of harm's way.

Even their aerial support could not turn back the tide. JT, Ben and the Coasters had been forced to leave the battle area, all of their airplanes out of ammunition and dangerously low on fuel. The Cobras were already on board, their valiant choppers shot up and similarly out of gas and ammo. Fitz knew that even Hunter's jumpjet must be depleted of weapons by this time.

Nevertheless, the Irishman called back to the Rangers, alerted them to the dire threat and rallied them to make one last stand.

Then, he grimly turned his binoculars on the approaching enemy troops and calculated that this, the *Freedom Express*'s last battle, would take no more than a few minutes to be consumated.

Hunter was speeding back to the scene — his sixth sense warning him just moments before he shot his last Sidewinder at Devillian's chopper that his colleagues on the train were in great danger.

And once again, his instincts proved damnably correct.

Even he was shocked when he saw the ten-thousand-man army of Burning Cross soldiers descending on the train. The long line of tractor-trailer trucks off in the

357

distance answered the question as to how so many troops could have gotten to the scene so quickly.

Now, as the first shots from the enemy were being fired as they closed to within a quarter mile of the motionless burning train, Hunter checked his weapons. He had about a quarter's worth of ammunition in his Aden gun pods and that was it.

But then, just as he was about to add his meager lot to the train's last stand, he felt a surge of excitement run through him.

Off to his left there was another line of figures approaching — fast.

"All right!" Hunter yelled. "The cavalry. . . ."

It was Catfish and the 1st Airborne, bearing down on the Burning Cross foot soldiers at full gallop on their herd of Kansas horses. They had made it to the battle through the sheer determination and stubbornness that had been the trademark of their last leader, the late Bull Dozer.

Having completely fooled Devillian by their retreat from Eagle Rock, the mighty 1st had been dropped off ninety miles from the southern rim of the canyon the night before, the nearest place that their huge C-5 transports could set down upon. After meeting up with Bad River and his main group of Piutes, the combined force had traveled all night, first through the brutal cold of the desert and then into its scorching sun, to arrive on the scene of the climactic battle — the right place at the right time.

Now Hunter put the Harrier into a screaming dive, a glimmer of hope burning in his heart.

"Just hang on," he silently urged the men inside the train. "Just a few minutes longer. . . ."

The final battle was brutal yet brief.

At the first sight of the approaching United American cavalry, many of the Burning Cross soldiers —

actually a hodge-podge of mercenary gangs deemed unsuitable to take part in the main canyon battle — turned and scattered. Those who ran to the south were met with a withering fire from Hunter's jumpjet. Those who fled north chose a slower, more painful death; there wasn't a piece of shade, a drop of water or a spot of civilization for a hundred miles around in that direction.

Most of the Burning Cross soldiers who stayed and fought were cut down by the mounted United American soldiers in brutal short order. By the end of ten minutes of sharp combat, those enemy soldiers still standing, threw up their hands in surrender.

The war was done. . . .

That evening, the scorched, battered but still-proud *Freedom Express* sat quietly in the middle of the Mojave Desert, less than two hundred miles from Los Angeles.

Although the men who had survived the horrors of the Grand Canyon were exhausted, many of them were spending several hours cleaning and repainting the train. Others were patching up the two workable locomotives in hopes that they would be able to pull the remainder of the railcars the last couple of hundred miles to their destination.

The UA leaders were not surprised at the *espirit de corps* of the men on the train. As one of them told Catfish: "We want to look our very best when we roll into LA. We took on the Badlands and won . . . and we want to look like winners."

Hunter and the other pilots pitched in, and before midnight the battle-scarred train had been at least symbolically restored to its former splendor and dignity. The two remaining locomotives now proudly sported the red, white and blue colors so cherished by the American people.

Despite their fatigue, Hunter and his friends talked far into the night, unwinding from the tremendous battle they had just won. Spirits were high and the booze was flowing.

"I've got just one regret, Hawk," Crossbow observed. "I wish I'd been the one to get Devillian. After what he did to my people, I owed him."

"Don't worry. When I put that Sidewinder into his Hind, it was for all of us," Hunter said.

"God, Jones better watch out," JT broke in. "Hawk's starting to sound like a politician; he'll probably want to run for president pretty soon."

"Not a chance," Hunter replied.

He had other plans. . . .

"I think the worst thing for Devillian in this whole thing," Catfish said, "was that a black man had a hand in beating him. That must have hurt almost as much as Hawk's missile."

"Not to mention that a bunch of Indians wound up on the winning side," Crossbow added. "I hope we are just rid of him for good."

It was the only piece of uncertainty left. Hunter had told them that while his last Sidewinder shot had been true, it had been hastily fired as he was turning in a hurry to get back to the train as it was being attacked by the last of Devillian's forces. Thus all the talk about the demise of Devillian left Hunter with a slightly uneasy feeling.

But he quickly shook it off when they were informed via the scrambler that General Jones would be on hand for their entrance into LA the following day.

"He wanted to be with us for the whole trip," Hunter said. "But his security people would never have allowed it."

Fitz smiled and raised his glass of beer in a toast. "I never felt for one minute that he wasn't here with us," he said.

That comment brought a few moments of silence, as

360

most of the men in the group recalled experiences they had shared in the past with the general. Finally Hunter raised his bottle of beer again and proposed a second toast.

"To the general—the *second* father of his country."

Chapter 72

For a long time, the man lay in the smouldering ruins of the helicopter, feeling nothing.

Finally, consciousness began to return. And with it came an overwhelming sensation of pain. His entire body felt as if it was broken in half. Much of his skin was burned. And the frigid desert night air was nearly as unbearable as the flames in the chopper had been.

But Duke Devillian was alive.

It took what seemed to be an eternity, but finally he managed to pull his battered body away from the wreckage and the gruesome skeleton of Lieutenant Kolotov. Everything started spinning around in his head, and he nearly collapsed again. But he fought the urge to pass out and, through sheer determination, continued crawling.

Slowly, his head cleared, and he was able to sit up and look around. It was freezing, the full moon mocking him with its display of false warmth. He painfully turned his head in every direction, only to find nothing but flat, endless desert and rocks.

Devillian began staggering across the barren landscape. For nearly an hour he wandered aimlessly, tripping over dozens of animal and human skulls lying in the desolation of the aptly named Death Valley. Finally, his battered body could carry him no farther, and he collapsed, facedown, in the ice-cold sand.

Just before dawn, a single helicopter appeared on the horizon.

It was a Soviet-built Hook, capable of flying long distances and carrying as many as two dozen people. The sharp-eyed female pilot spotted the body lying in the desert, and turned back for a second look. Flying low enough to see the man's features, the pilot called back to her crew to prepare to land.

Within five minutes the chopper was down and the unconscious body of Duke Devillian loaded aboard. Taking off shortly thereafter, the female commander of the Hook pushed a series of buttons on her console and sent a coded message back to the chopper's secret base, a location deep in the wilds of Alberta, Free Canada.

"Tell Elizabeth that we've found him" was all the message said.

Also shivering in the desert night air was Red Banner.

He had turned religious about twelve hours before, after one of the helicopters from the train fired a barrage of missiles into the gun and communication station where Banner had been doing his enforced play-by-play commentary of the Grand Canyon battle.

Miraculously, the missiles had killed everyone at the position but Banner.

It had taken him more than a couple hours to recover from the shock and to convince himself that he was indeed still alive and breathing. Then he spent another eight hours climbing down from the high, all-encompassing perch.

Now he was hiding behind a large boulder, watching as a huge helicopter took off and turned to the north. He had just witnessed the crew—all women, so it appeared—retrieving what may have been a wounded soldier from the desert floor.

He had surprised himself by not running toward the chopper as soon as it appeared. He'd been scanning the skies for nearby choppers all night and into the early morning, planning to flag down the first one he saw in an effort to get rescued. But something inside him—they could call it newsman's instinct he supposed—told him that he wanted nothing to do with this particular chopper.

Instead he waited for another hour when the sun was finally rising and the desert air was beginning to heat up. Within minutes of the dawn, the sky was filled with helicopters belonging to the Coasters as well as the LA militia, sweeping back and forth over the battle area, looking for survivors.

All it took was several waves of his bright red toupee for him to attract a Coaster Chinook, and soon Banner was on his way back to LA, already composing the speech he intended to deliver to Wild Bill which would list his demands for a doubling of his salary—at the very least.

Chapter 73

Preparations for welcoming the *Freedom Express* to Los Angeles dwarfed the festivities that had been planned for the ill-fated train of the Modern Pioneers, now more than a month before.

Nearly every citizen within reach of Los Angeles tried to jam into the vicinity of the hastily rebuilt Amtrak station, awaiting the arrival of the United Americans' famous train. Stretching for miles from the station into the outskirts of the sprawling city, the train tracks were lined with flags, banners, balloons, and more than a million people, all of them eager for a glimpse of their new heroes.

In downtown LA, hundreds of bands had gathered to greet the train with rousing, very loud, patriotic music. As one witness put it, the long-awaited earthquake that people for years had feared would split California apart from the rest of the continent might well be caused by reverberations from this "battle of the bands." The World Series quake of years ago would have seemed dull in comparison.

Red Banner, having survived his flight to LA by the Coaster rescue chopper earlier that morning, insisted that he was up to covering the arrival of the train for KOAS-TV. As many as twenty million people had listened to his "brave" and "stirring" commentary during the broadcast of the titanic Grand Canyon battle, making him as much of a hero as the men on the train.

Thus, the last thing he wanted to do was pass up the opportunity to bask in the sunshine of his mushroomed popularity.

But this time, he was keeping his feet solidly on terra firma. He had built a temporary broadcasting booth on a platform not far from the Amtrak station, giving him a good view—not an aerial, birds-eye view, but close enough—of the festivities. And just to be safe, he had insisted the booth was surrounded with bulletproof glass.

Bandaged and pleasantly sedated, Banner was warming up his audience now, assaulting them with a constant barrage of overblown language. "It won't be long now, citizens. Not since Hannibal crossed the Alps . . . not since Columbus crossed the Atlantic . . . not since man first traveled to the moon . . . has there been a journey to match this one. Take it from one who was there, never in the history of mankind has a group of brave, valiant souls overcome such odds, suffered such horror . . ."

Banner rambled on, never suspecting that the TV audience for his masterful performance, the epitome of his reportorial career, had been reduced to little more than a handful of shut-ins. Just about everyone else in the LA region was on hand in person to witness the train's arrival.

After hours of waiting, the crowd was rewarded with the first sign that the *Freedom Express* was coming.

Hunter's Harrier came into view from the east, flying low along the tracks, leading the way for the train. Then came the two Cobras, their blades flashing in the bright California sunshine. Finally, the *Freedom Express* itself—or what was left of it—roared into view, the two battered red, white and blue locomotives heralding its triumphant arrival.

There were only four cars still attached to the Dash-8's, the rest of the damaged railway cars having been disconnected at a switchoff near San Bernardino. However, this quartet of cars was covered with the surviving Football City Rangers as well as Bad River's Piutes. And serving as the caboose was the heavily damaged but still imposing weapons car carrying the gigantic cannon known as Big Dick, which had its share of Football City Rangers hanging all over it.

The City of Angels simply went wild at the first sight of the train. A mighty roar went up from the crowd, starting out in the valley and rolling like a huge tidal wave through the foothills, into downtown LA and to the shores of the Pacific.

On board, Fitz and Crossbow watched as the throngs thundered their welcome. Thousands of flags filled the air; guns fired ear-splitting salutes; bands blasted songs like "Battle Hymn of the Republic" and "When the Saints Go Marching In." The accumulated noise was louder than anything the United Americans had endured during the height of the Grand Canyon battle.

Finally, the train rumbled into the Amtrak station, where a huge, flag-draped platform had been erected for a welcoming ceremony. By this time, Hunter and the Cobras had landed nearby, and now they climbed onto the platform to join General Jones, Louie St. Louie, JT, Ben, the Wreckers and many other top officials of the United American Command. This distinguished group also included Catfish—whose troops were riding toward the city and were scheduled to arrive to another huge welcome later that evening—and the clearly bewildered, but very dignified Piute chief, Bad River.

General Jones took his place in front of the microphone, and at this point, the crowd's roar reached an even greater crescendo.

Jones tried to quiet the crowd, but each time he held up his hands, the tumult only grew louder. Finally, after twenty minutes of cheering, flag waving

367

and bursts of band music, the din began to subside enough for the general to start speaking into the microphone set up on the platform.

"My fellow Americans," he began, "today we're honoring an amazing band of patriots."

With a sweep of his hand, he indicated Hunter and the other key figures in the *Freedom Express* adventure who were standing on the platform behind him.

"Because of their heroism," Jones continued, "their willingness to risk their lives for a cause they believe in, they have opened a path of freedom through the heartland of this country."

This brought more cheers.

"Don't get me wrong, ladies and gentlemen," Jones said when it was settled down enough for him to speak again. "We still have much work to be done before our country will be completely safe again. But these men have taken the first, giant step toward taming our new frontier. They have served notice to all of our enemies out there, in the Badlands and elsewhere, that the American continent no longer will be held captive by the forces of terror, racism and oppression. . . ."

Jones' words stirred the crowd into a new frenzy, and it was several minutes before he could make himself heard again.

Finally he shouted, "And now, I want you to meet someone who you've all heard about . . . a man whose feats of bravery and skill have inspired all those who have served with him in countless battles over the past few years . . . a man who stands for the very best in America's past, present and future. . . . Ladies and gentlemen, Major Hawk Hunter!"

As Hunter reluctantly stepped forward to take Jones' place at the microphone, the entire city of Los Angeles seemed to explode with cheers. It was another ten minutes before this latest tribute died down and Hunter was able to address the crowd.

"I don't have that much to add to what General Jones already has said so eloquently," Hunter began. "Only that I was just one of many people who made this mission a success, And we just want you to know how much we appreciate this tremendous welcome today. As the general indicated, our work is far from over. But with your support, we will continue the struggle to overcome the enemies of liberty . . . and one day, in the not too distant future, Americans once again will stand proudly as the greatest monument to the freedom of the human spirit this world has ever seen."

Just then a voice up close to the stage yelled, "Would you do it again?"

Hunter managed to force his face into a smile.

"Not in a million years," he replied.

Chapter 74

Two days later, a CH-53 Sea Stallion helicopter set down briefly onto the virtually deserted mesa top that had been Duke Devillian's headquarters.

"Jesus Christ, will you guys listen to reason?" Studs Mallox pleaded with the members of the chopper crew and Michael Crossbow in particular. "If you leave me up here, I'll die. There's no way for me to get off."

"Sorry, Studs," Crossbow told him as he literally kicked the man out of the chopper's cargo bay. "You're lucky you're still alive."

On this point, even the Skinhead knew Crossbow was right. He had survived the Ten Miles of Hell ordeal, curled up in the fetal position inside of one of the *Freedom Express*'s weapons cars, whimpering and crying as the battle raged all around him. Wounds to both his knees—caused by severe cowering—were treated by a Coaster doctor upon the train's arrival in LA. But the injuries were bad enough to prevent Studs from walking without the aid of crutches. This meant any activity that needed the use of his legs—like rock climbing—was totally out of the question.

"But what about our deal, you bastards!?" Mallox

screamed at Crossbow as the CH-53 began to pull up and away. "You gave me your word that you'd let me go if I called my guys off."

"Tough luck, Studs," Crossbow yelled back to him over the roar of the chopper's blades. "Guess we're just a bunch of Indian givers."

With that the huge helicopter pulled up and away from the mesa. It immediately turned northeast, bound for Oklahoma Territory where Crossbow would have a long-awaited reunion with his tribe.

Mallox began crying again as the copter disappeared. He shakily looked around the deserted mesa top. It seemed like years—and not days—since he'd been snatched from its summit. Now, as he hobbled over toward a set of the barracks, he wondered how long he could hold out on the fortress top. There had already been a shortage of food and water when he was kidnapped; he couldn't imagine much of these necessities being left behind when the majority of the Burning Cross troops moved out for the disastrous battle in the Grand Canyon.

He heard the first voice just as he was about twenty-five feet away from the camouflaged barracks. At first, he was heartened at the sound; if there were still people on top of the mesa, then perhaps they would help him escape. But as he entered the barracks his last hope for life quickly evaporated.

There were five men gathered around a table at the far end of the small billet. The moment they looked up at him, he could tell they were all insane. Their eyes were glistening madly, but this was not what petrified him so. Nor was it the blood that covered their mouths and fingers.

No—it was the quick glimpse of what lay on the table in front of the five crazed individuals that convinced Studs that he was going to the *real* hell by a particularly painful route.

The food must have run out damn quick, was the

Skinhead's last thought in life as the five men approached him, fully revealing the half-eaten human body on the table before them.

Chapter 75

At about the same moment, one thousand miles to the east, a man named Frank Derrick looked up from tilling his small farm's tomato garden and spotted a strange speck of light in the sky that looked like it was heading right toward him.

Because Derrick lived in the rough and tumble woods of West Virginia, his rifle was always close by. Now, he instinctively reached for the carbine, still startled at the sight of the light that was rapidly descending toward his cornfield no more than fifty feet away.

"Ma! Get out here, quick!" he yelled to his wife. "And bring your gun, too!"

By the time the woman named Emerald Derrick appeared on the front porch of the farm house, the speck of light had come in close enough for her and her husband to see that it was a jet.

But not like one they'd ever seen before.

This jet was coming straight down, landing like a helicopter right next to their cornfield.

"What is it, Pa?" Emerald yelled, loading her own rifle.

But her husband could not answer; she saw that two streams of tears were pouring down his face.

"My God," the man was saying as he tentatively stepped toward the strange hovering jet fighter. "Could it be?"

His wife soon realized that he was looking at the person in the back seat of the plane's cockpit who was waving madly at the both of them.

Was it really her? Emerald dared to think.

Instantly, they both dropped their guns and were running toward the airplane just as it was setting down.

Through the wind and dust and exhaust the plane had kicked up, they could see that a miracle had just happened. Waving and crying from the airplane's back seat was their long lost daughter, Diamond, whom they had given up for dead after she'd been snatched by a band of raiding white slavers four years before.

The girl leapt out of the airplane, jumped down off the wing and was instantly crushed in the warm embrace of her parents.

"Oh, God," her mother was crying and laughing at the same time. "An angel has brought you back to us."

Even two hours later, after a quick meal of greens and cornmeal, Diamond's parents couldn't believe that their daughter was home again safe, never mind that she had been delivered by none other than the famous Hawk Hunter.

Now, as Hunter and the young girl walked back out to his Harrier, it was her turn to cry.

"Please don't go . . ." she weeped softly, hanging on tight to Hunter's arm. "Can't you stay, just for a while?"

"No, I have to go," he replied sadly, placing his fingers gently on the girl's lips. "You've meant a lot to me, Diamond. You helped me through the toughest time of my life. But my fight is just beginning again. I have to find my airplane, and then I have to find . . ."

He was surprised to hear his words trail off; he just

couldn't tell Diamond that he was dedicating as much time as it took to finding Dominique. He knew that this meant — in its own selfish way — that he cared very deeply for the young girl.

He opened his mouth to say something — anything — but still, he could not speak. So he simply kissed her on the lips one last time, then climbed into the Harrier and took off without another word.

Rising above the small farm, he throttled the jump-jet forward and roared off toward Washington, DC.

Sitting in her office on the banks of the Potomac River, Doctor Jocelyn Leylah was transfixed by what she was watching on her TV.

Footage of the Grand Canyon battle had just reached TV stations on the East Coast, and now, like their fellow citizens on the West Coast, millions of people east of the Mississippi were reacting in patriotic awe as they watched the valiant *Freedom Express* battle its way through the Burning Cross's seemingly invincible Ten Miles of Hell.

The news was full of exploits of Hawk Hunter, and Leylah could hardly wait to see him again. The TV report said that the Wingman was heading for Washington to address the newly formed House of Representatives on the recent action against the Burning Cross, and she intended to get a hold of him as soon as he landed.

They had many things to talk about, not the least of which would be whether he had ever fulfilled her subliminal learning experiment or not. To find out she would have to put him in a trance, of course, and undo the hypnotic suggestion that would have prevented him from remembering anything about listening to the subliminal-learning tape cassette.

Still keeping an eye on the TV, she stood up, made a drink and then retrieved the burgeoning file on

Hunter from her briefcase.

She couldn't help but laugh when she re-read the last entry she had made on his dossier during their romantic weekend about a month before. It was at that time that she'd selected the especially appropriate tape recording that Hunter promised to listen to—and then forget—as part of the experiment. If her theory was correct, it would take only a few seconds to release Hunter from her hypnotic amnestic suggestion.

Then—and *only* then—should he begin to remember everything he'd learned from the tape recording of the famous book that had guided warriors for five centuries called *Goo Dai Bau Dzein Dzuan*—or, in the Cantonese Chinese translation *The Ancient Book of the Great Sword*.

Chapter 76

The next day

When the huge Sky Crane helicopter finally set down in the midst of the Alberta wilderness, it was quickly surrounded by a small army of heavily armed, parka-clad women.

Juanita Juarez emerged from the aircraft first, her senses dulled from the long seven-day, stop-and-start journey north as well as from the biting cold.

Still, she was astonished at what she saw.

In a wide, open field nearby sat the partially wrecked hulk of a C-141 Starlifter, the cold Canadian winds just now peeling the name *Candlestick One* off the nose of its fuselage. Hidden throughout the woods nearby were lines of weapons—SAMs, artillery, howitzers, rocket-launchers—an arsenal that made Devillian's mesa-top fortress defenses pale in comparison.

But the subject of her greatest fascination sat high on a mountaintop nearby. Through the fog and clouds she could just barely see the outline of what looked like a great castle, a few twinkling lights sparkling away like jewels orbiting the fairy-tale structure.

"So it is all true," Juanita whispered.

The pilot stepped out of the helicopter and was immediately led away by a squad of guards—all males, but acting under the orders of a female officer who was definitely in charge.

As this was happening, a snow tractor pulled up to the chopper's doorway, and a woman in flowing white fur stepped out.

"And who are you?" the woman asked Juanita.

"A friend," the Mexican beauty responded. "I had heard only rumors about this place. I never really dreamed that it actually existed."

"It does," the attractive woman in the fur replied. "But we cannot allow just anyone to come here. Or to stay here."

Juanita had already made an intuitive connection with the woman in white; immediately she knew that she was being told that no interlopers would be allowed to leave this place alive.

"But I can help you," Juanita said, a tinge of desperation in her voice. "The women who whispered to me about this place said that you and your sisters have vowed revenge on the men who run the United American Government. Is that true?"

The woman in white nodded slowly. "Partially . . ." she said.

"Then I *can* help you," Juanita quickly continued. "I know many things about them. Things that can help you."

"Such as?" the woman in white asked.

Juanita took a deep breath, and as quickly as she could speak, she began to detail her association with Devillian and the plans to destroy the *Freedom Express*.

But halfway through her story, the woman in white held up her hand.

"We already know about this train," she said. "More than you do, in fact. It reached Los Angeles successfully several days ago."

Juanita was stunned, but not as much as when she heard the woman in white's next sentence.

"And the man who tried to stop it arrived here a

378

few days ago."

"Devillian?" Juanita forced herself to ask. *"Here?"*

The woman in white nodded again, this time with a marked loss of patience.

"So you actually have very little to offer us," she told Juanita. "I'm sorry."

A panic ran through the Mexican beauty as two of the mysterious woman's bodyguards turned their guns toward her.

"But I know of Hawk Hunter, too!" Juanita yelled out desperately.

The woman in white turned back to her and, after a few moments of silence, asked, "You do?"

"Yes," Juanita said. "I was 'with' him on two occasions . . . just in the past two weeks."

The woman in white drew so close to Juanita their breasts touched.

"And you made love with him?" the woman breathed.

"In a way . . . yes," Juanita answered.

The woman in white snapped her fingers, and immediately the two bodyguards lowered their guns.

"And will you tell me about it?" the woman asked, her voice almost panting with excitement. "Will you tell me about Hawk Hunter?"

Sensing her opportunity, Juanita reached out and caressed Elizabeth Sandlake's face lightly.

"Yes," she whispered, her own voice now lowering to a seductive tone. "Let me stay with you and I'll tell you *all* about it. . . ."

THE ONLY ALTERNATIVE IS ANNIHILATION . . .
RICHARD P. HENRICK

SILENT WARRIORS   (3026, $4.50)
The Red Star, Russia's newest, most technologically advanced
submarine, outclasses anything in the U.S. fleet. But when the
captain opens his sealed orders 24 hours early, he's staggered to
read that he's to spearhead a massive nuclear first strike against
the Americans!

THE PHOENIX ODYSSEY   (2858, $4.50)
All communications to the USS *Phoenix* suddenly and mysteriously vanish. Even the urgent message from the president cancelling the War Alert is not received. In six short hours the *Phoenix*
will unleash its nuclear arsenal against the Russian mainland.

COUNTERFORCE   (3025, $4.50)
In the silent deep, the chase is on to save a world from destruction. A single Russian Sub moves on a silent and sinister course
for American shores. The men aboard the U.S.S. *Triton* must
search for and destroy the Soviet killer Sub as an unsuspecting
world races for the apocalypse.

CRY OF THE DEEP   (2594, $3.95)
With the Supreme leader of the Soviet Union dead the Kremlin is
pointing a collective accusing finger towards the United States.
The motherland wants revenge and unless the U.S. Swordfish can
stop the Russian Caspian, the salvoes of World War Three are a
mere heartbeat away!

BENEATH THE SILENT SEA   (2423, $3.95)
The Red Dragon, Communist China's advanced ballistic missile-
carrying submarine embarks on the most sinister mission in human history: to attack the U.S. and Soviet Union simultaneously.
Soon, the Russian Barkal, with its planned attack on a single
U.S. sub is about unwittingly to aid in the destruction of all of
mankind!

*Available wherever paperbacks are sold, or order direct from the
Publisher. Send cover price plus 50¢ per copy for mailing and
handling to Zebra Books, Dept. 2892, 475 Park Avenue South,
New York, N.Y. 10016. Residents of New York, New Jersey and
Pennsylvania must include sales tax. DO NOT SEND CASH.*